THE LAST ANNIVERSARY

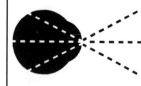This Large Print Book carries the
Seal of Approval of N.A.V.H.

THE LAST ANNIVERSARY

LIANE MORIARTY

KENNEBEC LARGE PRINT
A part of Gale, Cengage Learning

GALE
CENGAGE Learning®

Farmington Hills, Mich • San Francisco • New York • Waterville, Maine
Meriden, Conn • Mason, Ohio • Chicago

GALE
CENGAGE Learning®

LIBRARY OF CONGRESS CATALOGING-IN-PUBLICATION DATA

Moriarty, Liane.
   The last anniversary / by Liane Moriarty. — Large print edition.
     pages ; cm. — (Kennebec Large Print superior collection.)
   ISBN 978-1-4104-7529-9 (softcover) — ISBN 1-4104-7529-8 (softcover)
    1. Large type books. 2. Domestic fiction. I. Title.
  PR9619.4.M67L37 2015
  823'.92—dc23
                                        2014045461

Published in 2015 by arrangement with Harper, an imprint of
HarperCollins Publishers

Printed in the United States of America
2 3 4 5 6   23 22 21 20 19

For my parents,
Diane and Bernie Moriarty,
with lots of love

ACKNOWLEDGEMENTS

A special thank you to my friends Petronella McGovern, Marisa Medina and Vanessa Proctor for the time they spent reading and commenting on drafts of this novel. I'm also in debt to my sisters Nicola and Jaclyn Moriarty for all their suggestions and wonderful encouragement. My Grandma, Lily Dennett, provided lots of helpful information about the Depression, and my parents, Diane and Bernie Moriarty, helped with research and ideas and excursions on the Hawkesbury River! Thank you to my agent Fiona Inglis for being such a great supporter of my writing career. Finally, I am so lucky and grateful to have Cate Paterson as my publisher and editor — she made it a much better book.

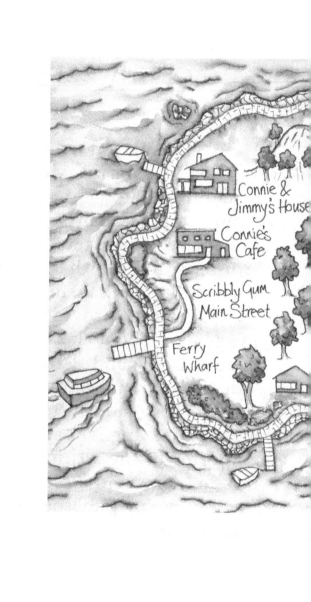

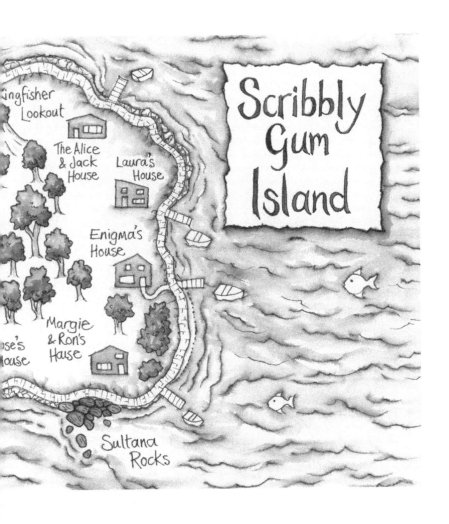

1

'Do you really think we can get away with it?'

'If I didn't think so, I wouldn't be suggesting it, would I?'

'We could go to jail. That's my third worst fear. First funnel-webs, then childbirth, then jail.'

'Neither of us is going to jail, you ninny. One day we'll be sweet little old ladies and we'll probably forget that it didn't happen the way we said it did.'

'I can't imagine us as sweet little old ladies.'

'It does seem unlikely.'

2

'A marriage is hard work and sometimes it's a bit of a bore. It's like housework. It's never finished. You've just got to grit your teeth and keep working away at it, day after day. Of course, the men don't work as hard at it as we do, but that's men for you, isn't it? They're not much good at housework either. Well, they weren't in my day. Of course, these days they cook, vacuum, change nappies — the lot! Still don't get equal pay in the workforce, though, do you? You've got a long way to go, you girls. Not doing much about it, though, are you?'

'Yes, OK, Aunt Connie, but the thing is I'm not interested in marriage in *general*. I'm interested in Alice and Jack's marriage. How would you describe it? Ordinary? Extraordinary? Cast your mind back! Even the tiniest detail would be helpful. Did they love each other, do you think?'

'Love! Pfff! I'll tell you something, something important. Write this down. You ready?'

'Yes, yes, I'm ready.'

'Love is a decision.'

'Love is a decision?'

'That's right. A decision. Not a feeling. That's what you young people don't realise. That's why you're always off divorcing each other. No offence, dear. Now, turn that silly tape-recorder off and I'll make you some cinnamon toast.'

'I'm stuffed full of food, Aunt Connie. Really. Look, I have to say you haven't been at all helpful. See, the Munro Baby Mystery is like a jigsaw puzzle. You're a piece of the puzzle. If I found all the pieces I could actually solve it. Imagine that! After all this time. Wouldn't you like that? Wouldn't that be *fascinating*?'

'Oh, Veronika, love, why don't you just get a job? A good steady job in a bank, perhaps.'

3

Out of the blue, just after the Easter break, Sophie Honeywell's ex-boyfriend, Thomas Gordon, calls her at work to ask if they can meet for a drink. He says he needs to talk to her about something 'quite serious'.

'But nothing *too* serious, I hope?' Sophie hears herself sounding bright and brittle. Her heart beats fast, as if she's just had a bad fright, and in fact it did give her a start when she heard that familiar but now strange voice. This is the first time they've spoken since their very messy break-up three years ago.

'Nobody's died, I hope?' she asks, all hale and hearty.

What a stupid thing to say. She never says that sort of thing. It must be nerves.

There is a pause and then Thomas says, 'Well, yes, actually, somebody has died.'

Sophie hits the palm of her hand against the side of her head. She has a moment of dithery throat-clearing and then, just in time, she remembers the polite thing to say to bereaved people. 'Thomas,' she says gently and sadly, 'I am so sorry.'

'Yes, thank you,' replies Thomas briskly. 'So, can we meet for a drink?'

'Yes, of course we can. But, ah, well, who died?'

'I'd rather talk about it tonight.'

All of a sudden it's like they have never broken up. Why can't he just come out and *say* things? Her mouth begins to gape into one of those silent shrieks of frustration that used to characterise so many of her phone conversations with Thomas. 'But I'll be worrying all afternoon wondering who it is. Who? Who died?'

He sighs heavily and says, as if proving a point, 'My Aunt Connie.'

'Oh.' Sophie tries not to sound relieved. 'I'm sorry.' She remembers his Aunt Connie well, but the old lady must have been at least ninety and it's not as if she had ever been likely to see her again, since she and Thomas aren't together any more. Surely, after three years of stony, betrayed silence, he hasn't asked her for a drink just to tell her that his Aunt Connie has died?

'I guess it will be in the papers,' she says.

15

'She was something of a celebrity, wasn't she?'

'Yes, it probably will. Look, I'll see you tonight. It will be nice to catch up. So, the Regent at six. Are you right to get there?'

The Regent is a five-minute walk from her office. 'Yes, of course. I'll see you then.'

She puts down the phone and slowly writes *'Thomas, 6 p.m.'* on a Post-it note and sticks it to her computer, as if there's a chance it will slip her mind. She had forgotten his habit of worrying about how women, being such helpless, fragile creatures, could cope with transporting themselves from place to place.

That's unfair. She gives herself a mental rap across the knuckles for pretending that Thomas is sexist, when in fact he is a sweethearted person who is always worrying about transport arrangements for both men and women. He is like everyone's worrywart of a dad.

Of course, he is now a real dad. It seems his heart has recovered from when she 'fed it through the paper shredder' (his words, written in a drunken, pitiful email full of weird metaphors) as he is now married to a girl called Deborah and they have a new baby, called Millie or Lily or Suzy, or something similarly cutesie.

16

She is only pretending not to know the baby's name. She knows perfectly well that it is Lily.

Sophie looks back at her computer screen. When Thomas called she had been in the middle of writing a memo to the Morale Committee. So far she has a heading:

☺ ☺ ☺ ☺ ☺ ☺ ☺

This is how she always cheerily begins her memos to the Morale Committee. She dislikes the Morale Committee because it is a ridiculous concept (in place before she started) and its members are all so relentlessly upbeat and self-righteously whiny about the need to have more 'fun in the workplace'. But it would not do for the Human Resources Director to disband the Morale Committee. Morale would surely plummet without the Morale Committee!

She types:

☺ COMMITTEE MEMBERS! IT'S TIME TO PUT YOUR THINKING CAPS ON! ☺

Then she types: GET A LIFE YOU LOSERS.

One of the sales reps walks by her office, taps on the glass wall and calls out, 'Yo, Soph!' She calls back 'Yo, Matt!' and waves a fist in the air like a homeboy.

She is such a fraud.

17

She taps quickly on the delete key, thinking with pleasurable horror of the reaction if she had accidentally clicked on 'send'. Their hurt, earnest faces!

What can Thomas possibly want, after all this time?

She finds herself remembering a sugary-brown smell. It is the smell of cinnamon toast, frangipani blossoms and Mr Sheen — the smell of his Aunt Connie's house.

Sophie had been going out with Thomas for nearly a year when she decided to break up with him. The decision was the result of weeks of agonised self-analysis. Yes, she loved him, but did she love him for the right reasons?

She knew, for example, that it was right to love a man for his kind heart, but wrong to love him for his bank account. It was fine to love him for his gorgeous blue eyes, but shallow to love him for his tanned muscles. (Unless, of course, they were uniquely *his* muscles, for example if they were as a result of his profession as a shearer or an acrobat, or from being in a wheelchair.)

But was it right or wrong to love a man for his marzipan tart? Thomas could cook like an angel and Sophie is a woman who likes her food. Watching him chop garlic could make her weak with desire, and eating a slice of his marzipan tart was equivalent to a multiple orgasm. His seafood risotto brought tears of joy to her eyes. But wasn't that a gluttonous, superficial basis for love? Especially when you sometimes secretly, shamefully wished he could just drop off the marzipan tart rather than having to stop and tell you some long, worrying story about his car registration.

And was it wrong to love someone because he was the grandson of the Munro Baby, and you'd always been just slightly obsessed with the Munro Baby Mystery? Wasn't that like loving someone because he was a member of the Royal Family, when you were really meant to fall in love with him when he was disguised as a simple peasant and then be pleasantly surprised when he turned out to be a prince?

It seemed to Sophie that she didn't love Thomas the way he deserved to be loved. He deserved to be with a woman who adored that fraught, scrunched-up expression he got whenever he had to do a difficult reverse park. He deserved a girl who thought it was cute the way he scrupulously read every line of the passenger safety card every time he flew, and took his responsibilities so seriously that when he was seated in the exit row he spent ten minutes asking a bemused flight steward questions about exactly what he'd need to do with the exit door in the unlikely event of an emergency.

Most importantly, Thomas deserved to be loved the way he loved Sophie. Once, she'd found a document on his computer called 'Sophie', which she opened of course, to find a list of reminders about how to be a good boyfriend. As if Sophie was a puzzle he could solve if he just followed the rules. It said things like: *'If S. suggests outdoor activity, don't mention possibility of rain. Pessimistic.' 'Don't say "whatever you feel like" when S. asks about weekend plans. Irritating.'*

Reading it made Sophie cry.

Thomas was good-looking, intelligent, very sweet, and occasionally — when he relaxed — quite witty, but Sophie had begun to feel terrified that she might be unfaithful to him. Once they had been out to dinner and a waiter had said to Sophie, 'Cracked pepper with that?' and she'd met his eyes and felt such a jolt of sexual attraction she'd had to look away.

Not that she hadn't enjoyed their sex life. It was just that sex with Thomas was so very pleasant and . . . clean. While he was giving her generous amounts of patient, gentlemanly foreplay, she'd find herself thinking wistfully that she'd quite like to be thrown on the bed and ravished. Of course, if she'd ever told Thomas that he would have dutifully thrown her on the bed, carefully so as not to bump her head, no doubt with that same worried expression on his face as when he reverse-parked.

Wasn't there more to love than this friendly, slightly irritable affection? Wasn't it morally wrong to stay in a relationship if you didn't feel weak-kneed passion for your partner? Wasn't there something noble about leaving a nice comfortable relationship and heading off on a quest for The One?

This was the deluded train of thought that led Sophie to recklessly break up with the nicest man she had ever dated.

Her timing for breaking up with him had been quite bad. Quite spectacularly bad, actually. She had deliberately picked a Friday because she thought that would give him the weekend to get the worst of his shock out of the way. He was a pathologist and she didn't want to be responsible for him misdiagnosing somebody's specimen.

Unfortunately, by horrible coincidence, Thomas had his own plans for that particular Friday.

It really wasn't her fault. How was she to know they were booked on a flight to Fiji that afternoon for a surprise holiday, which would begin with a marriage proposal on a white sandy beach bathed in moonlight while a string band wearing traditional Fijian dress serenaded them? How was she to know that he'd spent fifteen thousand, four hundred and twenty-five dollars on an engagement ring? How was she to know that at least a dozen friends and family members were excitedly involved in this careful, but not exactly covert, operation? There were the girlfriends who had secretly packed her bag with her sexiest lingerie; the various people who had been recruited to water her plants; her boss, who had agreed to give her time off work.

Naturally, all these people who had been sworn to secrecy had sworn at least three other people to secrecy too. It was annoying to discover that so many people knew about her forthcoming marriage proposal before she did, but that, of course, as Thomas so passionately pointed out, was no longer relevant.

'I need to talk to you about something,' she'd said bravely, on their way to what she thought was a new seafood restaurant in Brighton, although actually they were on their way to his sister Veronika's place, who was on standby to drive them to the airport.

'Well, I need to talk to *you* about something too!' said Thomas, rather gleefully she realised later. 'But you go first,' he said generously.

So she went first, and his eager face had crumbled and cracked like a six-year-old trying not to cry after he'd scraped his knee, and Sophie had had to look out the car window at the passing traffic and press a guilty fist against her stomach.

What would have happened if *he'd* gone first?

She would have put it off a week of course, and gone to Fiji. And when he proposed she would have said yes. How could she possibly have said no? It would have been farcical, with Thomas dolefully brushing white sand off his knee and signalling to the string band to stop playing by slicing a finger across his throat. Besides which, she loved nothing more than a romantic marriage proposal!

'I'm going to look like such a stupid fool,' he had moaned with his head down, hugging the steering wheel, after he'd pulled over in a no-stopping zone (evidence of his distraught state of mind that he didn't even check the sign) and revealed all his thwarted plans in a bitter, triumphant rush. He even pulled out the box with the ring heartbreakingly wrapped in bubble-wrap and hidden in a pair of black socks in the zippered compartment of his carry-on luggage.

'You're not going to look like a fool. *I'm* going to look like a bitch,' she had said, while she guiltily patted his hand and looked warily at that (really rather gorgeous, unfortunately) ring that had come so close to being hers and wondered if it would be in very poor taste to ask if she could try it on, just to see how it would have looked.

'Everyone loves you, Sophie,' Thomas had said bitterly. 'No matter what you do.'

She'd been flattered to hear that everybody loved her and then horrified at her own narcissism while poor Thomas was having his heart broken.

Actually, people had been upset with her, especially those involved in planning the secret proposal, as if she'd rejected them too. Thomas's sister Veronika, who was the reason Sophie had met Thomas in the first place, didn't speak to her for eleven months. (This was actually something of a relief, as Veronika could be hard work, and Sophie had found it difficult to show sufficient gratitude when Veronika magnanimously decided to forgive her.)

It seemed that Sophie had been both greedy and wasteful. Greedy for wanting something more than a perfectly nice, intelligent, good-looking man when she was in her mid-thirties and lived in Sydney, gay capital of the world. Wasteful of a perfectly lovely, expensive, carefully planned marriage proposal.

Of course, she'd got her comeuppance.

Thomas had been 'snapped up', just like his mother had cheerfully told Sophie he would be. 'Don't worry, Sophie. Some other nice girl will snap him up!' He got a refund for the Fiji holiday from a sympathetic travel agent — actually an excessively sympathetic travel agent called Deborah, who sensibly accepted his proposal just a few months later (remarkably similar in execution, except the location was Vanuatu and the string band was a string quartet).

Sophie, on the other hand, has been mortifyingly single ever since.

Over the last three years she has been on three first dates, two second dates and no third dates. She's had a drunken one-night stand after a charity ball, a drunken kiss after a fancy-dress fortieth, and a very weird sober kiss with a fat man in the hallway at a christening. (Who never called! The humiliation!) She has now been celibate for two years and sex has begun to seem as unlikely a possibility as when it was first explained to her in a disturbingly graphic drawing by Ann-Marie Morton when they were in second grade.

In spite of conscientiously accepting every social invitation, going to parties where she knows no one except the host, joining clubs and taking part in sporty, unpleasant activities likely to appeal to available men, she hasn't even come close to beginning a new relationship. It is laughable to think she'd been worried about being unfaithful to Thomas — just who did she think she'd be unfaithful with?

Last month, terrifyingly, she turned thirty-nine. It seems to make no difference that she still feels exactly the same person as when she was twenty-five, the birthdays just keep right on coming. She is actually going to turn forty — such a dry, grown-up-sounding age — and she's still going to be Sophie.

Lately, her biological clock, which has never given her much trouble before, has begun to tick with an increasingly feverish 'Umm, excuse me, don't you think you'd better hurry up, hurry up, hurry up?' She has caught herself staring at babies in strollers with the same resentful, lustful look that mid-life-crisis men give teenage girls. When she heard the news about Thomas having a baby, she said, 'Oh that's lovely', and then hours later, in the bath, she burst into tears and said out loud, 'You *idiot.*'

But by the next day her natural optimistic state had reasserted itself. She has a great career and a fabulous social life. She is hardly a lonely old spinster with a cat. She is out nearly every night of the week and she doesn't even like cats. Everything will be fine. He is just around the corner. He will turn up when she least expects him.

In fact, perhaps Thomas wants to see her tonight so he can set her up with a tall, dark, handsome friend? Ha. Funny. At least if she never finds anyone she'll always be able to laugh at her own hilarious wit while she eats baked beans on toast.

She wonders if Thomas will be smug. Surely even a man as sweet-natured as him would have to feel a bit pleased at the way things have turned out. Well, let him be smug, thinks Sophie as she goes back to typing her lively memo to the Morale Committee. (☺ *A fun idea from Fran!* ☺) You tore his heart to shreds. Be generous. Let him be smug.

4

Scribbly Gum Island, 1932

When they said they were sending out a reporter, Connie had imagined someone much older: an intimidating type with jaded seen-it-all-before eyes and those awful dirty yellow-tipped fingers, who would say 'good bickies, love' and act impatient and patronising if she took too long answering his questions. She had decided her answers would be brisk, with no unnecessary detail, and that she would probably not offer him a second biscuit.

But there was nothing jaded about Jimmy Thrum. Even his name sounded energetic. He could only have been a couple of years older than her, twenty-one at the most, skinny and long-limbed, with little-boy freckles on his nose and unusual-coloured eyes that grinned and glittered at her from beneath the shade of his battered brown hat.

Yes, Jimmy Thrum *thrummed* with life.

When she met him at the railway station he bounded up the stairs three at a time to greet her like a big lovable labrador. He chivalrously insisted on taking the oars when they rowed out to the island, even though she doubted that he'd even stepped foot in a boat before. She stopped herself from confiscating the wildly flailing oars or complaining about the sudden splashes of icy-cold river water — he was having far too good a time, gulping deep breaths of air as if it was the first day of a holiday, tipping back his head so the winter sun was on his face. He made her want to giggle helplessly like a child. She had to turn her head and pretend to be fascinated by the flight of a pelican.

Now, Jimmy Thrum the reporter was sitting at the Doughty family's kitchen table, gulping down his second cup of tea and munching into his third biscuit with a spray of crumbs, which he quickly tried to clean up by licking his finger and dabbing at them.

From the way he was listening to her, it seemed that he wasn't just interested in her story, he was positively enthralled by it. I hope he's not making fun of me, thought Connie with sudden suspicion. Shouldn't a newspaper man be a little less excited?

If he was faking it, he was doing a very

good job. A couple of times he'd even slapped his thigh.

She took the opportunity to covertly study him while he bent his head to scribble in his notepad. He had a knobbly neck. Unexpectedly hairy forearms. There were curls springing up one by one from his slicked-down hair. He was writing in a mixture of what Connie assumed were shorthand symbols and words. She could read *'Scribbly Gum Island'* and her own name, carefully spelled out: *'Constance (Connie) Doughty. Age: 19'.*

'This is a great story.' He looked up at her. She still couldn't work out the colour of his eyes.

'That's good,' said Connie, and thought, Don't make him think you're flattered, for heaven's sake.

It wasn't surprising that she was feeling a bit, well, to be honest . . . *charmed.* It was just a refreshing change to have someone with a bit of verve in the house, what with Dad the way he was, and Rose the way she was becoming. They both had such dazed, doleful expressions on their faces all the time that Connie sometimes seriously considered grabbing them by the scruffs of their necks and banging their heads together. Of course, Dad had very good reasons. As

Mum used to sigh, France clearly hadn't been a walk in the park. Whereas Rose: well, she just needed to bloody well snap out of it. Especially now there was a new baby in the house. A poor, defenceless baby who hadn't chosen to come into the world at this inconvenient time.

Jimmy finished writing in his notepad, shook his head in wonder and said, 'So, you say the kettle was actually boiling?'

'Yes, and the cake was still very warm. It could only have been out of the oven a few minutes.'

'What sort of cake?'

'A marble cake.'

'That's the one with all different coloured layers, right?'

He looked hungry as he said it. All the biscuits were gone and there was nothing else to give him. Connie wished she could feed him up with a big roast dinner like they used to have when Mum was alive. It would be so satisfying, almost *wickedly* satisfying, to feed a hungry, appreciative man like that, to keep on dishing out steaming helpings until he pressed one hand to his stomach and protested, 'No, no, I can't eat another thing.' One day, Connie would live in a house with a pantry full of food. It was not right. Skinny (handsome!) boys like Jimmy

31

Thrum shouldn't be hungry.

'Different layers. That's right.'

'And the baby was just lying there, crying, I guess?'

'No, no,' said Connie, a bit irritated by that. 'The baby was *smiling*. She woke up when we walked in and smiled at us.'

'Poor little mite,' said Jimmy Thrum sadly. 'With her parents vanished from the face of the earth! Does she seem to miss her mum and dad?'

'She's too young to know any different,' said Connie firmly. She wanted it clear that the baby was in good hands. She didn't want any rich do-gooders reading this article and turning up to help themselves to the baby. 'She's thriving. We'll take good care of her until her parents come back.'

'*If* they come back,' Jimmy pointed out. 'It seems unlikely, don't you think? Don't you suspect foul play of some sort?'

'I've no idea,' said Connie. 'It's a real mystery.'

'A mystery, eh? An unsolved mystery.' Was he giving her a keen, shrewd look? Was he holding her eye-contact for just a bit too long? Was he seeing right through her?

His eyes were the warm brown colour of cinnamon. Connie thought highly of cinnamon. After she fed him a roast dinner she'd like to feed him apple crumble with fresh cream. Later on, for supper, (*before bed!*) she'd give him a couple of very thick slices of sugary cinnamon toast and a strong cup of tea.

Perhaps she was misinterpreting his shrewd look. Perhaps it was actually an interested look. The dress she was wearing had a nice neckline and she'd noticed when she combed her hair that morning that her fringe had fallen just right across her forehead. Actually, he seemed more interested in the neckline than the fringe.

'You know what this is like?' said Jimmy. 'It's exactly like the *Mary Celeste*. Have you heard of the *Mary Celeste*?'

What luck. She wouldn't need to supply him with the comparison. It was exactly the extra edge the story needed.

'I think so,' she said, and pretended to sound a bit uncertain. 'The ship, right?'

'Yes! It was sailing from New York to Italy about sixty years ago and they found it adrift. All ten people on board had vanished without a trace! No explanation. There are lots of theories, but nothing satisfactory.'

Not ten, eleven people on board, thought Connie. Ten adults. One little girl.

'In this case, it's a house instead of a ship.'

Well done for stating the bleeding obvious, thought Connie, but she forgave him for the bright, excited look in his cinnamon eyes.

He continued, 'And of course, there is a survivor. The baby. But she can't tell us anything, unfortunately.'

'Unfortunately,' agreed Connie.

'The mystery of Alice and Jack Munro's abandoned house. The Munro Baby Mystery. Our very own *Mary Celeste*.'

Connie smiled encouragingly at him. 'Is this what you'd call a scoop?' she asked innocently.

'That's exactly what I'd call it! The scoop of 1932!' Jimmy looked delighted and bent back over his notepad to scribble some more.

'Have you been a reporter for very long?' asked Connie.

He seemed to sit up straighter and she realised she'd hurt his feelings. It made her feel tender towards him. 'I'm a cadet,' he said defensively, and smoothed his palm over the top of his head as if he'd just remembered how his hair was probably refusing to stay put.

So the newspaper hadn't thought it was much of a story after all. Still, maybe Jimmy Thrum's enthusiasm would be contagious.

'What do the police have to say about

this?' asked Jimmy, in a more formal voice than he'd been using previously. 'I assume you notified them when you found the baby?'

She spoke confidingly to mollify him. 'Actually, they weren't very interested in the beginning. They didn't think it was all that mysterious. The Munros were behind on their rent. People are abandoning their houses all the time these days. Often they go in the middle of the night. They're abandoning their babies too.'

'But normally they leave the baby at a church or on somebody's doorstep. They don't just leave a baby sleeping in the house.'

'Alice had asked Rose and me to go around for a cup of tea,' said Connie. 'I guess she knew the baby would be found.'

'But the kettle boiling! And the cake waiting to be iced!' Jimmy regained his former enthusiasm as he defended his scoop. 'And you said there was an overturned chair and blood stains on the floor!'

'The sergeant at Glass Bay Police Station said he'd be more interested if there was an actual body on the floor. I also think he would have been more interested if it was my father reporting it, not me, but Dad doesn't really get off the island much. My father isn't well. He was gassed twice in France. He's a bit . . . as I said, he stays on the island most of the time.'

She had been going to say her father was a bit soft in the head, but then she realised that wasn't relevant, or any of Jimmy Thrum's business, for that matter. Although for some reason she wanted to tell Jimmy all about how her dad had been even stranger since Mum died, and how worried she was about Rose, who seemed to be going a bit barmy too.

She continued talking. 'Anyway, the sergeant did come out eventually and poked around the house and scratched his head. He said they weren't *necessarily* blood stains on the floor. You'll have to see what you think, when we go over to the house. It sure looks like blood to me. He said he'd come out and have another look sometime next week if the Munros still haven't turned up. He seems convinced they'll be back to get their baby. I understand he's pretty busy, and I think he thought I was just a silly young girl. And people think it's such a bother to come out to the island. You'd think we lived on the moon, it's so inconvenient.'

'I don't think you're a silly young girl.'

'Thank you.'

Their eyes met and they both looked away and shifted awkwardly in their chairs.

'It's worth the inconvenience,' said Jimmy suddenly. 'This island. It's so beautiful. You're so lucky to live here. I don't know why people don't come here for picnics.'

Picnics. Exactly, thought Connie. Picnics will be the start. Then Devonshire teas.

There was a sudden kitten-like cry from down the hallway and Jimmy looked up.

'That's the Munro baby?' he asked, as if he was surprised by the coincidence of talking about the baby and it actually existing as well.

'Yes,' said Connie. 'My sister will pick her up.'

But the baby kept crying and crying, and after Jimmy and Connie looked at each other for a while, Connie got up and found Rose sitting upright at their mother's sewing machine, staring out the window, her face immobile and empty. She jumped when Connie said, 'Can't you hear the baby?' and answered, 'Oh, sorry, I was just doing some sewing.'

'It might help if you had some fabric then,' answered Connie, and thought, There is something quite wrong with that girl.

Connie scooped up the baby, who stopped crying and began making hopeful sucking movements with her mouth to indicate she was hungry. Babies were really no problem to look after, thought Connie, as she carried her back into the kitchen. Any fool could do it.

'Jimmy, I'd like you to meet our little Enigma.'

But Jimmy didn't even glance at the baby. Instead, he fixed his eyes carefully on Connie's forehead and said, 'I was just wondering. Well, I was wondering if you had a fellow?'

Not any more I don't, thought Connie Doughty, and hid her smile as she buried her nose in the sweet folds of the baby's neck.

5

(Excerpt from 'The Munro Baby Mystery', a DL-sized brochure printed in four colours on celloglazed 150 gsm stock and handed to every visitor to Alice and Jack's house on Scribbly Gum Island, Sydney, Australia.)

Welcome to the mysterious 'frozen in time' home of Alice and Jack Munro! Look, be intrigued, but please *do not touch*! It's *vital* that we preserve our historical integrity. This home, built in 1901, has not been touched since teenage sisters Connie and Rose Doughty stopped by for a cup of tea with their neighbours on 15 July 1932. They discovered the kettle about to boil, a freshly baked marble cake waiting to be iced, and a tiny baby waking for her feed — but *no sign* of her parents, Alice and Jack Munro.

The only clues that violence may have taken place were a few drops of dried blood on the kitchen floor and one upturned chair. (Please do not attempt to look under the chair.) The bodies of Alice and Jack have *never* been found, and over seventy years later their disappearance remains one of *Australia's most famous unsolved mysteries.*

The sisters, Connie and Rose, took the tiny baby home and reared her as their own child. They named her Enigma — you can guess why! Connie, Rose and little Enigma (now a Grandma Enigma!) are all still residents of Scribbly Gum Island, as are Enigma's two daughters, Margaret and Laura, and their families.

Note: For obvious health and hygiene reasons the cooling marble cake you will see during your tour is not the original cake but actually a freshly baked one, made to Alice's delicious original recipe. Enjoy a complimentary piece after your tour!

6

Grace Tidyman is dreaming. Her eyelids twitch irritably. It's one of those frustrating, muddled dreams.

Aunt Connie is really cross with her. She's pouring Grace a cup of tea from her blue china teapot and snapping, 'Of course I'm not dead! Where did you get that idea?' Grace is floundering, trying to remember why she thought such a thing. Suddenly, to Grace's horror, Aunt Connie puts down her teapot, throws back her head and begins to wail with a scrunched-up face like a baby. Grace puts her hands over her ears even though she knows she's being very rude, but she can't bear to hear that gruesome baby-cry coming from Aunt Connie's mouth. The sound keeps going on and on and on. 'I'm sorry!' screams Grace. She feels angry, astonishingly angry, with Connie. 'I didn't mean to hurt your feelings! I thought you were dead!'

'Grace? He's crying. Will I get him for you?'

'Mmmmm. What? Oh. Yes. OK. Good.'

Grace feels her husband leave the bed. She squashes her fingers hard into the sockets of her closed eyes and pushes herself up into a sitting position.

Aunt Connie *is* dead, she remembers. She died yesterday.

She hears her son's sharp wail and Callum's voice. 'You hungry, mate?'

She snaps on the lamp and winces at the yellow spotlight. Her arms in front of her, resting on the duvet, look strange in the light, as though they're not hers. She thinks of that American rock climber who had to chop off his own arm after he was trapped by a boulder. She imagines sawing diligently away at her own flesh, snapping her own hard, white, bloody bone: escaping.

Callum appears with the baby in the crook of his arm.

Grace thinks, Please just go away, and says, 'Come here, sweetie.'

7

'I'm positive I remember her saying that she wanted to be buried in that lovely burgundy suit she wore to Grace's wedding.'

'Enigma, you are a terrible fibber.'

'But I remember it quite clearly! It was that day we went to that Legacy luncheon. I complimented her on the suit and she said something about wearing it to her funeral.'

'She said she was wearing it to Molly Trasker's funeral, not her *own*! I can remember her saying that she didn't see the point in wearing anything at all. She said it was a waste of good fabric. "I came into the world naked, I'll leave it that way too." That's what she said.'

'She was joking, Rose! You can't bury your own sister in the *nude*!'

'Why not? It would give her a good laugh.'

Margie Gordon listens to her mother and Aunt Rose bicker while she cuts almond cake to have with their cups of tea. She gives herself a small piece for comfort and motivation. It's difficult sticking to a diet when you've got a big, complicated funeral to arrange. Margie feels quite overwhelmed when she thinks about everything she will have to do over the next few days. She needs a tiny sugar burst.

'I expect Connie has it written down somewhere what she wants to wear,' she says to them as she pours tea. 'You know how organised she is.'

She *was*. Oh my goodness, fancy there being a world without Connie. It seems as though everything on the island will surely fall apart without Connie's iron-hard certainty, her irrefutable opinions, her snap-fast decisions. Margie feels a seasick sensation at the thought. How will they cope without her?

It had been a nasty shock finding Connie's body yesterday morning, her face sickly grey against the pillow, her eyes glassy slits, her forehead ice-cold under Margie's palm. For a moment she'd had to fight a childish desire to run away and find a grown-up, but of course *she* was the grown-up, over fifty years old and a grandmother to boot, so she had to 'bite the bullet', as they say, and take care of things.

'Pale blue always suits Connie.' Rose's

age-spotted hand trembles badly as she lifts her teacup. 'Not too pale, of course.'

Rose looks awfully frail today, worries Margie. Even her beautiful peach-coloured cardigan is buttoned up wrongly, which is unlike Rose.

'You'd think Connie would have mentioned what she wanted to wear when she brought around all that minestrone soup,' says Margie's mother, Enigma. Her eyes are shiny with tears, but her grey hair is so bouncy, her cheeks so pink with good health, it seems almost disrespectful to Connie. ' "Put it straight in the freezer, Enigma," she said, and I said, "Goodness, Connie, what are we stocking up for? Are you going away?" I didn't know we were stocking up for her blooming death, did I?'

The three women fall quiet, and Margie feels grief wrap its lethargic arms around them, making their shoulders slump.

'Thomas is going to see Sophie tonight,' she says.

'That's good,' says Rose. 'I wonder what she'll say.'

'Maybe they'll get back together!' says Enigma brightly, conveniently forgetting Thomas's wife and new baby.

'Oh *Mum,* don't be so *ridiculous,*' snaps Margie, because she wishes that too.

8

In fact, Thomas doesn't seem in the least smug, and the first few minutes of their meeting at the Regent are surprisingly pleasant — considering that the last time Sophie had seen him he was handing her a laundry basket in which he'd collected every gift, letter and card she'd ever given him throughout their relationship.

Sophie asks him about his baby girl and Thomas speaks with quiet pride and joy. It is obvious that he is very happy. He is so happy he probably doesn't need to be smug. He is beyond smug.

Listening to him talk, doing an imitation of the 'grrr' and 'meow' sounds that Lily brilliantly makes whenever she sees a dog or a cat ('*without* any prompting whatsoever!'), Sophie realises that she will always love Thomas, a little.

But she also realises, as she observes the slight suggestion of a well-fed double chin, that breaking up with him is not, after all, the biggest mistake of her life. She doesn't want to be Deborah at home with pretty, growling, meowing baby Lily. She really doesn't. She would rather be single, desperate-for-a-man Sophie. This revelation makes her feel euphoric with relief and she takes a handful of peanuts and settles back in her chair, ready to enjoy all the things she used to like about Thomas.

Finally, he gets down to business.

'So, as I said on the phone, Aunt Connie died yesterday.'

'Yes, I'm very sorry,' says Sophie. 'She was such a sweet lady.' She'd actually found Aunt Connie ever so slightly terrifying, but now she is dead 'sweet' seems an appropriate description.

Thomas clears his throat. 'The reason I needed to see you is because I've been through her paperwork and it seems that Aunt Connie has left you something in her will.'

'Oh! Gosh. That's unexpected.'

Sophie feels awkward. Nobody has ever left her anything in a will before, and it seems to her that if someone is going to do something so thoughtful it is only courteous to be devastated by their death. Ideally she should be crushed, red-eyed and sniffly, clutching a soggy hanky. She should certainly be a few levels higher up the grieving stakes than 'a little sad'. At the same time, she is flattered and even — she hates to admit it — a bit covetous, wondering if it is something nice, perhaps an antique plate, or a lovely old-fashioned piece of jewellery.

She says, trying not to sound too interested, 'So, what exactly did she leave me?'

Thomas places his drink down squarely on its coaster and meets her eyes. 'She left you her house.'

'Her *house*?'

'Yep, her house.'

'Her house on Scribbly Gum Island?'

'That's the one.'

Sophie is staggered. Her ex-boyfriend's aunt, a woman she barely knew, has left her a *house.* A beautiful house. An extraordinary house.

It is very inappropriate and it is probably, somehow, her fault.

So she blushes.

Of course she blushes. Sophie is a blusher. It isn't cute or funny. It's a disorder. It even has a name: 'Idiopathic Craniofacial Erythema', or 'severe facial blushing'. Her blush isn't a petal-pink virginal stain stealing disarmingly up her neck; it's a burning, blotchy, all-enveloping beetroot, a phenom-

48

enon which is impossible for even the most tactful person to ignore, or the least observant person to miss. Her fair skin doesn't help. Like fine porcelain, her mother says proudly, as if she'd purchased her complexion at David Jones. Like a corpse, her friend Claire says.

She's been blushing since she was seven. She knows this because she can remember her first blush. Her mother had dropped her off at school and Sophie was trotting into the playground when she heard the toot of a horn and turned to see her mum leaning out of the car window waving her teddy bear and calling, 'Sophie, darling, did you remember to kiss Teddy goodbye?!' A dozen kids witnessed this profoundly humiliating incident, including Bruno Tripodopolous, the most glamorously wicked boy in her class. (Twelve years later she dated Bruno for two weeks, during which time they had a lot of vigorous sex and only spoke when absolutely necessary. Even when she was seven, before she knew what sex was, some part of her must have known that Bruno would be good at it.) When Sophie heard Bruno making smacking sounds with his lips she was shattered. Her face went boiling-hot purple. Bruno stopped snickering and looked at her with scientific interest, calling over his friends to 'Come check out what's happened to Sophie's head!' Her mother instantly grasped the enormity of her error and quickly withdrew Teddy from the car window, but it was too late. Sophie was thenceforth a blusher.

'What colour is red?' the boys used to yell, squashing their cheeks together like gargoyles. 'Sophie's face, Sophie's face!' 'Oh, poor Sophie is *embarrassed,*' the girls would snigger with fake sympathy. 'Poor Sophie is *shy.*' For the rest of that year she spent every recess and lunchtime hidden under the tuckshop stairs with another outcast, a boy called Eddie Ripple, who had a horrendous facial twitch. They were the school 'retards', until Eddie left and Sophie, in the same way that fat kids learn to be funny, learned to be extremely social and eventually became popular, so much so that she was voted school captain in high school. She can now walk straight into a cocktail party of strangers and within five minutes be part of the group that's laughing the loudest and making everyone else feel jealous and left out. But she has never managed to fully vanquish the blush and it continues to make regular appearances at the most inconvenient times.

'This must be a mistake,' she says to

Thomas as her face heats up as reliably as a hotplate. 'She can't have left me her house. That's ridiculous.'

Thomas looks everywhere except at her. He is one of those people who writhe in empathetic embarrassment whenever she blushes. They really had been quite incompatible.

'I've seen the paperwork,' he says. 'It's all very clear.'

Sophie picks up a piece of ice from her glass and holds it against her forehead. 'But I would have thought she'd leave the house to you or Veronika. Or your cousin. The beautiful one who does the children's books. Veronika said she just had a new baby. What is her name again? Grace?'

'Yes, Grace. Well, Grace has just moved into her mother's place on the island. Aunt Laura has gone travelling for a year and Grace and her husband are building a home. Maybe Aunt Connie thought they didn't need another one. Anyway, apparently she has left all three of us some money.'

'But she hardly knew me! And my history with your family isn't that good, is it?'

Thomas smiles slightly and doesn't say anything.

'What does your mother say? Oh, God,

what does Veronika say? I hope they don't think I somehow manipulated your aunt! I complimented her on her house, that's all. I didn't mean I *wanted* it!'

'I know,' says Thomas. 'I was there.'

But Sophie is in agonies of guilt because this sort of thing has been happening to her all her life — although on a much smaller scale. She admires some person's belonging, and the next thing she knows they are absolutely insisting she take it as a gift, which naturally causes Sophie to blush. 'Darling, don't be so *heartfelt* when you like something,' her mother advises her. 'It's when you get that shiny-eyed look.'

She probably did have that shiny-eyed look when she visited Aunt Connie's house, because she loved it. She absolutely loved it.

'The thing is,' says Thomas, 'Veronika doesn't know yet — and you're right, she probably will be upset. Have you heard about her latest idea? She reckons she's writing a book about the Munro Baby Mystery. She's got a bet with Dad that she's going to solve it. She was interviewing Aunt Connie the night before she died. Mum thinks she probably talked her to death. Anyway, if I know Veronika she'll still want to go on writing it, and of course it would suit her right down to the ground to live in Aunt Connie's house. She hasn't really got herself settled since the divorce. She's living in a share house and driving her flatmates insane; they only put up with her because they like her cooking. Anyway, I wouldn't be surprised if she gets it into her head to contest the will.'

'Well, that's the solution, then!' says Sophie. She can feel her face settling back to normal. 'It's obvious. I won't take the house. Veronika can have it!'

'I think Aunt Connie was worried you might say something like that,' says Thomas. 'She left you this letter.'

From his jacket pocket he pulls out a plain white envelope with the word 'Sophie' written on the front in firm black letters. 'Just read it first before you decide anything. If you decide you want the house then I won't let Veronika contest the will.'

Sophie says, 'That's very kind of you.' Thomas shrugs and gives a small grimace. She opens the letter, reads it slowly, carefully refolds it, puts it back in the envelope and smiles, a touch flirtatiously, certainly fondly, at Thomas.

'I guess I'd like to keep the house.'

He grins back at her. 'Knew you would.'

Then he opens his briefcase and pulls out

a Tupperware container with a piece of marzipan tart. 'Here. Your favourite.'

It seems that Thomas stills love her, just a little, too.

9

'Do you feel you've been hard done by in a will?'

Veronika's hands freeze in the middle of vigorously kneading 'extra volume for fine or flat hair' shampoo into her scalp.

'The good news is you could be entitled to contest it.'

Veronika throws back the shower curtain so hard that plastic rings go pinging across the room. The radio is sitting on the bathroom cabinet. With the shower still running she skids wild and naked across wet tiles to turn the dial up to shouting volume.

'AT O'SHEA SOLICITORS WE SPECIALISE IN WILLS AND PROBATE. WE CAN LET YOU KNOW YOUR LEGAL ENTITLEMENTS. CALL US NOW ON . . .'

Pen! she thinks frantically.

In desperation she writes the number with the tip of her finger on the steamed-up bathroom mirror, opens the bathroom door, dripping copiously, and sticks her still foamy head out in search of a passing flatmate. Rivulets of shampoo run into her eyes. 'Is anyone awake? It's an emergency! I need a pen!'

There is an anguished cry from down the hallway. 'Veronika! Do you realise what time it is?'

'Good morning! It's six a.m., it's a beautiful day and I need a pen!'

Veronika pulls open the bathroom cabinet's drawer, grabs a lipstick and traces the fading numbers in bright fuchsia. She stands there, feeling resourceful and determined.

How could Aunt Connie have been so cruel? Sophie! Of *all* people!

10

'Thomas's Aunt Connie died. It looks like she's left me something in her will.'

'Well, how thoughtful of her! Is it something nice?'

'Yes. Her house.'

'Oh *no*. Sophie, darling, I'm afraid you'll have to give it straight back.'

'Mum, I think she really wanted me to have it.'

'You mean her house on Scribbly Gum Island? Her actual house?'

'Yes, her actual house.'

'Really? It's extraordinary. It's exciting! But oh dear. Oh goodness. It doesn't seem appropriate after Thomas, does it? Look, I'll call you straight back. *Survivor* is about to start. Did you forget? Do you need me to tape it for you?'

'No, no. I'm watching it. Call me in the first ad.'

11

WELCOME to the Scribbly Gum Island website. Scribbly Gum Island. *'A little island. A big mystery.'* You are the 1,223,304th visitor!

About the Island
Scribbly Gum Island is one of Australia's most fascinating, favourite tourist attractions. Located north of Sydney on the stunning Hawkesbury River, near Glass Bay, the island gets its name from the beautiful Scribbly Gum trees that can be found there. (The Scribbly Gum is a eucalyptus tree with

a creamy pale trunk covered in dark brown lines — as if somebody has taken a pen and scribbled all over it! These scribbles are actually made by the larvae of the tiny scribbly moth.)

Scribbly Gum Island's two most famous residents were Alice and Jack Munro, who mysteriously vanished from their home during the height of the Great Depression in the 1930s, leaving behind a two-week-old baby. Visitors can take a tour of **Alice and Jack's home,** exactly as it was when the Doughty sisters, Connie and Rose, found the Munro baby. They can also share Devonshire teas with Baby Enigma (now a grandmother!) and the Doughty sisters.

The **Doughty Family** has owned Scribbly Gum Island since 1882, when a poor blacksmith named Harry Doughty won a bet with its rich owner, Sir Charles McKay. The bet was over the outcome of a test match in England. Australia had never defeated England away from home and appeared unlikely to do so this time. Sir Charles famously said, 'I'll bet this island that Australia will not defeat England.' *Guess who lost his island!* Australia narrowly defeated England in a sensational match that was reported as the 'death of English cricket' and became the origin of the

'Ashes' series. Sir Charles was forced to hand over his island, much to the jubilation of young Harry Doughty (who, not surprisingly, was a keen cricketer!).

Today, the only full-time residents of the island are Harry Doughty's granddaughters, Connie and Rose, as well as Baby Enigma and her two daughters (Margaret and Laura) and their families.

Scribbly Gum Island is the perfect location for a day out. There's just so much to do!

- Take the tour of Alice and Jack's intriguing house and learn more about the Munro Baby Mystery. This is a must! Only $15 for adults, $10 concession.
- Take a break at Connie's Café. Here you'll find the most delectable blueberry muffins and Devonshire teas in Australia!
- Treat the littlies to an exquisite face-painting by Rose Doughty. Just $10 per little face!
- Put some *natural* colour in your cheeks — walk the marked **bush tracks** which criss-cross the island. The most invigorating is the walk up to the top of Kingfisher Lookout. As you walk through the forest in the centre of the island you'll see so much beautiful plant life, including scrib-

bly gum (of course!), banksia, blueberry ash and dwarf apple. Watch out for white-cheeked honeyeaters, pygmy possums, brush-tailed possums, sacred kingfishers and the red-bellied black snake! When you reach Kingfisher Lookout, catch your breath and enjoy your reward: breathtaking views of the island and the dramatic sandstone cliffs that line the Hawkesbury River, which sparkles like a sapphire in the sunshine.

- Enjoy a refreshing swim followed by a picnic lunch at glorious Sultana Rocks on the south side of the island. Pre-packed picnic baskets available from Connie's Café.

- Don't forget to keep an eye out for Alice Munro's ghost. She is said to haunt the island at twilight, wearing a beautiful green dress. (Don't worry — she's friendly!)

Camping is not permitted. All non-residents must leave Scribbly Gum Island by 8 p.m. This rule is strictly enforced.

12

Once, a long time ago, Grace left Callum a love letter in their microwave.

Dear Callum,
Here are five reasons why I love you.
1. You dance with me even though I can't dance.
2. You buy Fruit and Nut even though you prefer boring Dairy Milk.
3. Your gigantic hairy-caveman feet.
4. The way you always laugh at your mum's terrible jokes.
5. The three little freckles in a triangle on the back of your left shoulder.

Love from your Grace.
xxxxxxxxxxxxxxxxxxxxxxxxxxxxxxxx

PS. STOP! Avoid splattering. Put Glad-wrap over whatever you're about to microwave!

Sometimes she still leaves letters for him in the microwave, but now they consist of just one word written in capitals on a Post-it note:

GLADWRAP!

It is the day after Aunt Connie died and Grace's first day alone with the baby. Callum had taken two weeks off but today he is due back at work. It is time for their new lives playing Mummy and Daddy to begin.

'I could extend it,' Callum offers as they sit down to breakfast. 'Death in the family.'

'I'm fine,' says Grace.

Actually, she has woken up with a headache unlike any other headache she has ever experienced. Her head feels like mashed potato. When she tentatively puts her fingertips to her scalp she is surprised that it still feels hard, not soft and pulpy.

She remembers her horrible dream last night about Aunt Connie. Perhaps the headache is grief, but this seems unlikely considering that when Grace thinks about Connie dying she feels absolutely nothing. Grace loved Aunt Connie. She knows that as if it were a biographical fact about somebody else's life. It is just that there is no time to feel things any more. Looking after the baby is like taking some sort of terrifying, never-ending practical exam. All she does is respond to what the baby is doing. Feed baby. Change baby. Wash baby. Keep baby alive. Prepare for when baby wakes again.

When will it all be over? When will she have time to think and feel again? Presumably not till the baby is a teenager and can safely fend for himself. Although, of course, teenagers need to be taught to drive and say no to drugs and wear condoms. She wants to say to Callum, What have we done? We must have been mad! We can't do this!

Except that Callum *can* do it. He holds the baby non-chalantly in the crook of one arm and talks on the phone with the other. When they can't get the baby to sleep, Callum puts him over one shoulder and waltzes around the room, humming Mozart's Violin Concerto No. 2 to him.

Callum is a high-school music teacher. He tells Grace all about something called the 'Mozart effect' and how classical music can develop Jake's 'spatial-temporal reasoning'. Whatever *that* is. Grace is pretty sure she lacks it. It is extremely unlikely that her own mother ever hummed Mozart to her.

The first time she ever saw Callum he was

dancing. They were at a mutual friend's wedding and Grace was sitting at a table drinking champagne to take away the taste of the worst crème brûlée she had ever eaten in her life, when she caught sight of a guy walking onto the dance floor. In spite of his perfectly nice suit there was something strangely loutish about him. His shoulders were a bit too big, his arms a bit too long. But oh my word, as her Grandma Enigma would have said, could that man dance! He danced as naturally as if he were walking. There was no self-conscious 'Yes, yes, we all know I'm the best dancer in the room' smirk. Grace quickly put down her champagne glass, wondering if she was drunk because she had never felt so instantly attracted to a stranger in her life. That big dancing gorilla made her insides go as soft as butter.

She had been thirty years old and she'd never fallen in love so hard or so fast or, well, at all. She had always thought she just wasn't the type to fall in love, not in that abandoned way that other people could: she was too uptight, too hard-headed, too tall. Romantic scenes in films made her toes curl; she wanted to avert her eyes from heartfelt looks the way other women looked away when there was too much blood. When men started to get those sappy expressions on their faces she always felt an inexplicable desire to sneeze.

So when Callum came to pick her up to take her to the movies on their third date, and she opened her front door and her heart fluttered and her legs trembled, it was such a foreign sensation that she genuinely thought, Oh dear, I must be coming down with the flu. When it finally dawned on her that the reason love songs on the radio were starting to sound so poignant was because she was in love herself, it was like discovering a hidden talent, like waking up one day and finding you could sing. So she wasn't a Cold Unfeeling Frigid Bitch after all (the last words of an ex-boyfriend before he slammed down the phone). She was a real, red-blooded woman in love with a high-school music teacher who looked like a labourer but played the cello with his eyes closed, a man with size twelve feet and a secret stash of ballroom-dancing trophies, a man who ate spaghetti straight out of the can while listening to symphonies, a man who seemed fascinated by her every thought and feeling and memory, a man who never kissed her hello or goodbye without whirling her around in a waltz or making her go all weak and giggly with a dramatic cheek-to-cheek tango. He never actually danced *with* her because she couldn't. 'Wouldn't,' Callum said. '*Move,* woman!' But then he'd dip her to the floor and kiss her and she'd think, *Oh God, I'm so happy it's embarrassing.*

Of course, now, four years later, it turns out they are just another ordinary, run-of-the-mill married couple. She is fine with that. She is *so* fine with that. After all, she's a realist. Callum doesn't dance her around the room quite so often, but that is to be expected after all this time. You have to expect the passion to wane. You have to expect these hot flares of irritation, like lit matches.

They are having one of those flares now, at the breakfast table.

'Are you sure you're OK for me to go back to work?' Callum asks. He is eating Crunchy Nut Cornflakes and his spoon clinks against his teeth with each mouthful. When Grace watches television she apparently jiggles her knee up and down. He clinks, she jiggles. One annoying habit cancels out the other.

'I *said* I was sure.'

'OK. I'm just asking.'

'What, do you think I'll drop him without you here to monitor me?' Grace's terror that she will do exactly that makes her voice sound its meanest and most sarcastic.

Callum once asked her why she sometimes spoke to him as if she hated him. 'I do not!' she'd said, surprised and guilty.

'I do not think you'll drop him,' he says now, in a resigned, I'll-be-the-mature-one voice. 'I do think you're looking a bit pale.'

'Thank you, but I'm fine.' She doesn't tell him about her headache. She wants him to go back to work. Maybe it will be easier without him there. She can stop worrying that he might notice she is all wrong as a mother. Perhaps the problem is just that she feels self-conscious.

'I'll make sure I can get the afternoon off for the funeral,' says Callum.

'Good,' says Grace vaguely. She watches him stand up, stretch and go to leave the room, with his breakfast bowl still sitting on the table.

'I'd better get dressed for work.'

'Do you think you could put your plate in the sink?'

'Sorry.' He turns around and puts the bowl in the sink and conscientiously fills it with water.

She is still eating her toast. He puts one hand on her shoulder and she tilts her head and presses her cheek against his hand.

Jab, jab, truce! This, it seems, is marriage

— or their marriage, anyway.

She has regained the high ground with the cereal bowl. He'd felt guilty, she can tell. He has been making a huge effort since the baby was born.

'I'm Callum Tidyman,' he had told her at the wedding, much later in the night, when they were all waiting outside the reception place for the bride and groom to hurry up and leave on their honeymoon. They just happened to be standing next to each other, thanks to some careful shuffling on Grace's part. He was sweaty and messy from his dancing, his shirt coming out the back of his trousers.

He continued, 'And I'm not.'

'A tidy man?'

'That's right. I'm a slob. I've rebelled against my name.'

'Yes, well that's nothing to be proud of,' she said sternly and flirtatiously, already noticing with interest that she was behaving differently than she did with other men.

Back then, she would never have believed it possible that they would one day have an operatic fight over a wet towel left on the bed, or that the sight of a breakfast bowl with a concrete-hard ring of leftover cereal could make her want to bash her head against a wall. Now, when she hears Callum perform his 'tidy man' joke for other people, her smile is a stiff grimace. Oh, ha, ha.

Of course, this whole tidiness issue has got out of hand since they moved into her mother's house — her childhood home — on Scribbly Gum Island.

Even though her mother Laura is thousands of miles away, on a meticulously planned world trip, Grace can feel her presence in every domestic move that she makes. She finds herself holding glasses up to the light, squintily inspecting them for streaks. Every third day she pulls on long, yellow rubber gloves and gets down on her hands and knees to violently scrub the kitchen floor. 'Feet,' she says sharply to Callum whenever he walks in the door, and then waits for him to kick off his shoes with a bemused expression.

'Do you think she'll ground you if we leave a mark on the place?' he asked her once, before the baby was born.

'Oh, we're leaving marks,' said Grace. 'I'll be hearing about them for years to come.'

He said, 'We don't have to live here, you know. If it makes you unhappy.'

'Don't be silly.' Grace made herself laugh. 'It would be stupid to pay rent when this place is sitting here.'

Grace and Callum are building their

dream home in the Blue Mountains. 'Building your dream home is a fast-track to divorce,' one friend helpfully told them, just after they'd signed all the contracts. When Laura had offered her home on the island while she was away for a year it had been too good an offer to refuse. Grace was pregnant and she and Callum had been spending a lot of time at the kitchen table with a calculator, calculating how far they were in over their heads. It would have been madness to turn down Laura's offer. It was such a normal, everyday thing for a mother to offer and a daughter to accept.

'Fantastic,' Callum had said.

'Scribbly Gum isn't the most convenient place to live,' offered Grace.

'Yes, but *free*,' he'd said cheerfully. Things to do with family are simple and straightforward to Callum. There are no murky depths of unexplained feeling.

Grace can't even explain to herself her resistance to accepting favours from her mother. After all, they are perfectly civil with each other these days. Sometimes they even *laugh* together, just for a few seconds, and then there is always an awkward silence — but still. In fact, they'd become so close to normal that at the airport seeing her off, Grace had almost said, 'I'll miss you', but then she had a disconcerting memory of her mother's face looking right through her, smiling slightly, humming a tune while thirteen-year-old Grace beat the insides of her wrists on the edge of the dining-room table and begged, 'Please, Mum, can we please, please stop it now?' So Grace hadn't said, 'I'll miss you', and her mother hadn't said it either.

Callum, of course, had thought that living on Scribbly Gum Island would be a wonderful adventure, but then Callum thinks that anything new is a wonderful adventure, from trying a new brand of tomato sauce to having a baby.

'Sleeping like a baby,' he reports now when he comes back into the kitchen, looking unfamiliar and grown up, wearing a shirt and tie for the first time in two weeks. 'You won't hear from him for another two hours at least, I'd say.'

Watching him, Grace realises that Callum will actually miss the baby while he is at work. All his Daddy instincts have clicked so neatly into place, unlike her missing Mummy instincts.

'Are you taking Vic?' she asks.

'You bet. It's the only fun part of going back to work.'

When they first moved onto the island,

Grace had shown Callum Laura's little outboard motor boat.

'What's she called?' he'd asked.

'It's just called the tinny,' said Grace. 'It's not like a sailing boat.'

Callum had replied, 'You can't just call her the tinny, like she's a can of beer. At least call her Victoria Bitter, after the world's best beer. Vic for short.'

So now the old tinny was called Vic, and Grace feels an obscure sense of failure that she'd never thought to give it a name. It looks perkier now it has a name.

'Get the ferry back if it's raining,' she tells him.

'It'll be fun in the rain.'

'I can assure you it won't.'

'OK, Island Girl.' He kisses her goodbye. 'I'll be home early.'

'It's OK,' says Grace. 'I've got lots to do.'

The first thing she does is spend an hour and a half staring at a milk carton.

It isn't her intention to spend an hour and a half staring at a milk carton. It is an accident. After Callum leaves, it is as though a leaden blanket of silence shrouds the house. The silence is like a sound: a hollow, shrieking sound.

'Right,' Grace thinks, loudly in her head,

73

busily, pretending not to notice the silence. 'Lots to do before the baby wakes. First thing: marble cake.'

Living on the island means performing certain duties for the family business, and this afternoon Grace is giving a tour of the Alice and Jack house. Aunt Connie always insisted that the tours be given by someone who could claim a personal connection to the Munro Baby Mystery. She and Aunt Rose were the sisters who first discovered the Munro Baby, Grandma Enigma was the baby herself, Aunt Margie and Grace's mother Laura were the Munro Baby's daughters, while Grace and her cousins Veronika and Thomas were the grandchildren.

It's been years since Grace has given a tour and she hopes she'll remember her lines. She'll have Jake with her, she remembers with a start. A real live baby. Before Aunt Connie had died, she'd suggested to Grace that she pop Jake in Enigma's crib to give the tour an authentic touch. 'You can bet your bottom dollar some silly ninny will ask if it's the same baby,' Connie had snorted, and slapped her thigh with a withered hand.

One of the responsibilities of giving the tour is making the marble cake to be left cooling on the kitchen table. It's meant to be made to Alice's original recipe, but every member of the Scribbly Gum family bakes a slightly different version. Grandma Enigma puts in two tablespoons of honey, while Aunt Rose likes half a teaspoon of grated nutmeg. Thomas uses one egg, Veronika uses two, and Grace uses three. Nobody, not even Laura, would ever dare to use a packet mix.

Marble cake, thinks Grace. You need to start the marble cake, *now*. But she just keeps sitting there, staring at the carton of milk that Callum used for his breakfast cereal and, of course, left sitting on the table.

She thinks through exactly what she needs to do:

Stand up.

Pick up the milk.

Walk to the fridge.

Open the fridge.

Place the milk in the fridge.

Close the fridge door.

But to do all that she needs her brain to send electrical impulses to her legs, her arms and her hands, and it seems that her brain is refusing to cooperate. She knows about electrical impulses from a science teacher from her school days who once set up an elaborate display of dominoes on the classroom floor in the shape of a human body. The idea was to demonstrate how your brain transmitted electrical impulses through your nerve cells. That's how you moved.

Instead of toppling like dominoes, Grace's nerves are rigid, waiting for electrical impulses that aren't forthcoming. Her brain is having a black-out. It is quite possible that she has a brain tumour.

She needs to pick up that milk carton. She has things to do. She is very busy. Mr Callahan. That was the science teacher's name. In her memory it was always winter when Mr Callahan taught science. He wore brightly coloured jumpers and often had a phlegmy, hacking cough that repelled the girls in his class. 'Mr *Call*ahan, maybe you could take some sort of medicine because that's so disgusting!'

It must have taken him so long to set up all those dominoes before the class.

Grace looks at the milk carton and grief sweeps over her. She thinks of Mr Callahan's excited pink face. That poor, sweet man. Some girl had flicked one of the dominoes before he'd finished his explanation. He had probably thought, Now this will intrigue them. This will stop all that talking and giggling!

Grace puts her head in her hands and weeps inconsolably for Mr Callahan's disappointment.

Finally, she stops crying and looks again at the milk carton.

Move, she tells herself. Stand up. Put the milk in the fridge. Make the marble cake. Do a load of washing. He'll be awake soon.

She reads, *'If this product is not to your satisfaction, we will cheerfully refund your money.'* She imagines a cheerful lady, in a floral apron, cheerfully refunding her money. 'There you go, dear! Can't have you not happy!'

But I'm so unhappy. I'm so very, very unhappy.

The cheerful lady says, 'Oh, sweetheart!' and pats her hand.

Oh for Christ's sake, now she is crying over some imaginary cheerful lady. She cries and cries and cries. Every tear is fresh, fat and salty. They run down either side of her nose and into her mouth.

Finally she stops, wipes the back of her hand across her face and looks again at the milk carton.

Stand up, Grace!

She glances at her watch. And that's when she discovers it's nine thirty. She claps her hand over her mouth. It can't be right. It has only been five minutes. Ten at the most. But according to her watch she has been sitting in this chair, staring at a milk carton, for an hour and fifteen minutes.

How can she complain about Callum not doing enough around the house, if she spends her days staring at milk cartons?

The telephone rings and Grace's nerve cells finally topple like dominoes. She gets to her feet, puts the milk in the fridge and calmly answers the phone.

'Grace! Is it a bad time? A good time? How is the baby? Asleep? Awake? This is Veronika, by the way. I hate people who just expect you to know who it is, don't you? Have you heard? Have you heard what Aunt Connie has done?'

Grace's cousin Veronika rarely requires answers to her questions. 'She's like a breathless, busy little ferret!' said Callum, fascinated, the first time he met her, as if Veronika was some unusual creature he'd seen on a nature programme. It is true that Veronika has sharp, pointy teeth and darting brown eyes.

That's why I was crying, thinks Grace. I'm grieving for Aunt Connie. I miss Aunt Connie. Of course I do.

'I know that she left her house to Thomas's

78

ex-girlfriend, if that's what you mean. Your mum told me.'

'Did your jaw drop? Mine did! Of *all* people: Sophie! A complete stranger! If it wasn't for me, Aunt Connie would never have even known of Sophie's existence! And then she just ignores her own flesh and blood!'

Veronika is an intelligent girl but sometimes she says things that are so easy to refute that Grace has to wonder if she does it on purpose.

'Yes, but we're not Aunt Connie's flesh and blood, are we?'

'But we are! Well, perhaps not *biologically,* but spiritually and morally and perhaps legally! I mean, Aunt Connie and Aunt Rose brought Grandma Enigma up as their own baby! If they hadn't found her that day, she would have died. A baby can't survive long without care. Well, you know that better than anyone! A new mother!'

Grace thinks about Jake, asleep in his crib, blue-veined eyelids fluttering. How long would he survive if she followed her great-grandmother's lead and vanished from his life? Baby Enigma had thrived. According to Aunt Connie and Aunt Rose, she'd been sleeping peacefully, and when they looked into her crib she had opened her eyes and

79

given them the sweetest smile they had ever seen.

Grace says to Veronika, 'What does it matter? None of us want Aunt Connie's house, do we? You always said you'd rather die than live on the island again. You said it makes you feel trapped. Actually, I think I recall you saying that to Aunt Connie, which might have been your downfall.'

'This isn't about me wanting the house. It's the principle of the matter. Sophie broke Thomas's heart!'

'So? He seems to have recovered. Last time I saw him he was so disgustingly happy it put me in a bad mood.'

'That's not relevant!'

Grace begins to feel exhausted. Her mother doesn't own a walkabout phone. The phone is kept on an antique table in the hallway, so you have to stand up with your shoulders back while you talk. No cosy, curled-up conversations in armchairs. She slides down to the floor with her back against the wall.

'Look. If this is what Aunt Connie wanted . . .'

'Sophie could only have met Aunt Connie twice at the most!'

'Well, she obviously had an impact.'

'Yes, what a conniving, manipulative witch!'

'I thought she was your friend?'

Veronika ignores that. 'This morning I heard an ad on the radio for solicitors who actually specialise in this sort of thing. I'm thinking that we all contest the will.'

Suddenly Grace is angry. 'We haven't even had Aunt Connie's funeral yet! I don't want anything to do with contesting the will. Aunt Connie was perfectly sane and had every right to leave her house to whoever she wanted.'

Veronika's voice bubbles up and over, relishing the opportunity to argue. 'You have no sense of family, Grace! No sense of history!'

'I'm hanging up. The baby's crying.'

'I don't believe you. I can't hear the baby. You've always avoided confrontation!'

'And you've always sought it. I'm hanging up.'

'Don't you dare hang up on me! Face this conflict!'

Grace hangs up. She lets her head drop forward onto her knees.

There is a sharp, cross cry from upstairs. Grace looks at her watch, terrified that another hour has vanished without her. What if the baby has been crying and crying without her hearing?

It's fine. Only a few minutes have passed. The incident in the kitchen was an aberration.

She gets slowly to her feet like an arthritic old woman. With her hand on the banister for support she walks up the stairs, hoping with each step that this time she'll feel it. But when she walks into the baby's room and picks up her screaming son, she feels nothing except intense boredom. A drab, dreary sense of nothing much at all.

She changes his nappy and takes him into the bedroom and sits on the end of the bed, unbuttoning her shirt with one hand. The baby's agitated mouth sucks at the air for her nipple. Finally she manages to get him to latch on and his eyes roll back in ecstasy while he sucks feverishly.

Grace's aunt, Margie, had mentioned yesterday that she didn't know about any 'Mozart effect' but she had certainly sung to Thomas and Veronika when she was feeding them as babies. 'It did seem to keep them focused on the job!'

Dutifully, wearily, Grace begins to sing.

In the afternoon, Grace puts Jake in his state-of-the-art stroller. It's one of those ones you can jog behind, but she can't imagine having the energy or desire to ever go for a run again. She and Callum had practised running around the shop with it. They'd made other shoppers laugh and there'd been a chummy community feeling about it. That sort of thing was always happening with Callum.

Outside, it is cold and bright and still; the river is flat and hard.

Grace looks worriedly at the cooling marble cake in her mother's cake tin, sitting on top of the stroller. She had to throw it together in a frantic rush and she's not even sure it's cooked all the way through. It's just her luck that it's a group of older women doing the tour rather than school kids.

Aunt Connie had told her about the group booking just a few days before she died.

'Are you sure you can manage it?' she'd asked. 'I wouldn't ask you, but Enigma, Rose and I are going to that recital at the opera house and Margie has her ridiculous Weight Watchers meeting. It's like a new religion for her. She can't miss one session.'

'I'll be fine!' Grace had said. 'At this age they're still so portable! It's not like he's a toddler.'

She'd stolen that 'portable' line from a friend. She'd even stolen her happy, casual, motherly tone of voice. Grace doesn't think babies are portable at all.

'Well, if you're sure,' Connie had said doubtfully. 'The booking is for the *Shirley Club*. A club for women called Shirley. Isn't that the funniest thing you've ever heard? There are fifteen of them. Fifteen Shirleys. "You're not serious," I said. She said, "Oh, but we are!" I said, "Well, give me your credit card details, *Shirley*." '

Grace wonders who will handle the bookings now that Connie has died. Perhaps Sophie will take that responsibility along with the house. That would infuriate Veronika.

The Shirleys are an excitable bunch of women in their fifties and sixties, all wearing similar brightly coloured, comfy parkas, long scarves, beanies, and sunglasses that are too large for their faces. They giggle and chat like girls on a school excursion. Perhaps being called Shirley guarantees you a cheerful personality.

They'd caught the train and then the ferry from Glass Bay, and are full of praise for the weather, the scenery, the island and the hot chocolates down at the wharf.

'It's the most beautiful island! Have you lived here long, love?'

'I grew up here,' says Grace. 'But I only

just moved back about six weeks ago, before my baby was born.'

'Are you a model, sweetheart?'

'No, no, I'm a graphic designer.'

'Well, you *could* be a model. Couldn't she, Shirl?'

Jake is passed around from Shirley to Shirley and looks perfectly content in each expert pair of arms. Grace wonders if she should be worried about letting so many strangers hold him, but decides it's worth it. He is being topped up with all the proper motherly love he is missing out on. Besides which, these energetic women are far too cleanly scrubbed to harbour germs.

She stands on the front porch and begins the speech she, Thomas and Veronika were all taught to give when they turned sixteen and were considered old enough to take their turns at the Alice and Jack tours.

'Welcome to the home of my great-grandparents, Alice and Jack Munro. Some of you may have heard of a famous, mysterious ship called the *Mary Celeste*. It was found adrift in 1872, sailing itself across the Atlantic Ocean. The crew and passengers had vanished. There were no signs of struggle and the ship was in perfect condition, with plenty of food and water. Well, this house is similar to the *Mary Celeste*.

When Connie and Rose Doughty visited this house in 1932, there were no *immediate* signs that anything was amiss, yet Alice and Jack had vanished into thin air. The difference is that in this case there *was* one survivor. A tiny baby was just waking for her feed. That baby was my grandmother.'

And pause, one, two, three.

Aunt Connie had told them to always pause at that moment for dramatic effect. Grace considered herself quite good at the pause, unlike Veronika, who spoke much too fast and added too many of her own peculiar opinions to Aunt Connie's carefully drafted script, and Thomas, who was painfully shy at sixteen and delivered his tours in a barely audible monotone.

Jake gives a little whimper and the Shirleys all cluck. 'Imagine! A tiny baby like you! Your mummy wouldn't leave you on your own even for a *minute,* would she!'

Grace looks at her son, his face blissfully squished against a Shirley's large purple-T-shirted breast. He seems very content.

'I'll invite you all now to enter the house. Please remember that the house has not been disturbed in over seventy years, so we do ask that you refrain from touching anything.'

She opens the front door of the house and

in they troop, all bright-eyed beams and exclamations, while Grace mentally checks off the list of things she needs to cover:

Cake.

Kettle.

Blood stains.

Connie and Rose.

Alice's diary.

Jack's love letter.

Theories.

Questions.

Souvenirs.

She'd never been very good at the souvenirs part. That was where Veronika excelled. She could bully anyone into buying anything.

After the tour is finished, Grace stands on the veranda of Alice and Jack's house and waves the Shirley Club goodbye, a colourful gaggle of women winding their way back down the hill towards the ferry, arms swinging, energy unflagging, going back home to cook their husbands' dinners.

Jake is sound asleep in his pram, a smudge of a Shirley's lipstick over one eyebrow.

I should have asked them to adopt you, thinks Grace. Fifteen no-nonsense, happy, laughing, loving mums. What a perfect life. But your daddy would miss you.

She doesn't allow herself to think about whether she would miss him too.

13

'Don't tell me! Salmon and salad on multi-grain. No butter, no beetroot, no onion!'

'You got it!' shouts Sophie across the crowd of people at the sandwich shop. She is actually a little bored with salmon and salad sandwiches, but Al, the man who owns the shop, takes such professional pride in remembering her lunch order that she doesn't feel she can change it. Once she'd said, 'I think I might have ham and cheese today,' and he'd said, 'Oh, feel like something a bit different, eh?' and looked hurt, his tongs hovering uncertainly over the sandwich fillings. After all, salmon and salad is a delicious combination. Sometimes she does go to other places for lunch, but then, the next day, Al cries, 'We missed you yesterday! Where were you?' and Sophie thinks, This is ridiculous. Why don't I just admit I had won ton soup at the Chinese takeaway? But Al seems so convinced she is in a monogamous relationship with his sandwich shop that she has to pretend to sneeze to cover up her guilty blush. 'Ah, you had the flu!' Al says kindly. As a result, he has decided she is a rather sickly sort.

'Keeping up that vitamin C, Sally?' he asks today as he expertly compiles her sandwich. That's the other problem with Al. He thinks her name is Sally. Sophie is sure she must have tried to correct him at least once but now the moment for setting him straight has long passed. He has been calling her Sally for three years. Once, he confided to her that was how he remembered her sandwich order. 'I just think to myself, here comes Sally Salmon!'

That had given her such a bad attack of the giggles she'd had to pretend to sneeze six times in a row, causing Al to worriedly suggest garlic tablets.

'Actually, you're looking well today, Sally,' he says now. He nudges his wife who is chopping up boiled eggs. 'Look. Sally is glowing today. She looks even prettier than usual.'

'Hmmph,' says his wife, who doesn't seem to like working in a sandwich shop or being married to Al.

'Is love in the air, perhaps, Sally?' asks Al. He flutters a hygienically gloved hand like a butterfly.

'Perhaps,' says Sophie. 'Oh, well, not really.' She feels her heart lift as she thinks about Aunt Connie's letter, sitting safely in the zippered pocket of her handbag. 'But I got some good news.'

'Did you now,' says Al, and then his eyes flicker to another regular in the crowd. 'Don't tell me! Avocado and salami!'

'You got it,' says a resigned voice.

Sophie picks up her brown paper bag, gives avocado and salami a sympathetic smile and pushes her way through the crowd and out onto the streets of Sydney. She walks down into the Domain to her usual spot to eat her lunch under a Moreton Bay fig, where she can read her book and watch the sporty types from nearby offices playing netball and soccer in their lunch breaks. It is the middle of winter and the air is frosty cold but the sun is hot and summery. The sporty types are red-faced and sweaty.

'*Pass,* Jen!' calls out an anguished netballer. 'I'm here! Would you *pass*!' Jen, a rather large girl with black hair, flings the ball wildly and the other team intercepts it. There are groans of disgust and Jen looks doleful, hands on her hips, chest heaving. She is probably a high-powered lawyer, thinks Sophie, but every Wednesday at lunchtime she is the kid who nobody wants on their team. Sophie watches the game for a bit and then pulls her book from her bag. She is starting to get to know far too many of these people and has already identified a blossoming romance between the tall Goal Attack and a married-to-somebody-else soccer player. If she isn't careful these lunchtime games will become her own personal reality TV programme, and she is already unhealthily hooked on too much socially unacceptable television. One should *not* be listening to a very interesting lecture on ancient Greek mythology, like she was last Monday night, and realise that one is actually thinking about who is the most likely candidate to be voted off on tonight's episode of *The Bachelorette.*

She catches herself hiding the cover of her book in her lap and defiantly holds it upright for the world to see. Reality TV is one thing, but it's silly to be ashamed of her choice of reading material. After all, these books are often extremely well written and meticulously researched. They are historically interesting, witty and clever. She should just come right out and tell people: 'It so happens I quite enjoy a good . . . regency romance.' She'd caught the habit from her mother, who isn't in the least concerned about what people think and even belongs to a Regency Romance Readers' Club. Once a year they have a party where everyone has to dress up as lords and ladies. Sophie's dad always goes along, stoic and ridiculous in his cravat, breeches, stockings and waistcoat. Now that's true love: a man who is prepared to wear a cravat for you.

Many of Sophie's friends blame regency romances for what they describe as her 'unrealistic' approach to her love life. Recently, there has been an aggressive campaign to get her to join an Internet dating site.

'There is nothing sleazy or desperate about Internet dating,' declares Lisa, who met her boyfriend in a Paris bookstore.

'I know so many people who are doing it, you don't need to feel ashamed,' says Shari, married to a paramedic who fell in love with her when he was winched down by helicopter to rescue her after she broke her ankle in a bushwalking accident.

'It's *fun,* it's *great* fun, it's so *easy* and *convenient,*' cries Amanda, who actually did meet her husband on the Internet. Sophie doesn't really like Amanda's husband, and she suspects that Amanda doesn't like him much either, which accounts for her demented enthusiasm on the topic.

She is resisting the Internet idea, not just because of Amanda's husband but also because she doesn't want to one day tell her children that she posted an ad on the Internet, interviewed twenty-five hopeful applicants, and finally their father turned up and looked good in comparison with the rest of them. It just doesn't seem right.

Anyway, when she thinks about a truthful description of herself it makes her wince.

Thirty-nine-year-old moderately successful Human Resources Director. Interests include regency romances, reality TV, and baking large novelty birthday cakes for other people's children. Hobbies include drinking Tia Maria and eating Turkish delight in the bath and dining out with her mum and dad. Wanted to be a ballerina but didn't end up with a ballerina body; however, has been told she is an impressive dirty dancer when drunk. Knows her wine, so please just hand the wine list over. Godmother to nine children, member of two book clubs, Social Club Manager for the Australian Payroll Officers' Association. Suffers from a severe blushing problem but is not shy and will probably end up better friends with your friends than you, which you'll find highly irritating after we break up. Has recently become so worried about meeting the love of her life and having children before she reaches menopause that she has cried piteously in the middle of the night. But otherwise is generally quite cheerful and has on at least three separate occasions that she knows of been described as 'Charming'.

Yep, that about summed it up. What a catch. If Sophie was a man she wouldn't date herself. She'd run a mile. 'Jeez,' she'd say, '*regency romances*! Give me a scuba-diving, marathon-running, catamaran-sailing woman!' The problem is that Sophie wouldn't want to date the sort of man who would want to date her. She imagines too skinny a man with too nice a complexion, saying, 'Oh, regency romances, how interesting!' Blah.

She looks up from her book to watch a family group setting up a picnic nearby. The daddy in his business suit, the mummy in a pretty pink cardigan and skirt, two frolicking angels with white-blond hair. They've come in to meet Daddy in his lunch break and he's so chuffed to see them! Good God, they look like something from a television commercial. Daddy is caressing Mummy's hand and she's giggling at something he's said. Is Mummy looking over and wishing she was a free, single career-woman like Sophie? Nope. No way. She's so blindingly happy it hurts to look at her.

Oh stop it. You are not going to turn into one of those embittered, jaded single women. They're a lovely family. If you knew them, you'd be their friend. One of the blond angels comes toddling over to where Sophie is sitting under the tree. He holds out a grubby fist to her and shows her a piece of bark.

'Wow!' says Sophie. 'That's very pretty.'

'Sorry!' The mummy runs over and scoops up her child. 'Don't disturb the lady.'

'It's OK,' says Sophie. It's perfectly OK that you appear to be at least ten years younger than me, and you already have two children, and I'm a 'lady' who doesn't even have a boyfriend. No problem. It's fine.

There is something so undignified about being single when you're nearly forty. It's not glamorous any more, or funny. It's sad and sometimes it's lonely, even when you do have a Christmas card list numbering over one hundred and you can remember the birthdays of at least forty different people, not even counting their children.

For God's sake, even the girls on *Sex and the City* all got matched up in the final episode.

On Saturday afternoon, Sophie had talked to a friend who described what she'd done that morning: two loads of washing, grocery shopping, driving children to soccer and ballet, and so on and so forth. She might even have baked a cake. It was quite extraordinary.

'What have you been doing?' asked the friend.

'Oh, cleaned the bathroom, paid a few bills, you know, just pottering,' said Sophie, stifling a yawn.

Actually, she was still in her pyjamas and all she'd achieved that morning was getting out of bed. She hadn't even managed to feed herself breakfast yet. It made her feel like a frivolous flibbertigibbet from one of her regency romances, except that frivolous flibbertigibbets don't have wrinkles that appear on either side of their mouths when the bathroom lights are too bright, and they don't feel sick when they see magazine articles about the decreasing fertility of women in their late thirties.

She remembers a woman at her first job who used to sit at the desk next to her doing data entry and saying at regular intervals, 'Oops! Stuffed it up, buttercup!' It seems an appropriate description for Sophie's life: *Oops! Stuffed it up, buttercup. You forgot to get a family!*

She reads a page of her book. The heroine in her regency romance engages in sparkling banter with her dashing suitor.

Maybe Sophie should try out Internet dating. Maybe she is unrealistically romantic. Maybe she does think her life is a friggin' fairytale, like her friend Claire had said once when they were both very drunk. 'Sophie, your problem is that you think life is a friggin' fairytale. You're so friggin' optimistic you don't just see the glass as half-full, you see it as *full,* of, of . . . pink champagne! And the thing is, *the glass isn't full,* Sophie! It's half *empty!*' Claire said 'friggin' a lot when she was drunk. It was funny. She always denied it the next day.

Sophie munches her way through her sandwich without really tasting it. She should just come clean with Al and tell him she's sick to death of salmon and salad and she wants something really loopy like curried egg and asparagus. She is in a rut. That's the problem. These sandwiches are a symbol of a life that's going nowhere.

Ah, but then again, how could she have forgotten? Her life isn't in a rut! It's at a crossroads, a turning point. Her life actually *is* like a fairytale and Aunt Connie is her fairy godmother. She puts down the book and takes out the letter from her handbag to re-read it for about the hundredth time. It's weirdly compelling reading something written 'from the grave', so to speak.

You would expect a letter from an old lady to be written in spidery handwriting on lavender-scented notepaper — it's typical of Aunt Connie that hers is perfectly typed in Microsoft Word and looks like a business letter. Apparently she did a computer course when she was eighty.

Sophie tries to visualise Connie sitting at her computer to type it. She remembers an upright, white-haired woman with powdery, papery skin, a longish, fine-boned face and intelligent brown eyes that dared you to even think about treating her like an old person. Some elderly people look like they've always been old, but Connie looked like a young person who had aged a great deal. She was frail, and moved slowly but impatiently, as if she was driving too slow a car. You could tell that once upon a time she'd been the sort of person who never sat still.

It had been a summer's day when Thomas had taken Sophie to visit, and there was the smell of an approaching storm in the air. Sophie was feeling flippant and skittish, while Thomas was in one of his stodgy grown-up moods that made Sophie want to act like a rebellious teenager. He didn't like going to visit his family on Scribbly Gum; he preferred it when they came into Sydney. 'It's such a hassle getting out there,' he'd say, in an exhausted tone, as if it involved a mountain trek. He'd only taken Sophie out to the island two or three times while they'd been dating, in spite of the fact that Sophie was always hopefully suggesting it.

They'd had lunch first with his parents, Margie and Ron. It was Margie who had said it might be a good idea to stop in and say hello to Connie before they caught the ferry back. Connie's husband Jimmy had died just a couple of months earlier. Thomas hadn't complained — he was a good, dutiful son — but he was anxious to get off the island.

'I just start to feel a bit trapped when I'm here for too long,' he'd told Sophie as they walked down the hill towards Aunt Connie's place. 'It's so *small,* you know what I mean?'

'Not really,' Sophie had answered, taking in a deep breath of salt-tanged air.

Connie had seemed graciously, if not effusively, pleased to see them. She made them cinnamon toast and chatted articulately with Thomas about his favourite topics: federal politics and cricket. Sophie could sense in Connie a terrible restrained grief for her husband. She had sad pink half-moons under her eyes and Jimmy's presence was still everywhere: an old man's cardigan draped over the back of a chair, a pair of muddy black boots on the front porch, framed prints of newspaper articles he'd written, including, of course, his story breaking the news about the Munro Baby Mystery.

Connie had given Sophie a slow, painful tour of the house, and she'd seemed to appreciate it when Sophie said how much she liked it, so Sophie hadn't held back with her compliments. Not that they weren't genuine. She'd never been in a house which had appealed to her so much before; she'd never been in someone else's home and thought to herself, 'I'd give anything to live here.'

Oh dear, thinks Sophie now, perhaps I didn't just think that, maybe I actually said it out loud to Aunt Connie. Still. She hadn't meant it as a *hint.*

She'd just honestly fallen in love with that

house. Ever since she got the news from Thomas she has felt like hugging herself with glee each time she remembers something new. The jasmine-covered archway at the top of the garden path leading to the front door. That gigantic green claw bathtub. Honey-coloured floorboards. Stained-glass windows reflecting reds and blues in the late afternoon sun. Glittering pieces of river from every window. The tiny looping staircase to the main bedroom. The window seat where you could curl up with a regency romance and a Turkish delight. It really was like a house in a fairytale.

But is it wrong to accept it? She reads the letter one more time, trying hard to be objective, trying to see herself through Aunt Connie's eyes. She lingers over the PS. She is trying not to take the PS too seriously. Nothing will come of it, of course. It's just a bit of fun. Just a bit of heart-lifting fun.

Sophie's mobile rings and she answers it, her mouth full of sandwich, still thinking about the PS.

'Sophie, this is Veronika.'

Sophie makes a strangled sound. 'Oh, *hi*!' she says brightly and falsely, as guilty as a murderer.

'I just thought it was polite to let you know that we'll be contesting Aunt Connie's will. Everybody in the family is terribly hurt by what you've done.'

Sophie holds the phone slightly away from her ear. Veronika always speaks too loudly on the phone, and when she is angry it's even more painful than usual.

'Just remind me exactly what I've done?'

'Ha! You know, I used to pride myself on being a good judge of character but it just goes to show how wrong you can be. I would never have thought you capable of this! Manipulating a defenceless old lady like that! I thought you were a *friend*! I even thought you were a *good* friend! But, oh, I see *exactly* what you are now. You may think you can walk all over Thomas but the rest of us aren't quite so stupid. I just got off the phone from my cousin Grace and she could hardly bear to talk about it, she was so appalled by what you've done.'

'Really?'

For some reason the thought of Grace, who Sophie barely knows, thinking badly of her is more distressing than Veronika, her friend of many years, thinking she is an evil manipulator of old ladies. Sophie has only met Grace just once, years ago, at Veronika's wedding, but she has a schoolgirl crush on her. Grace is beautiful — achingly, ridiculously beautiful: the unfair sort of beauty that made it a painful pleasure just to look at her. Plus, there is that comment in Aunt Connie's letter about Grace.

'Tell Grace not to be upset with me,' she says frivolously. 'Tell her I'm a big contributor to her royalties. I'm always buying her books as presents!'

Ever since Veronika had mentioned that Grace wrote and illustrated a series of children's picture books about an evil little elf called Gublet, Sophie has been buying her books as presents for her friends' children. The illustrations are gorgeous, full of detail and an intriguing touch of menace that kids, especially the brattier ones, seem to love. The Gublet books only add to Grace's mystique.

'You're not even taking this seriously!' explodes Veronika. 'I have nothing more to say to you, Sophie. I forgave you for what you did to Thomas but this is genuinely unforgivable. My family will be fighting this all the way to the highest court in the land. And I will not say another word to you in my *lifetime*!'

'Starting from . . . now?' asks Sophie.

But Veronika is true to her word and hangs up.

She must be genuinely upset to actually stop talking.

Whenever Veronika gets on her high horse about anything, from her opinion on a movie to her views on abortion, it brings out a flip, sarcastic side of Sophie's personality. Afterwards she always feels bad, and now she feels particularly guilty.

Part of her had been thinking that this whole thing with Aunt Connie's house had been all about destiny. It had been her destiny to become friends with Veronika, even though it was an annoying friendship at times. It was her destiny to date Veronika's brother, Thomas, even though it had all ended so horribly. It was her destiny to live in Aunt Connie's wonderful home on Scribbly Gum Island. That was the final pay-off. She deserved it!

But now it occurs to Sophie to wonder if perhaps she had been subconsciously manipulating her destiny.

She remembers when she first met Veronika at a friend's baby shower. Sophie was supervising the cutting of the cake — one of hers, of course — featuring a pair of baby booties made out of cup cakes, when she heard somebody saying in a clear, sharp voice that she'd grown up on Scribbly Gum Island.

'Did you really?' Sophie had chimed in, leaning across another woman to hand the stranger a piece of booty. 'What was that like?'

Sophie had a thing about Scribbly Gum Island. She'd adored it ever since her first visit on a school excursion when she was a child. She disagreed passionately with people who described the island as 'a bit twee, don't you think?' She'd done the Alice and Jack tour a dozen times, staring with fresh fascination at the clothes still hanging in the cupboard, the baby's crib, the newspaper sitting open on 15 July 1932 — the crossword halfway completed. She'd picnicked at Sultana Rocks, had birthday lunches at Connie's Café and convinced friends that the blueberry muffins and hot chocolates were worth the train and ferry ride, especially on a cold winter's day. She once had a terrible fight with a boyfriend when they were holidaying in the Greek islands over whether the view from Kingfisher Lookout on Scribbly Gum Island was prettier than the view from their hotel window in Santorini. (She said it was, he said she was deliberately being ridiculous.)

When Sophie learned that Veronika was the granddaughter of the Munro Baby, she was as thrilled as if she'd met a favourite celebrity.

It was true that Veronika had been the one

to rather aggressively pursue the friendship. She had invited Sophie to lunches and drinks and bullied her into doing a belly-dancing course with her. Sophie had enjoyed the course. She thought it was a hoot. When she managed to restrain her gales of laughter she was rather good at it — the teacher's pet in fact. Veronika was the worst in the class but took it all terribly seriously, listening intently to the instructions and zealously trying to jiggle her skinny hips. That was when Sophie became fond of Veronika. Sophie's other friends would have been collapsing with giggles or refused to really try. There was something endearing about Veronika's hopeless persistence.

Still, the Scribbly Gum connection probably helped make the friendship more attractive and made up for Veronika's more aggravating characteristics, such as her energy-draining intensity over *everything*. One of the guys at work had openly admitted to cultivating a friendship with someone who owned a yacht. What if Sophie had subconsciously been doing the same with Veronika, even while she was congratulating herself on her saintly fortitude?

But what would she have been hoping to achieve? Veronika hadn't even taken her to meet her family on Scribbly Gum Island —

'Oh, why would you want to go there? *Boring!*' It wasn't until Sophie had started dating Veronika's brother that she got to visit. Unless, of course, dating Thomas had been the next step in her dastardly plan.

She looks at her watch. It's time to get back to work. She has a meeting at two. She will read Connie's letter to her parents tonight over dinner and see what they think. If they say it's wrong to accept the house she won't take it.

I'm a good person, Sophie reminds herself. Everybody loves me. I give to charity. I recycle. I buy things I don't want from door-to-door salesmen. I've been a bridesmaid seven bloody times. I'm not the sort of person to manipulate an old lady.

'NOOOOOO!'

Sophie looks up to see the angelic blond toddler in the middle of a ferocious tantrum, flipping his body back and forth while his mother tries to strap him in his stroller and yells at the other child to 'STAY STILL, HARRY'. The daddy has escaped, striding back to work, his tie swinging.

Actually, thinks Sophie, as she stands up and brushes crumbs off her skirt, she's quite looking forward to her meeting on graduate recruitment strategies.

14

Gublet McDublet was a very naughty little elf.

Every day, his mum said to him, 'Now, Gublet, do you think it's going to be a Good Gublet day or a Bad Gublet day?'

Every day, Gublet answered the same way, 'A GOOD Gublet day!'

But guess what? Every day turned out to be a Bad Gublet day.

One day, Gublet said, 'Oh fuck it, Mum, you're a boring old hag,' and he took a knife and lopped off his sweet mummy's head.

Grace looks at the line drawing she has scribbled of a ferociously grinning elf with blood dripping from a butcher's knife. Oh dear. It isn't going to be a Good Gublet day for Grace, is it? Next thing she'll have Gublet raping his best friend, Melly the Music Box Dancer — ripping off Melly's sparkly tutu and giving it to her right there on the pink satin music-box floor.

Where are these perverse and strangely bitchy thoughts coming from? They aren't at all appropriate for a new mother. Her head should be full of lullabies and bunnies, not blood and rape.

Grace pulls the sheet of paper from her sketchbook and screws it up into a hard ridged ball.

It is eleven a.m. on her second day at home alone with the baby. He is asleep upstairs, fed and burped and clean and swaddled ('like wrapping a burrito' Callum said when the nurse showed them at the hospital) and, most importantly, breathing. She is successfully keeping him alive and so far she hasn't broken any important rules or made any fatal errors, but still, every move she makes continues to feel fake and forced, like she's pretending to be this baby's mother and the real mother will be along soon to look after him properly. She can't shake a constant, underlying feeling of terror.

All new mothers are nervous, she tells herself.

Not like this.

Yes, of course they are.

It's perfectly normal.

I am perfectly normal. I am a new mother sitting down with a cup of tea.

She tries again to draw Gublet's familiar features. He stares back at her with a new cold, bland expression.

This hasn't happened to her before. It has always been such a pleasure to work on Gublet. She was never stuck for inspiration; all she needed was time.

Grace has been working on her Gublet McDublet books for over four years now. He started as a doodle. Whenever she was talking on the phone, a wicked elf character would appear on her notebook. She became fond of him and eventually, just for fun, not really thinking too hard about it, she made up a funny story about Gublet's first day at school. It was Callum who secretly sent it off to a children's book publisher he'd picked out of the *Yellow Pages* and, astonishingly, they agreed to publish it as a hardbound picture book for three- to five-year-olds. So far she hasn't made enough money to be able to give up her day job as a graphic designer for a company that specialises in beautiful annual reports. There isn't that much money in the children's picture-book market unless you are phenomenally successful, and besides which, so far each of the two Gublet books has taken her over two years to complete. 'Two *years!*' people always say with disbelief and a hint of derision. They seem to think she should be able to knock one off in a couple of weeks, when each illustration is actually an oil painting on canvas, a labour of love one generous reviewer described as 'exquisite works of art'.

When her first book was launched, the local pre-school invited her to read her Gublet book to a group of cross-legged, squirming four-year-olds. She was nervous. Children made her feel huge and awkward and she was never sure exactly how to correctly pitch her conversation for their age group, worrying that she was speaking to them as if they were retarded or deaf. When friends suddenly (bizarrely!) put their heavy-breathing toddlers on the phone to talk to her, Grace would more often than not just sit there in tongue-tied silence. What in the world was she meant to say? 'So, what have you been up to lately?' 'Hear you just learned to walk, hey? How's that going, then?'

She was convinced the pre-schoolers wouldn't like her. After all, people generally didn't. Friends were always cosily informing her how much they'd disliked her at their first meeting. 'You just seemed so cold and standoffish.' The children probably wouldn't hide their dislike like grown-ups. They'd probably boo and hiss. Maybe they'd all suddenly attack her like rabid little rats. Who knew what they'd do? They were another species.

She was sure that she sounded ridiculous as she read her own words to the pre-schoolers, but then she got her first laugh. It was the part where Gublet jumped up and down on his mum's yucky pumpkin pie like a trampoline. The children whooped. One got up to demonstrate how he would jump in a similar situation. The teacher, sitting at the back of the room, gave her a thumbs-up, as if she knew Grace had been nervous, and the kids sat back down and looked up at her with open flower-like faces, eyes shining expectantly, ready for the next funny part. So *this* was what people saw in children.

After she'd finished reading, when the teacher asked them if they had any questions, every hand shot in the air, straining high for her attention.

'Is Gublet so naughty all the time because he wishes he didn't have pointy ears?'

'Would Gublet like to come to my party? Do you think he would jump up and down on my cake? My mum would be pretty cross with him!'

'Gublet is *funny* when he's naughty! I laughed so much! I laughed until *forever*!'

'That time when Gublet's mum sent him to the moon for being naughty and he rang up Melly and then they ran away to Mars, well, guess what, that happened to me too! But guess what, it wasn't real! It was a *dream*!'

Hearing a client say 'The CEO was quite impressed with your design concepts' could never compare with the intense pleasure Grace felt hearing a four-year-old say 'I laughed until *forever*!'

So that was the day she decided that what she really wanted to do with her life was work full-time on her Gublet books. When she got pregnant and her mother had offered them her house on Scribbly Gum, she and Callum had gone out to dinner and worked out a whole life plan.

She would take maternity leave from the graphic-design studio, but hopefully she'd never have to go back. When the 'baby' (it was so amazing to think that there really *would* be an actual real baby, separate from herself) was asleep, she'd work serenely on the third Gublet book and get it finished by the end of the year. Meanwhile, Callum would take on extra music students outside of school hours. The builders would do what they said they were going to do and their dream home in the mountains would be finished in plenty of time for them to move in when Laura returned from overseas. Within two years they would save up enough money so that Callum could start up his Music School for Adults. They would work out a sensible investment plan. They would take multi-vitamins and drink carrot, celery and apple juice every day. (They would need to buy a juicer.) They would be healthy, happy and successful. They would have one more child. Maybe even two more! Why not? So far it seemed pretty easy!

Callum wrote it all down on a notepad. Grace added amusing sketches to illustrate each point. They ate duck with crab-meat sauce. They were pleased with themselves.

Grace draws her pencil back and forth across the page in deep zig-zags, remembering that night. Their plans had been so very, very *pat,* hadn't they?

She remembers how she'd poked at her stomach to make the baby kick back and how she and Callum had laughed, high on the possibilities of their future. What was so different about her imagined life from the reality of it? It's all going according to plan. Here she is, with her baby sleeping, sitting at her mother's dining-room table, ready to do Gublet — and everything seems bland and pointless, just plain old yawning dull.

Gublet. A trite, not especially original picture book in an overcrowded market which doesn't sell that well or make that much money.

Her marriage. She remembers all that fuss she'd made when she first met Callum. So prissy and girly. *Oh, oh, I just love him so much!* Did she really feel any of that? He is just a man, for God's sake. A slovenly man who doesn't do enough around the house, who is getting a bit fat around the tummy, who has really horrible breath in the morning, who is infuriatingly convinced he is always right.

She says out loud, 'Oh, stop being such a *bitch,* Grace.'

She remembers the day the call came through from the publisher about Gublet. 'There's someone on the phone for you,' Callum had said, failing to repress an enormous grin. Grace, mystified, had taken the phone, and Callum had carefully watched her face until he saw her start to smile, at which point he'd performed a wild, silent victory dance around the kitchen.

How can she not love Callum?

Well, she does love him. Of course she loves him.

The baby is crying. She looks at her watch. It has happened again. Two hours vanished.

This is not normal.

15

From inside the warm restaurant, Sophie looks down at the crowds of people walking back and forth along the quay, heads bent against a chilly wind. A non-descript couple rugged up in black coats, hurrying and holding hands, slowly metamorph into the familiar figures of her parents, like a special effect in a movie. Sophie smiles involuntarily and tries to keep watching them with the eyes of a stranger. A perfectly ordinary middle-aged, quite stylish, definitely married couple with a relaxed, happy air about them, as if they are on holidays. They are both on the short side, giving them a cute, compact look. The woman stops and demonstrates something: a hammering movement with hands. The man shrugs, grabs her hand and pulls her along towards the restaurant. Sophie laughs to herself and feels the anticipation of relief. She is going to read them Aunt Connie's letter and let *them* decide what she should do. Whatever they say, it will be said with unconditional, soothing approval of Sophie.

She watches them come in the door, pink-faced and peeling off their coats. Her father, in a smart grey suit with a red tie, has a roundish face, old-fashioned gold glasses and a lovely smile, which he gives his wife as he helps with her coat. Her mother, who is wearing a soft blue dress, is checking herself in the glass-mirrored wall and trying to smooth down her irrepressibly curly hair. The wind has given her a slightly crazed look. They chat away to the maitre d' as if he is an old, dear friend and there is a loud burst of laughter. Sophie's parents create flurries of laughter wherever they go.

Finally, they look Sophie's way and she raises a hand. Her parents beam in unison, as if it has been months since she'd seen them last, not a mere two weeks.

Sophie's friend Claire, on meeting the Honeywell family for the first time, said, 'Now I get it why you're so popular. You've always been adored. You expect to be adored and so you are.'

'I do not expect to be adored. Anyway, all parents love their children,' retorted Sophie, feeling embarrassed because she knew it was true.

'Not like yours love you,' said Claire. 'It's borderline dysfunctional.'

'Hello, darling,' says her mother. 'That's a gorgeous new top. Can you believe my hair? I look like I've been electrocuted.' She bulges her eyes and vibrates her head to demonstrate her point.

'Hello, Soph,' says her father. He pulls out a chair for his wife and kisses Sophie on the cheek. 'Your mother accepts full responsibility for our lateness. No drink yet? Two points off? This lighting is a bit *too* moody I think. I can hardly see you.'

Every third Thursday, Sophie's father takes his wife and daughter out for dinner at a carefully chosen restaurant. The Honeywell family specialises in fine dining. They'd applied their own elaborate rating system to restaurants in Paris, London, New York and, of course, Sydney. It is one of their shared family hobbies, along with opera, Scrabble and reality TV.

Her mother, Gretel, enjoys telling people about how they used to take Sophie out to restaurants when she was just a toddler. They would prop her up on two cushions so she could reach the table and she'd be *'good as gold!'*, solemnly pretending to read the menu which was *'twice the size of her!'*. The waiters made her pretend cocktails exactly the same pink colour as her mummy's. Sophie also smoked pretend lolly-cigarettes, just like Mummy and Daddy's, blowing pretend smoke out the side of her mouth (*little actress*), but Gretel generally leaves out that part of the story because it makes people stop saying 'Ohhhh' and say uneasily 'Oh?' Plus, Gretel doesn't actually like to think about the number of cigarettes they smoked in their daughter's presence. Sophie only has to give the tiniest cough before Gretel is clutching her husband's arm. 'Listen to that! Passive smoking! What were we thinking? We probably destroyed her poor little lungs!'

Sophie's Dad's name is Hans. Hans and Gretel. When they were teenagers they had mutual friends who found the idea of them becoming a couple so uproarious that they engineered a meeting. Hans and Gretel were determined not to like each other but accidentally fell hopelessly in love the moment they were simultaneously pointed out by chortling friends on opposite sides of the Prince Albert Park ice-skating rink. If it had been a movie, it would have switched to slow motion and a romantic soundtrack as Hans and Gretel glided over the ice into each other's arms. In reality, neither of them had been skating before, so they bravely made their way across the rink with spaghetti legs and flailing arms, met in the middle, went to shake hands and crashed to their bottoms on the ice. 'I hit my tailbone,' said Gretel. 'I was in excruciating pain but I was so blissfully happy it was like I was drunk. I *knew*, you see, and I knew he knew too. I quickly peeked a look at my watch so I'd always remember the exact moment that I met my husband. Twenty past two, eleventh of June, 1962.'

It doesn't matter how many times Gretel tells Sophie this story, they both still sniff at the end. Not that it takes much to make mother or daughter sniff. They are, after all, addicted to anything romantic: romantic comedies, regency romances, romantic TV ads.

The Hans and Gretel romance ended with them living happily ever after — well, pretty much, anyway. The only mildly unhappy thing in their lives is that they couldn't have any more children after Sophie. Both Hans and Gretel came from small families and they had planned to have 'a few dozen kids', but as her mother says cheerfully, it just wasn't meant to be, and besides which they hit the jackpot first time.

It seems to Sophie that her parents are the sort of parents who should have had a whole brood of shouting, messy, sticky-fingered children. Her mum should have been one of those distracted mums serenely presiding over a crammed table, dishing out gigantic, nutritious casseroles, ruffling one kid's hair, slapping another one's knuckles. Her dad should have been one of those dads flipping sausages on the BBQ in between tossing kids in the air like juggling balls and saying funny things to visitors like, 'Who are you? You one of mine?' while his own children squirmed, 'Aww, Dad!' Sophie herself would have been the perfect older sister: kind and loving, firm but fair. She would have let her younger sisters use her make-up under supervision and dispensed judicious dating advice. She would have driven her dear little brothers to their soccer games and helped them with their homework. She probably would not have had a blushing problem if she had been an older sister.

But instead there is just Hans, Gretel and Sophie. They are like three guests at a party where no one else has turned up, doing their best to create the impression of a much larger, rowdier group, and doing so well that it turns out to be the party everyone is sorry they missed. People always comment on how extraordinarily close a family they are, how much fun they have, how they seem like three best friends. When Sophie was a child, her friends were thunderstruck when she invited their parents to join in with games, just like her own parents did. She thought all parents were just extra-large-sized kids. (How she blushed when this terrible faux pas was pointed out to her. 'Mum isn't even *allowed* inside the cubby house, Sophie. She can't play with us. That's sort of . . . weird.')

This Thursday night the Honeywells are trying out a new restaurant at the quay, with ceiling-to-floor windows revealing the white sails of the Opera House like a gigantic, gold-lit sculpture. The three of them sit in grave silence, studying heavy, hard-bound menus, with sighs of indecision and lots of flipping back and forth of pages. They put their menus down, frown, pick them up again and continue flipping. Finally, hands clasped over closed menus, they each present their selections as if they are explaining complex mathematical solutions.

'Confit of Tasmanian ocean trout with roe,' says Gretel. 'Followed by marinated scampi with pawpaw, cucumber and tonburi.'

Sophie and Hans shake their heads in admiration.

'Salad of sea scallops,' says Sophie. 'Followed by — if you're thinking the salmon, Dad, you'd be wrong — lobster ravioli with tomato and basil vinaigrette!'

'Oh, no!' Her father puts a hand to his forehead. 'I had the ravioli!'

'Back to the drawing board, darling,' says Gretel.

There is a rule that nobody ever has the same dish. It is an unfair rule because Hans always chivalrously insists that Gretel and Sophie say their choices before him.

He heaves a dramatic sigh, pushes his glasses back up his nose and picks up his menu, squeezing his bottom lip with two fingers. In the meantime Sophie's mother has tipped slightly back on her chair with a dazed expression on her face. It means that a conversation at the next table has caught her attention. She, like Sophie, is an avid eavesdropper.

Sophie looks to see who she is listening in to. It is clearly a family group. Grandparents, daughter and son-in-law, or son and daughter-in-law (Gretel will confirm in a few minutes), together with a silent, unseen baby in a pram. Sophie can sense by the way they are all sitting slightly self-consciously, with their heads cocked towards the pram, that the baby is a new addition to the family.

It is bad enough that Sophie's parents have only one child, but now they are in their early sixties, when they can quite reasonably expect to be grandparents, their only daughter isn't even in a relationship. Sophie's mother has a group of friends who she has been playing tennis with for over twenty years and Gretel is the only one in that group who isn't a grandma. Sophie can't bear to think about her mother politely listening to all those women showing off about their grandchildren. The worst part of it is that her parents never put pressure on her. There are never any loaded questions like, 'Met anyone interesting lately?' Sophie would feel less guilty if Gretel was like her friend Claire's pitiful mother, who nags and cajoles and begs, accusing Claire of deliberately not having children just to spite her.

'The mozzarella and chilli salad followed by the slowly poached veal shank, if anyone is still interested.' Hans closes his menu. 'Your turn to choose the wine, Soph.'

Gretel leans forward and lowers her voice to a hoarse secret-agent whisper. 'First night out with colicky new baby,' she informs Sophie. 'Mother-in-law about to make daughter-in-law cry.'

'Fascinating.' Hans doesn't approve of his wife and daughter's eavesdropping habits. 'Do you think we could concentrate on our own family now?'

'I am *terribly* sorry,' says Gretel in a Royal Family accent. 'How *frightfully* rude of me.'

'I happen to think it is,' says Hans sternly, although Sophie knows he is trying not to laugh. Nobody chuckles louder than Hans at his wife's repertoire of accents and funny voices.

Sophie watches her parents acting as if they have just reached that nice stage in a relationship where you pretend to be annoyed with each other in public. There is a mean feeling in her chest like heartburn. It takes her a few seconds to identify that it is actually envy. She puts down her glass of water with a thud. Well, this is getting beyond a joke. Yesterday she'd been pounding away on the treadmill at the gym watching a documentary on one of the television screens. It was about a woman with no arms and no legs who had to get around on a skateboard. A touching story of courage in the face of terrible odds. But even while she was blinking back tears of sympathy, Sophie had, just for a second, actually felt a tiny bit *envious* of the woman. Why? Because of her nice, good-looking (fully limbed) husband!

As punishment she had given herself an extra twenty minutes on the treadmill to show her appreciation of her two rather short, but perfectly functional, legs. (Still, she couldn't quite get the thought out of her mind: if an arm-less, leg-less woman on a skateboard could find a man, surely Sophie was doing something very, very wrong? How did this woman meet him? Pull on his trouser leg as she rolled by him in a nightclub?)

Now here she is, feeling jealous of her own sweet parents. She is a very bad person. A spoiled only child. A brat.

She says, 'Don't you want to hear my letter from Aunt Connie?'

'Oh, *yes*!' Her parents are immediately all attention.

Sophie takes the letter out of her handbag, clears her throat and reads,

'Dear Sophie . . .'

A waitress appears at their table as though she has been waiting for this very signal. 'Good evening. Did you need any more time, or may I take your order?'

'My daughter is just reading a letter from someone who left her a house,' Gretel beams up at her. 'This woman barely knew her! It's all very intriguing.' Sophie's mother believes discretion is the height of rudeness.

128

'Oh, well, that is — ah — intriguing.' The waitress is obviously unsure whether to make her face happy or sad about this revelation and settles for confused.

'What's more intriguing is whether the veal comes with vegetables?' Hans looks up over the top of his glasses and treats the waitress to his sweet smile.

When their orders are taken and Hans and Sophie have managed to restrain Gretel from generously inviting the waitress to stay and listen to the letter, Sophie begins again:

Dear Sophie,

Well, my dear, today I decided to leave you my house. It is an odd decision, but not, let me assure you, a whimsical one or a senile one. I have thought about it at length. No doubt this decision will create something of a hoo-ha and Veronika will be in a state, but it is my house and I've decided I want you to have it. It would have been easier if you had stayed with Thomas but I'm not at all surprised, in fact I'm rather pleased, that you didn't.

I don't really know you from a bar of soap, do I? But there was something about you and your reaction to my house. You know that my husband Jimmy

129

and I built it together. It is very special to me. Every brick, every floorboard, every windowsill has a memory for me. (Goodness me, I smile when I look at that silly toilet-roll holder!)

As much as I love them, I couldn't bear to think of Veronika crashing about, pulling things down, or Thomas carefully repainting the place in some dreadful neutral colour. As for Grace, I don't think she should live on the island at all — afraid it has unhappy memories for her.

I haven't stopped missing Jimmy since the day he died. It's like waking up with a stomach ache every day. Well, this will probably sound quite barmy but there is something about you that reminds me of my husband. The reason I fell in love with Jimmy, the reason I'm still in love with him, was his capacity for joy. That man could be happy in a way my family has never been. (I'm afraid we can be a miserable lot!) There was a moment when you were standing out on my balcony and you saw our resident kookaburra. You looked back towards me, and I thought, she's got it too. Jimmy's joyful look. I want someone joyful to live in my house. I also think the island needs someone like you — someone with that rare capacity for joy. It will be good for the house, good for everyone. Probably good for the business!

By the way, if Grace is still living on the island, perhaps you could consider a friendship. I think you would like her. Please excuse me for meddling. As my sister Rose will tell you, I've been a terrible meddler all my life. Still, as she may one day tell you, it seems to have all worked out rather well.

Well, that's all I have to say.

Enjoy the house. I have attached a list of instructions you may find helpful. Don't throw them away or I shall haunt you.

It was such a pleasure to meet you, Sophie, love.

Yours sincerely,
Connie Thrum

PS. I'm sure you have dozens of beaux, but there is a rather nice young man I feel would be very appropriate for you, who I hope you will meet as a result of moving into my house. I won't say who he is, because although most of my meddling has been successful, I've had no luck at all matchmaking Rose and I've been trying to do so for over seventy years. All I'm saying is keep an eye out for him.

Sophie looks up to see her mother smiling radiantly, as if she has just read out a glowing report card, while her Dad has his shrewd fatherly 'nobody's going to put one over me' expression.

'A rare capacity for joy,' says Gretel. 'That's lovely. I expect you inherited it from me. Well, I've changed my mind. I think you should absolutely accept the house!'

Hans says, 'I'm betting she's put in some sort of clause that says you can't sell it. She obviously wants you to live in it. Now, how expensive is the upkeep? Is the place falling apart? That's what I'd like to know. And do you really *want* to be living there, Sophie, spreading your message of joy?'

'Sarcasm!' scolds Gretel.

They are interrupted by the arrival of the wine: a Gewürztraminer Sophie had selected. She tastes the wine as she's been trained to do since she was thirteen years old: swirl, sniff, slosh in mouth, reflect with serious expression, smile decisively up at waiter and say graciously, 'Lovely, thank you.'

'It's not exactly a convenient location,' continues Hans when the wine is poured.

'They don't allow cars on the island, do they? How would you get to work?'

'There's a ferry,' explains Sophie. 'The families all have their own motor boats and they keep their cars in a padlocked parking area on the mainland. So I'll take my boat across, hop in my car, drive to the station and catch the train into the city.'

She tries hard to look casual, so her father won't guess how enchanted she is by this idea, but her mother spoils it by clasping her hands and saying out loud everything that Sophie is secretly thinking. 'How wonderful! I can just see it! The sun shining on the water! Your own little boat chugging across the river while you wave hello to other islanders!'

'That will all seem very romantic right up until the first day it rains,' says Hans. 'Or you're running late for work. Or you're coming home late at night.'

Her mother says, 'Oh no, darling. I don't think she could drive her little boat late at night! I don't think boats have headlights, do they?'

Hans gives her an exasperated look. 'Well, she can't stay home every night, can she?'

'She could come and stay with us if she's out late.'

'That's hardly practical.'

'I don't see why not.'

'Because she might want to — you know — she might have a — she might like — she could — bugger it, you know what I'm trying to say!'

'Oh, well, she could stay at his place!' says Gretel blithely and then frowns. 'If he seems nice. And clean.'

'Mum. Dad. I'm very grateful that you're both so concerned about my sex life but I'm sure I'll be fine,' says Sophie. These assumptions by Aunt Connie that she has 'dozens of beaux', and by her parents that she actually has sex on a regular basis, are both flattering and depressing.

There is a disturbance at the table next to them. The younger woman stands up suddenly, with a face she is trying hard not to let crumple, and walks off quickly to the ladies.

'Told you so,' whispers Gretel, looking sympathetic and triumphant. 'I wonder if I should go after her?'

'I might not even get the house,' continues Sophie. 'Veronika rang me up and told me she's going to fight me all the way to the highest court in the land.'

Her father snorts. 'I've checked up on it. I really don't think she has a chance. One, she's not even related to this woman. Con-

134

nie doesn't have any living relatives, does she?'

'Yes, she does,' says Gretel. 'The younger sister who was with her when they found the baby. The face-painting lady. Remember, we met her when we took Sophie to the island when she was young. What was her name?'

'Rose,' says Sophie.

Hans says, 'Well, even if Rose wanted to contest it she'd need to prove that Connie wasn't of sound mind, or that she was somehow manipulated. It's clear from her letter that wasn't the case. She just took a liking to you. Anyway, this is all premature until you hear from the lawyers and what the will actually says.'

'But I don't know,' says Sophie. 'Is it morally right for me to take the house?'

'Of course it is,' says her mother. 'Now I've heard that letter I've decided it would be morally wrong not to take it! Connie wanted you to have it.'

'If you think you could be happy living there, then you should,' says Hans. 'It's a windfall, darling, that's all. No need to feel guilty about windfalls.'

'I'm going to check on that poor girl,' says Gretel.

■ ■ ■ ■

The next day, Sophie models possible outfits to wear to Aunt Connie's funeral, while her friend Claire lies on Sophie's bed eating a gigantic bag of salt and vinegar chips.

Claire can eat and eat and eat and still retain a malnourished look. She looks a bit like a junkie, a skinny young rock chick, although she's actually a forty-two-year-old physiotherapist.

'Is the funeral on the island?' she asks, as Sophie stands in front of her wardrobe flicking through hangers.

'No. The island is tiny,' says Sophie. 'It's Sydney's smallest suburb. Only six houses. Haven't you ever been there?'

'Nope.'

'You've never done the tour of the Alice and Jack house?'

'How could I if I've never been there?'

'Right. Well, when I live there you can come and visit me. We'll do the tour together. I'll make you cinnamon toast.'

At the thought of living in that house, walking out onto that balcony in her PJs and having a cup of tea in the morning sun, watching the reflections of the gum trees in the river, Sophie feels an intense shot of pleasure. It will be bliss. It is like the life she's always wanted without ever knowing it — and this lovely old woman has just handed it to her — 'here, take this life' — a glittering gift, like something in a fairytale.

'There's a kookaburra that comes and sits on the balcony every night,' she tells Claire as she pulls a shirt over her head and zips up a skirt.

'I know,' says Claire. 'You told me. Sounds thrilling. That outfit is far too insipid.'

Sophie looks down at her grey skirt and white shirt. 'I think insipid might be exactly the right look. I'm not even sure if I should go. It's not as if I would have gone if she hadn't left me the house, but it seems ungrateful not to be there now. So I sort of want to be there and not be there at the same time. Plus there will be Thomas and his wife, and Veronika, and all the family who I haven't seen since the break-up. Oh God, it's going to be excruciating.'

Claire says, 'Wear the black dress you wore when you snogged that fat guy at Melissa's christening.'

'He wasn't fat. He was stocky. Anyway, I don't want to wear black,' says Sophie. 'People will think I'm pretending to be sad when they all know I didn't really know her.'

She shoves Claire's hand aside so she can reach in the bag for some chips.

'Sixteen, seventeen, eighteen,' says Claire. At Sophie's request she is counting the number of chips Sophie eats, with orders to stop her at twenty.

'I think you look really sexy in that black dress,' says Claire. 'Nineteen, twenty, that's it, no more.' She folds the top of the chip bag with a straight, firm crease and begins licking her fingers, efficiently, one by one, like a cat grooming itself. Sophie will not get another chip now even if she goes down on her hands and knees and begs for it.

'I don't want to look sexy. I want to look demure and non-manipulative.'

'You should look sexy,' says Claire. '*He* might be there.'

'Who?'

'Oh, don't pretend you haven't thought about it. The guy Aunt Connie thinks would be right for you. Your new *beau*!'

In fact, Sophie hasn't thought about him being at the funeral at all. When she thinks about him, which she does quite a lot, she imagines him knocking on her door a few days after she's moved in to Connie's house. She'll be wearing overalls with one strap dangling down and her hair will be tousled and cute. She might have a darling smudge of dirt on one cheek. He will walk in, probably wearing muddy boots for some reason, and he will glance down at her piles of books and exotic, interesting ornaments demonstrating what an exotic, interesting woman she is, and he will make some sort of funny, perceptive, intelligent (but not scarily intelligent) remark, and at that exact moment there will be some sort of minor crisis. Something will explode or flood or burst into flames. They will work *together* to overcome this crisis, which ideally will require some bicep-bulging strength on his part, and when it is over they will flop down together, laughing with relief, and their eyes will meet and they will both just *know*. That will be the moment Sophie will sneak a look at her watch to check the time that she met her future husband, so she can tell her future children.

One problem is that she doesn't own a pair of overalls. Or any exotic, interesting ornaments. She'll also have to hide away her collection of regency romances. She hates the condescending expressions new boyfriends get on their faces the first time they see her regency romances, as though she's an adorable puppy.

'Oh, him,' says Sophie vaguely. 'I'd forgotten about him.'

Claire gives a long, exaggerated snort of disbelief.

'Well, she wrote that letter months ago,' says Sophie defensively. 'The guy is probably with someone now. Single men don't last long in Sydney, remember? They're "snapped up". Besides which, what do I know about Connie's taste in men?'

'You said you saw photos of her husband. You said he was a spunk.'

Sophie grins. 'That's true.'

'Look, you really can't risk looking insipid the first time you meet this guy. You've got to go for it. It could be your one chance. You're not —'

'— getting any younger. Yes, thank you, Claire.'

'I'm just saying, if you seriously do want to have a family, you haven't got much time. You've got to take every opportunity. You're about to miss the baby boat.'

There's that bossy, big-sisterly tone Claire adopts whenever she talks to Sophie about her love life, or lack thereof. She herself has been in a long-term relationship for eleven years and doesn't want children because she and her partner have a 'lifestyle', which means they go on trekking holidays and have white wool carpet. However, she is very respectful of Sophie's desire to have children, maybe a bit *too* respectful because she is vigilant about Sophie slacking off on her man-hunting. She doesn't believe in fate or destiny or that 'Mr Right will turn up just when you least expect it'. She believes that finding a man to be the father of your children before your fertility drops to zero is no different from any other goal, like finding the right car or the right property.

Sophie sighs and pulls another hanger out of her cupboard. 'Don't you think it's a bit much to expect Aunt Connie to provide me with both a house and a man, as if she's my fairy godmother? You're the one who says I think life is a friggin' fairytale.'

'Put the sexy black number on, Cinderella.'

Veronika rings Sophie again the night before Aunt Connie's funeral. 'Tell me you don't have the *gall* to come tomorrow.'

'I thought you weren't saying another word to me in your entire lifetime.'

'You're not welcome. You're not family.'

'Gosh, Veronika,' says Sophie sweetly. 'I thought I *was* like your family. I seem to remember you making a speech about how I was like the sister you never had.'

Naturally, Sophie had been Veronika's bridesmaid. It is cruel and bitchy of her to

141

remind Veronika of her wedding to Jonas when it had ended so quickly in divorce, but this is getting tedious.

'May I remind you that it was at my wedding that you got together with my brother!'

'I don't deny it, but what's the relevance?'

'The relevance is that you rejected him. You rejected our family. And now you think you can waltz back in, Miss Butter-wouldn't-melt-in-my-mouth.'

She means, you rejected *me*. Sometimes Sophie thinks she'd hurt Veronika more than she'd hurt Thomas. Veronika had been ecstatic when Thomas and Sophie got together. If Sophie is honest with herself — and oh, how she strives to be honest with herself — Veronika's effusiveness is probably one of the reasons why she had to break up with her brother. There is something about Veronika that makes Sophie want to fold her arms tightly across her chest and say, 'You can't have any more of me.' Sophie has an irrational dislike of Veronika's intense interest in the most trivial details of her life. She remembers everything, as if she is stockpiling ammunition to prove . . . what? That she knows Sophie better than she knows herself? She would say in front of other friends, 'Oh, no, that date is no good. Sophie wouldn't be able to come. It's the third Thursday — it's her dinner night with her parents. They rate restaurants, you know.' She remembered what books, food and movies Sophie did and didn't like. 'Sophie hates tortellini.' 'Sophie loved that movie.'

Why do such innocuous comments aggravate Sophie so much? It feels like if she spends too much time with Veronika there will be nothing left of her. She's like a vampire sinking her fangs into Sophie's neck and sucking her dry.

'I thought you'd forgiven me for breaking up with Thomas.' Sophie softens her voice because Veronika just wants to be her friend, that's all. She's not really a vampire. 'I thought you said it was time to move on.'

Veronika ignores that. 'I bet you were trying to get your claws into Aunt Connie at my wedding.'

Sophie is outraged. '*What?* I barely spoke to her!'

Connie had been far to busy having a good time, remembers Sophie. Her husband Jimmy had still been alive. They had danced the Charleston: an elderly, white-haired couple who still somehow managed to flutter their fingers and kick in perfect timing, crossing their hands across their knees and giving Sophie a split-second glimpse of the vibrant young couple they had been. Everybody had applauded madly. They were gorgeous.

Veronika switches topics again. 'Look, you're just going to upset people by turning up tomorrow. Mum, Grandma Enigma, Aunt Rose — none of them wants you to be there.'

'Veronika, your Aunt Rose phoned me today to ask if I was coming.'

There is silence, which is so unlike Veronika that Sophie thinks they must have been cut off. 'Veronika?'

Her voice is strained. 'I don't believe you.'

Of course. The worst betrayal for Veronika is when she is left in the dark about something.

And now Sophie is back to feeling guilty because Veronika is right. She isn't part of their family. She has a handful of memories about Aunt Connie when Veronika has a whole lifetime. It isn't fair. Sophie has charmed an old lady into leaving her a house. It doesn't matter that it wasn't deliberate. It's wrong.

'I'm sorry, Veronika,' she says.

Veronika's voice is full of icy, righteous hurt. 'I'm sorry I ever met you.'

16

'Do we tell Sophie the truth about Alice and Jack? Do you think that's what Connie would have wanted?'

'Yes, I think so, but not until she's forty. Just like the others.'

'How old do you think she is?'

'I don't know. They all look about twelve to me.'

17

Did Alice and Jack Munro deliberately abandon their baby, knowing that Connie and Rose would stop by and that their family could give the baby a better start in life than them? Surely not. It was far too boring an explanation, and luckily it didn't account for the boiling kettle, the marble cake or those satisfyingly mysterious blood stains on the kitchen floor. And why not opt for the simple baby-left-on-doorstep solution?

Did Jack kill Alice in a fit of rage because he hated marble cake, dump the body and leave the baby to die? *Or* did Alice kill Jack in a fit of rage because he said something derogatory about her marble cake, dump the body and leave the baby to die? Certainly the diary found in the Seventies would suggest something along those lines.

Did the *baby* kill Alice and Jack?

The last one was ten-year-old Veronika's suggestion, made on the beach one day to

Thomas and Grace, who fell about laughing, imagining the baby (their Grandma Enigma!) leaping out of its cot to strangle Alice and Jack with tiny hands.

It is the day before Aunt Connie's funeral and Grace is bathing her baby and thinking about the mystery of her great-grandmother Alice Munro.

Grace hates bathing the baby. When he is dressed and wrapped tightly in a rug he is a solid, manageable football. But when he is naked he is all flimsy and breakable, skinny legs all bent up at angles like an uncooked chicken. The fragility of his tiny limbs makes her feel sick. He seems to know how horribly vulnerable he is when he is naked because the moment she starts undressing him he screams and screams, which does something to her brain like the shrieking scrape of nails across a blackboard. When she holds him in the bath, his legs and arms thrash. The possibility of drowning him seems more likely than not; it is as if the point of each bath is to save him. She feels that her nails, although she deliberately keeps them short and filed, will surely tear his purplish paper-thin skin.

Of course, Callum loves bathing Jake. Grace could let him do it every day but she has the feeling that she is on some sort of treacherous journey, and if she stops, even for a moment, then she might never get up again. It is better to just go doggedly on and on.

Grace wonders how Alice Munro had bathed her baby. It had been winter when they vanished, just like now. The island gets very cold. Alice didn't have hot water or electricity or warm gas heating. No TV to blank out her mind while she was breast-feeding. No CDs to drown out the sounds of a silent house. No refrigerator. No washing machine. No dryer. No gleaming white-goods at all. They had been very short of money, like everyone. 'You children have no idea,' Aunt Connie used to say. 'You think terrible things happened on the battlefields, but terrible things happened in ordinary suburban homes.' Jack was unemployed. Seventy years later their combined savings of two shillings and sixpence are still sitting in the tin on the shelf above the sink. Guests on the Alice and Jack tour are allowed to peer in the tin as it is rattled under each nose by the tour guide. ('No need to rattle quite so *loudly,* Veronika,' Aunt Connie would say.)

Grace can't imagine how her great-grandmother coped, although then again, in light of what happened, perhaps she hadn't.

She'd made a marble cake, though. That was indisputable. That indicated coping, didn't it? Well, of course it didn't. You can still bake a perfectly good cake while losing your mind. Grace remembers watching Aunt Margie in her kitchen efficiently grating lemon rind for a lemon meringue pie while she cried great wrenching sobs over her father's cancer diagnosis. Aunt Margie had been closest to Grandpa out of any of them. Who knows what thoughts were going through Alice's mind while she baked that marble cake. Did she know it was the last cake she'd ever bake?

Grace takes the baby from the bath and lays him on his back on the change table. At least he can't roll over yet. When he learns to roll over he'll be in even more danger. He'll be like a slippery glass ball. Just thinking about it gives her a drilling sensation behind her eyes.

What did Alice think of her new baby girl? Was she besotted with her like a mother should be?

It's strange really that she's never thought much about the fact that she is Alice Munro's great-granddaughter. It had been hard enough for Grace and her cousins to get their heads around the fact that grey-haired Grandma Enigma was the same person as the tiny abandoned baby who had smiled so sweetly at Aunt Connie and Aunt Rose. Alice Munro never seemed particularly real or even that interesting to Grace. It was Veronika who was forever coming up with new and more macabre solutions to the mystery.

She clicks together the press-studs on Jake's pale green babygro suit, buttoning him back up into a standard, cared-for baby with a standard, caring mother.

She wonders if the something that held her great-grandmother together, the something that kept her neat and tidy and allowed her to get out of bed each day and bake marble cakes, had been loosening moment by moment, pulling and straining, until one day her husband said or did something quite innocuous and it snapped: the real snarling, biting, furious Alice was unleashed with terrible consequences. Grace wonders if that propensity to snap had been encapsulated in a gene that is now floating around in her own DNA. She wonders if perhaps it would be more sensible to take action *before* that gene has a chance to hurt anyone.

After his bath, Jake falls into a deep drugged sleep halfway through his feed. She puts him down and looks at him dispassionately. He is a very good, obedient baby. He is doing everything as per the books that Thomas's wife Debbie has lent her.

Before Jake was born, Grace had visited Thomas, Debbie and baby Lily at their spotless West Ryde home. There were children riding bikes up and down the street and the smell of freshly mown grass. Debbie served them home-made Anzac biscuits. Thomas showed her their new pergola. There was a tangible sense of relief emanating from Thomas. It was as though all his life these achievements — home, wife, baby — had been weighing heavy on his mind, and now he'd finally checked them all off he could relax and benignly observe the rest of the world still flailing about trying to reach their own little islands of security. 'Sophie is still single, you know,' he told Grace sadly, without a trace of triumph, just ponderous concern. 'The chances of having a Down Syndrome baby increase every year after the age of thirty-five. She really needs to hurry up.'

Debbie began a hefty percentage of her sentences with the phrase: 'I'm the sort of person who . . .' Debbie was the sort of person who could *instantly* and *accurately* judge a person's character and she could tell that Grace was going to be a wonderful mother. Debbie was the sort of person who believed knowledge was power, that's why she had bought so many books on good parenting. Debbie was the sort of person who didn't mind at all lending her books to someone like Grace, who was family, but she was the sort of person who would like to get them back in good condition. Debbie was the sort of person who had a very high tolerance for pain, but when she was in labour it was like being torn in two and she screamed so loud that she burst a blood vessel in her eye. Debbie was the sort of person who didn't really like kids but the moment she saw her daughter Lily she felt the most euphoric feeling, the most intense love she had ever felt.

'I fell instantly in love with her,' said Debbie. 'I'm the sort of person who doesn't exaggerate, and honestly, truly, it was like nothing I've ever experienced before. I just adored her. I'd give my life for her. I'd throw myself in front of a semi-trailer for her. I just sobbed when she was born, didn't I, Tommy? You'll see! It will be the same for you. It happens to every mother.'

Three months later, at four in the morning, Grace saw her baby son for the first time. The midwife, a snappy skinny girl who

Grace hated, put him on her stomach. Grace waited for the euphoria. Instead she felt the most intense sensation of *nothing*. She didn't like or dislike this greasy creature. He was a stranger: nothing to do with her. All she could feel was relief that it was over, that it was out of her, that nobody was shouting instructions at her any more.

She has her own labour story now, but she can't imagine cheerfully sharing it with anyone, like Debbie had done, in excruciating detail, over Anzac biscuits. It had been, quite simply, grotesque. She had lost all control of herself — her mind and her body — and she never wanted to again.

'He's so small!' Callum was standing next to the bed in a white hospital gown, pale and red-eyed. There was some blood on his gown. He looked like a doctor on *ER*. Grace saw her husband's face all scrunched and silly with joy. So, *he* was feeling it.

She thought perhaps the euphoria was running late and it would eventually hit her. One day she'd look at her son and fall in love with him like a proper mother. But Jake has been in the world now for three weeks and Grace is beginning to wonder, with a sort of tired inevitability, if she will never feel anything except the enormous responsibility of keeping his tiny heart beating, his tiny lungs breathing. It seems she might have to fake it for the rest of her life. She imagines him taking his first steps, dressed for his first day of school, playing his first soccer game, standing up, all awkward and gangly, to do a speech at his eighteenth birthday party, and all the while there would be Grace, his fraudulent mum, becoming greyer and wrinklier and *still not feeling it.*

She watches Jake sleeping and says out loud, 'Well, Debbie, guess what? I'm the sort of person who can't love her own child.'

As Grace is walking back down to the kitchen she begins to cry. She feels somehow separate from her crying, as if her body is experiencing a series of involuntary symptoms — a salty discharge from her eyes, a convulsing chest. It continues on and on until she is mildly astonished; she didn't know it was possible to cry for so long.

Eventually she decides it isn't necessary to stop functioning just because she is crying. She should just get on with what she needs to do.

She sobs as she does a load of washing and wails into the cold wind as she puts the washing on the line. She fries mince for Callum's favourite meal, lasagne, and lets the tears slide off the edge of her chin and into the sizzling meat.

'Oh, this is ridiculous,' she thinks. 'That's enough now.'

She doesn't want to be all puffy and red-nosed when Callum comes home. She wants dinner in the oven, a CD on the stereo, a sleeping buttoned-up baby in his crib and a nice bottle of red wine already opened. She wants everything calmly in place, like the way she imagined it would be before the baby was born.

She wants to be good at this. Being a mother is just like any other new skill, like driving a car or playing tennis. At first it seems impossibly difficult, but then, by gritting your teeth and trying again and again, you get your head around it. She just has to get her head, her stupid aching head, around this new skill.

When Callum had got home after his first day back at work he'd found Grace deeply asleep on the couch. He'd touched her arm and she had apparently said, without opening her eyes, 'Look! All you need to do is add two eggs! It's not rocket science!' before rolling over and going back to sleep again. Callum had found this very amusing. She had heard him telling his mother about it on the phone, sounding very loving and husbandly. 'Very tired, of course,' she heard him say. 'But no, she's fine.'

Stop talking about me as if I'm a retarded child, she wanted to scream. His mother was so nice! *He* was so nice! He'd cooked dinner (microwaved some leftovers and made a salad with a great deal of stirring and clattering and leaping around the kitchen as if he was cooking a three-course meal, but still) and even packed the dishwasher and wiped bench tops without being asked while she breastfed the baby. It had all made Grace feel unreasonably aggravated. He seemed so happy, he was doing everything right and he hadn't even been the one who particularly wanted children! It was Grace who had pushed for the baby.

Why had she done that? It seemed to be more to do with the fact that she didn't see herself as the sort of person who would choose not to have children than the fact that she actually wanted to be a mother herself. She didn't identify with those people who talked about not having children as a 'lifestyle choice'. There was something suspicious about people who seemed so proud of going against convention. Grace saw nothing wrong with convention. That's why when she turned thirty-three she decided it was about time she and Callum had children.

Not the best reason for having a child, she thinks now. Surely a reprehensible reason, to have a child just because you didn't want to be the sort of person who didn't have one.

Oh, her head, her poor papier-mâché head.

The meat spatters oil on the white tiles behind the cook top and Grace immediately wipes them clean with a paper towel, as though her mother isn't thousands of miles away on the other side of the world (Turkey, according to the typed fifteen-page itinerary hanging on the cork noticeboard next to the fridge) but could walk back into the room at any moment.

She wipes her eyes with the paper towel and thinks how repulsed her mother would be by this excessive crying. 'Don't be a drama queen, Grace,' her mother used to say when she cried as a child.

She goes to the pantry for the spices and stops to look out the window with watery eyes. Her mother's house, like all the houses on the island, is built up high on a block of land sloping gently to the waterfront. All the windows along the front of the house have views of the river. It is twilight and the sunset is turning the river bronze. All their friends turn into real-estate agents the first

time they see this view: 'Stunning.'
'Panoramic.' 'Breathtaking.'

'You grew up with this view!' they say to
Grace. 'I bet you just took it for granted. I
bet you never even looked at it, huh?' Actually, she did used to look at it, sometimes
for hours at a time, sitting at the window
and imagining a boat appearing at the house
jetty with her father in it. 'I'm back!' he'd
say cheerily. 'Sorry I took so long.' Her
father had left when Grace was a baby. 'A
lot of abandoning of babies in my family,'
she'd told Callum when they were sharing
family histories. Except there was no mystery about Grace's father. He was a dentist
who fell in love with his dental nurse and
moved to Perth.

When Grace was a child she assumed that
the first thing her father would look at when
he came back to collect her would be the
state of her teeth, so she brushed them so
rigorously that her dentist told her she was
wearing away the enamel. She still thinks of
her father whenever she flosses. She flosses
religiously, twice a day. Her teeth are perfect.

As she watches the river, she hears the
putt-putt of an engine and a boat does appear, trailing a wide curve of whitewash. It
is Callum, sitting very straight, one hand

behind him on the tiller, the sky all fluffy orange and pink, like something in a religious poster. She can't see his face but she knows he'll be smiling.

Shit, shit, shit. He's early. She can't even complain about her husband working long hours and not being supportive, for Christ's sake. She doesn't want him home just yet. The lasagne is not in the oven. She is still crying. She turns around from the window and her elbow knocks against the bowl she's been using to mix up the tomatoes and spices. It falls in slow motion to the floor. There is time to catch it but she just stands there stupidly, as if she wants her mother's good china mixing bowl to shatter violently on her flawless white kitchen tiles.

With comic timing, the baby begins to cry, louder than she's ever heard him cry, as if he's been crying for hours.

'Please don't say anything,' says Grace without turning around when she hears Callum come into the kitchen behind her. She stands looking at the mess in front of her.

He silently tiptoes past her to get the broom.

Later that night, after they've eaten the lasagne and watched TV and packed the dishwasher and given Jake his ten p.m. feed,

Grace's mother calls from Istanbul.

Grace sits down on the hallway floor with her legs straight out in front of her and drums her fingers against her thigh. Callum says he can tell whenever she is talking to her mother. 'You become very still and alert,' he says. 'Like a commando.'

She carefully tries to sound like a daughter, not a commando. 'Hi, Mum!'

'Oh my word!' Her mother's voice is clear and sharp in her ear. 'It's a very good line, you sound like you're next door!'

'Oh my word' is a favourite phrase of Laura's own mother, Grandma Enigma. It is the first time Grace has ever heard her mother use it. Perhaps everyone is turning into their mothers.

'So, Istanbul . . . are you having fun?' she asks.

Her mother answers in a rush of words. She sounds slightly manic.

'Well, yes and no. The food, for example, is quite inedible. It's swimming in oil. I'm eating nothing but tomato. The tomatoes are all I can stomach. Still, that's a good thing. I ate far too many carbohydrates in France. How is your weight, by the way? It took me six months to get back to my pre-pregnancy weight after you.'

'I haven't weighed myself.'

'Well, the scales are right there in my bathroom. You need to be vigilant about your weight. Look what happened to Margie. She blew up like a balloon while she was pregnant with Veronika and stayed that way. She wore a size twenty to your wedding. I checked the label on the jacket when she went to the bathroom and I nearly had a fit. Size *twenty*.'

'She looked fine to me,' says Grace.

'Oh don't be ridiculous. She's monstrous.'

Poor, cuddly Aunt Margie. Grace thought she'd looked quite uncomfortable in that blue suit. She probably should have had a size twenty-two.

She says, 'So, but apart from the food you're enjoying yourself?'

Her mother's voice drops and becomes almost emotional. 'Oh, Grace, you can't imagine the state of the toilets. In some of them you have to *squat* right down on the ground. It was the most horrific experience of my life.'

Surely you've had worse experiences than squatting on a toilet, thinks Grace. How about your husband leaving you for his dental nurse? Or your father dying of cancer?

'Good for your thighs,' comments Grace. 'Squatting.'

161

Laura brightens. 'Yes, that's a point.'

'Have you bought a rug?' asks Grace.

'Oh, yes, I've done the tourist thing. Sleazy men ran around giving us all apple tea. So sugary-sweet! Terrible! I bargained as well as I could. No doubt they were laughing their heads off at the price I paid. I probably won't be able to get it through customs back in Sydney. I wouldn't blame them. I'm sure it's not hygienic.'

'Is it nice and hot?' tries Grace. 'It's very cold here.'

'Oh, the heat! The *humidity*! I'm so dehydrated. Terrible.'

'Right,' says Grace.

She doesn't really understand why her mother is taking this world trip. She doesn't seem to be enjoying it at all. It's like she is forcing herself to undergo one of her more rigorous diet and exercise regimes.

She says, 'Mum, I'm afraid I've got some bad news . . .'

But Laura doesn't seem to hear her. 'How is Jake?' she asks urgently.

For a moment, Grace can't think who Jake is. Her mother said the baby's name in such a grown-up way.

'He's fine.' Grace feels a dead feeling in her stomach. 'Beautiful.'

'Breast-feeding OK?'

'Yes.'

'I didn't breast-feed you. I couldn't stand the thought of it. I remember saying to Margie, I'm not a *cow,* I'm not a *pig!* Still, I wasn't informed. We thought that formula milk was just as good. I should really have breast-fed you.'

Oh my word, thinks Grace. Is she drunk?

'And any other news on Scribbly Gum?' asks Laura.

'Yes, there is. I'm sorry. I tried to call yesterday but I couldn't get through on the number on the itinerary. Aunt Connie died. The funeral is tomorrow.'

There is a sudden hissing silence on the phone.

'Mum? I'm sorry to break —'

Her mother's voice overlaps her own. 'Was it pneumonia? I told her a thousand times she'd catch pneumonia. She would never wear anything warm around her neck. I gave her a perfectly nice skivvy last Easter. She acted all hoity-toity about it. She said, "Would you wear this, Laura?" And I said, "Well, I might if I was approaching ninety, Connie!" '

'It wasn't pneumonia. She just died in her sleep. Aunt Margie found her. They all think she knew she was going to die. She had all her papers in a pile next to her bed.'

'I suppose I'd better call. How are they taking it?'

'Grandma Enigma has been crying a lot.'

'I can imagine,' says Laura disgustedly, sounding more like herself again. 'Mum *likes* to cry. I've tried to tell Margie that.'

'The other news is that apparently Aunt Connie has left her house to Thomas's exgirlfriend, Sophie. Aunt Rose told Thomas. There was a letter for her.'

'That's contemptible! That is just so *Connie.*'

'Veronika wants to contest the will.'

'Good for her. Someone should stand up to Connie. She's been bossing this family around for far too long.'

'Yes, well, she's dead now, Mum. She's not going to be bossing us around any longer.'

Laura says, 'But Sophie's the one who left poor Thomas at the altar!'

'Not exactly at the altar.'

'How very tactless of Connie.'

Seeing as her mother had once told Thomas to stop being such a 'soppy sap' when he was grieving over Sophie, Grace doesn't think she is qualified to give a lecture on tact. She changes the subject. 'Veronika thinks that Aunt Connie always knew the secret of what really happened to

164

Alice and Jack. She thinks the secret will die with her.'

'Oh, Alice and Jack,' says Laura dismissively. 'Do you know, I'm so bored with the whole Alice and Jack business. Travelling has really put things like that in perspective for me. All my life — Alice and Jack, Alice and Jack. *I'll* tell you what happened to Alice and Jack!'

There is another hissing pause and then Laura says irritably, 'How old are you?'

'Sorry?'

'You're thirty-four, aren't you?'

'Yes. What's that got to do with anything?'

'Oh, I don't know. Look, Alice and Jack is a business. A profitable business, which we've all done very well out of; I'll give Connie that. And as she always said, if the mystery was solved it would be bad for business. There is probably some dull solution, but who really cares?'

'Veronika cares. She's always cared. And now she wants to write a book about it.'

'No doubt she'll find some new project before she gets past the first chapter.'

It's true that over the last three years Veronika has started three different university degrees, a novel, six new jobs, a children's book to rival Harry Potter, dozens of community college courses, a pet-washing business and a 'clear your clutter' consultancy. Veronika has always been flighty, but since her divorce she has become quite frenzied.

'Probably.'

'Oh shit! This ridiculous phone card is —'

The line goes dead.

Grace hangs up. That had been a very strange phone call. Her mother had sworn too. The 'shit!' had been just as out of character as the 'oh my word'.

'What did she say?' calls out Callum from the living room.

There is plenty of material from the conversation that Callum would enjoy hearing. The tomatoes, the Turkish toilets, Aunt Connie's skivvy, the implication that Laura knows more about the Alice and Jack mystery.

He comes into the hallway and looks down at her eagerly. Grace feels her head begin to cave in again with that horrendous headache. It is just too much effort to be funny and entertaining and loving. It is just too much effort to talk, really.

'What's the gossip?'

'Nothing,' she says. 'I'm going to have a bath.'

18

A thin layer of frost makes the Scribbly Gum wharf glitter in the sun. The island is closed for business. Family members still on the island are catching the ferry across for Aunt Connie's funeral.

'Oh, would you just *look* at him!' clucks Grace's Aunt Margie, peering into the stroller at Jake, who stares back at her solemnly, his chin wet with dribble. 'He looks adorable. You dress him so beautifully, Grace! Of course, you dress yourself so beautifully too. You get it from your mother. I'm afraid I have no style whatsoever, do I, Ron?'

Her husband, immaculate in a dark suit and dark glasses, stops his pacing up and down the wharf. 'I'm assuming you don't actually require an answer to that inane question, Margaret. Good morning, Grace.'

When Grace was a child she thought her Uncle Ron, so handsome and debonair, so cleverly sarcastic, was exactly the sort of man she would like to marry one day. When she got older she decided he wasn't clever at all, he was just nasty and Margie was a stupid fool for putting up with it. Now, she just accepts them. After all, Thomas and Veronika don't appear at all concerned by their parents' relationship. Every marriage, every family, has its mysteries.

'You look very stylish, Aunt Margie,' says Grace.

In fact, Margie looks her usual frumpy, cuddly self. She is wearing a white blouse and a black skirt straining valiantly to hold her in.

'It's hard to know what to wear to a funeral these days,' says Margie. 'Everything is so much more casual. You don't think I look like a *cocktail waitress,* do you, Grace, darling?'

'Not in the slightest.' Grace thinks that Margie actually looks like a lovable diner waitress in an American road movie. All she needs is the pot of coffee and some gum.

'I've been going to my Weight Watchers quite regularly,' confides Margie breathily, leaning forward while her eyes dart over to her husband. 'Your mother will be relieved. She thinks I'm grossly overweight.'

Grace looks at her aunt's carefully

made-up face, brown foundation collecting in the pores of her nose. 'Oh, no, I'm sure she doesn't,' she says finally, wondering if she waited too long to answer. She has a strange, not unpleasant sense of disconnection from everyone, as if she is floating somewhere high above her head and operating her body by remote control. Stretch lips to smile. Fold palms of hands around pram handle. Tip head towards child in motherly fashion.

The night before, Jake had woken up at one a.m. and refused to settle after his feed. He would pretend it was his intention to go to sleep and then all of a sudden he'd give a violent shudder and scream furiously, his face bright red and wrinkled tightly like a walnut. Grace had turned on lights and paced the house, grimly rocking the baby as she walked around the perimeter of each room, upstairs and downstairs. When her route took her past the main bedroom she would see the silhouette of Callum, asleep, flat on his back, snoring blissfully. It was because he'd drunk red wine at dinner. It always made him sleep like a corpse. He would have wanted Grace to wake him but she preferred to play the martyr. She was the mother. It was her job. It was her duty. It was her punishment, for God knew what terrible crime she'd committed. At five thirty in the morning, Grace looked down and realised that the baby had finally fallen asleep, frowning deeply, his cupid's-bow lips slack. Grace had got back into bed beside Callum and stared with burning dry eyes at the ceiling until seven, when Callum had sleepily rolled onto his side, pulling her to him, asking, 'Did you sleep well?'

'You look a little pale, darling,' says Margie. 'How is the baby sleeping?'

'Beautifully,' answered Grace. She steals Callum's joke. 'Like a baby.'

'Like a baby!' giggles Margie. 'Oh, that's a good one, Grace! Ha, ha!'

Grace tries to laugh and is horrified at the weird sound that comes out of her mouth, but Margie doesn't seem to notice.

She imagines telling Margie the truth:

'Here's the thing, Aunt Margie: it's just that I really, truly don't *like* being a mother. It's not that I'm tired or a bit emotional. It's just not the job for me. It's not that I'm having a few problems bonding with my baby; I don't even *like* him! I feel nothing. I want out. Oh, please, please, I want out.'

Margie sighs and tugs at the waistband of her skirt. She glances at her husband, who is standing at the end of the wharf, his back very straight, one hand shading his eyes,

170

looking out for the ferry. She smiles brightly back at Grace and shivers theatrically. 'Isn't it *cold*! It was quite hot on Tuesday! It's been such a funny old winter, hasn't it? Well, darling, I think it's going to be a really lovely funeral. We've done everything just as she wanted. Not that Connie left anything to chance. She had a manila folder with step-by-step instructions. It's called "Instructions for my Funeral". She's practically done all the catering for her own funeral, you know. That freezer of hers! Oh, I'm going to miss her so much. I don't know how the island is going to get by without her. I thought we'd have her for another ten years at least. Oh my, would you look at what they're wearing!'

Grace looks up to see her grandmother and Aunt Rose coming down the hill, the two of them sitting erect on their 'mobility aid' scooters. There is a missing space where Connie should have been. It was normally Enigma, Rose and Connie, three abreast, although with Connie just slightly ahead. They were like an elderly biker gang, zooming around the island's one road, going as fast as the bikes would let them, which was pretty fast because one day Connie had called up one of Jimmy's nephews who was a mechanic and said, 'I want you to "hot up" our bikes for us, Sam. They're too slow. It drives me mad.' Sam had responded to the challenge with alacrity, replacing the engines with ones from lawn-mowers. Connie had given him a high five the first time she revved up her new engine. 'We're real hoons!' Grandma Enigma always said. 'We hoon around the place!' Enigma really enjoyed saying the word 'hoon'.

'The wharf might be slippery!' cries out Margie frantically. 'It's frosty! Be careful, Mum, Rose! Oh why must they always go so fast!'

'Oh, relax, darling.' Enigma comes to a neat stop next to them. 'My word, it's chilly. But otherwise a lovely day for it, isn't it?'

'I must say, you two look very . . . colourful,' says Ron.

Enigma, who comes up to Ron's waist, is wearing a fire-engine-red jacket with a diagonally striped skirt. With her short, permed purplish-grey hair and apple-pink cheeks, she looks like a brightly wrapped lolly. Rose is tall and ethereal, with long, impractical white hair that she still wears the same way she wore it when she was sixteen, clasped at the back with the same tortoise-shell hairclip. For Connie's funeral she is wearing a gorgeously coloured turquoise suit with a matching long, filmy scarf that changes from blue to green in the sun. She has tied a piece of the same material around her walking frame. Actually, they look quite presentable; Grace knew Margie had been worried they'd have flowers or birds painted on their faces, which did cause people to stare.

'Yes, we do look colourful!' says Enigma snappishly. She doesn't take any rubbish from her son-in-law. 'That's because we're celebrating Connie's wonderful, *colourful* life!'

'Colourful,' says Ron. 'That's an interesting choice of word, Enigma. Makes it sound like Connie might have rather unsavoury secrets in her past.'

There is a moment of strange, loaded silence. Margie wrings her hands. Enigma punches her fists into her sides and narrows her eyes ferociously. Rose's nostrils become pinched and regal. 'What a remarkably inappropriate thing to say,' she announces with devastating disdain, and gives Ron a look as if he were a filthy boy, caught in the act of doing something truly repugnant.

It is always interesting to see Rose switch from vague and dreamy to crushing and cold; unless, of course, you are on the receiving end, which Grace had been occasionally when she was a teenager, especially when she went through her brief but memorable pierced nose and shaved head stage.

'My sincerest apologies, Rose.' Ron is as smooth as expensive liqueur. 'You're right. It was a poor attempt at humour. I should leave the jokes to my witty wife, shouldn't I, Margie?'

19

The morning of Aunt Connie's funeral there is frost on the grass outside Sophie's flat.

'Sophie, Sophie, Jack Frost has been!' Gretel used to call on mornings like this, with such excitement in her voice that Sophie would leap from her bed and run to her window to see their white-spangled front lawn.

Sophie had believed in Jack Frost, the Tooth Fairy, Santa Claus and the Easter Bunny for an embarrassingly long time. It was her mother's fault. She was too good an actress. For example, she described accidentally running into Santa Claus one night in the kitchen when she went to get a glass of water in such authentic-sounding detail: Santa had had such a fright that he'd said 'Lordie me!' and had to sit down and have a Milo and an Iced Vo Vo. He'd got crumbs in his beard. From outside on the driveway Gretel could hear the sleigh bells jingling in the breeze and the reindeers snorting and pounding their hooves.

On Christmas Eve and frosty mornings Sophie still feels a faint shivery tingle of that old magic. It makes her feel better as she eats her porridge. Aunt Connie's funeral seems like some sort of horrible public-humiliation test.

She wears the black dress because Claire had been so adamant that it was right. Sophie has lost all confidence over what is right or wrong about this whole thing.

The funeral is at noon at Glass Bay. She plans to go in to work for a couple of hours and then catch a train from the city to Glass Bay, where she can get a cab to the church. She has allowed an hour and a half, to give herself plenty of time. Timing is crucial. Too early will appear too eager: *OK, let's get this over with so I can get my hands on the old biddy's house.* Too late will appear blasé: *Just dropping by to pay my respects . . . by the way, where are the keys to this house I've been hearing about?*

In the end she is running late. A girl tumbles excited into Sophie's office to make a report of sexual harassment. She has clearly not been sexually harassed (you should be so lucky, Sophie catches herself thinking, rather unprofessionally) but these things must be gently defused like a ticking explosive device.

Then the train stops inexplicably for twenty minutes in between stations. By the time she gets to Glass Bay and she is pelting up the stairs in her stilettos, she is hyperventilating with a mix of guilt and nerves.

There are pounding footsteps behind her and a man in a suit is suddenly running by her side. 'You're not going to Connie Doughty's funeral, are you?'

'Yes, I am,' she says breathlessly as they both keep running.

'Me too,' he says. 'We'll share a cab then. That train — could you believe it? I was bashing my head against the window.'

Sophie laughs. 'I was thumping my fist against the seat in front of me.'

She manages to get a fleeting impression of a big nose and deep laugh-lines. He is running easily, his briefcase held under one arm.

Stop it, she thinks. Stop it. It's not him. If you think it's him, it won't be him.

'Here's one!'

She watches him run ahead and flag down a cab.

Nice square, broad back. *Stop it!*

He turns around and smiles at her. 'Our

luck's changing.'

Well, mine certainly is. His smile is funny and friendly and sexy all at once. *Stop it, stop it, stop it!*

He opens the cab door for her and she slides across the seat. He hops in beside her and gives the cabbie the address of the church. It seems like the space in the back of the cab is very small and intimate. She can smell his aftershave. As he pulls back his sleeve to check the time she can see his very masculine-looking forearm. Oh, for heaven's sake, Sophie!

'Well, hello,' she says. She can feel her smile is radiant and possibly beautiful. 'I'm Sophie Honeywell.'

'Aha,' he says. He raises one quizzical eyebrow, James Bond style. He really is extraordinarily sexy. 'So *you're* Sophie.'

Oh God, it seems like it has been years since the last time she has felt this. Instant mutual attraction. She is not imagining this. Chemistry is frothing and fizzing all over the place. She can feel it in her kneecaps.

He reaches out to shake her hand. 'Hello, Sophie.'

Sophie puts her hand in his: warm, dry, enfolding hers. She lets her eyes drop to her watch. It's five to noon.

I knew. I knew the moment we sat in the

cab and your father shook my hand. It was
five to noon on Thursday the second of . . .

'I'm Callum,' he says. 'Callum Tidyman. Grace's husband.'

20

Rose sits right at the end of the front pew of the church next to the aisle, with her walking stick propped up beside her. The seat offers no support for the lower back and already she can feel a stabbing pain. Oh, *sugar*! It hurts. It really hurts. She has to stop herself from crying out, that's how much it hurts. If her back had ever hurt like this when she was twenty she would have been hysterical, demanding painkillers and cups of tea in bed, but she has found that nobody is especially surprised to hear you're in pain when you're in your eighties. *You* might find it astonishing, but nobody else does.

People are murmuring to each other, or sitting silently, hands clasped carefully on their laps, looking self-consciously solemn. Occasionally there is a hollow-sounding cough. Funerals all have the same smells and sounds. The cloying, nose-twitching scent of lilies. That muted rustling. Sometimes, a sudden, shocking, uncontrollable sobbing. Although there is not much sobbing at the funerals Rose seems to spend so much of her time attending these days. People would consider it excessive and rather Italian if you started wailing at the death of an elderly person. Instead, you say things like, 'Well, he had a good innings, didn't he!'

No surprise you're in pain, no surprise you're dead. You're old. That's what is meant to happen. We don't care that *you* forget you're old. We *know* you're old.

Rose thinks of that poem she used to like and is pleased with herself when she can remember the first few lines.

Do not go gentle into that good night.
Old age should burn and rave at close of
    day;
Rage, rage against the dying of the light.

That's right, she thinks. We should all be raging and raving and brandishing our walking sticks: *We don't want to go! And by the way, we want our legs and arms and backs to stop HURTING!!*

She will ask Thomas to find the rest of that poem on the Internet for her. He can find anything on his lap computer. He's a sweet boy, Thomas. Such a pity it didn't work out with Sophie. They'd all liked Sophie.

'What's the hold-up? It's so chilly in here!'

Enigma is sitting on Rose's left, jiggling around in her bright red outfit. Her feet don't quite touch the ground. When Rose looks straight ahead she can almost believe that it's still a little girl sitting next to her, not a seventy-two-year-old Enigma.

'Rose? Isn't it cold! You'd think they'd have a heater. No need to make us feel like we're in a morgue just because we're at a funeral, eh? Rose?'

Rose ignores her. She doesn't feel like talking. Enigma makes an offended sound and turns to talk to Margie, who is sitting on her other side and never ignores her mother.

Rose and Connie had chuckled, just last week it was, about how funerals had become their new hobby. Throughout their lives they'd taken up various convivial pastimes together — tennis, art classes, lawn bowls. Now they'd taken up funerals.

Their friends had got so old that whenever Connie bought a get-well card she also bought a sympathy card at the same time, to save herself the trouble of going back to the newsagent when they didn't 'get well'. Rose had thought that was just terrible, but Connie always liked to be the practical one.

The light inside the church is like twilight, shadowy and strange, making it hard for Rose's eyes to distinguish anything except the giant stained glass picture at the front, which makes her flinch with its assault of colour: ruby, emerald and sapphire. The picture features a handsome, melancholy Jesus stretching out an imperious, drooping hand to his poor mother, who kneels distraught at his feet. Both Jesus and Mary have glowing circles around their heads, like psychedelic motorcycle helmets, and they're surrounded by macabre baby-faced angels.

Why did you want a church, Connie? Is this your last shot at pretending we're good Catholic girls?

It is unbearable to think that she won't ever hear Connie's acerbic response.

Above the stained glass there is a window revealing a square of pale blue sky and a wispy cloud. The sky looks comfortingly mundane compared to the garish kaleidoscope of the stained glass. It makes Rose yearn to be reliving any one of a thousand ordinary days spent with her ordinary older sister, who has now done this extraordinary thing and died.

A lifetime of ordinary moments crowd her head. Teenagers, sitting in a train station, picking at the green peeling paint of their chair and bickering desultorily over something to do with a pair of shoes. In their forties, driving somewhere, running late, looking for a parking spot. 'There! On your right! Too late, you ninny!' Little girls, fishing off Sultana Rocks: Connie holding a frenzied flapping slimy-silver fish trapped with her foot, while Rose crouched down to remove the hook, saying 'I'm sorry!' to the begging-for-mercy eye. Whole afternoons with baby Enigma on that old red checked rug in the backyard when the jacaranda tree was in full purple bloom. They didn't have the slightest inkling of how to look after a baby. They made it up as they went along and played with her like two children with a doll.

Thousands of cups of tea. Thousands of conversations about what to eat and what to wear and how to get there. Thousands of shopping trips. Thousands of circuits of the island: running when they were children, strolling languidly when they were teenagers, power-walking with hand-weights when they were middle-aged and worried about cholesterol and osteoporosis, and then slower and benter and even slower, until they bought their 'hotted-up' bikes, the best thing they ever did, and once again they were children again, with the air skimming their cheeks as they soared around the new unfurling sandstone footpaths that always reminded Rose of the yellow-brick road in *The Wizard of Oz*.

I didn't properly appreciate one damned moment.

Someone starts a CD and music begins to play. 'What a Wonderful World' by Louis Armstrong. It must be Connie's choice. According to Margie, Connie has specified every tiny detail for her funeral.

Rose didn't even know she liked this song.

People turn their heads towards the back of the church, keeping their faces blank, reminding themselves that they're here to see a coffin, not a bride. Rose twists slightly in her seat and her back shrieks in pain. There is no surprise about Connie's choice of pallbearers: Jimmy's four nephews who used to come and stay on the island for school holidays.

The boys are men in their fifties now, but to Rose, as she watches them walk down the aisle, they don't seem all that different from the four little boys they were. None of them have lost their hair: they still have identical curly mops, like clowns. They were

185

extremely naughty children, always breaking things. You had to watch them like hawks. As they walk down the aisle of the church, each with one shoulder hunched to carry the gleaming coffin, their heads solemnly bent, Rose realises she is still carefully monitoring their behaviour, as if at any moment they'll let the coffin crash to the ground and go pelting off to play with their water pistols.

Connie was always very good with the boys, whereas Rose felt a bit scared of them and tried to cover it up by acting too strict and schoolmarmish. Connie cooked them enormous meals and she and Jimmy had midnight water fights with them, whooping around the island in the moonlight.

It should be Connie's own sons carrying the coffin, not Jimmy's sister's children. Jimmy should have let her adopt. He'd let her do anything else she wanted. Rose feels a fresh surge of anger, as if it had all happened yesterday. She should have spoken up after the war, when it became clear that Jimmy and Connie would not be contributing to the baby boom. She should have said, 'Don't be so stubborn, Jimmy. It doesn't suit you. Pick something else to be stubborn about, if you must prove yourself a man, but let her adopt a baby for heaven's sake!' People thought bringing up Enigma gave Connie all the mothering she needed. Rose was the only one who knew why Enigma wasn't enough. Rose was the only one who knew, without ever talking about it, how much Connie yearned for her own babies. The problem was that Jimmy got in a bad mood when he learned the truth about Alice and Jack. That was his ace and he played it. Connie should never have told him. It offended his pride. Made him feel silly. 'You women have all been sniggering behind my back!' he kept saying.

The coffin passes and Rose looks at her lap. Next to her Enigma is sobbing with abandon into a man's handkerchief. Ever since she was a baby, Enigma has cried when she's unhappy and laughed when she's happy. For a person whose whole life is built on a mystery, she is very un-mysterious. There is nothing enigmatic about Enigma.

The boys lower the coffin onto its pedestal and walk back down the aisle, separating to go to their wives and children. Rose tries to smile at them but they have their heads bowed.

Another song starts.

'Danny Boy.'

Oh, Connie, *really*!

The sly old thing. Rose can just imagine her chuckling as she threw that one in. 'This will get the waterworks going!' Enigma is now howling like a two-year-old. Like the two-year-old she was. Margie is making soothing sounds. Like the two-year-old *she* was. Margie was born motherly.

Rose carefully shifts again to see which members of the Funeral Club have turned up and their expert reaction to 'Danny Boy'. Good Lord. The first person she sees is Mick Drummond, with his ancient bobbing head. Would that man never die? Was he immortal? Was he *real*? Would he outlive them all? He'd been old for decades, it seemed. Wait till she tells Connie!

She turns back around and sees the coffin again, lustrous black, like a grand piano. It hits her with a horrible lurch that she won't be eating cinnamon toast tonight at Connie's kitchen table and telling her all about her own funeral. It is pointless saving up the good bits. Rose's big sister is lying flat on her back in her good burgundy suit, inside that shiny box, with her face collapsed and her lipstick perfect but somehow not quite right.

I'm the only one left in the Doughty family, thinks Rose. You've all abandoned me. She wants to wail and sob and stamp her feet. She is five years old and stuck in a dreadful old woman's body that aches and creaks. Mum, Dad, Connie! How could you just leave me here all alone? It's not right. I'm the youngest! I shouldn't be left here on my own!

21

'We are here today to celebrate the life of Connie Thrum.' The priest stands behind the pulpit with hands outspread. He is a fresh-faced boy. No surprises there. Children are running the dashed world, thinks Enigma, while tears slide down either side of her nose, trailing pink rivulets through her face powder. Doctors, policemen, politicians, newsreaders. Children everywhere, acting so important! They think they've always been in charge, which is sweet, although sometimes inconvenient, such as when the doctor refuses to give Enigma the prescription she requests and tries to come up with her own ideas, when Enigma knows exactly what it is that she needs. They all take themselves so damned seriously. Sometimes Enigma has to try not to laugh. All this talk about Australia's 'aging population' when anybody with eyes can see it's not aging, it's young-ing, or whatever the opposite word to aging is — Connie would know the right word. Connie filled in every single square of the *Sydney Morning Herald* cryptic crossword puzzle every single day. The clues are all nonsense to Enigma.

Connie was always a real smart woman. Enigma remembers the night they all sat around doing the National IQ Test on television and Connie got the highest score. Ron had been furious and made accusations of cheating, pretending he was being funny but everyone could see right through him. Veronika had accused her father of being a misogynist and Thomas had told Veronika to stop acting like a pseudo lesbian intellectual. Enigma didn't understand either accusation. Rose had dreamily refused to take part in the IQ test. Luckily Thomas got quite a high score, nearly as high as Connie, which was a relief because ever since Enigma dropped him when he was a baby she has been secretly observing him for signs of brain damage. (Nobody knows about this — she has never told a soul, it wasn't her fault, he was such a *slithery* baby!) Even when Thomas went on to study at the university, she never completely relaxed, worrying that perhaps he was some sort of idiot savant.

Enigma leans back and peeks a look down

the aisle at Thomas, sitting next to his wife, dull-as-dishwater Deborah, with dear little Lily on her lap. Oh dear, Thomas looks quite stupid today with his mouth hanging open like that. He probably does have a touch of brain damage. Certainly, it was stupid of him not to hold on to Sophie Honeywell, who was so funny and pretty and really enjoyed her food!

Rose hasn't cried at all, Enigma notices. She is sitting very still, looking at the priest with that gracious blank expression she gets. You can never tell what she's thinking. That Rose is an odd fish all right, Enigma's husband Nathaniel used to say.

'Connie played many roles in her life,' says the boy-priest. 'She was an outstanding member of the community, a successful businesswoman, a loving sister to Rose, loving wife to Jimmy, and loving adoptive mother to Enigma.'

Yes, well, excuse me but that's not strictly true, she never actually adopted me. Enigma remembers coming home from school one day and asking Connie if she could call her 'Mum'. 'No, you can't,' Connie had said. 'One day, when you're forty years old, I'll explain why. This is nothing to cry about, Enigma. Save your tears for something worthwhile.'

Enigma had still cried. She didn't need to save them up; her tear ducts never let her down. When the other kids teased her for being the Alice and Jack baby and having a funny name, she would plonk herself on the ground, bury her face in her hands and bawl luxuriously until they got bored with yelling things like, 'Your dad stabbed your mum in the guts!' and 'Enigma's mum was a Murderer!'

She liked being the Alice and Jack baby. It made her feel special and exotic, like a girl in a film. And she loved a good cry! Afterwards she always felt serene and slightly sleepy. Once she revealed this to her granddaughter Veronika, who told her that when you cry your body releases a chemical like a sedative. 'You're probably addicted to that sedative, Grandma Enigma,' Veronika had said. 'You're like a druggie.'

A druggie! That child talked such rubbish at times. Margie should have smacked her more when she was little.

Enigma leans forward to see Veronika sitting at the end of the pew, her skinny face all twisted in a ferocious expression. She'll give herself wrinkles. Probably still sulking over Connie leaving her house to Sophie. It is a poky, old-fashioned house anyway. Difficult to clean. Enigma doesn't know why

Veronika is making a fuss over it.

Such a pity that Veronika's marriage to Jonas had been a flop, but then Jonas had been a wishy-washy sort of fellow. No match for Veronika. She needed a good, firm man in her life.

Actually, what that child needs, thinks Enigma, sniffing noisily, is a real good fuck.

She sits back in her seat with a satisfied nod and rummages through her bag to find her Tic-Tacs. She enjoys thinking deliciously shocking thoughts from time to time. It does her good.

'How many calories in a Tic-Tac?' wonders Margie, as her mother rattles the little plastic box in her face.

Surely not many. Perhaps none at all. She holds out her hand and Enigma tips a white lolly into her palm. Margie puts it into her mouth, sucks, and immediately begins to viciously attack herself. 'This is why you're so fat, you blubbery whale, you greedy pig! Calories are *insidious*! Why do you say yes every single time food is offered to you? Why are you so weak? Why are you so pathetic? Can't you feel how the waistband of your skirt is digging into your pasty, doughy flesh! And *you don't even like Tic-Tacs*!'

She remembers a tip she learned at the last Weight Watchers meeting. *If you don't love it, don't eat it.*

Surreptitiously pretending to cough, she is about to spit the Tic-Tac into her hand when her mother suddenly shoves against her arm as she leans across her to offer the Tic-Tacs to Ron. This causes Margie to gulp and swallow the Tic-Tac and all the calories it contains, without even tasting it.

It's probably one of those deadly, calorie-packed food items. Like cashew nuts. They have been warned to avoid cashew nuts.

Margie gives her mother a reproachful look, which Enigma doesn't notice at all. 'Tic-Tac, Ron?' she is hissing.

For heaven's sake, surely it's disrespectful to be passing Tic-Tacs down the pew during a funeral! The priest is trying to talk. A minute ago her mother had been crying her eyes out into one of Dad's old hankies, and now here she is cheerfully handing out Tic-Tacs! Margie has always secretly suspected that her mother is just a bit shallow.

Ron takes a Tic-Tac of course, just to amuse himself, and offers, by raising his eyebrows and inclining his head, to pass the Tic-Tacs down the aisle to other members of the family. He is doing it to make fun of Enigma and she doesn't even know. He thinks he's superior to everyone. Has he always been like this? Margie can't remember.

'. . . and I know Connie's wonderful blueberry muffins will be sadly missed.' The priest gives them a gentle, sad twinkle and there is a ripple of fond laughter. Margie, who told the priest to say that, chuckles along with them.

My thighs certainly won't miss them, she thinks. At least with Aunt Connie dead there won't be so much fattening, calorie-laden food on the island. No more Connie turning up with a freshly baked caramel fig loaf or a tray of honey cakes, even though she knew perfectly well that Margie was trying to lose weight.

What a selfish fat-person thing to think. She loved Aunt Connie. Although she did always feel a bit relieved when Connie left the room.

She'd noticed that whenever Connie left she could feel herself exhaling just slightly as if she'd been holding her breath. Connie could make her feel slow and bovine; the way she'd suddenly snap her head around and bark a question that would leave Margie fumbling for an answer. Even if it was a perfectly ordinary question like, 'How are you, Margie?' it sounded like a test. Connie always seemed disappointed with her answers, as if she'd expected more, although Margie never knew in what way. She'd certainly never shown the slightest sympathy for Margie's attempts to lose weight. 'You're too old for such rubbish! Of course you want a second piece!'

Connie was very skinny.

The waistband of Margie's skirt is cutting cruelly into her waist.

It's a wonder Connie hadn't specified what everyone should wear to the funeral. Her list of instructions had been so meticulous, leaving nothing to chance. There was even a *running sheet* for the service.

Margie is quite convinced that Connie just *decided* to die that night. She can imagine her thinking to herself, 'Right, that's it. Time to go.'

For the last three days Margie has had Connie's voice in her head.

NO SICKLY SWEET SPEECHES.

NO FLOWERS.

HEAT SPINACH AND RICOTTA TRIANGLES AT 300 DEGREES FOR 15 MINUTES. <u>DO NOT MICROWAVE.</u> THEY GO SOGGY.

It has been tiring, organising this funeral, along with all her normal work. Margie would quite like to curl up in a corner somewhere and go to sleep. She wishes her mother or her daughter had asked if she needed a hand. She would have said 'No, thank you' of course, but still, just for the recognition. Everybody likes a 'pat on the back', as they say. Ron seems quite convinced she sits around all day watching television.

With Connie gone she'll have a bit more time to herself. That's horribly disloyal to think but it's true. People were always going on about how remarkable it was that both Connie and Rose managed to look after themselves at their ages. 'Tough old biddies!' they'd say admiringly. It's true that Connie and Rose were remarkable for their ages, and Margie was so proud of them: their minds were as sharp as tacks! But a fair amount of 'behind the scenes' work had gone into ensuring they thought that they'd been managing just as well as they had ten years ago. Not that she begrudged the extra washing or ironing or cleaning or shopping.

'Don't do so much for them,' her sister Laura was always saying, 'then they might realise they need to go into a retirement home.'

'They'll go into a retirement home over my dead body,' Margie had retorted.

'It probably will be your dead body,' Laura

had told her very unsympathetically, before she jetted off to Europe, leaving her daughter with a brand-new baby! (Fancy deliberately choosing to take yourself to the other side of the world when your first grandchild was about to be born. Still, 'each to their own', as they say.)

Next to her, Ron shifts slightly and sighs. She can smell the contemptuously classy smell of the aftershave he buys at the airport when he travels away on business. His legs next to hers, encased in newly dry-cleaned Armani suit trousers, with sharp straight creases down the centre, are masculine and controlled.

Margie is nothing but soft, oozing, spreading thighs and breasts and bottom.

I'll show all of you, thinks Margie with sudden determination. I'll lose weight. I'll lose kilo after kilo after kilo and then I'll emerge from all this flesh, skinny and hard and light and free.

The priest seems to think he is a fucking talk-show host. Ron looks at his watch. He has a meeting in the city at two. Margie promised him the service would go on for no more than an hour, but Margie just says whatever it is she thinks you want to hear, with no particular regard for the facts. If this goes on for much longer, he'll just get up and walk out.

For some reason his eyes keep returning to that shiny, expensive-looking coffin. He wonders how much it cost and considers leaning over to ask Margie, just to see her panicky mortification. He doesn't know much about the funeral industry but he suspects the margins are excellent.

So, you carked it, Connie. He feels a flicker of triumph, as if he has won something. He does not bother to analyse this feeling. He is not into naval-gazing.

Ding dong, the witch is dead.

He *did* respect the old bird. She never fussed. Generally women waste a lot of time fussing. Fuss, fuss, chat, chat. Never get to the point. Whereas Connie said exactly what she meant. When he'd first met her, over thirty years ago now, she could throw a frisbee like no woman he'd ever seen. A good straight pass that sliced the air. Margie always did these feeble, pathetic tosses, as if her arm was made of plasticine. Back then he thought that was cute. Back then he was thinking with his dick.

Yes, Ron had always respected Connie, even though he suspected the feeling was not mutual. That doesn't concern him especially. He doesn't need to be liked. A lot of people don't like him. It is their problem. Not his.

'Connie was a woman of strong Christian ideals,' says the priest.

What a load of crap. Connie was a hard-nosed manipulator who conned the whole bloody country. The island has lost its dictator. Now who will tell them all what to eat for fucking breakfast?

Ron stops listening to the priest and lets his eyes glaze over.

It doesn't bother him that Connie, or any of the women, have never once asked him for his advice about the business. He just finds it ironic. He is, after all, a Business Consultant. Quite a successful one. Executives with MBAs who are running multi-million-dollar corporations come to him for advice, but not the old women in his own family. It doesn't seem to have ever occurred to any of them, not even his wife. They ask him to open jar lids and change light globes. They don't ask him to look at their financial statements. In fact, he has never even seen the financial statements for Scribbly Gum Enterprises, although he has often idly attempted to calculate its net worth. As a shareholder, Margie would have access to the figures, but she has never asked for his help interpreting them. It wouldn't surprise him if she didn't even know the difference between a balance sheet and a profit and loss.

They don't invest much, but then Connie and Rose have always been so careful with their money. It's a legacy of growing up during the Depression. Ron has an uncle who is incapable of putting more than a speck of butter on his toast.

He would quite like to see the Scribbly Gum figures. He is ready to be impressed by the capabilities of a trio of old women.

He is no misogynist, in spite of what his daughter Veronika might think.

Thank Christ. The priest seems to have finally wrapped up the eulogy and is moving on to the procedural part of the day. Move it along, mate. A fast funeral is a good funeral.

Ron is not *completely* sure what the word 'misogynist' means. He keeps forgetting to look it up in the dictionary because he doesn't have a dictionary. Proof that he is not a misogynist is that when his son Thomas was growing up, Ron fully expected him to turn out to be gay and he was *fine* with this. He would have said, 'No problem, mate.' That's how open-minded he is. He's almost disappointed that Thomas ended up so bloody conventional. Look at him, sitting there holding hands with his bland sex-less wife. He should have held on to that Sophie. Now *she* was a sexy little thing.

Someone is opening the double doors at the back of the church. Daylight spills in and people turn, disapproving and interested, to see who is so late.

Speak of the devil. Here she is.

Yes.

Far too sexy for poor old Tom.

22

Grace turns around and sees Callum at the back of the church, holding the door for a girl with a wedge of honey-brown hair falling over one eye. Even from this far away, she can see the girl's face is aflame with colour.

Veronika, who is next to Grace, holding the baby, makes a disgusted sound and mutters something under her breath, nostrils twitching and eyes darting like a mad person.

It's that Sophie Honeywell, Grace realises. She recognises her from when she was bridesmaid at Veronika's wedding. She remembers now feeling charmed by some funny, self-deprecating story Sophie had told her about the stupid things the wedding photographer had made them do between the church and the reception. She'd pulled faces and mimicked the photographer.

Sophie is obviously hoping for somewhere to sit at the back. She is desperately craning her neck while people stare comfortably back at her. Callum has seen that there is space at the end of the front pew next to Veronika and Grace. He makes an affable gesture for Sophie to go ahead of him but she is all in a fluster. Callum places a hand on her shoulder, gently propelling her forward, and Sophie has no choice but to walk down the aisle.

The priest stops talking and waits with elaborate priestly patience while everyone in the front row turns their legs sideways to let Callum and Sophie shuffle past.

'Incredible!' hisses Veronika, bitterly shaking her head. She rocks the baby furiously and slides down towards the end of the pew.

Callum sits down next to Grace. 'Sorry I'm so late,' he whispers and puts his hand over hers. Sophie sits down on the other side of him and looks straight ahead, while Veronika makes an exaggerated show of squeezing even further away from her.

The priest raises his hands again and at that point the baby begins to cry.

Automatically, Callum turns and reaches across Sophie to take the baby from Veronika. Tenderly, expertly, he holds Jake over one shoulder, pats his bottom and sways slightly in his seat. The baby stops crying immediately.

Grace watches Sophie watching Callum and the baby. Sophie's eyes, which seem to be the same honey colour as her hair, are lingering on them both with the yearning, enchanted expression of a child standing in front of a magical Christmas display in a shopping centre.

23

Scribbly Gum Island, 1999

It was thirteen weeks since her husband's funeral. Connie Thrum stood at her stove browning lamb shanks and rubbing her neck with her free hand.

Jimmy used to stand behind her when she was cooking and rub her neck while he offered enthusiastic, exceedingly dumb suggestions. 'How about a bit of parsley, Con?' It bugged her. She didn't need her neck rubbed when she was cooking and she didn't like people watching her. She liked to present them with the completed meal, nicely arranged on a good-quality plate and see their eyes light up. 'Scat!' she'd say to Jimmy. 'Stop *lurking*! Can't you find something better to do?'

Now, when she was cooking, she missed him rubbing her neck so much it gave her stomach cramps.

Until he died she hadn't realised just how

often Jimmy had touched her: a kiss on the forehead in the morning when he brought in her morning tea, sudden bear-hugs if they met in the hallway. When they watched the six o'clock news together they'd sit thigh-to-thigh on the sofa and he'd absent-mindedly stroke her arm while he concentrated on the news, frowning heavily and muttering beneath his breath at the politicians' lies. He'd run his fingers up and down her spine while they read together in bed. And patting her bottom — well, the man couldn't leave it alone! 'What's so fascinating about it?' she'd asked him once. 'It was the first thing I noticed about you,' he told her. 'Your pretty bum.' Really! He must have patted and pinched it a dozen times a day. She could never train him out of the habit. Sometimes he'd sneakily try to do it in public, which she found disgraceful and he found hilarious.

The problem was that after all those years her body seemed to have adapted to being touched. Now the touching had stopped, just like that, with no warning, and it was a shock, like a blast of cold air. Jimmy hadn't even been sick. They were going to do the fruit shopping one ordinary Thursday morning and she walked into the kitchen and there he was, lying on the floor, sending her heart flying into her throat. *'What are you doing?'* she shrieked out foolishly, into the silence. The last thing he'd said to her, only seconds before, was, 'I can't find my bloody wallet, Con.'

Now her untouched body felt like a plant drooping without water. Her skin was drying up and shrivelling before her eyes, becoming astonishingly ugly, as if the touch of Jimmy's fingers had been keeping it alive. Lately she had been secretly stroking her neck when she cooked, patting her arm when she watched the news, wrapping her arms around herself when she went to sleep. Once, ridiculously, she even patted her own bottom.

Still, it was better than crying so hard you felt like you couldn't breathe.

She took the shanks out of the pan and began layering the base of her good oven pot with chopped-up onion, mint leaves and garlic. Lamb shanks with Guinness. Jimmy's favourite. She kept making his favourite dishes, as if that would make him feel closer, as if that would make up for the fact that the last words he'd heard from her were, 'For heaven's sake, you'd lose your head if it wasn't screwed on.'

She'd noticed over the years of their marriage that they were always going through patches — good ones, bad ones, so-so ones. For example, there was that really enjoyable time in the early Eighties when they discovered apricot massage oil from Avon. Goodness me. That had certainly spiced things up in the bedroom (and once in the bathroom and quite a few times in the living room!). But then of course there were the bad times, like after the war, when she'd told him the truth about Alice and Jack. He was furious. He got such a *wounded* look on his face, she never forgot it. And when he refused to see the doctor about why she wasn't getting pregnant. She'd hated him for a while over that. Really hated him. But then she just got tired of hating him and started loving him again. It was easier.

And then, interspersed between the really good times and the really bad times, were the so-so times, where they didn't take all that much notice of each other, just ambled along, like a brother and sister really, maybe a bit snitchy at times. They were in the middle of a snitchy patch when he died.

Perhaps the poor man hadn't been feeling well.

Good Lord. She held on to the counter for balance. Sometimes the pain of missing him was so bad it almost knocked her off her feet. She poured stock and Guinness into the pot and bent, one hand on her back, to put it in the oven. It was the first time she'd hosted a dinner party since Jimmy died. There would be ten people: Enigma, Rose, Margie, Ron, Thomas, Veronika, Laura, Callum, Grace and — ah, their guest — oh for heaven's sake, what was the fellow's name? She knew it perfectly well. She was good at remembering names. Jimmy was hopeless. When they went to parties, someone would catch sight of Jimmy and their face would break into a grin — because everyone loved him — and Connie would lean over, barely moving her lips, like a ventriloquist: 'Paul Bryson, tennis, local council', and Jimmy wouldn't even blink, he'd cry, '*Paul,* mate! How's that killer serve of yours?!'

Now for the sticky caramelised apples. Thomas's favourite dessert. Poor old Thomas, according to Margie, was eating nothing but rice crackers he was so distraught over the Sophie business. Sophie had broken it off two weeks ago, just before he was going to take her to Fiji, of all the ridiculous places, to propose. (What was wrong with right here on Scribbly Gum Island?) The family was up in arms about it; they were probably more upset about Sophie's defection than Jimmy's death.

The fact was that Connie was actually upset about the Sophie business too. She'd been quite taken with her the few times she'd met her. Not that she'd met her that often. It was like pulling teeth getting Thomas to come to the island these days. But she'd come to the house for afternoon tea a month or so after Jimmy had died and Connie had felt marginally better just looking at her. It was those dimples — a thumbprint on either side of her mouth. The dimples were still there, even when she wasn't smiling.

Her enthusiasm for the house and Scribbly Gum Island had reminded Connie of Jimmy, the way he was that first day he rowed her out to the island, his cinnamon eyes all shiny. For years, before she packed away those dreams forever, Connie had imagined hers and Jimmy's child. She'd always thought they'd have a son, a miniature version of Jimmy, but when Connie looked at Sophie she found herself imagining what it would have been like to have had a daughter. It was strange, feeling that old pain for a child, like hearing the notes of an old song.

When Sophie had seen Jimmy's boots still sitting there on the back veranda, she'd stopped, put her hand on Connie's arm and said, 'You must miss your husband so much.' Not in a sappy, sentimental way. No. She looked genuinely sympathetic. 'Yes, I do,' Connie had said, and had had to suppress a tremor in her voice. 'Yes, I do.'

Everyone in Connie's family seemed to expect her to just get on with it, as if the death of your husband was to be expected. Five days after Jimmy died, Enigma actually had the hide to say, 'What a grumpy face you have today, Connie!' *Grumpy!* But Sophie said, 'You must miss your husband so much.' Such a simple thing to say, and the girl was probably being polite, just well brought up, but for some reason Connie had found it profoundly touching. How wonderful to have a daughter like that!

Sophie wasn't right for Thomas, though. Connie could tell. He was too damned grateful to have her. A woman wants to be adored but she doesn't want reverence. Thomas was trying too hard. He had the strained expression of a man who is under-qualified for his job. He laughed too loudly at her jokes and sat too close to her. Sweet, serious, worried Thomas; he needed a woman who made him feel like a man and Sophie needed a man who could give her a run for her money. He was just plain too wimpy for her.

Still, it would have been nice to have had Sophie there at family events. She clearly loved the island. She might even have convinced Thomas to live there. She would have brightened up the place, like Jimmy did. Yes, Jimmy's daughter would have been just like Sophie, and maybe the island would have been a different place with her light-hearted touch. She was the missing ingredient they needed. The hint of nutmeg.

Connie stirred brown sugar in melted butter and watched the sugar dissolve. Would six apples be enough? There had to be enough food and it had to be perfect. If her standards slipped, Laura would be on her case about getting somebody in to help, or even suggesting she move off the island to a retirement village. She, Connie Thrum, in a *retirement village* filled with doddering geriatrics!

It had been terrible the first time Connie washed sheets after Jimmy died and she realised he wasn't there to pull them out of the machine for her and carry them out to the line. She'd leaned over, tugging uselessly at the wretched heavy things, which had got all twisted around the rotor, and when she realised it was hopeless she'd kicked the washing machine in futile rage and really hurt her foot. Then she'd found herself sitting on the laundry floor, sobbing like a baby. It just seemed so unfair and undignified that after all the hard work of her life, all the striving and the planning and the worrying, she would end up defeated by two wet sheets. She didn't know what she would have done if Margie hadn't turned up and made her a cup of tea and kept up a meaningless stream of comforting Margie-babble while she lifted the sheets out of the washing machine and pegged them on the line for her. Now, whenever Margie came over she quietly helped herself to a load of washing (even stripping the sheets off the bed and remaking it) and brought it back the next day all neatly pressed and folded. It wasn't necessary of course, Connie wasn't a helpless old woman, but still, bless her.

Anyway, Connie could still damn well cook them all a bloody good meal.

What *was* that extra fellow's name who was coming tonight? It was driving her batty trying to think of it. It was right there on the tip of her tongue.

Two hours later she still hadn't remembered his name and there he was at the other end of the table, nodding politely as Veronika ranted away about something.

Looking around at the self-absorbed faces of her family, Connie felt an overwhelming desire to send everybody home and eat cinnamon toast alone in front of the television.

There was Ron, sitting in Jimmy's place with such a smarmy, self-satisfied expression on his face that Connie wanted to give him a good slap. Good Lord, he'd been a shy, gawky teenager when he first started courting Margie, and now look at him, sniping away at her. And there was Margie, pretending so hard to be happy when she'd been unhappy for years. It made Connie furious. The silly ninny was on some new diet where she ate nothing but 'protein'. This apparently meant she couldn't eat Connie's roast potatoes. 'Don't be ridiculous!' Connie snapped, and spooned out three for her. 'You've loved my roast potatoes since you were a little girl.'

'Oh, Connie,' said Margie reproachfully.

'Aunt Connie, you're sabotaging Mum's diet!' cried out Veronika.

'Nobody actually force-feeds your mother,' said Ron. 'She could just leave them on her plate.'

'Nobody supports her either,' said Veronika.

'*I* support her!' said Laura. 'I keep inviting you to join my tennis club, Margie.'

'Yes, well, I am thinking about it,' said

Margie uncertainly.

'I wouldn't bother, Aunt Margie,' said Grace. 'Mum's tennis friends spend more time worrying about their manicures than actually playing tennis.' Grace's tone was light but Connie noticed she didn't look at Laura as she spoke. It was Jimmy who had first pointed that out to Connie. 'Have you noticed that Grace never looks at her mother if she can help it?' he'd said. 'There's something not right there.'

Something not right with my whole bloody family, thought Connie now.

'Well, the potatoes are delicious, Mrs Thrum,' contributed their guest. It seemed that everyone was determined to be as unhelpful as possible by not saying the fellow's name.

'Thank you, dear,' said Connie. He had a nice, kind look about him, that boy.

'My friend Janet rang today,' announced Enigma. 'I'm very upset about it.'

'Here we go,' muttered Laura, picking up her wine glass.

'She's going to become a great-grandmother for the second time and she's *younger* than me!' said Enigma. 'The only news I had to tell her was that my grandson had just broken up with his fiancée!'

Thomas, all pale and hunched over his

217

dinner plate, said, 'Sophie wasn't my fiancée, Grandma. I hadn't asked her yet.'

'You had the ring! I saw the ring! It makes me cry to think about it.' Enigma gave the table a watery, martyred smile.

'It's not Thomas's fault, Grandma Enigma!' said Veronika. 'Sophie dumped him!'

'I never saw it coming.' Thomas gave a morose shake of his head. 'Never saw it coming. I thought she felt the same way.'

'Of course you did,' said Veronika.

'You'll meet someone else, darling.' Margie had polished off all her potatoes. 'Miss Right is waiting just around the corner!'

'She might not be, you know,' said Enigma darkly. 'June's grandson is forty and can't find a woman to marry him. He has to live with another man. Two sad bachelors!'

'Two gay bachelors, I'd say,' said Laura, while Ron smirked.

Grace, bless her, changed the subject by telling Enigma that Callum's mother was dying to meet her.

'She had a book of unsolved mysteries when she was young,' explained Callum. 'And the Munro Baby Mystery was one of her favourites.'

'It would be a pleasure to meet your mother, dear,' said Enigma graciously. 'You can take her home an autographed photo of me if she'd like.'

Connie asked Callum, 'What were some of your mother's other favourite mysteries?'

'Well, she does love a good grisly murder, my mum. She used to talk about the Pyjama Girl Mystery and, oh, what was it, the Bread Board Murder. She was a young girl when they both happened.'

'I've never heard of either of them,' said Grace.

Connie said, 'The Pyjama Girl was a woman found in her pyjamas near Albury in the 1930s. It was a horrible, brutal murder and they couldn't identify who she was for ten years. They kept her body preserved in a bath filled with formalin for all that time. The Bread Board Murder was a man who was found sitting at his kitchen table with his face in his breakfast. He'd been hit over the head once with a bread board.'

'Oh, but they were just normal run-of-the-mill murders,' said Enigma dismissively. 'Not as interesting as *our* mystery! And they solved the Pyjama Girl Mystery!'

'Yes, but there was a big cover-up! I read a book about it and it looks like they got the wrong man,' said Veronika, who always seemed to know everything about everything. It was a wonder the child hadn't solved the Munro Baby Mystery for herself.

'I bet the wife did the Bread Board Murder,' said Laura caustically. 'He probably complained about his eggs and she thought, That's it, I've had enough.'

Yes, well, with that sort of attitude it's no wonder your husband ran off with his dental nurse, thought Connie.

'What's your favourite unsolved mystery, dear?' asked Margie, bringing the visitor back into the conversation.

'That's easy. The pyramids. I went to Egypt last year and they were extraordinary.'

But Enigma had no interest in mysteries other than the one involving her. She sighed, 'I was just thinking, you know, Sophie would have been such a *pretty* bride!'

'Mum, please!' Margie made exaggerated gestures at her son, but Thomas, Connie could see, was in the mood for wallowing.

'Well, she would certainly have been a *blushing* bride,' said Veronika.

Connie said, 'Don't be spiteful.'

'I'm being factual, not spiteful,' said Veronika (rudely, thought Connie), and turned enthusiastically to the visitor. 'Sophie has a blushing disease. You've never seen anybody go so red. The first time I saw her do it I couldn't believe it.'

'It's not a disease,' said Thomas. 'It's a condition.'

'Whatever,' said Veronika.

'Is she very shy?' The visitor probably thought they were all mad, but he was certainly doing an excellent job of acting interested.

'Oh, no!' contributed Margie. 'That's what's so funny about her! She's very social!'

'Everyone loves her,' said Veronika. 'She's manipulative.'

'For heaven's sake, is anybody else tired of the Sophie topic?' asked Laura.

'I don't know,' sighed Thomas. 'Maybe she was out of my league.'

'Oh bullshit!' said Veronika, causing Rose to flinch as she came back to the table. Certain words didn't agree with her. 'She's just average-looking! It's not like she's as good-looking as Grace, for example.'

'Veronika!' Grace dipped her head while Callum beamed.

'I thought she was the most beautiful woman in the world,' said Thomas. He turned to the visitor. 'Do you want to see a photo of her?'

'Sure,' said the poor fellow, with what seemed to be genuine interest. He had such beautiful manners!

Thomas pulled his wallet out from his

jeans, flipped it open and reverently handed the picture over.

'Oh, she's very attractive,' said the visitor immediately.

At that point Thomas put his elbows on the table, buried his head in his hands and began to make strange wheezy gasping sounds.

'Oh for Christ's sake,' said Ron.

'Let it all out, darling!' said Margie.

'Maybe not at the dinner table,' said Laura.

'We should sue Sophie for emotional distress,' spat Veronika.

'Why don't you ask her to marry you again?' said Enigma. 'Maybe it's worth a second shot. Take along some marzipan tart. And did you mention to her that we're quite wealthy?'

Connie was the only one to notice that the visitor had quietly taken the opportunity to slide the photo back across the table and steal a second look.

Did you see that, Jimmy? I think our Sophie has an admirer.

24

It is a misty-grey Sunday afternoon and Sophie is driving down the freeway towards Brooklyn, practising not blushing.

On the car seat next to her is a freshly baked coffee and walnut liqueur cake in a Tupperware container and a bottle of expensive sauvignon blanc in a brown paper bag.

Sophie is going to lunch with Grace and Callum on Scribbly Gum Island, and she hasn't felt this nervous about a social event, since, well, since Aunt Connie's funeral the week before.

And it isn't as though she can comfort herself with the thought that Aunt Connie's funeral hadn't turned out to be that bad after all. It turned out to be far worse than her worst imaginings. First of all there was the humiliating incident in the taxi when she decided that Grace's husband was the father of her future children. Sophie makes pitiful 'ouch' sounds each time she remembers it. She tells herself again and again that there is no need to feel embarrassed. It's not as if she threw her arms around him, crying, 'My love, at last I've found you!' So she imagined some non-existent chemistry. So what? Big deal! Happens to everyone! It is extremely unlikely he somehow guessed she was checking her watch so she could tell their future children exactly what time it was when they met.

She reminds herself that everyone has thoughts they wouldn't care to share with the world. Many people have quite perverse thoughts about doing things with animals or fruit, or being spanked by nurses. The difference, of course, is that their thoughts are securely locked away behind bland faces, whereas Sophie's are always in danger of being revealed to all in a sudden flood of colour.

Generally she is quite resigned to her blushing. If minor disabilities were being distributed, she would, for example, still choose blushing over a horrendous facial twitch like her old school friend Eddie Ripple had suffered. Blushing is just her thing. It's like having an extraordinary sneeze. 'I'm sorry I look like a tomato,' she says to people. 'Don't worry. It's not contagious.'

But she does not want a situation to develop where she blushes each time she sees a particular person, such as Callum Tidyman. If she blushes every time she sees him, people will most definitely notice and start to comment and assume she has a sweet little crush on him. It will ruin everything. She'll feel sick each time she walks outdoors. The last time something like this happened was when she was fifteen and developed an automatic blush every time she saw the man who lived two doors down. Mr Fisk had a large moustache, a wife and three small children. He was not at all attractive. It was just that one day when there was a neighbourhood BBQ, Sophie was appalled to find herself eating her sausage sandwich and imagining what it would be like to have *sexual intercourse with Mr Fisk! Mr Fisk's dick! Mr Fisk's moustache scraping against her upper lip!* Naturally, it made her blush, and after that, just like Pavlov's dogs salivating when the bell rang for dinner, Sophie blushed whenever she saw Mr Fisk mowing the lawn or washing his car, or talking to her dad about the cricket. It was a tremendous relief when the Fisk family moved to Adelaide.

So, this lunch is her opportunity to put a stop to any such neurotic behaviour with

Callum. She will develop a friendship with both Callum and Grace, just like Aunt Connie had asked in her letter. Sophie is excellent at making new friends. She is quietly proud of this skill. If she can just get through those first few moments blush-free, she will be fine.

Of course, the problem with Callum might be the very least of her worries, because Sophie isn't quite sure of the purpose of this lunch. There's something a bit odd about it.

After Aunt Connie's funeral was over, all she could think about was getting away as fast as possible. She couldn't believe that she had ended up being late and having to make such a public entrance, and then, horror of horrors, sitting in the front row, with the family and next to Veronika, of all people, who had twitched and muttered for the next half-hour like someone with Tourette's syndrome. Directly behind her was Thomas, with his wife Debbie and baby Lily on her lap. Sophie could feel Debbie's eyes drilling triumphantly into the back of her neck, as if they had been involved in a competition for Thomas and Debbie had won. At one point Lily had reached forward and grabbed a handful of Sophie's hair. 'Sorry,' Debbie had whispered, sounding not at all sorry as she dislodged Lily's pudgy hand. Had she somehow trained her baby to pull Daddy's ex-girlfriend's hair?

After the funeral had finally ended she had talked to Enigma and Aunt Rose on the church steps, who had asked if she was coming to the afternoon tea.

'We haven't seen you in so *long!*' said Enigma. Sophie had seen Veronika's grandmother crying during the funeral but now she seemed quite cheerful, reapplying bright red lipstick as she spoke. 'We've missed you! You *must* come back with us.'

'I'm actually going to have to get back to work now,' apologised Sophie.

'You mustn't worry about Veronika, if that's what you're thinking,' Enigma said. 'She's just sulking. She'll get over it. She wasn't smacked enough when she was a child. Were you smacked? I'm a great believer in smacking.'

'Oh, all the time,' lied Sophie. In fact, her mother had never even so much as raised her voice at her without later buying her a special treat to make up for it.

'You're very welcome to come along, dear,' said Rose. 'Connie would . . . yes, Connie . . .' Her voice drifted off and she seemed to forget she was speaking, her pale eyes looking dreamily past Sophie as she leaned heavily on her walking frame, the turquoise of her dress glimmering richly in the sun. She was like an aging fairy princess.

'I love the colour of your dress,' commented Sophie. Rose had always been her favourite of the three old ladies.

Rose blinked and caressed the fabric. 'Yes. It's beautiful, isn't it? The fabric is quite good quality too. This is my favourite colour. Once I . . . well.' Rose looked around nervously, as if she'd forgotten her lines and was waiting for the prompt.

'Ahem, ahem!' said Enigma meaningfully. 'Are we having an Alzheimer's moment, Rose, dear?'

Sophie didn't know what they were talking about but gave a surprised giggle and Enigma chortled with her, looking proud. 'I heard that on a television programme. "Alzheimer's moment." It's funny, isn't it? I say it all the time to my friends. Some of them get quite annoyed with me. Of course, I can be senile myself — I do forget things sometimes.'

Sophie said, 'I'm always forgetting where I've left the car, or dialling a number and then forgetting who I'm phoning.'

Unfortunately Veronika happened to walk out of the church at exactly the moment Sophie and Enigma were laughing. Her face contorted.

'Oh, pet, don't pull faces like that!' said Enigma. 'The wind might change!'

'Grandma Enigma!' Veronika looked enraged and as if she might burst into tears.

'Veronika,' began Sophie, not knowing what she was going to say but feeling bad for her, because there had been some schoolgirl spite in Enigma's remark.

'Don't you talk to me!' hissed Veronika. All around them ears quivered as guests sensed interesting funeral conflict.

'That's enough now, Veronika,' said Enigma sharply, looking as if she wanted to give Veronika a smack.

'I've really got to go,' said Sophie desperately. 'Thank you so much for having me. I had a lovely time. OK. I really must go!'

She practically sprinted from the church, inwardly hollering, OH, YOU HAD A LOVELY TIME, DID YOU? AT A FUNERAL?

It must have been stress that had caused her to recite the words her mother used to make her practise in the car before she went to a birthday party. 'Thank you for having me, Mrs Blake.' Smile. Don't hang your head. Look Mrs Blake in the eyes. 'I had a lovely time.'

A lovely time? Her toes were blushing.

229

She had nearly escaped to the freedom of the street when she heard footsteps behind her and felt a touch on her arm. It was Grace. Oh, the mortification of feeling attracted to a man who slept every night with a woman who looked like that. Translucent, flawless skin. Clear green eyes. Heartbreakingly full lips. They were a different species. If Grace was a gazelle, Sophie was a ground mole.

'I'm Grace,' she said. 'I don't know if you remember me. I'm Thomas and Veronika's cousin. Callum said you shared a cab today. I just wondered if you'd like to come for lunch next Saturday?'

'Lunch?' repeated Sophie. She had to tip her head back to look at Grace. Her voice sounded hoarse and feeble, as if even her larynx recognised its inferiority.

'Callum and I are living in my mother's house on the island. I thought it might be nice because . . .'

She stopped and seemed to be searching for a reason why it would be nice. Perhaps Rose or Enigma had forced her to issue the invitation.

'. . . we're going to be neighbours!' she finished, and smiled expectantly at Sophie. Her smile was exquisite but remote. She was like a world-famous celebrity talking by video-link to a sycophantic journalist.

Sophie wondered why she'd liked Grace so much at Veronika's wedding. She was generally slightly resentful of people who made it obvious they didn't care less whether you liked them or not, because she herself was conscious of an unattractive need to please. Sometimes when talking to somebody she was suddenly revolted by herself, aware of how eagerly she was leaning forward, chin jutting, mimicking the other person's gestures, moving with them, nodding and smiling, gently nudging their conversation along with a constant stream of appreciative chuckles, soothing 'hmmms' and surprised exclamations. 'Really!' 'Did he?' 'You're *kidding!*' *Love me, love me!* People like Grace didn't change their body language depending on the other person. They set the pace. They stood, elegant and still, while people like Sophie fluttered around them.

Well, Sophie wouldn't be doing any fluttering around Grace.

Her mother had trained her in the delicate art of suddenly remembering an invented social engagement. Sophie, like Gretel, was extremely good at it and never even came close to blushing because it was crucial that the other person didn't guess you were faking and have their feelings hurt.

'Saturday?' she said brightly. 'That would be really nice. I'm sure I'm free. Oh, no, wait!' She crunched her forehead regretfully and gave her handbag an annoyed little slap. 'I'm not free! I've got a friend's birthday lunch on that day. Oh what a pity. I don't even want to go, to be honest. Well, perhaps another time.'

'Oh. But, well, what about Sunday?' asked Grace, and suddenly she didn't seem cold, she seemed desperate, as if she was pleading for Sophie to come to lunch.

Well, if she was *needed*, that was different! Sophie felt her heart melt on cue. 'You're a soft touch, Soph,' her dad, who was the softest touch of all, always told her. She abandoned her mythical 'such a bore' BBQ and went straight into normal flutter-like-a-moth mode. 'Oh, Sunday would be lovely. It's so nice of you to ask me.'

So now here she is, driving that familiar route down the freeway, seeing her first glimpses of the river, mysterious slate-grey today, beneath a heavy layer of pearly mist hovering just above the water.

In just a few short hours it will all be over and she will be in the pub with Claire, telling her about it. That's the way to get through today's lunch; it's just a new story

232

to tell Claire, so the worse it is the better it will be for comedic value. The funeral had provided Claire and her boyfriend Sven with virtually a whole night of entertainment. Actually, thinks Sophie, she seems to spend a lot of her time providing entertainment for her couple friends. They love having Sophie over for dinner, sympathising with the latest disasters in her life, saying to each other, 'There must be someone we can set her up with!' The men flirt outrageously with her and the women tell her they're jealous of her single state. Sophie suspects that after she leaves they always have better sex than normal. She gets at least one dinner invitation a week. One couple even eagerly suggested she become their flatmate and move into their spare room. For some reason, Sophie is the perfect third partner in a non-sexual ménage à trois. She gives them something they need. She doesn't know what, but it's nice to be helpful.

She wonders if Grace and Callum will expect her to fill a similar role. They'd probably love to know about her attraction to Callum; it might invigorate a stale relationship. Although it seems unlikely that women who look like Grace are ever in stale relationships.

Rain splatters on the windshield. Sophie

puts on the windscreen wipers and leans forward slightly to concentrate more on the road ahead. It's easy to forget to think about driving on these long, straight roads.

Yes, Grace had been odd when she issued this lunch invitation. Perhaps she is very shy. Or just not a very nice person. Or devastated by Aunt Connie's death. Or perhaps she was behaving oddly because Sophie is going to be forced to undergo some bizarre Scribbly Gum Island initiation ceremony, with chanting and incense and walking across hot coals. Or maybe the whole family is going to confront her about Aunt Connie's will. It will be like an intervention, or a mock courtroom, with Veronika presiding as judge. Sophie will be found guilty, of course. 'We find the defendant GUILTY as charged!' They will blindfold her and frogmarch her to the highest point of the island where they'll toss her over to certain death on the vicious rocks below. After all, the family is probably perfectly capable of murder. They're all a bit strange. Look at their mysterious history. Look what happened to Alice and Jack — *the last non-family members to live on the island!* But then, against all odds, Sophie will survive! She'll need extensive plastic surgery, of course, and months later she'll come back even more beautiful than Grace (but essentially still Sophie) to confront them all with their crime. 'Gad, who is that intriguing woman?' Callum will say, peering through his eye-glass, inexplicably dressed and talking like a regency gentleman.

Sophie chuckles out loud in the car at her own fantasies. She has a special, slightly dirty-sounding chuckle she only uses in private. As her mum always says, one of the advantages of being an only child is that you have no trouble amusing yourself.

As she pulls off the freeway at the Glass Bay exit, Sophie feels her heart lift, like it did when she was a child and her parents were taking her for a day out on Scribbly Gum. At this point her father would always make the same joke. 'Only another hour to go, Soph!' when really they were only minutes away. Daddy was being a trickster!

The opening bars of a new band's song comes on the radio and Sophie quickly flicks up the volume. A good omen. She's been listening out for the song for ages. She's in the early stages of falling in love with it, where she knows the chorus but not the verses and she makes up pretend words so she doesn't have to stop singing. She sings lustily, enjoying how stupid she must look to other people, with her mouth open-

ing and shutting and her face twisting in
rock-star anguish.

By the time she pulls in at the ferry wharf
she is in a fine and feisty mood.

25

Gublet McDublet was running away from home. He'd had enough of Mummy and Daddy and his best friend, Melly the Music Box Dancer.

LEAVE ME ALONE, he wanted to shout, but you weren't allowed to shout. It wasn't nice. So he was going to live on the moon all by himself. It would be dark and cool and silent. He would be weightless and free, taking giant floating footsteps inside his big spacesuit.

Or maybe he would just kill himself. Commit hari-kari like a Japanese samurai. Or put a gun in his mouth and pull the trigger. He hadn't really decided yet.

Grace is brushing Jake's hair for Sophie's visit. It's raining hard now and Callum has gone down to the wharf to meet her with a big golf umbrella.

It's the first time Grace has used the soft little blue hairbrush with the teddy bear on the handle. It came in the huge cellophane-wrapped basket she got from the girls at work. 'Ohhhh,' everybody said when she held up each new item.

The baby seems to like having his hair brushed. He looks up at her with ruminative, wise-old-man eyes. He has an ugly pimply rash across both his cheeks, which is apparently *very* normal, according to Aunt Margie and Enigma, but Grace wishes he didn't have it at the moment. 'A face only a mother could love,' Ron said the last time he saw him, glancing briefly in the pram, and Grace was filled with a rage so murderous she had to avert her head.

She brushes the baby's hair flat with a part down the side and his whole face is transformed into that of a 1950s geek. All he needs is the bow tie. She fluffs it back up again so he looks like a baby. His head is so soft.

She imagines smashing his tender head with the side of the hairbrush, again and again and again. He would cry but he wouldn't try to wriggle away because he doesn't know how. He'd just lie there inert, while his head was transformed into a mess of blood and bone.

Grace trembles. Her heart races.

She stands up with the baby held lightly in her arms and walks rapidly to the pram. She breathes shallow short breaths as she places him flat on his back.

The baby is crying as she walks carefully out of the room and stands in the hallway. She silently pummels her body with clenched fists, punching the tops of her arms and thighs, slapping herself across the cheeks. The pain is exquisite.

After about a minute she stops. Her body aches, her cheeks sting. She breathes in deeply through her nostrils and then turns her head and practises smiling in the empty hallway — a warm, welcoming smile to no one.

The baby wails. Outside, the rain picks up.

'It's all right,' she says softly, to him and to herself. 'Everything is going to be all right. I'm going to find a way to fix it.' Sophie's coffee and walnut liqueur cake recipe had called for one cup of finely chopped walnuts. The sides of the cake are decorated with half-walnuts carefully pressed into the icing in a pretty pattern.

It is an especially nutty cake, which is unfortunate because Grace has a life-threatening allergy to nuts. If she eats even the tiniest mouthful of Sophie's cake she'll experience anaphylactic shock. Her throat and mouth will swell up, her heart will race and she'll collapse. Within seconds she'll be dead. She has something called an 'EpiPen', which must be jabbed into her leg, straight through her clothes, giving her a dose of adrenaline. 'Wham! Just like that scene in *Pulp Fiction*,' explains Callum, cheerfully demonstrating with his fist.

'It's a beautiful cake,' says Grace. They are all standing in the kitchen observing Sophie's deadly offering and listening to the rain, which is now pounding down relentlessly. Grace is holding the baby up over one shoulder. The baby has a single drop of milk hovering on his bottom lip, and flushed cheeks. His arms flail. Sophie is entranced by the delicate curve of his floppy dark head.

'All that work you put into baking it,' says Grace. 'I'm so sorry I can't eat it.'

'I'm so sorry I brought it!' says Sophie, while Claire and Sven guffaw in her head.

'It's not your fault,' says Callum. 'How would you have known?'

The thing is that Sophie actually *did* know about Grace's nut allergy. Both Thomas and Veronika have on different occasions regaled her with the legendary story of Thomas's

sixteenth birthday, when Grace had kissed a
boy who had just finished eating three satay
chicken skewers. There had been a terrifying, exciting race across the river on Uncle
Jimmy's speedboat to the waiting ambu-
lance. The boy she'd kissed had been quite
traumatised by the event and later turned
out to be gay. Apparently his mother still
blamed Grace for what she considered to
be her son's unfortunate choice of sexuality.

But Sophie had forgotten all about the
nut allergy when she'd made the cake.

'Actually, I think I *did* know but I forgot,'
she admits, and battles unsuccessfully with
a blush. Too late. Here it comes. Oh *shit*!
These are the worst situations, where she
really *isn't* embarrassed. After all, it's
perfectly understandable that she would
forget Grace's allergy, and this sort of situation must happen to her all the time. She's
like the growing gluten-free, wheat-free,
dairy-free brigade, constantly having to say,
'Oh, no, I couldn't possibly eat that.' So
even though it's a bit mortifying that her
cake is so *conspicuously* nutty, she doesn't
feel that bad. Unfortunately, the moment
there is a likelihood that other people might
conceivably think she could feel awkward,
she blushes, and is therefore embarrassed
by the blush, not the original situation.

Yes, it is a cruel disorder.

Her face throbs.

Her neck burns and blotches.

She watches Callum and Grace slide their eyes away to opposite corners of the kitchen. I'll take the twitch next time, thinks Sophie.

'Thomas and Veronika both told me about the birthday party where you nearly died,' she says, talking normally, calling upon thirty years of blushing experience to get her through.

'Aha! Satay-stick boy!' crows Callum, and he looks Sophie straight in the eye, grinning, as if she isn't blushing at all. 'I think Sophie is trying to bump you off, Grace. Lucky we uncovered her cunning plan. The walnuts all over the cake were a bit of a giveaway.'

Oh bloody, bloody hell. She really, really likes him.

'People forget about my stupid nut allergy all the time,' says Grace nicely, but still with that perceptible touch of ice. 'My own mother forgets. Please don't worry about it. Callum can have my piece. I'm still watching what I eat anyway. I'm trying to get back to my pre-pregnancy weight.'

Grace is wearing jeans and a pristine long-sleeved white shirt. She is tall and slender and utterly perfect.

'As long as he doesn't kiss you after he eats it,' teases Sophie, a bit daringly, as if they are all old friends. She stands there with her scarlet face, like a silly mask, resigned to it.

'Actually, I never forget Grace's allergy. I'm in a constant state of terror I'll have to use the EpiPen on her,' says Callum, and Sophie, watching him watching Grace, sees that he truly adores his wife. Well, of course he does.

'I'll have two, no, three pieces of cake,' he continues. 'Just so you don't feel bad, Sophie, but then I'll gargle with disinfectant.'

'A disinfected mouth doesn't sound very kissable,' says Sophie.

'Yes, I think I'd rather risk it with a walnut mouth.' Grace smiles and her whole face is transformed.

There is a cosy moment of three-way camaraderie in the kitchen. Oh dear, thinks Sophie. I think I'm falling in love with both of them.

But Grace's smile vanishes like sunlight obliterated by a cloud and she seems impatient. 'All right, well, why don't you two go and sit down in the dining room and I'll just finish off making the lunch. It's a pity the weather is so bad. Otherwise we could have sat on the balcony. Here, Sophie, would you like to hold the baby? He's just had his feed so he's in a good mood.'

Before Sophie can answer, Grace dumps the baby in her arms.

Sophie makes a strange 'ha!' sound and clutches the baby tight. Although she adores babies she is also terrified of them. As godmother to nine children (it's very expensive, and two of them she secretly dislikes, to her intense shame) she has extensive experience with first-time mothers. Generally, they are quite wearing. Sometimes they hand the baby over only to immediately snatch it back, and Sophie can always feel their eyes on her and their baby, watching her like a hawk, which only adds to her nervousness. Grace, however, instantly turns her back and is chopping an eggplant into cubes, the knife thudding hard against the cutting board, thud, thud, thud. Her back in the white shirt is very still; Sophie imagines all the muscles contracted. She feels sudden, unaccountable pity for Grace. *What is it, honey? What's the matter?* Well, how ridiculous. Grace is a woman leading a dream life.

Callum leads Sophie into the dining room. She walks stiffly, imagining tripping or accidentally banging the baby's head against something. She's always slamming her own elbows against doorways. Callum and Grace probably wouldn't be quite as understanding as they were about the walnut cake if she smashed their baby's head. It's a relief when she is seated.

The dining room, like the rest of the house, is elegant but austere, like a display home. There isn't enough real 'stuff' lying around. The colours are too neutral. The surfaces too shiny.

'Do you like living here?' she asks Callum when she is settled with relief at the table, the baby a comforting weight in the crook of her arm.

Callum sits at the head of the table, next to her. He's wearing jeans, a long-sleeved shirt with a T-shirt on underneath. His jaw is unshaven, unlike at the funeral. He obviously doesn't shave on the weekends. He's a big lumbering lump of a man really, but there is just something delicious about him. Oh for heaven's *sake,* Sophie! Get a grip. You obviously need to have sex with somebody, anybody, very soon. Celibacy is sending you mad.

If you blush again I'll murder you.

'I like living on the island,' says Callum. 'It's great. I'm not so fussed about living in my mother-in-law's house. It's all a bit stiff and clean for me. I grew up in a house with six boys.'

'Five brothers!' Surely one of them is single. Another version of him! An identical twin, perhaps? Perfect! She hadn't made such a mistake in the cab. She'd just had a slight, understandable mix-up between brothers.

'Yep. I'm the baby. We're all married with kids now. Jake is the youngest of sixteen grandchildren.'

Of course not. There is no such thing as a single man. They're all gone. They were sold out by the early Nineties.

'Gosh. Fifteen cousins.'

Callum is re-filling Sophie's wine glass with the sauvignon blanc. He takes a sip from his own glass and smacks his lips. 'Even a philistine like me can tell this is really good wine.'

'I've been trained since birth. My parents used to take me on wine-tasting trips for school holidays.'

'That's the difference. My parents took me to Budgewoi Caravan Park. Were you a spoiled little princess?'

'If you hid a pea under my mattress I wouldn't sleep a wink.'

This is most certainly not chemistry. This is a beautiful woman's husband who is so happily married he can afford to be nice to plain, single women.

Sophie looks down at the baby and finds herself doing that thing women do where they ask babies who can't talk questions meant for other people.

'Who do you look like, Jake? Your mum or your dad?'

Callum obligingly answers her, leaning forward to look at the baby in Sophie's arms. She can smell his aftershave. 'I'm hoping he'll get Grace's looks rather than mine, for obvious reasons. I don't think he really looks like either of us at the moment. I think he most closely resembles an elderly monkey.'

'A little monkey, eh?' Sophie bares her teeth in a monkey-face and makes a chattering sound at Jake. The baby looks up at her with wandering dark eyes, and all of a sudden they pause and it's like he's caught sight of his first ever fellow human being. His eyes lock on to hers and a corner of his mouth curves up tentatively in a wonky attempt at a grin.

'Was that a *smile*?' Callum leans forward on his chair, his arm pressing against Sophie's. 'I think that was his first smile!'

Jake's eyes waver and then focus on Callum. He gives his father an even bigger lopsided smile. This time his eyes crinkle at the corners. Callum almost tips forward off the chair in ecstasy. 'Hello there, mate! You don't look like a monkey at all! No, you're a good-looking guy!'

There is a tender, teary feeling in Sophie's chest.

Grace walks in at that moment, carrying a gigantic platter of food.

Callum grabs Grace around the waist. 'He smiled at us! You should have seen it. Sophie made a monkey face and he smiled for the first time! Do it again, Sophie!'

Feeling like an idiot, Sophie makes a half-hearted monkey noise, thinking, I'm sure she's really going to appreciate missing her baby's first smile.

But the effort of trying out brand-new facial movements has obviously tired Jake out and he is suddenly fractious. As Grace leans towards him he throws back his small head and gives a screeching, red-faced wail.

'Oh,' says Grace.

Sophie expects her to take the baby from her, but she just gives a wintry smile and sits down on the other side of the dining-room table, indicating the platter.

'Just a few starters. Those ones are tuna spring rolls, that's bruschetta, of course, and those there are egg rolls with smoked salmon. The rest is self-explanatory, I think.'

'Gosh,' says Sophie feebly. The baby continues to cry and she experiments gamely with a few ineffectual rocking motions.

'Let me take him, so you can eat,' says Callum. He casually swoops the baby up and out of Sophie's arms and plonks him over one broad shoulder, rapidly patting his large nappied bottom. The baby whimpers a bit and then stops crying. Callum caresses the back of Jake's downy head and says, 'You'll have to smile for your mum later, or she'll think we made it up.'

Grace is not even looking at her baby. Sophie has seen all types of new mothers: the ones with besotted, glazed-over eyes; the cool, casual 'this is a piece of cake' types; the teary, terrified ones, and the exhausted, overwhelmed ones who speak obsessively of how many hours' sleep they managed the night before. Grace doesn't seem to fit in any of those categories. She's like a woman playing a mother in a moisturiser commercial. Actually, thinks Sophie, she's quite weird.

Sophie hears herself start to gush. 'This food looks wonderful, Grace. That's so impressive when you have a new baby. I have some friends who say they don't even have time to get dressed in the morning, or go to the toilet, or comb their hair!'

'Oh, well, none of this was very difficult.'

'Grace's family take food *very* seriously,' says Callum. He takes an enormous bite of an egg roll. 'It's like my family and music. What's your family's obsession, Sophie?'

'I don't know if we've got one. Oh, yes, I know. We're hedonists. We take pleasure very seriously. My parents have always meticulously planned their weekends for maximum pleasure.'

'They sound great,' says Callum. 'My parents get nervy if things are going too well for too long.'

'What's the opposite of hedonism?' says Grace. 'Masochism, I guess. That's my mother. She plans her life for maximum misery.'

She is smiling at Sophie, folding a piece of prosciutto in half and wrapping it around a sun-dried tomato. She is not weird at all. She is perfectly normal. Sophie is obviously prejudiced because of her beauty. Beautiful people probably suffer from terrible discrimination just like other minority groups. Sophie should think of Grace's beauty as a handicap, like blushing. Ha, ha.

'Isn't your mum travelling around the world at the moment?' asks Sophie. 'That doesn't sound too masochistic.'

'Everywhere is too dirty, too expensive, too hot or just too different. She's revelling in a sort of exotic, international misery now.'

'I think he's dropped off.' Callum turns his shoulder slightly to show them Jake's flushed, sleeping face. 'I'll put him down.'

'No, no,' says Grace. 'I'll do it.'

She disappears from the room with Jake and is gone for ages. Callum refills Sophie's glass again and starts interrogating her about her taste in music. She receives a thumbs-up for Cowboy Junkies, a quizzical eyebrow for Pearl Jam and a pained wince for Shania Twain. When she reveals that she has the soundtrack to *Titanic* he writhes, waving his arms at her to stop while he chokes on a mouthful of wine.

They are laughing when Grace comes back into the room and immediately stop and turn expansively towards her, smiling too eagerly to make sure she knows they've been having a good time, but not *too* good a time.

'Titanic,' explains Sophie inadequately.

'I'm afraid our guest has shocking taste in music,' says Callum.

'Oh, well, I can't even converse about music,' says Grace, sitting down.

'That's not true,' says Callum.

251

'Yes it is.' Grace immediately stands up again. 'I'll get the main course now,' she says.

'Sit down!' says Callum. 'Let me get it. You've been rushing around all day.'

'What can I do to help?' Sophie is half out of her chair.

'No, no.' Grace quells them both like over-eager puppies. 'You *stay*. Chat!'

So they stay. And they get on to the music of their youth, Eighties music, Wham, Duran Duran, Boy George, Madonna. They sing lines of songs to each other. They keep exploding with laughter. They discover they were at the same Pseudo Echo concert back in 1986. (It was probably my destiny to meet him at that concert, thinks Sophie. Just my luck, I was in the toilet, readjusting my shoulder pads.)

It's turning into one of those conversations at a party where you've both got just the right amount of alcohol in your bloodstreams and you're making each other laugh and you both know you fancy each other and you're ignoring the party happening around you, and you're so pleased because you didn't want to come in the first place and any minute now you're heading for first-kiss time, and you know that after he kisses you he's most definitely going to ask for your phone number and he's most definitely going to call.

Only it's not one of those conversations, because this type of euphoric tableau does not normally incorporate a beautiful wife in the kitchen fixing lunch, or a sleeping baby son down the hallway.

This is getting just the tiniest bit dangerous. They are flirting with the idea of flirting. What is Grace *doing*?

'Wine at lunchtime goes straight to my head,' says Sophie suddenly, as if she's explaining something.

'Me too. I'll get us some water,' says Callum as if he's explaining something back, and as he stands up his eyes meet hers with a fleeting uncomfortable glance and Sophie knows, the way you just know some things without question, that in another parallel world he *would* have asked for her phone number if she'd met him at the Pseudo Echo concert or the imaginary party. She didn't imagine the chemistry in the cab. It's just bad luck.

There is a sudden rapping on the glass windows of the dining room. 'Yoo hoo!'

Callum and Sophie both jump. Two figures are outside on the balcony, tapping on the windows with their umbrella handles as they walk past them towards the front door.

'Enigma and Aunt Rose.' Callum is smiling with something that looks suspiciously like relief.

Enigma and Rose come into the dining room, awkwardly peeling off sopping wet bright yellow raincoats, squeezing out water from their straggled hair, puffing, pink and wrinkled. They are obviously rather exhilarated by their daring as they say things like, 'Torrential!' 'I couldn't see a thing!' 'We're absolutely *drenched*!'

They collapse on the sofa, full of themselves and their adventure, like prematurely aged teenagers.

'We *hooned* over on our bikes, dear,' explains Enigma to Sophie. 'We're real hoons! Oh my word, is that a nice white wine there I see? Rose and I will have a glass, won't we, Rose?'

'I think there's going to be the most tremendous storm,' says Rose. 'I love storms. Especially thunder. That big powerful *boom, kaboom* as if something is breaking. Connie loved storms too. When we were young we used to run around the island when there was a storm. Sometimes we took our clothes off. You'll see wonderful storms from Connie's balcony, Sophie.'

Callum hands them both glasses of wine and Sophie sees that Rose's hands are trembling slightly.

Grace appears in the doorway. 'You two will catch pneumonia,' she says.

'You sound just like your mother, dear,' says Enigma.

'Are you staying for lunch?' asks Grace.

'Oh, no, dear, we wouldn't dream of it, we just stopped in to say hello to Sophie,' says Enigma. 'What have you made?'

'Mum's salmon risotto.'

'Ah, Laura's risotto — with the goat cheese! — well we'd only need small portions, wouldn't we, Rose? We eat like little birds these days.'

'It's OK, there's plenty. Will you get them towels, Callum? They've got to get dry. Maybe you should both use my hairdryer.'

Sophie watches Grace and Callum share a husbandly-wifely look. They will laugh and complain about this unexpected visit in bed tonight.

'I'll give both their heads a good rub,' promises Callum.

'Oh, *you*!' says Enigma coquettishly.

When Callum and Grace are out of the room, Rose and Enigma lean forward confidentially towards Sophie.

'We've brought you the keys to Connie's house,' says Enigma.

Sophie is a bit thrown. She has an appointment to see Connie's solicitor on Tuesday. She had assumed the whole process would take weeks. There's also the Veronika issue.

'But, ah, Veronika mentioned — that you — that maybe the family wasn't too happy about Aunt Connie leaving the house to me.'

'Oh, she's a rascal, that Veronika,' says Rose fondly.

'You mustn't take any notice of her,' says Enigma. 'I often sing a little song in my head until she's finished talking. The thing is, Rose and I think it would be fun if you moved into the house quite soon.'

'But won't there be paperwork?' asks Sophie.

'Oh, but we don't *like* paperwork!' says Enigma. 'No need to dilly-dally. Sooner the better.'

'You won't be lonely,' says Rose. 'And the garden needs you.'

'We'll drop in on you,' says Enigma. 'As often as you like!'

Rose smiles radiantly at her. 'And when you turn forty we'll tell you the truth about Alice and Jack.'

Enigma starts and looks terrified. 'Good Lord Rose, have you gone stark raving *mad*!'

'Oh. I haven't mixed up the ages, have I? Forty. Yes, no, that's right Enigma. Connie said, we tell them when they're forty.'

'Yes, but we don't tell them we're *going* to tell them, do we!' Enigma is agitated. She gulps at her wine and turns to Sophie.

'You must excuse Rose, pet,' she says. 'She's so upset about Connie. She's not herself. She's talking gibberish, of course.'

'It's OK,' says Sophie. So, they actually *know* what happened to Alice and Jack?! Wait till she tells her parents! Does Veronika know? Veronika isn't forty, so presumably not.

Enigma says, 'I need to ask a favour, dear.'

'Of course.'

'I need to ask you not to mention what Rose just said to anybody. It's all nonsense, of course, but it could upset the family. This is quite serious. Although not at *all* serious, of course! But still, you need to keep it a secret, dear.'

'Keep what a secret?' asks Callum, his arms full of towels.

'Secret women's business,' says Sophie, and she gives Enigma a wink.

Outside, the rain sounds harder, pelleting against the roof, as if someone has increased the volume.

'That's hail,' says Rose. 'It's exciting but it flattens the flowers. Connie won't like that.'

26

Margie is at her Weight Watchers meeting listening to a woman tell the story of her 'Amazing Weight Loss Journey'. The woman has lost sixty kilos — a whole person! There has been a four-page article about her in the *Australian Women's Weekly*. She is in the running for the Weight Watcher of the year. She is an inspiration. A movie star! She was a size twenty-two in a caftan. Now she is a size eight in *leather pants.* The whole room is mesmerised by those shiny black leather pants.

'I *despised* myself when I was fat,' says the woman, holding toned, skinny arms wide. 'You should have heard my self-talk. I used to wake up each morning and say to my reflection, "Good morning, Slovenly Sow!" '

Everyone laughs slightly quivery laughs.

'Does anyone else do that? Negative self-talk?'

'I don't need self-talk,' contributes a pretty woman who is about the same age as Margie's daughter Veronika. She has round apple cheeks and hurt eyes. 'I have husband-talk. He calls me Chubby Chops. He's not exactly Brad Pitt either.'

'I'll *bet* he isn't!' a man cries out angrily at the other end of the aisle, and when everyone turns to look at him he suddenly looks horrified. 'Oh! I don't mean that you — I meant that in a *good* way!'

Oh just leave your husband, darling, thinks Margie. You could marry that nice man and have lots of dear little plump children together.

'So what I did was change my self-talk!' says the woman, whirling around to give them a glimpse of her neat leather buttocks. 'Instead of saying, "Good morning, Slovenly Sow" when I looked in the mirror, I changed it to "Good morning, Sexy Goddess!" You know why? I'll tell you why! *Because the body believes the mind.*'

The man sitting next to Margie shifts uncomfortably in his chair and lowers his chin. 'Ms Leather Pants is getting a bit tiresome now, don't you think?'

The man has a bright red face and layers of chins. Ron would call him a Heart Attack Waiting to Happen.

Margie looks around nervously. She never talked in class at school but she doesn't want to be rude to this poor man. His heart attack might happen. And it's nice of him to try and be funny like that.

Daringly, she whispers back, 'Yes, she is a bit!'

He lowers his chin again and Margie is frantic. That's enough! *We'll get into trouble!* She looks straight ahead with bright attention at the speaker.

The man wheezes into her ear, 'Would you like to have a skim cappuccino with me after the meeting?'

Good Lord! Surely he isn't trying to 'pick her up', as they say? He's probably just lonely. Perhaps he wants to sell her some 'business opportunity'. Or he's a Christian. Or he might be a *dangerous kook!*

'All right,' she whispers back.

Sophie and her mother are at the Korean Bathhouse in the city. They've been coming here for years, since Sophie was a teenager. First they have a full body scrub, followed by a long, languid soak in the baths, then yum cha in Chinatown, shopping, and a cocktail or two at the Opera Bar.

They sit in one of the hot baths, their heads resting against the wall. Naked female forms stroll through the steam, lowering themselves into the water. Everyone covertly checks out everyone else's bodies through half-lowered eyelashes.

Sophie is telling her mother about how she got Jake to smile for the first time.

'He's adorable,' she says.

'You sound very clucky.' Gretel's hair has gone into corkscrew curls in the heat, and she has hectic pink circles on her cheeks.

'I guess I am a bit,' says Sophie, and she's shocked by a sudden swell of grief. 'But I'm just going to have to accept it, aren't I? I'm not going to be a mother. When I think about my fortieth birthday it's like a big iron door slamming in my face. There just isn't *time* to meet somebody and I *know* that's just life, but sometimes, Mum, I just *ache* for a child.'

'Oh, Sophie.' Gretel sits upright and agitatedly pats her shoulder. 'Sweetheart! Of course there's time! We just have to fix this! I didn't realise it meant so much to you, darling. I'm so stupid! I thought you were happy being a career girl. Oh, dear, how can we fix this?' She looks around her frantically, as if a spare baby is likely to go floating by any second and she can quickly scoop it up and hand it over to Sophie.

A woman, a sleek brunette, sitting close to

them, leans over confidentially and says, 'I
hope you don't mind me listening in, but
I've got a friend who is single and wants a
baby and she's doing it on her own. She
just said, bugger it, this is what I want, and
off she went to the sperm bank. Picked out
a donor. He's tall with red hair and his
interests are scuba diving, Thai cooking and
playing the violin. My friend said she always
dreamed of having a red-headed baby.'

'Goodness,' blinks Gretel.

'What a pity she couldn't *meet* the red-
headed sperm donor at a Thai cooking
course and fall in love with him,' says
Sophie.

'Ah, you're a romantic,' says the brunette.
'I bet you believe in fate and all that crap.'
She elbows the woman sitting next to her.
'Give her a reading, Caitlin.'

'Caitlin is a psychic,' she explains. 'She's
very accurate.'

Caitlin doesn't open her eyes. 'Would you
like it if I went around suggesting you give
people a free haircut? If people want a reading they can make an appointment and see
me at my offices.'

The sleek brunette is unfazed. 'Oh don't
be a bitch. Give her a sample of your wares.'

'It's OK,' says Sophie. 'Thanks anyway.'

Caitlin groans and heaves herself up to

262

squint at Sophie. 'You've got a strong aura,' she says irritably.

'Oh well done, darling,' says Gretel.

'What colour is it?' asks the sleek brunette.

The psychic squints. 'Ah. It's caramel.'

'Oooh, a caramel-coloured aura!' Gretel is enchanted. 'That sounds delicious. What does it mean?'

'Umm, well it generally means a positive career change.'

'Oh.' Gretel looks disappointed. 'We're not so interested in her career. What about her love life?'

The psychic sighs heavily and says, 'Give me your palm.'

'I'm really fine,' says Sophie. 'Perhaps I'll get your number and make a proper appointment to see you.'

But Caitlin takes her hand in a firm, professional grasp. 'OK,' she says tiredly. 'You've got an excellent life line. Very strong.'

'Oh yes, she's always been *very* healthy!' says Gretel.

'Now your fate line is strong too, but with lots of breaks — so in other words you're overcoming barriers.'

'That's right, she's overcome lots of barriers,' says Gretel sagely, as though Sophie was paralysed and had to learn to walk again at one point in her life.

'OK — your heart line, now that's not so good. It's all over the place. I'd say your love live is a real fiasco.'

'Thanks,' says Sophie.

'What about kids?' asks the brunette. 'Is she going to have kids?'

The psychic pulls Sophie's palm closer to her face and shakes her head regretfully. 'Gosh, you know, I've never seen anything like it. See, under your pinkie, this is where you're meant to have lines indicating your potential number of children. Well, you've just got completely *smooth* skin —'

'OK, that's enough!' Gretel grabs Sophie's hand. 'You couldn't possibly read her palm properly when it's all pruney from the water. Come on, Sophie, it's time for us to go.'

'Typical. People only want to hear good news,' shrugs the psychic, subsiding back against the side of the pool.

'Charlatan!' Gretel hops out of the pool, quivering with maternal indignation. 'Come on, darling, it's time for yum cha.'

Sophie meekly follows her mother to the changing rooms where her knees finally give way and she dissolves into helpless giggles, only made worse by her mother furiously muttering things like, 'I'll give her a caramel aura!'

■ ■ ■ ■

Veronika is doing Boxercise for the Broken Hearted.

It's an aerobics class at her local gym especially for people recovering from bad relationship break-ups. The room reeks of fresh, sweaty misery. Veronika loves it. Grim-faced men and women work out to angry, punch-the-air sorts of songs like 'You Oughta Know', 'I Will Survive' and 'These Boots were Made for Walking'. The teacher yells ordinary instructions like 'Lift those knees!' interspersed with motivational comments like 'It's time to move on!' They do boxing exercises where they are encouraged to imagine assaulting their ex-partners. 'Left hook! Right hook! They hurt you! Hurt them back! Smash their skulls in! Jab, jab, *kick*!' Afterwards, during the 'cool down', the teacher's voice switches to tender. 'Stretch your right hamstring and release your anger. Stretch your left hamstring and know that you are strong. Breathe in. Breathe out. It's time for a new beginning.' Often there is a piteous sob from the back of the classroom. Veronika normally leaves before this part. She doesn't think it's necessary to cool down.

She started doing the class two years ago after the morning her husband Jonas gave her a funny sad look and said, 'Don't you think we'd better get a divorce?' He was handing her a cup of tea at the time. She slopped it all over her hand and burned herself. 'I don't know what you want, Veronika,' he'd said. 'But I know it's not me.'

Most people only need to come to Boxercise for the Broken Hearted for a couple of months before that crazed look in their eyes starts to fade. Their jabs become less vicious and more comical. They start smiling instead of scowling, which isn't nice for the newly broken-hearted. Eventually they stop coming and take their healed hearts back to the cheery classes like 'Move 'n' Groove'.

But Veronika still comes, week after week. Her broken heart may have healed but she can always find something or someone to be angry about.

She's angry with that snooty market-research woman who told her last night she talked too much in the focus group about tinned tuna. (Wasn't that the point? Wasn't that what she was being paid for? To give her *opinions*?) She's angry with the man who swerved into her lane on the way to the gym and raised an apologetic hand, as if *that made it OK!* She's angry with that Asian girl in the red and green top over there who consistently kicks with the opposite leg to the rest of the class and doesn't seem to notice. She's angry with Sophie for being so manipulative and cutesy, Grace for being so beautiful, Aunt Connie for being so patronising and now so dead, Aunt Rose for being so dippy, Grandma Enigma for being so cheery, Thomas for being so sappy, Mum for being so fat and tragic, Dad for being so cruel to Mum. She's angry with her third-grade teacher and the woman who fitted her for her first bra.

She combines them all into one giant sumo wrestler of humanity and punches him again and again in his big flabby stomach.

'HA!' yells Veronika with the rest of the class, doing a jump kick followed by a slice to the neck. Her sumo wrestler flinches but doesn't fall.

On the way home in the car, still puffing from her workout, Veronika listens to a radio interview with a criminal psychologist, who is talking about the difference between male and female serial murderers.

Veronika turns up the radio. She is interested in murder.

'Men *stalk,* women *lure,*' says the criminal

psychologist.

'So we lure our victims with our irresist- ible feminine wiles?' says the interviewer ir- resistibly.

'You could put it like that. In fact, you tend to already know your victims,' says the criminal psychologist, apparently happy to let the interviewer act as a representative of female serial killers.

'Aha! Watch out for your wives and girl- friends, listeners!' says the interviewer.

Veronika shouts at the radio. 'Shut up, you fatuous twit! You moronic cow! This is *interesting*!'

'You tend to smother or poison your victims,' says the criminal psychologist.

'Ooh, here's a lovely dinner I've baked for you, honey!' chortles the interviewer. Veronika gives the car radio a left hook and it really hurts her hand. She hadn't intended to connect.

She turns off the radio and pulls up with a screech of brakes at a red light. She hates this intersection. The traffic lights are clearly faulty. Her lane is always treated unfairly. Look at that! The fools doing a right-hand into Condamine Street have had *two* green lights in the time she's been sitting here! She's already written once to council about it. Perhaps it's time for a visit. Personal confrontation seems to be very effective when dealing with bureaucrats.

Afterwards, she will be fascinated by the complex workings of her own brain. Because there she is, busily pondering the issue of faulty traffic lights, while *simultaneously* her smarter, more intuitive subconscious mind is considering the topic of murder. And then, without warning, her subconscious lobs a clear, precise, perfectly articulated thought straight into her consciousness. It's not so much a thought as a fundamental *truth.* A truth she has probably always known, somewhere deep within her psyche, ever since she was a small child and first heard the (SO OBVIOUSLY FABRI- CATED!) story of Alice and Jack.

Aunt Connie was most definitely a murderer.

Well of course she was. Alice and Jack didn't just vanish. They were murdered. Poison probably, artfully sprinkled on cinnamon toast!

Veronika smiles, oblivious to the fact that the lights have changed and the car behind her is tooting with increasing irritation.

27

I want my ashes scattered one night, at the stroke of midnight, by Rose and Enigma at Kingfisher Lookout. (No, it is NOT necessary for any of you younger ones to accompany them, thank you. They are perfectly capable.) Afterwards they can celebrate with a feast of my cinnamon pear tartlets and some nice champagne. The pies are in the freezer. Thaw overnight and cook at 250 degrees for twenty minutes. They should still be warm by the time you get to the top. You can take that champagne I won in the Legacy Raffle.

PS. Don't stand too close to the edge when you throw the ashes, girls, or you'll be joining me sooner rather than later.

'It will be her last midnight feast at Kingfisher,' says Rose. 'I can remember the first time we did it. We must have been about thirteen.'

'All very well for you Night Owls,' says Enigma. 'I'd rather be asleep at midnight. I can remember you dragging me up there when *I* was about thirteen. All I wanted to do was sleep.'

'Rubbish. You loved it,' says Rose.

'Well of *course* I loved it. I was thirteen,' says Enigma. 'But I'm too old for it now, for heaven's sake. Are you nearly finished?'

Rose is painting a silver moon and stars on Enigma's cheeks. She's already done an identical design on her own face. It was Connie's favourite. She chose it for her fiftieth birthday party and wore a midnight blue and silver dress to match. Rose gave Jimmy a colourful sunrise on his forehead. She remembers Connie sitting on Jimmy's lap, pressing her cheek to his. 'Opposites still attract! Even now we're old fossils!' In fact, they were extraordinarily young, thinks Rose with surprise, who at the time had believed that they were all astonishingly old.

'You used to be much quicker,' grumbles Enigma.

'You used to be much more patient.' Rose dips her brush into the midnight blue. She watches her hand's tremor. Every day it distresses her afresh, the way her body doesn't belong to her any more.

'What does it matter if it's not perfect just

271

this once?' says Enigma querulously. She is sitting opposite Rose, her face tipped forward, an unwilling canvas, with her glasses clasped in her lap. 'No one is going to see!'

'Enigma *Anne*!' Rose uses the same quelling tone of voice she and Connie both used when Enigma was naughty as a child. They were imitating their own mother's scolding tone.

Enigma subsides and pushes her lower lip out slightly. Rose turns to share a meaningful face with Connie and remembers yet again that she is not there. She will never get used to that either. Every day she will forget and remember, forget and remember.

She dabs metallic silver paint over the deep crevices in Enigma's cheeks. When she was a little girl she had such firm, velvety, kissable skin.

'Connie and I used to love kissing the back of your neck,' she tells Enigma. 'We showered you with kisses.'

'Hmmph,' mutters Enigma, but Rose feels her face soften beneath her brush.

When Rose is finally finished and they are ready to go, Connie's ashes have gone missing. They get irritable and snap at each other until Enigma remembers putting the container in the fridge.

'The fridge?' repeats Rose. 'Did you think

272

they would go off?'

'Yes, I know it sounds silly,' says Enigma. The moon and stars on her face give her a puckish look. 'But I was clearing the table and I couldn't think what it was. I have a little rule: when in doubt, put it in the fridge!'

'Imagine Connie's face!'

'She'd be absolutely furious!'

They look at each other and they have to sit down while they giggle, resting their heads on their hands.

Outside, it's bracingly cold. They rug up in beanies, scarves and gloves. Connie's ashes are safely stowed in a picnic basket together with the hot, foil-wrapped tartlets and the cold champagne.

'Look at the stars!' says Rose as they climb astride their bikes. 'It looks like they've put extras out for us tonight.'

They drive slowly up the winding paved road towards Kingfisher Lookout. Rose has a pleasant sense of anticipation, as if this ceremony will make everything OK, as if by following Connie's instructions to the letter they'll get her back.

At the top they light candles and place them around the edges of the picnic rug. The moon is a big yellow coin creating a floodlit path across the river.

'Did you see that illustration in Grace's last Gublet book?' says Rose with pride. 'I said to her, "That's midnight at Kingfisher Lookout." She said, "You're right, Aunt Rose." She's a very talented girl. I knew it from when she was five years old.'

'It *is* very pretty up here,' says Enigma. 'It only seems like last week that we came up here for my fortieth birthday. I remember, Connie said, "Enigma, you're old enough to know the truth about Alice and Jack!" My word, I thought, this is a turn-up for the books! Old enough! I thought I was ancient!'

'I didn't think we should have waited that long,' says Rose. 'But Connie had that theory about forty being the "precise age where you're old enough and young enough to handle a revelation". It wasn't a scientific theory. She just made it up! But she's so *certain* about things, isn't she? Whereas I'm uncertain about everything.'

Enigma is looking at her with a strange expression. The moon and stars on her face scrunch up with concern.

'Are you losing your marbles, Rose? You're starting to worry me. Some of the things you've been saying to Sophie! It will be awful if you lose your marbles.'

Rose thinks of marbles pouring from a jar

in a clattering torrent of coloured glass.

'I'm not losing my marbles,' she says. 'I'm just shook up by Connie dying.' And as she says the words for the first time, 'Connie dying', she feels a new steely sensation.

She picks up the container of ashes and stands near the little fence that Jimmy built after the war.

'We'll do it together,' she says to Enigma. 'Come on.'

'We've still got another twenty minutes before midnight.'

'Oh, for heaven's sake! It won't hurt her if we're twenty minutes early. She was always so bossy!'

But now she can't unscrew the lid on the container.

'Oh sugar!' she swears.

'Give it to me,' says Enigma. She taps around the edges of the lid with a knife from the picnic basket. 'This is what Margie always does with the tomato sauce.'

'That doesn't do anything,' says Rose.

Enigma grunts as the lid finally comes free and holds it towards Rose. 'Here you go!'

They hold it together, their hands overlapping.

'Shouldn't we say something?' says Enigma.

'Goodbye, Connie,' says Rose. 'Thank you

for the cinnamon pear pies. Thank you for always being so strong and so clever. We'll miss you.'

'We love you!' Enigma starts to sob. 'We'll make sure everything stays the same!'

Together they shake the container and watch the fine grey ash stream down into the moonlit river below.

'Goodness!' says Enigma through her tears. 'Connie's ashes look exactly like the dust when I empty the vacuum cleaner.'

But Rose's steely feeling has vanished and she's crying for the first time since her big sister died.

28

Margie, wearing her black one-piece swimming costume, stands in front of the mirrored wardrobe in her bedroom with her eyes shut.

She has deliberately avoided actually looking at herself in a swimming costume for many years, quickly averting her eyes if she happens to pass her reflection. But now, even though it's the middle of winter, she must, as they say, 'face the music'.

Because tomorrow she is going to allow a man she barely knows to take a photograph of her in a swimming costume. 'I have a proposal for you,' the man from Weight Watchers had said to her, stirring Light and Low into his skim milk cappuccino. Margie still can't believe she'd said yes. Immediately. Without even thinking about it. 'Sure I will,' she'd said. She hadn't even sounded like herself. She'd sounded like a confident American. She might even have put on a bit of an American accent, as if she were on a TV show. It was very odd.

Margie takes a deep breath and opens her eyes. She squints. A shadowy figure squints back at her.

She sighs. Where are they this time? After a few minutes walking around the house talking through her previous movements — 'So, I came in the front door from visiting Rose and the phone was ringing and I was dying to go to the toilet' — she finally finds her glasses on top of her handbag, puts them on and once again stands in front of the mirror with her eyes shut.

Surely it won't be *that* bad. Will it?

Whenever Ron sees her in a swimming costume he starts talking about beached whales. Oh, he doesn't say, 'You look like a beached whale, Margie.' No, he just gets an innocent sly look on his face and starts telling a story related to whales. He has a whole selection of them. His favourite is about a beached whale in Oregon that the authorities tried to blow up with dynamite. Apparently they thought it would turn into convenient bite-sized pieces for the seagulls. 'Imagine it!' Ron always says with enthusiasm. 'Massive chunks of smelly whale blubber raining from the sky. Only the Yanks, eh?'

'Why are you telling me this story?' Margie always asks. 'I hate this story! The poor whale!'

'No reason,' Ron says. 'It just came into my head.'

When Ron and Margie were first married he used to hide her nightgowns so she'd sleep naked. When she put on her red crochet bikini in the Seventies he used to embarrass her by putting two fingers in his mouth and doing a loud wolf-whistle. He didn't know any stories about beached whales back then.

'One, two, three,' says Margie out loud.

She opens her eyes.

'Oh Lordie me.'

It is worse than she thought. All that crinkly white flesh like an uncooked chicken. Saggy, baggy upper arms. Thighs like pork sausages. The tummy. Oh, dear, the tummy! Like a big watermelon.

What happened to pretty petite little Margie McNabb and her twenty-three-inch waist? Always one inch smaller than her sister's waist! No matter how hard Laura tried she couldn't manage it. (The sweet, secret triumph!) Before Veronika was born Margie could still just squeeze into her wedding dress.

The only consolation is that her new

friend will surely not look any better in his swimming costume.

She remembers him sitting across from her in the coffee shop. He was very . . . *wide,* reflects Margie. His body sort of kept on going and going.

Although, of course, a fat man isn't nearly as pathetic as a fat woman.

Her new friend's name is Ron. This is a coincidence that Margie should have exclaimed over the moment he introduced himself. 'Fancy! That's my husband's name!' she should have said, but she didn't for some reason. She avoided talking about her Ron at all. Instead she'd concentrated on Fat Ron and his 'proposal'.

Not Fat Ron, she decides. That's cruel. Rotund Ron. That's nice. Like a jolly character in a fairytale.

'I think it will be a laugh,' Rotund Ron had said, 'if nothing else.'

'It will be a hoot,' Margie had said in her new confident American-sounding voice. Then she'd amazed herself by reaching over to shake his hand. *Initiating* a handshake. She'd never initiated a handshake. She was becoming a women's libber!

Well, it *will* be a hoot, thinks Margie, taking off her glasses so that the fat lady in the mirror is blurred.

And maybe, just maybe, I'll show them all.

29

'I'll be very, very sad if you go and live on the moon,' said Melly the Music Box Dancer, looking rather glum.

Gublet felt angry. 'Don't make me feel guilty, you frilly pink bitch!'

Melly started to cry. 'You hurt my feelings very, very badly!' She stood up on her pointy toes and twirled around in circles so fast that her tears splashed off her face just like a garden sprinkler.

Gublet stamped his foot. 'Oh, fuck it!' Then he had a clever thought. He would find a NEW best friend for Melly so she wouldn't be lonely when he went to live on the moon. It was SUCH a clever thought!

The baby has got the hang of smiling after Sophie's visit. Grace has taken digital photos of him grinning gummily up at his father and emailed them to friends and family. She has also printed off thirty copies of one of these photos and turned them into charming thank you cards for all the gifts they've received. Grace has never done such a thing before; it seems like the sort of sweet girly motherly thing someone like Sophie would do. She has written a personal message on each card. *Your rattle is Jake's favourite toy! Jake looks so sweet in your outfit! Your teddy is Jake's favourite toy!* She has addressed, stamped and posted the envelopes. The effort to do all this was so colossal that when she let them slide into the post-box she felt the weak-kneed relief of someone who has finished writing a thesis or running a marathon. 'Good God, handmade cards!' said a friend the next day, breezily bitchy. 'Talk about a superwoman! You don't always have to be so perfect, you know, Grace. Give the rest of us ordinary mortals a chance.' Grace hung up and threw the portable phone against the wall, screaming, 'Oh fuck it, fuck it, fuck it.' There was a mark on the wall. It took half a tub of her mother's Gumption to scrub it away.

Today, Grace sits at the kitchen table paying bills over the phone, while Jake lies in his bouncinette that Aunt Margie gave to

Grace. 'Deborah didn't want it for Lily,' Margie had confided to Grace when she brought it around. 'I didn't want to sound like an interfering mother-in-law, so I just said, "Well, dear, your own husband used to gurgle away for hours on this very bouncinette, kicking his fat little legs." Oh dear, it's a terrible thing to say, but I did prefer Sophie to Deborah.'

Grace rocks the bouncinette with one foot while she pays bills, dutifully pressing numbers followed by the hash key as instructed by the robotic lady.

Jake frowns as he experiments with a new sound: a low, humming gurgle. He smiles radiantly up at her as he gurgles. *Did you hear that?*

He is adorable. She can see that. She just can't feel it. She looks at him and it seems so evil, so *dirty,* that she feels nothing for this cooing, gurgling child. She can't even smile back at him. Even when she makes a tremendous effort, tries to squeeze out a loving feeling, pushing as hard as when she was pushing him out of her body, she feels nothing. In fact, the harder she tries, the less she feels.

Grace thinks about the day Sophie came to visit. She stood in the doorway holding the platter, watching Callum lean over

284

Sophie to see Jake smile for the first time. Sophie was pulling a funny face. Callum had his hand on Sophie's shoulder. They were both so natural. Proper, real, feeling people. When she'd made herself walk in, Grace felt like she used to feel on the dance floor as a teenager, surrounded by gyrating figures, her cheek muscles hurting from her fake smile, her body like marble. She'd always known she was a bit unnatural. Now it was proven. Her emotional responses were somehow never quite right. When she met Callum she thought he'd saved her, but obviously it was only temporary.

Everyone would be better off without her. There would be a lot more laughing. The problem is that Callum wouldn't think so. Mystifyingly, he still loves her. He genuinely seems to miss her if she goes away for one night. He might fall apart. Callum is, at heart, an old-fashioned family man. He loves saying 'My wife'. After they got married he couldn't stop saying it. He needs a wife; and the baby needs a mother, otherwise who would take care of him while Callum was at work? He'd have to put the baby in day-care. Callum would be stressed and he'd eat badly and the house would be a pigsty and Jake would catch colds from all the other children and, no, it wouldn't do.

Grace needs to have a replacement woman waiting in the wings, an understudy, someone who is already like part of the family, someone who *wants* the role, someone better qualified for it in the first place.

Sophie Honeywell is such a perfect, obvious candidate, it's like it's meant to be.

The vague half-thought Grace had at the funeral begins to solidify into a sensible, logical plan. When she'd seen Sophie looking so longingly at Callum and Jake she'd felt an overwhelming desire to just give them both to her, to see her face light up. *Here you go. They're yours. No, really. You can keep them. They'd look better on you.*

It was quite obvious that Sophie liked Callum, and it seemed from the way that they were chatting at lunch that Callum liked her. Grace just needed to fan that spark of attraction into something more. If Sophie and Callum have begun falling in love, Grace can leave them without feeling guilty. She can erase herself.

Sophie is a sweet, kind, smart girl who would never, ever think of smashing a hairbrush against a baby's head. She makes funny faces. She talks to Callum about music. She would fit right in with Callum's huge circle of extroverted friends, whereas Grace still feels like the new girlfriend even after all this time. Sophie made Callum do his helpless sort of teenage-boy guffawing laugh that Grace hasn't heard in ages and she made Jake smile for the first time ever. She even made Grace smile, for God's sake. Jake will be much better with Sophie as his mum. After all, Grandma Enigma was brought up by Aunt Connie and Aunt Rose, and look what a happy life she's led! Grace is just following a fine family tradition of handing over babies to more suitable people.

Tomorrow Sophie is moving into Aunt Connie's house, which will make her much more accessible. It should be easy to make sure that Callum and Sophie spend as much time as possible together. Just as they're about to fall in love, Grace will conveniently disappear.

One spoonful of sesame seeds and she'll be out of everybody's way. No need for sleeping pills or jumping off cliffs. She can already imagine how her throat will feel as it begins to swell and close up. That part will be awful but it will only last a few seconds, and the great clean void of nothingness that follows will be wonderful.

30

Bellbirds. Sunlight gentle on her face. Lapping water. Salty air. Pine-O-Clean scrubbed floors.

Sophie opens her eyes on the first morning of living in Aunt Connie's house and feels almost drunk with first-morning-of-a-holiday happiness. She knows she will remember this time in her life the way you remember the first few months of a new relationship; a time with its own special smell and taste, a time where everything, even ordinary objects like shower curtains, look sharper and more significant, as if you've taken a hallucinogenic drug, as if all your senses had been muted before. She's in love with this house. It's so perfect it makes her want to laugh. The butterflies that suddenly swoop down the hallway in front of her, the way the polished floorboards turn gold in the afternoon sun, the constant background sound of the river, the resident kookaburra, the state-of-the-art dishwasher that leaves glasses sparkling, the funny china toilet-roll holder!

It is comforting to know that she can experience joy like this without it involving a man. She frowns. Although, then again, there is something a bit *sexual* about this drunken happy feeling. Her body feels all soft and yielding, as if she's woken up from a night of sleepy lovemaking. This isn't how she expected to feel after moving into an old lady's house. Perhaps Jimmy and Connie had an excellent sex life and all those sighs of satisfaction over the years have soaked into the atmosphere.

She stretches her arms languorously above her head. She definitely had some rather enjoyable dreams last night. There was a lot of kissing involved. Lovely, romantic kissing. Somebody with wide shoulders. They were in a boat together. Now who was the guy?

Oh.

It doesn't mean anything. You can't help who chooses to march into your dreams and start kissing you without your permission.

Mmmmm.

Yes, well, no point lingering on *that* particular topic.

Anyway, the point is, she feels very happy

and right now she does not need a man at all. In fact, perhaps — she grins wickedly at the ceiling — it's time she invested in a nice, expensive . . . vibrator! Forget all these romantic ideas about sex and get practical. Claire is always offering to buy her one for her birthday. ('They're perfect when you're in a hurry,' Claire told her. 'I'm never in a *hurry* to have an orgasm,' Sophie had said.) Yes, the bellbirds, the lapping of the river and the gentle hum of an efficient, state-of-the-art vibrator.

She laughs out loud.

And who cares about kids anyway? Messy, noisy, ungrateful things. She'll sponsor another World Vision child or something. Connie and Rose never had children and they led satisfying, happy lives. Perhaps they made judicious use of vibrators.

Oh, that's *enough*! The prudish side of Sophie's personality slaps her hands together with disgust.

She should get up. The place is filled to the rooftop with boxes. Her parents will be over later today to see the place. Her father will bring his toolbox, light globes, spare fuse wire and picture hooks. He will frown a lot and bang on all the walls with his fist. He'll worry about things like the hot-water system and security. He doesn't like the fact that she has moved in without the deeds to the property. So far she has only talked briefly to Aunt Connie's solicitor on the phone. Unlike Enigma and Rose, Hans finds paperwork soothing and necessary. Sophie's mother will bring Turkish Delight chocolate, champagne, bubble bath and some new regency romances. Gretel will dance around the house pretending she's Sophie: 'Here I am eating my dinner!' 'Here I am talking on the phone!'

Just another few minutes and then she'll get up.

The ceiling of Connie and Jimmy's bedroom slopes at sharp angles with beautifully carved cornices. Her eyes linger on the cornices and she realises that the pattern is actually curved eucalyptus leaves. She remembers Connie telling her that Rose did all the designs for the cornices and tiles around the house and that she got her inspiration from the island. When Sophie lifts her chin from the pillow she can see the river from a row of uncurtained picture windows. Lying here feels like being in a boat bobbing along the river.

Sophie has been brought up to send charming handwritten thank you letters on pretty notepaper and it is a terrible pity that she can't send one to Aunt Connie.

Dear Aunt Connie, thank you for my brand-new life. What a thoughtful gift.

Sex in the morning. Sleepy, sticky, cosy sex. Like sex in a tent. Or sex in a sleeping bag. Faster, quieter and a bit dirtier than sex at night. A simple, satisfying, tender, loving fuck.

It is six a.m. on a Saturday and Callum Tidyman is lying in bed, on his side, with an optimistic erection, looking at his mother-in-law's cream curtains and thinking about sex in the morning. He's thinking about how only a few months ago he would have just rolled over and pulled Grace to him, if she hadn't already done the same to him. Now that seems as wildly inappropriate as grabbing a stranger's breast on a bus. (When he was a teenager he used to frighten himself, imagining what would happen if he suddenly went mad and shoved his hand down the front of some woman's dress, how her face would instantly switch from benign to appalled, how he'd no longer be a gawky kid carrying a gigantic cello case but a psycho. You wouldn't be able to go back once you'd done something like that. You'd cross a line. It was like imagining throwing yourself off a cliff — terrifyingly compelling because *you could so easily just do it.* It was only your self-control that stopped you, and what if you lost it for a second?)

He can feel Grace's foot against his calf and maybe a few strands of her hair, which always gets all over the place, at the back of his neck. He lies very still.

It would be highly inappropriate to wake up one's wife for sex when one knows that she was awake at two a.m. feeding one's son. That would be something a Selfish Bastard Typical Man would do. Grace has never called him that, but other women in his past have and you need to be vigilant because it can happen without a moment's notice, when you're not concentrating — all of a sudden they're furious with you, crying even, because you've hurt their feelings, clomping about with your big insensitive ways.

Sometimes Grace pretended to stay asleep when they had sex in the morning. She'd let her head flop around, even do a few fake snores, and then suddenly she'd open one green eye a fraction and give him a lazy, intimate wink, '*Good* morning'. Afterwards she would stretch her legs and arms with luxurious abandon, yawning gigantically. Grace's yawns always end with a strange yelping sound. It sounds like 'iip!' She takes forever to wake up properly, stretching and moaning; while Callum, who wakes instantly (except when he's been drinking red wine) watches this performance with fascination.

'What a fuss. It's like you come out of a coma each morning.'

'Yes, and you just had sex with a girl in a coma, you sick pervert,' she'd say without opening her eyes.

Callum really loves his son but he really misses sex with his wife.

They have (had?) such a *good* sex life. That's the thing. Sex with Grace was so easy and uncomplicated, sometimes funny, sometimes beautiful, sometimes nothing special but still satisfying, like spaghetti on toast. All the women Callum dated before he met Grace had ended up using sex like an ace up their sleeves. Louise used to have a special irritable little sigh that meant 'oh not *again*!'. He can still remember the humiliation of tentatively touching her on the shoulder and hearing that impatient exhalation of breath. 'Forget it if it's a bloody favour,' he'd said once, and Jesus Christ, the drama, the tears, the phone calls to girlfriends! He was such a chauvinist pig. He was so insensitive to her needs. He was such a Selfish Bastard Typical Man.

Maybe it was because of Louise, or maybe it was some sort of inferiority complex dating back to when he was a skinny, pimply teenager who played the cello and did ballroom dancing on Saturday mornings, but Callum suffers from a mild neurosis about the whole concept of sex as a dull duty women perform for men. He doesn't laugh when sitcom couples do their clichéd comedy routines about sex. He doesn't join in jokey dinner-party conversations about husbands 'getting lucky' after they've done the vacuuming. (Grace never joins in with those conversations either. Sometimes he looks across the table at her and her eyelid will lower in the barest suggestion of a wink. One of the hottest things about Grace is her winks. It's because they're so unexpected and out of character. An ice queen winking at you.)

When Callum had met Grace he'd only just recovered from a very badly broken heart. Pauline. She was the one after Louise. One day, after two years together, while they were eating lunch on a Sunday — toasted ham, cheese and tomato sandwiches — Pauline calmly informed him that she'd accepted a transfer to South Africa and she didn't expect him to come because she 'couldn't be herself' with Callum and she needed to 'get herself back'. He can still remember how his mouthful of sandwich turned into a hard lump in his throat. 'Be yourself! How am I stopping you from being yourself?' he'd said, and she'd just looked at him contemptuously, as if she wasn't going to fall for his sneaky tricks, and in his head he was yelling, *What the fuck are you talking about?* It was so humiliating. He'd seriously thought they were happy. He'd thought they were going to get married and have kids. It took him months and months to wake up without a sick sense of vertigo when he thought about filling the day ahead. But he got over it; of course he got over it. He decided — and he truly meant it — that he would be a bachelor forever. He would enjoy the company of his nieces and nephews. There was music. There was work. There was travel. There was a whole interesting world out there. He would never even bother asking a woman on a date. He was obviously not good at relationships in the same way that he was not good at tennis. It wasn't his thing.

And then he'd gone to that wedding and met Grace. She was like a reward for all those months of misery. She was too good to be true. She was like winning the lottery when you hadn't even bought a ticket. Even after all these years of marriage he still feels immense gratitude, relief and surprise when he thinks about how his life could have been if he'd never met Grace.

Of course, their marriage hasn't turned out to be quite as fairytale perfect as he'd blissfully expected it to be in those early days. They have fights, horrible in their banality. Callum had truly thought that if they ever fought, *their* fights would be operatic and passionate, over big, complex issues, and they would probably end up in bed. He didn't envisage these petty, pathetic spats. He hates that hatchet-hard tone she can get in her voice over something as trivial as a wet towel left on a bed or a breakfast bowl not put in the sink. And that *look* she gives him. Sometimes he clicks his fingers in front of her eyes when she does that. 'Grace? Are you in there? Or have you been taken over by a cold-hearted alien?' He's disappointed that she keeps herself a bit aloof from his circle of friends. He wishes they could go out dancing together, or even just dance alone in the living room. He wishes she wouldn't jiggle her leg when they watch TV. But even while he is frustrated with her, or hurt by her, or plain irritated by her, he still loves her, he still has a secret crush on her, he is still awed that someone this beautiful is with him. When she told him she was pregnant he even caught himself thinking, 'She can't leave me now'.

One of his brothers had told him, 'Don't be surprised if you don't feel anything when you first see the baby. It takes a while to get your head around it. It's different for women. They've got hormones. It's an unfair advantage. The fact is mate, a baby is a baby. They all look the same. You might have to fake it in the beginning. Just do the Proud Daddy act. I just thought about the night we played at the Basement. Remember? Best night of my life. Anyway, when I was holding Em for the first time, feeling absolutely nothing, I thought about that night, and Sara's mum was saying, "Oh look at the proud daddy, he's got tears in his eyes!" '

But Callum didn't have to fake it. He got his head around Jake immediately. His *son.* He said it over and over in his head. My son. I have a son. That's my son. I'd like to introduce my son.

Now should be the happiest time of their lives, so why isn't it? It isn't just that sex has stopped. He was ready for that. His brother had warned him of that too. 'Forget about sex. It's a sweet, distant memory.'

But he thought even if they stopped having sex they'd still be able to laugh about it, or even talk about it all. He thought they'd still be *them.* Before the baby was born the doctor had told them they could have sex about six weeks after the baby was born. *'Six weeks!'* Grace had said on the way home from the doctor. 'I'll go mad without sex for six weeks!'

It's now been eight weeks. Jake is two months old. Not only has Grace not mentioned anything about sex but she has stopped touching Callum.

Grace isn't a touchy-feely type. She's not the sort of woman to snuggle and cuddle and lavish him with kisses. But she does (did?) touch him. She gets very cold hands and feet. When they're watching television she has a habit of warming her hands by putting them under his clothes, snaking her hands up his sleeves. She doesn't do this any more. When he was shaving at the bathroom mirror with a towel wrapped around his waist, she used to stop and kiss his back on the three freckles like a triangle that he'd never even known existed till she told him. She doesn't do this any more either. He's started taking note. It's not that she flinches when he kisses her hello or goodnight. She doesn't move away when he hugs her in bed. But she completely avoids touching him at all.

Is that normal? He wants to ask someone

but he can't bear the jokes. He doesn't want his brother to give him that complacent big-brotherly look: 'I told you, mate. Forget sex!'

Sometimes in the middle of the night he wakes up with his heart pounding, a terrifying thought in his head: *Grace doesn't love me any more.* He remembers how everything changed in an instant with Pauline, as they were eating those sandwiches. That time of his life was so terrible, and he realises now that he didn't even love Pauline! Not the way he loves Grace. In the morning he laughs at himself. Everything is fine. Everything is perfectly normal. He is thirty-five years old with a beautiful wife, a brand-new baby, a career and a mortgage on a house which is being built when it's not raining.

Except that sometimes when they're eating dinner and he's watching Grace move her fork to her mouth and he's talking about his day at work, he has a sick, frightened feeling in his stomach as though he's teetering on the edge of a terrible chasm where one wrong move will send him flying off the edge.

'Good morning,' says Grace, next to him.

'Good morning. Did you get back to sleep OK?' Callum turns over but already Grace is out of bed, walking towards the bathroom, pulling at the strap of her nightie which has slid down over one shoulder.

She seems to wake up instantly these days. No more Girl in a Coma.

I miss you, Grace, thinks Callum. *I really miss you, honey.*

31

Aunt Connie's solicitor is about forty, well dressed, tall, with a crooked grin, gentle brown eyes and a tiny v-shaped scar on his left cheekbone. His name is Ian Curtis. On his desk there is a photo of him knee-deep in snow, with a small, cute nephew sitting on his shoulders. After Ian finishes explaining the rather peculiar terms of Aunt Connie's will, he takes Sophie to a coffee shop and makes her laugh unexpectedly three times. He says, 'Mrs Thrum told me I'd like you. She was never wrong, that woman.' He asks Sophie if she'd like to go out to dinner one night after she's settled into Connie's house. She says yes. She does not blush. She also does not even come close to looking at her watch.

Sophie's girlfriends shriek down the phone lines. Everyone had a *feeling* she was going to meet the right guy very soon. There is no doubt that this is the 'nice young man' in

Aunt Connie's letter. It's just so *obvious*. It's just so *perfect*. Finally!

32

The man employed full-time to look after gardening and maintenance on Scribbly Gum Island is called Rick. He is muscular, tanned and shirtless. He has a tattoo of a small green turtle on his right shoulder. He meets Sophie in Connie's back garden one afternoon and makes her feel quite breathless as he gives her very firm instructions about taking care of the roses, the freesias and the busy lizzies. He says, 'Mrs Thrum told me she was leaving her house to a very pretty girl. She was never wrong, that lady.' He asks Sophie if she'd like to go for a picnic at this beautiful spot down the river, once she's settled into the house. She says yes. She does not look at her watch and she does not blush.

Sophie's girlfriends become quite deranged. There is frenzied debate. It's brains versus brawn! But solicitors can be brawny! Gardeners can be brainy! Aunt Connie was clearly referring to the Sweet Solicitor. Aunt Connie was clearly referring to the Gorgeous Gardener. Aunt Connie's opinion is no longer relevant. She must *not* sleep with either of them. She must *definitely* sleep with both of them. She must have a passionate fling with the gardener and then marry the solicitor. She must weigh up her pros and cons. She must go with her heart. She must go with her head. She must take her time. She must hurry up or she'll lose them both.

Sophie's girlfriends are starting to annoy her, just a bit.

33

'Do you think Grace is coping OK with the baby?'

'Oh *yes,* darling! She's so organised! She's amazing! And she never takes offence — even when I'm giving her all this advice she probably doesn't want. She's always been so lovely and polite that way, even when she was a little girl. Not like Veronika. I shouldn't say this but there were times I could cheerfully have swapped daughters with Laura!'

'Yeah. I just sometimes —'

'That's just between us, of course. I wouldn't want Veronika to know I thought about swapping her for Grace. I mean, I didn't *really* want to swap!'

'No, of course not.'

'Well, one thing, Grace has certainly got her figure back, hasn't she! Lucky girl.'

'She just sometimes doesn't seem quite right to me. I even wondered if she could have postnatal depression.'

'Oh, no, darling, I'm sure she hasn't! Look at those beautiful thank you cards she sent out to us all. Now, I can assure you a woman with postnatal depression would not be able to manage that.'

'I suppose so.'

'She's just a bit distracted by the baby. That's the thing with us women. We fall in love with our babies and maybe we don't pay quite as much "attention" to our husbands as we normally would.'

'Oh, I didn't mean I wasn't getting enough —'

'I know you didn't, darling. Don't you worry. Grace certainly does *not* have postnatal depression.'

34

'Callum told me he was worried Grace has postnatal depression. He's such a sweet boy.'

'I don't believe in postnatal depression. Of course you feel depressed after you have a baby! Who wouldn't? It's when you realise how much damned work they are and that you're stuck with them forever! I cried solidly for the first six weeks after Laura was born. I thought my life had ended. Your father just pretended not to notice. I remember my teardrops sizzling in the pan while I cooked his chops.'

'That's not normal, Mum! *You* probably had postnatal depression.'

'Rubbish! I was just tired. Anyway, I like a good cry. Grace is fine. She's always been a tough cookie, that one. Never cries. Postnatal depression! Pfff! Look at those pretty cards she sent out!'

'Yes, that's what I said. Still, I'll keep an eye on her. Maybe she would like to come jogging with me. I'm taking up jogging. Why are you laughing? It's not funny! Well, it's certainly not *that* funny. I'm getting you a glass of water. Oh, for heaven's sake, Mum!'

35

It's the second weekend since Sophie moved into Connie's house and she's out on the back balcony watering Connie's herb collection that has been thriving for over forty years, and which Sophie is pretty sure she'll manage to kill off within the next two weeks. Already the parsley looks sad and wilted.

She rests her elbows on the balcony and breathes in deeply, the sun on her face. The island is just close enough to the ocean so that there is always a hint of summer holiday in the air.

Yep, even the air she breathes is different. Over the last week her life has been transformed.

Instead of waking each morning to the muted roar of traffic, she is woken by a symphony of chiming bellbirds. ('I expect you'll be in the market for a sniper gun soon,' said a guy at work, causing Sophie to throw a floppy disk at his head.) Instead of eating a muesli bar while she blow-dries her hair and then pelting to the bus stop and squashing herself onto a misery-packed city bus, she eats a leisurely nutritious breakfast on the balcony, looking beatifically out at the river. Then she climbs into Connie's dinghy, starts the outboard engine with a deft flick of her wrist (she loves that part, she is so pleased with herself when it roars into life, like an obedient pet) and putt-putts capably across a shimmering vista of water, past silently majestic sandstone cliffs and rolling bushland. She doesn't care that it takes an hour and fifty minutes to get to work each day. It's like starting each day with an aromatherapy massage.

Instead of coming home to fumble in her handbag for her security-door key under a flickering light, then climbing four flights of stairs breathing in other people's dinner smells, she walks up a paved footpath fragrant with honeysuckle, from her own private jetty, and opens a tiny green wooden cupboard helpfully marked 'Key'. When she flings open her door each night the house seems delighted to see her. Her sterile, stuffy old apartment had never shown the slightest interest when she got home from work.

But best of all, for the first time in her

life, she feels like she's part of a big, quirky family. Enigma, the island's most accomplished fisherwoman, has taken her fishing at sunset and shed tears when Sophie caught a respectable bream with a hook she'd baited herself. Rose has asked her if she would like to come one day next week for an early morning swim. Margie has turned out to be another closet reality-TV addict and has been around to watch *Survivor* with her, clutching Sophie's arm and gasping when someone unexpected was voted off. Even Ron turned up on her doorstep late one night to ask her opinion about whether a bottle of wine he'd received from a client was corked or just awful. ('Both,' said Sophie, after one sniff.)

And, most importantly, there are Grace, Callum and the baby. Since their lunch, Sophie has been around to dinner twice and watched a video with them. It's true that she seems to be getting to know Callum better than Grace, but that's because Grace keeps going to bed early, or just vanishing for ages at a time, leaving them to chat. Sophie even went along with Callum to a concert when Grace couldn't go at the last minute.

There is nothing untoward going on, of course. It's just an innocent platonic new friendship with a really nice guy. She doesn't know why she needs to keep telling herself this because it's perfectly true. Besides which, she really *likes* Grace. She's a bit distant, but Sophie will break through eventually, and they'll all be friends.

Nothing is going to go wrong. It's one of the happiest times of her life. She resolutely ignores that whiny, pessimistic voice telling her she must be heading for a fall.

At work, in meetings, watching people talk, Sophie can't help but smugly imagine their dull suburban homes and soulless city apartments. *She* lives on an island. *She* can start an outboard motor. *She* owns a brand-new pair of gum boots! She feels different. Outdoorish. A touch tomboyish. Glowing with fresh air.

'Actually, you do smell different,' says Claire when she comes to visit that afternoon, pulling at her sleeve and sniffing at Sophie's shirt. 'Sort of mouldy. Old-ladyish.'

'I expect I smell fragrantly *earthy*. Rivery. May I remind you that over the next few days I have "engagements" with not one but two very eligible, good-looking men?'

'Yes, *that's* true.' Claire gives Sophie a suspicious look.

'What does that mean?' asks Sophie. 'You're my only friend who isn't mad with excitement about these two guys. You just get this really annoying expression as if you know something I don't.'

'All I know is that when you talk about a certain neighbour, who is supposedly happily married to somebody else, you get a very interesting expression on *your* face. It's Callum this and Callum that. Whereas when you talk about your two eligible men, you look a bit ho-hum. I still can't believe you postponed your date with Ian the sexy-sounding solicitor so you could go to that concert with Callum stupid-name Tidyman.'

'They had tickets. Grace couldn't go at the last minute. I was just doing them a favour. I was being neighbourly. What's the poor guy's name got to do with anything?'

'Don't pretend you don't have the hots for him.'

'What a charming expression. I like Callum as a friend. I like Grace as a friend too! I babysat for her the other day.' She says this with pride. As well as being able to start an outboard motor she can rock a baby back to sleep. She is becoming extremely accomplished.

Claire doesn't look impressed. 'Yes, and that's another thing. She's just had a new baby, Sophie. She's probably lost confidence in her body and then along you come, sashaying around —'

'I told you, the woman is a supermodel!' Sophie is surprised at her rising irritation with Claire. She's ruining her happy mood. 'I look like a hobbit next to her. I'd never have a chance with Callum.'

'But you'd like a chance, wouldn't you?'

Her words have such an uncharacteristically bitchy edge that they both look startled.

'Gosh,' says Sophie.

'Oh, well, *sorry,*' says Claire ungraciously.

They sit in silence for a few seconds while Sophie remembers that prat of a law student who cheated on Claire when they were in their twenties. Claire had been a white-faced wraith for months. 'You've just got to snap out of it,' they all told her kindly. 'You've got to have your dignity.'

'I'm not going to have an affair with Callum,' says Sophie. 'I promise. I like Grace too much.'

Claire still looks doubtful. 'It's just that I don't want you wasting your time falling in love with a married man. You'll only get hurt and then the next thing you know your chances of having a family will be gone forever. You're all feelings, Sophie. You let your heart rule your head, and I think your heart is interested in Callum, isn't it?'

'It's not,' says Sophie. 'I'm going to fall very sensibly head-over-heels in love with the nice young man Aunt Connie has got picked out for me. I just have to work out which one it is. And now because I'm all *feelings*, I *feel* that both our glasses are empty and I'm going to get us some more of the wine that you bought, which I *feel* was a very nice choice.'

Claire lifts her hands in surrender.

Claire is being overdramatic, thinks Sophie that night. Nothing is happening. Nothing is going to happen. Sophie is a *good* person. Callum is a good person. They're becoming good friends. That moment at the concert when his hand knocked (brushed?) against hers during the interval when he handed her the chocolate magnum had meant absolutely nothing.

(Actually, she thinks it *had* meant something. Because he looked embarrassed, and you don't look embarrassed about touching someone unless you secretly like them a bit. But nothing was going to happen. She didn't want anything to happen. She wouldn't like him if he cheated on his wife. She could tell he loved Grace. It was just that . . . it was just that . . . well, it was just nothing really. And there was no need to keep remembering that moment over and over. It wasn't like they kissed. It was just a brush of hands. It just made her happy to spend time with him. That's all. You feel happy when you spend time with new friends.)

36

It's Sunday on Scribbly Gum Island. Rose
sits on her back veranda with an old shoe-
box filled with photos on her lap. She can
see the ferry, a speck in the distance, on its
way over from Glass Bay, filled with visitors
and their cameras and their picnic baskets
and their shouting and their litter . . . and
their purses and wallets, Connie would say,
so stop your complaining.

Rose picks a photo at random from the
box. Connie and Jimmy on the dance floor
on their wedding day. Enigma was flower
girl and Rose was bridesmaid. Jimmy is
looking adoringly down at Connie's dark
head. What would it have been like to have
a man love you like that? Would it have
changed something fundamental in your
psyche to wake up each morning knowing
that you were loved, that someone wanted
to touch your body even when it got all old
and wrinkly?

But the thought of a man touching her hand, her shoulder, her breast, as if they were all separate possessions of his, makes Rose want to gag. Move this way. Move that way. Open your mouth. Lift your hips.

She pushes the box off her lap, so that some of the photos fall to the floor. A breeze snatches up the photo of Connie and Jimmy and twirls it whimsically away down towards the river. She lets it go. It seems nice to let them float away together on the breeze.

She is going to make herself a nice cup of tea, but first she will clean her teeth again to take away that unexpectedly nasty taste in her mouth.

So much to do. So much to do. Margie slides her marble cake in the oven and tears her floury apron over her head as she heads up the stairs to get dressed. She's on the roster to give the Alice and Jack tour this morning, and before that she has to pop around to Rose's place to drop off her prescription from the chemist.

Also, she's going to have a chat with Rose about hiring a cleaner. A lovely girl called Kerrie. She's Rotund Ron's daughter and she's starting up her own business called Ms Mop-it's and Margie wants to encourage her entrepreneurial spirit. Connie always disapproved of hiring cleaners but Margie has had enough. Even her mother has started injecting an old-lady tremor in her voice and innocently suggesting that Margie might like to help her out by just 'running the vacuum around' for her. Kerrie can come once a fortnight and do her house, Rose's house and Enigma's house. They can afford it!

She notices she flies up the stairs two at a time. When she walks now her steps seem longer. She gets places faster.

She pulls off her about-the-house dress and grabs that nice skirt from last winter. She zips it up and it falls straight to the ground around her ankles.

Goodness me.

Dumbfounded, Margie stares at the skirt.

She reaches down and pulls it up. Did she not zip it up properly? No, it's zipped all the way up. She lets go and once again the skirt slides straight to her feet. It's far too big for her.

Last winter that skirt was too tight. She's going to have to take it in, or even better, give it away, airily and generously, to somebody fatter than her!

Light-headed with elation, she swings her new hips from side to side and then she dances around her skirt, singing softly at first and then louder and louder.

Enigma is on her way out the door to go to a Tennis Club do. She and the girls kept playing tennis until well into their sixties, but then they decided it was getting too hard to hear what someone was saying if you were right down the other end of the court and trying to have a chat, so why not forget the tennis part and just go to 'interesting' functions instead.

Today they're seeing some woman speaking about her autobiography, which describes growing up on an Italian vineyard, or something foreign like that. It doesn't sound especially amusing to Enigma. Her own autobiography would be far more intriguing.

She has made an appointment to have her hair done at the hairdresser's in Glass Bay beforehand, just in case the vineyard woman writer is really a cover-up and Mike Munro is going to appear on the stage and say into the microphone, 'Enigma McNabb, this is your life!' and shine the spotlight on her. For the last few years she has been convinced she is going to be on *This is your Life* any day now. After all, she's the Munro Baby! She's an Australian celebrity. It would make a very good, inspiring episode. There have been far less interesting celebrities on the show. It's getting a bit stressful, though, wondering when they'll surprise her, and making sure she always looks her best.

The phone rings and she nearly doesn't bother answering it, but she does just in case it's a journalist or something who wants to do a profile on her.

It turns out that it's Veronika, who does want to write a book about the Munro Baby Mystery, but that's hardly the same thing as a journalist, because it's just *Veronika;* and also she's far too intent on actually *solving* the mystery, which is, of course, problematic.

'I was just on my way out, pet,' says Enigma impatiently.

'OK, Grandma, but can you just tell me when you're free so I can come over and hypnotise you?' asks Veronika.

'I beg your pardon?'

'Well, I realised the other day that it's very likely you have repressed traumatic memories which could be brought to the surface under hypnosis. I could probably solve the Munro Mystery just like that.'

There is a clicking sound as if she has snapped her fingers.

Well, for heaven's sake!

'I'm not going under hypnosis, thank you

very much. I don't want to go under anything. I have high blood-pressure! It could
be extremely dangerous for my health.
Anyway, what makes you think you can hypnotise me? What do you know about it?'

'I've read up on it. It seems like a piece of
cake to me. It's perfectly safe, Grandma,
and who knows what could come out.'

'No, thank you very much indeed. I don't
like the sound of that at all. And don't you
secretly try to hypnotise me when I'm not
looking, or I'll be very cross with you! I have
to go now, Veronika. You can come and
interview me with your tape recorder, but
that's it!'

There is silence and Enigma immediately
gets suspicious. 'You're not hypnotising me
now, are you?'

'No, Grandma, I was just thinking. OK,
don't worry, it doesn't matter. I've got
another idea.'

Sophie has Grace, Callum and the baby
over to her new house for lunch on her
balcony. She spent hours agonising over
what food to serve, looking through Connie's old recipe books, and finally just
played it safe and bought some mushroom
soup and crusty bread from the takeaway
section of Connie's Café.

It's a beautiful day and her guests seemed happy enough with their soup. Now she is serving them Belgian chocolate and Grand Marnier, her own area of expertise.

'Do you believe in public or private education, Sophie?' asks Grace.

Sophie has noticed Grace has the oddest habit of suddenly focusing her attention on Sophie and asking her opinion about a subject seemingly unrelated to anything they've been talking about. She listens carefully to Sophie's answer but then doesn't seem to want to proffer her own opinion on the matter, changing the subject or immediately moving on to something new. It makes Sophie feel like she's attending an ongoing job interview.

'Why is that on your mind? Are you thinking about enrolling Jake in school?' Sophie tries to make it more like a normal conversation.

'Oh, I'm just interested in whether you have any philosophical views on the subject,' says Grace, and Sophie notices Callum, who is holding Jake, giving his wife a gentle puzzled look.

'Well, I guess it depends on the child,' says Sophie. 'I think you should find the right school for your child's personality and ability, the one which will be the right environment for them. I think too many parents pick schools as if they're ordering a certain brand of child.'

'*Exactly!*' says Callum. 'That's exactly what I think. Some kids thrive in big, competitive schools with lots of activities, and others need a smaller, friendlier school with more one-on-one attention.'

They both look at Grace expectantly but she doesn't say anything, just nods her head in a satisfied way and looks back out at the water.

Sophie stands up to go and put the coffee on and Callum's mobile phone begins to ring. 'Hello? Oh, right, yeah, hi, just a sec.' He hands the baby over to Sophie without asking and walks off to the other end of the veranda to take the call.

'It looks like a stressful phone call.' Sophie watches Callum gesticulating.

'It's the builder,' says Grace. 'I could tell by the way his voice dropped an octave when he took the call. The house is taking much longer than they promised.'

'I hear they always do.'

'Hmmm.' Grace's thoughts appear to drift off. She is very difficult to talk to at times.

'Oh, look, Jake,' says Sophie to the baby. 'Here's our kookaburra arrived for a visit.'

'He's got a friend with him,' comments Grace.

They watch the two kookaburras in silence for a few seconds.

'Umm, what are they doing?' Sophie turns her head on one side.

'Are they fighting?' Grace also turns her head on one side.

'Oh!' says Sophie suddenly.

'Aha,' says Grace.

The kookaburras are having furious, pornographic sex on the balcony railing. Sophie puts a hand over Jake's eyes and Grace starts to giggle helplessly in a way Sophie has never heard before. It's contagious and soon they are both laughing that silly, adolescent, stomach-hurting laughter you can only share with another girl. Sophie has always thought that the first time you get the hysterical giggles with a new female friend is like the first time you sleep with a boyfriend; it takes your relationship to a new, more intimate level.

The two kookaburras are certainly taking their relationship to a new, more intimate level.

Callum comes back from his phone call, just as the male kookaburra finishes off with a violent thrust and flies off, leaving the female kookaburra looking ruffled and dazed.

'Talk about wham bam, thank you, ma'am,' says Sophie, which isn't funny at all really, but is enough to set them off on a new wave of laughter. Grace puts her hands on her hips and bends forward to catch her breath as if she's been running a race. Sophie's eyes stream as she hugs Jake to her.

'What?' Callum raps his knuckles against the table with a sensible-man expression. 'What's so funny?'

But that just makes them laugh even more.

It's later that night. Callum is marking assignments and Grace is trying to settle the baby, but he is in a tetchy mood, and nothing she does pleases him. He keeps behaving like he's absolutely starved, sucking feverishly at the air, but then as soon as she gets him on her breast he gives up after a few seconds, turning his head disgustedly as if he hates her. He does hate her, she knows it. She's tried rocking him in a dozen different positions, bathing him, putting him in the stroller and pushing it up and down the hallway, giving him the dummy, taking the dummy away, closing the door and leaving him in his cot, but he just cries and cries.

It's a pity, because on her way from Sophie's place this afternoon Grace had felt almost normal for a few minutes. That silly hysterical laugh over the kookaburras had somehow cleansed out her head, and when Callum put his hand on her shoulder it felt comforting, not like a heavy weight. On the way home she had decided to make salmon pasta for dinner, because she knew Callum would be starved after only having soup for lunch, and that felt like a good, definite, controllable decision. She knew exactly how she would make it and she had all the ingredients, and maybe she'd have a glass of wine while she cooked.

And maybe she didn't need to go ahead with the Plan after all. Maybe it was going to be OK. Maybe that clamping sensation around her head was gone.

But then, as they opened the front door, the baby started crying, and hasn't let her be since. Callum said he didn't really feel like dinner anyway — he'd had enough to eat at Sophie's. (Soup, with a couple of bread rolls!) He was in a bad mood because the builder had called with more problems, something to do with the bathroom tiles, and the budget isn't looking good, and he sat for ages reading the building contracts at the coffee table with his back hunched, chewing nervously on his bottom lip, while the baby cried and cried.

Now Grace's thoughts are a tangled black mess again, and the clamping feeling is worse, more painful, because of the promise of relief earlier in the day.

'Well, what do you want then?' she hisses at the baby. '*What?* I'll do it!'

Friends have told her that sometimes babies simply refuse to settle, and you just need to be calm and wait it out, but she didn't realise it would feel like he was doing it deliberately. She knows she is imagining that malicious satisfaction in his cry. She knows he is a baby, not a person — he is not making a conscious decision to do this — but it doesn't matter what she knows because she believes in her heart that he is mocking her efforts. He doesn't like her, and she doesn't like him, and if he doesn't shut up soon she might throw him against a wall. Hard.

'Callum!'

He comes out of the study immediately, looking startled.

'What is it?'

'I know you're working but I just have to go for a walk. I'm really sorry, but I have to go for a walk right now.'

Your son is not safe with me.

'That's OK,' he says soothingly. 'Get some fresh air.'

He is a much better husband than she is a mother. She dumps the baby in his arms and virtually runs for the door.

'You'd better put something warmer on,' calls out Callum, but she pretends not to hear and it takes a super-human effort to close the door, not slam it.

The cold air makes her eyes sting as she half-walks, half-runs down the steps and out onto the paved footpath that circles the island. It's like the yellow-brick road, Rose always says, but didn't the yellow-brick road go somewhere, not just round and round in an endless suffocating circle?

I nearly did it.

Grace trips and clumsily rights herself and keeps on walking, her arms swinging heavily, her legs stodgy. Grace? Grace? What sort of name is that for someone like her? She thinks of the way Callum automatically handed Jake over to Sophie when his phone rang today. They already looked like a family.

I nearly threw him.

37

- Sophie must occupy the house.
- Sophie must repaint the house to suit her own tastes.
- Sophie must have Veronika over for dinner within a few weeks of moving in. Cook my Honey Sage Chicken for her, Sophie, page 46 of the Blue Book. She'll soon stop her sulking. Tell her she never liked my house much in the first place.
- Sophie must take her turn at the Alice and Jack tours. (Grace must be responsible for Sophie's training.)

'I thought *I* was a control freak,' Ian, the Sweet Solicitor, had commented, when he was explaining the terms of Aunt Connie's will to Sophie (before he'd asked her out and turned into a potential boyfriend).

'I don't mind any of the conditions,' Sophie had said. 'Although I don't know if Veronika will come to dinner. You know she wanted to contest the will? It's amazing that Connie could tell that was going to happen. Although, not so amazing, I guess.'

'I think I've convinced her to drop that idea. There are no possible grounds. Anyway, Veronika, Thomas and Grace all received substantial bequests from Connie. She was a very wealthy woman. I don't think you'll have any more problems with Veronika.'

He's right. When Sophie feels resilient enough to make the call, Veronika says yes, she will come to dinner, in a tone of voice that suggests it's about time she was asked.

'You know what I read on my desk calendar yesterday?' she asks Sophie.

'What?' Sophie is cautious. Veronika sounds quite genial, almost whimsical, which is frankly terrifying.

' "If you cannot get rid of the family skeleton, you may as well make it dance," ' quotes Veronika. 'George Bernard Shaw. I've decided it's time to make our family skeleton dance. And *you're* going to help me.'

Sophie speaks in a careful, neutral voice, as if she's negotiating the release of a hostage from a mad terrorist. 'Gosh, Veronika, that sounds intriguing.'

'Yup,' says Veronika. 'I don't suppose you need me to bring anything, do you? And obviously I don't need your new address. I'll stay the night, shall I?'

Sophie recoils as if she's been shot in the stomach. She silently bangs her fist against her forehead and says, 'Of course. We can have breakfast together.'

'Maybe,' says Veronika in an if-you're-lucky tone. 'But I should see Mum and Enigma and Aunt Rose while I'm there on the island. And Grace and the baby of course. Anyway, if I can fit in breakfast with you I will.'

'That's all I can ask,' says Sophie faintly.

'Gotta run! See you next week!' shouts Veronika, as if she's run off somewhere and is calling back over her shoulder. She slams down the phone.

Making the family skeleton dance, thinks Sophie. Oh dear, Veronika. Something tells me it's not meant to dance for you until your fortieth birthday.

Veronika brings a housewarming present when she comes to visit. It is a sculptured abstract figure of a woman raising her hands in consternation as if at some new puzzle of life. It's both beautiful and funny.

'Oh Veronika, I just absolutely love it,' says Sophie truthfully, feeling quite overwhelmed with gratitude in the circumstances.

'Of course you do!' Veronika has a very bad cold. She sucks ferociously on a cough lolly. 'I knew you would. I bought it for you the same day I was really angry with you. Very expensive too. That's the thing about you. You make people want to please you. It's not a compliment, by the way. No need to blush.'

'I'm not blushing,' says Sophie. Veronika is the only person Sophie knows who not only doesn't look away when Sophie blushes but actually provides a running commentary on progress. 'Oh, look, it's reached your forehead. I wonder if your *scalp* blushes?!'

'So, you haven't changed the place much, I see.' Veronika marches through the house like a nosy landlord, opening cupboards and drawers, even ripping back the shower curtain in the bathroom. Sophie trots behind her, full of pride and pleasure as they enter each room.

'Are there any of Aunt Connie's old papers or anything still here?' asks Veronika suspiciously when they get to what used to be Connie's office.

'No, your mum cleaned out the whole place before I moved in. The house was sparkling. She's so lovely, Margie. And she works like a Trojan, doesn't she?'

'Well, she obviously finds time to eat.'

'She's lost ten kilos so far at Weight Watchers! She's doing very well.'

'I *know* she's going to Weight Watchers! You don't need to tell me about my own mother. It was my present to her for Christmas. I'm sick of hearing Dad tease her about her weight. He treats her like a dirty doormat and she acts like one. It makes me sick watching them. I don't know what I'm going to do about that.'

'Maybe losing weight will give her new confidence to stand up to your dad?'

'I hope it gives her enough confidence to leave him.'

'Really?'

'Yes, *really.*' Veronika puts on a prissy voice to mimic Sophie. 'We don't all have a fairytale mummy and daddy like you.'

Oh this was going to be such a fun night.

'My parents send their love, by the way.'

'Are they proud of the way you got your hands on this house?'

Sophie breathes deeply. She is Audrey Hepburn in *The Nun's Story.*

'I hope you're hungry. I've cooked your Aunt Connie's recipe for Honey Sage Chicken.'

'I'm not actually that hungry.' Veronika marches into the kitchen. She opens the oven door and peers inside. 'It looks ready to me. Don't overcook it.'

'Her instructions were very firm about cooking for exactly fifty minutes,' says Sophie. She had felt Aunt Connie's presence peering over her shoulder the whole time she was cooking.

'You've got to follow your own instincts when it comes to cooking, you know, Sophie.' Veronika slams the oven door shut and sits down at the kitchen table. She taps her fingers rapidly. 'Did the recipe call for a spoonful of arsenic?'

'Not that I noticed.' Sophie rather desperately opens the fridge to look for the white wine she'd bought to go with the chicken.

'I wonder what poison she used to murder my great-grandparents.'

Sophie gapes at Veronika over the fridge door. 'You don't seriously think your Aunt Connie killed Alice and Jack. She was only nineteen!'

'Oh and nineteen-year-olds aren't capable of murder. Ha, ha!' Veronika gives Sophie the tired look of a hardened crime investigator who has seen many a brutal sight you couldn't even imagine, young lady.

Sophie finds two wine glasses and pours their wine. 'All right then, well, what was her motive?' It's rather enjoyable using words like 'motive' in casual conversation.

It makes her feel like one of those tough, resourceful forensic experts on TV shows like *CSI*. Sophie flicks her hair back, squares her shoulders and sticks her breasts out. Those women always have very confident breasts.

Veronika takes a gulp of her wine while still chewing on her cough lolly. Sophie winces. It is doubtful that the cough lolly is contributing much to the chardonnay's buttery undertones.

'Well, obviously Connie was having an affair with Jack Munro,' says Veronika. 'His wife had probably lost interest in sex, you see, after Enigma was born. Men always feel neglected after their wives have babies.'

'Oh I see,' says Sophie. She wonders if Callum feels neglected. Just a little bit? She hopes so. *Oh, stop it, you foolish, idiotic girl. You don't even mean it. Some crime-scene investigator you are.*

Veronika continues with her explanation. 'So Jack keeps promising Connie that he'll leave Alice and he never does. You know, the way they always promise they'll leave their wives and they never do.'

'So I've heard.' Sophie feels suitably chastised.

'Connie finally realises this. She goes mad with jealous rage, poisons them both and

337

helps herself to the baby.'

'Why not just poison the baby too?'

'She wasn't a *complete* monster.'

'And what happened to their bodies?'

'Chopped up, I expect.' Veronika smacks her lips. 'Did you know that Connie and Rose's father was a butcher? *Very* handy for body removal. I don't know for sure, of course, but I wouldn't be surprised if the bones are buried in those big flowerpots with the busy lizzies all along Scribbly Street.'

'And what about Rose?' asks Sophie. 'Was she in on it too?'

'Accessory after the fact,' pronounces Veronika. 'Helped with the cover-up.'

Sophie thinks about that day at Grace's house when Rose said, *'We'll tell you the truth about what happened to Alice and Jack.'* It is extremely tempting to reveal this information to Veronika, just for the satisfaction of telling her something she doesn't know, but Sophie has never broken a promise, especially not one made to an old lady with fervently pleading eyes.

'It seems a bit odd to make a tourist attraction of the crime scene.' Sophie raises a wry, detective-like eyebrow at Veronika.

'The woman had balls,' agrees Veronika.

'Really?' Sophie widens her eyes. 'Gosh.

How did Jimmy feel about that?'

'This isn't funny. She *murdered* my great-grandparents and she got away with it! She probably laughed all the way to her grave!'

Veronika blows her nose noisily and Sophie feels remorseful, because if Aunt Connie *did* kill Alice and Jack she'd find it more intriguing than dreadful. Murders that happened over seventy years ago don't seem quite as serious as murders that happen today. After all, the victims would be dead by now anyway, so the point seems sort of moot. But Veronika acts as if it all happened last week.

'Would you prefer a hot lemon drink to the wine?' Sophie asks Veronika.

'No,' snuffles Veronika. 'The wine is OK. Look, I want you to help me prove that Aunt Connie killed Alice and Jack. Then I'm going to write a book about it. I'll mention you in the acknowledgements, of course. You owe me. You wouldn't have got this house if it wasn't for me.'

'But how could I help you?' Sophie is aghast. It doesn't seem good etiquette to help prove someone a murderer after they've left you a house and a selection of potential new boyfriends.

'You can talk to my family. Rose and Enigma. Even Mum and Dad,' says

Veronika. 'They're all hiding something. I know it. I've always known it. I used to hear comments all the time. Once I overheard Mum and Dad fighting and he said, "I could blow this whole Alice and Jack thing sky-high at any time," and Mum just laughed and said she didn't mind, it would be Aunt Connie he'd have to face. I confronted them of course, and they just laughed at me. It happened when I was about fourteen. I keep forgetting about it for years at a time and then remembering and getting angry. It's a cover-up! My own family is involved in a cover-up and *I don't know the truth.*'

Sophie thinks about how hurt Veronika would be if she knew what Enigma and Rose had said to her. Now Sophie is involved in the cover-up too. Even though she has no idea of exactly what she's covering up. It's quite exciting.

'I really think you should ask them yourself.' She tries to sound soothing and not patronising.

'Oh, you think I haven't? Like a million times? My family likes you better than they like me!' Veronika drains her wine glass and pushes it towards Sophie for a refill. 'Not one of them would back me up about Aunt Connie's will. They didn't want to help me contest it. They didn't want me to have the house. They wanted you to have it. They'd rather have you living here than me. I annoy them. I'm fundamentally annoying. Are we going to eat soon? Do you think you should check that chicken again?'

Veronika crunches her cough lolly between her teeth and looks meaningfully towards the oven, seemingly determined to prove that she is indeed fundamentally annoying.

At that moment the oven timer shrieks like a fire alarm and they both jump.

'I think Aunt Connie might be cross with us,' jokes Sophie a touch nervously as she opens the oven for the chicken.

Veronika shakes her fist at the ceiling. 'I'm going to prove you did it, Aunt Connie! You always told me I needed to focus; well, I'm focusing all right. I'm focusing on you! *Murderer!*'

Sophie puts the chicken on top of the stove, noting hopefully that it smells delicious, and watches Veronika curiously. 'Are you OK? You look a bit pale.' And you're acting even nuttier than usual.

'I guess I shouldn't be drinking when I'm taking antibiotics.' Veronika's words are softening at the edges. 'Also, I think I forgot to eat today. Oopsie!'

And at that point her eyelids droop and

the top half of her body tips forward in slow motion until her forehead rests gently on the table.

The next morning Sophie leaves Veronika sleeping in Aunt Connie's spare bedroom. She is lying flat on her back, breathing snuffily through her mouth, one thin arm thrown dramatically across her eyes as if she can't bear the sight of something. It's strange to watch Veronika sleeping; she's so rarely quiet. Watching someone sleeping, thinks Sophie, is a bit like sneaking through their house when they're not home. Sophie notices for the first time that Veronika has elfin, pointy-tipped ears and she feels a rush of motherly affection for her, so much so that she even considers tucking the blanket under Veronika's chin, except she doesn't want to risk waking her and feeling her affection evaporate.

After stealthily leaving a cup of tea, a glass of water and some Panadol next to Veronika's bed, she tiptoes out of the house. It's Sunday, and Sophie is meeting Grace for her first training session on the Alice and Jack tours.

She reaches the Alice and Jack house via the paved private footpath that snakes along the island shore. It still gives her a thrill to ignore the friendly but firm signs saying, *'Sorry! Only Scribbly Gum residents past this point!'*

The river is different every day. Today it's grey-blue and choppy, like someone vigorously shaking out a picnic rug. A huge pelican makes an ungainly landing on the rocks just beneath her. 'Good morning!' calls out Sophie. The pelican modestly lowers its swooping beak and shoots her a glinting glance from its mean squidgy yellow eyes.

As she rounds the corner she sees Grace already waiting at the house. No baby. Callum must be minding him. Grace sits on the steps at the front of the house, wearing black jeans and a cream-coloured fleece, her hair scraped back from her forehead and tied in a single plait, looking like a supermodel in a perfume ad, but without a scrap of make-up. Each time Sophie sees Grace it takes a few seconds to adjust to her beauty. It really is a bit much first thing in the morning. Sophie goes to wave but then stops when she sees Grace's demeanour. She is sitting completely still, her hands resting limply on her knees, and the expression on her face is one of terrible desolation. Sophie feels a punch-in-the-stomach feeling of fear. She runs towards her. Something terrible must have happened. The baby? Callum?

'Grace?' Her voice cracks. 'Is everything OK?'

But Grace looks up and smiles her gorgeous glacial smile. 'Of course. Why?'

'You looked so sad. Actually, you looked devastated.' Grace stares at her with polite interest and Sophie feels as if she's just said something embarrassingly indiscreet.

'I must have been deep in thought.' Grace stands up, pulling on the knees of her jeans. 'I was trying to remember all the things I'm meant to tell you. Aunt Connie will be looking down at me, saying tch, tch, tch, if I get a word wrong.'

Oh, rubbish, thinks Sophie crossly. That was the saddest face I've ever seen. Who do these *private* people think they are?

'I wanted Margie to come and help me,' continues Grace. 'She does most of the tours these days. But she was off to some Weight Watchers all-day meeting today.'

'All day? On a Sunday?' says Sophie. 'Oh dear. I was going to go around after this and let Margie know that Veronika is sick in bed at my place — I mean Aunt Connie's place —' She stops, feeling awkward about claiming ownership of Connie's house.

'It's all right. It *is* your place now. Not

344

Aunt Connie's.' Grace gives Sophie a half-glimmer of a smile. 'You should be the one looking devastated if you're nursing Veronika.'

Sophie laughs, somewhat overenthusiastically. She tries to encourage these moments when it seems Grace is relaxing enough to tease her. It gives her a glimpse of the friend she could be, if she'd just loosen up a bit, like that day when they laughed at the kookaburras. (Maybe they should get drunk together next and talk about sex?) 'Veronika is more manageable when she's not talking. Actually, last night she was talking about this book she wants to write. She has a theory that Aunt Connie killed Alice and Jack and hid their bodies. She thinks Connie was having an affair with Jack.'

Grace doesn't look especially interested by this. 'Veronika has been coming up with new, more outlandish theories for what happened to Alice and Jack since we were children. I don't think it was anything as exciting as that. I think they just did a runner. They were behind on their rent. People were abandoning houses all the time during the Depression.'

'But what about the boiling kettle? The cake! All their clothes still in the cupboards. And why would they abandon their *baby* like that?'

Grace shoves her hands in the pockets of her fleece and gives Sophie an odd, narrow-eyed look. 'Maybe it was a split-second decision. Maybe the baby was crying and crying and Alice couldn't stand it any more. Maybe she thought she was going mad. Maybe she thought the baby would be better off with someone else. Maybe she just didn't like her baby!'

Is she imagining it, or is there a note of rising hysteria in Grace's voice?

'Maybe,' agrees Sophie gently. This family! Was it in their genes? Something in the water? In-breeding? Surely Grace wasn't implying that she didn't really like her own beautiful, kissable, heart-melting little baby?

'Veronika is just so irritating sometimes.' Grace brushes away an invisible insect. 'Aunt Connie always said it would be terrible for business if the Alice and Jack mystery was ever solved. She said the whole point of a mystery is that it's unsolved. So, look, shall we get started?'

'Sure.'

'Here's the script you'll have to learn off by heart. Aunt Connie didn't approve of reading from notes. I used to scribble cheat notes on my hands.'

She hands over a typed document and

Sophie reads: '(SPEAK LOUDLY, CLEARLY AND DRAMATICALLY. IF ANYONE TALKS DURING YOUR PRE-SENTATION, STOP AND LOOK PO-LITELY AT THEM UNTIL THEY STOP.) *Welcome to the home of my great-grandparents, Alice and Jack Munro!* (OPEN ARMS WIDE AND SMILE.)'

'You'll have to take out all the references to great-grandparents, of course,' says Grace. 'Even though you are practically family now.'

Is that an edge to Grace's voice? Sophie looks up, but Grace just surveys her impassively.

Sophie continues to read: '*Some of you may have heard of a famous, mysterious ship called the* Mary Celeste.'

'You'll see the script makes a lot of comparisons to the *Mary Celeste,*' comments Grace. 'It's like Scribbly Gum's "Sister Mystery". I've got an old book of Aunt Connie's about the *Mary Celeste* if you'd like to read it. Anyway, come in.'

Grace turns and opens the door to the Alice and Jack house with a large old-fashioned key and Sophie feels a frisson of excitement. All the other times she's been in the house she's been one of a shuffling, head-craning tour group.

'Did Thomas ever give you a private tour of the house?' asks Grace as they enter the gloomy hallway.

'No. He didn't even like coming to the island much. I could never understand it. It's so beautiful.'

'I think it's different when you grow up somewhere like this. It's like people who grow up in a small country town and want to escape to the big city. When I was thirteen I wrote in my diary, "This island is like *jail*" and drew a very dramatic picture of me peering out from behind bars. Connie gave us each a boat — just a second-hand tinny — for our sixteenth birthdays, so then at least we could come and go as we pleased, more or less. But mostly we just imagined how great it would be to order pizza whenever you wanted, or go to the movies without travelling for two hours.'

'I can remember seeing the three of you playing when I visited the island as a child,' says Sophie. 'Have I ever told you that? The last ferry was leaving and I looked back and saw you all playing some sort of game on the beach. I was so jealous. I thought you were like children living in a storybook.'

But Grace, in her disconcerting way, stops acting like a normal person and abruptly gets back to business.

'OK. Rule number one. Keep an eye on your tour group at all times. We've had a lot of trouble with people trying to steal souvenirs. It's always the most unlikely people too. Once, Veronika insisted this old lady empty her handbag and she'd taken two lace doilies. She said they reminded her of her childhood home.'

'Oh, poor thing,' says Sophie.

'Rule number two. You probably know this from when you've done the tour yourself. Nobody except you goes into the corded-off rooms. They have to stand in the doorway while you point things out. Some of them will beg you to let them in. I remember one man even offered Thomas a bribe.'

'He told me about that. He was horrified, of course.'

'Yes, he's always been a good boy. If it was Grandma Enigma taking the tour, she'd probably have negotiated for more.'

Grace unhooks the red cord from the doorway of the kitchen and gestures for Sophie to go ahead of her.

'Now, for a proper Aunt Connie — authorised tour, you should really come in early and light the fuel stove, and then just before the tour starts you put the kettle on.' She gestures at the large copper kettle sitting on top of the squat fuel stove. 'That way, as you're leading the group down the hallway the kettle can actually be whistling while you're saying, "As sisters Connie and Rose walked down the hallway they could hear the sound of the kettle boiling and smell a freshly baked cake. *Nothing seemed amiss.*" But, to be honest, I think Margie is the only one who still bothers with actually boiling the kettle these days. The one thing you do have to remember is to cook the marble cake. The brochure says it's made to the original recipe but I'm afraid that's slightly misleading. Well, completely misleading. We all have our own versions. I'll give you my recipe.'

'Oh, I'm sure I could find a good packet mix for marble cake,' says Sophie.

Grace laughs politely as if she's making a joke, and Sophie thinks, Oh dear. She tiptoes reverently across the brown lino floor of the kitchen. 'It gives me goose-bumps with just us being in here.'

'Probably because it's freezing.' Grace bounces up and down on the balls of her feet, her hands tucked into her armpits. 'So, when you're describing the kitchen you leave the chair and the bloodstains until last. Explain how Alice had to cope without running water or electricity or food processors or microwaves. No fridge. They didn't even

350

have an icebox. There's something called a Drip Safe out on the veranda. If you've got any women over seventy in your group, expect lots of interruptions. They'll want to tell you about how their lives during the Depression were even harder than Alice's. It's a mistake to look in the slightest bit interested. They'll never shut up. Aunt Connie used to say, "You must tell me about that after the tour." By the way, make sure you don't touch anything while you're walking around the kitchen. People take the "nothing has been touched" line very seriously.'

'Nothing has been touched, has it?' asks Sophie, who is one of those people.

'Margie does the dusting and she's very careful. But Enigma is picking up things all the time, and once Veronika was doing the tour and she tripped over the upturned chair and knocked the crossword and pen flying. So, I'd say the crime scene has been pretty well contaminated.'

Sophie looks closely at the crossword sitting on the scrubbed kitchen table. The page from the newspaper is folded into a square and a Bic pen is sitting on the paper. Whoever was doing the crossword was halfway through writing out the word 'brilliant' in 3 across.

'I wonder if it was Alice or Jack doing the crossword.'

'Jack, I would think, while poor Alice was slaving away baking the cake.'

'It looks like a woman's handwriting to me.'

'Does it?' Grace makes a non-committal sound and continues on with her instructions. 'So, once you've painted a picture of domestic bliss, you point out the chair and the blood stains. Somebody will ask how you can be sure they're blood stains. Just give them a frosty look and say, "We can't be sure. We can't be sure about anything in this house except that it's a *mystery.*" '

Sophie crouches down to examine the trail of brownish stains leading from the back door to the chair. 'It doesn't look like enough blood for somebody to die.'

'I'm quite sure Aunt Connie didn't kill anybody,' says Grace. 'Veronika just can't forgive her for leaving her house to you. Shall we do the bedroom next?'

The bedroom is tiny, almost filled by a double bed with a pale pink eiderdown. Next to the bed is a wash stand with a basin and jug, and, of course, the crib.

'Make sure you point out the indentation in the pillow where the baby's head was,' says Grace. 'They love that.'

Sophie peers in the crib. 'Actually, I can't see it.'

Grace puts her hand in the crib and smooths out a hollow in the shape of a baby's head. 'There you go.'

Sophie shakes her head and laughs. 'You're starting to spoil the magic.'

'Aunt Margie washes the linen every month.'

'Oh.' Sophie pauses. 'I wonder how your Grandma Enigma feels when she sees this crib,' she says to Grace. 'Her parents obviously cared for her and she never knew them, or even knew what happened to them.'

'Oh, sometimes she pretends to get all sentimental about it, but really she loves being the Alice and Jack baby. Wait till you see her swanning around at the Anniversary next month.'

'Maybe, deep, deep down in her subconscious she's still yearning for her real mother,' says Sophie. 'They say babies can recognise their mother's voice by the time they're born.'

'Babies don't care who looks after them, as long as they're fed. And clean.'

'You don't think Jake would miss you if you disappeared?'

'He wouldn't miss me in the slightest.'

'Oh, of course he would!'

'He wouldn't. He'd grow up and he wouldn't remember a thing about me.'

'Well, maybe not *consciously.*'

'So do you think adopted children are all subconsciously yearning for their real mothers?'

Grace looks far too involved in this conversation. It's so strange the way one minute she's distant and the next she's practically interrogating Sophie. Oh, God, was Grace *adopted*? Has Sophie insulted her by implying she is psychologically damaged?

'No, I didn't mean that. I don't know what I meant. I don't really know anything about babies.'

Grace tucks in a corner of the mattress in the crib and doesn't look at Sophie. 'Would you like to have one?'

Gosh. Here comes the job interview again.

'Yes. Very much. But I can't seem to find a man to have one with and my biological clock is ticking very nervously. I'm thirty-nine. I might have to accept I'm probably going to miss the baby boat.'

Blab, blab. Reveal your deepest fears, why don't you? And meanwhile Grace won't even tell you how she feels about the WEATHER.

'But you must have lots of men interested in you.'

'Well, thank you, but no, not really.' *Your husband's hand brushed against mine the other night. Does that count?* 'I seem to have been going through a very long dating dry-spell. Although of course, I told you, I've been asked on dates by *two* separate men in the last few weeks.'

Grace looks at her sharply, almost angrily. 'You didn't tell me that!'

'Didn't I? I know I told Callum. You mustn't have been there.'

She waits for Grace to do the obligatory flutter of female excitement but she just looks irritated. 'Are you interested in either of them?'

'It's too early to tell.'

'Well, that's just great.'

'I'm sorry?' Sophie stares in bewilderment at Grace, who has begun massaging her forehead with her fingertips. 'What's just great?'

Grace looks up. 'Sorry. I keep getting these horrendous headaches and I can feel another one coming on. Do you mind if we finish this another day?'

'Of course not. You poor thing. You must get home and lie down.'

As they are locking up the house, Grace

says urgently, 'I'll talk to you soon, OK?'

Sophie watches Grace walk off down the hill, her hands jammed in the pockets of her fleece, her shoulders slumped.

It must be a very bad headache.

'Why didn't you tell me that Sophie has two men after her?'

Callum glances briefly up at Grace from his newspaper with unfocused eyes, all his attention still on whatever he's been reading. 'I don't know. I guess I thought you already knew.'

'I didn't.'

'Well, now you do.'

He's reading again. Grace feels a surge of teeth-grinding irritation. The stupid man is going to let her slip through his fingers!

'I don't think either of them is very well suited to her,' she says. 'Actually, I think *you'd* be a better match.'

Callum chuckles and turns the page of his paper. 'Pity for her I'm taken.'

Grace digs her nails into the palms of her hands. This isn't working. He doesn't even sound that interested! She's going to have to plant the idea in his mind. 'Actually, I think she really likes you.'

'As a friend.'

'No, she *like*-likes you. I've seen the way

she looks at you.'

Callum looks up properly now. 'What is this? You're not seriously worried about Sophie, are you?'

Retreat, retreat! He's so bloody principled, if she acts jealous he won't have anything more to do with Sophie. She just needs him to feel flattered. 'Of course not. I'm just saying that if you were single I think she'd be after you.'

'Well, I'm not single and I don't want to be single ever again, thanks. I hated being single.' The expression on his face is so guileless and genuine that Grace has to look away, embarrassed by his naked, sooky niceness.

He says, 'Are you OK, honey? Is everything OK? You don't seem yourself.'

'No, you just don't *want* this to be myself.'

'I beg your pardon?'

'This *is* myself. You've always had some idea of me that doesn't exist.' As she says this she feels that it is, in fact, true. He has refused to see her true ugliness. It's exhausting and not very fair having to pretend all the time.

Callum carefully folds the newspaper and runs his thumb along the crease. 'What do you mean, Grace?'

'You just see what you want to see.' She

lets her cheeks and her mouth be dragged downwards into the face of a sad clown. Let him see.

'I don't know what you're accusing me of. I don't even know what we're talking about.' There is just the slightest tremor in his voice.

'You don't know me.'

'Oh for Christ's sake, Grace, you're my wife. You're the mother of my child!'

'No need to get dramatic. You said I don't seem myself, and I'm telling you, *this is myself.* Take it or leave it.'

He flinches as if she's slapped him. His eyes are watery and frightened.

Grace leaves the room, her legs trembling.

38

Join us for a night of intrigue and illumination! The Anniversary of the Mysterious Disappearance of Alice and Jack Munro in 1932 is one of the most exciting events on the Scribbly Gum Island calendar. It's the one night of the year when non-island residents are allowed to stay on the island after sunset. The main street of the island is lined with food stalls, lit by hundreds of glittering fairy lights and warmed by giant heaters. (But please do rug up, as it can be chilly!) The theme of the night is MYSTERY! There will be MYSTERY LUCKY DIPS, MYSTERY PRIZES and MYSTERIOUS ENTERTAINMENT, such as magicians, dancers, fire breathers and tarot-card readers! Meet some of the people involved in the Alice and Jack Mystery — like ROSE DOUGHTY, one of the two sisters who first discovered the abandoned home, and ENIGMA McNABB, the baby (now a Grandma!) who was found in such mysterious circumstances! FREE FACE PAINTING FOR EVERY GUEST!

HURRY! LIMITED TICKETS AVAILABLE! Only $75 (including GST) a head.

SPECIAL NOTE: THE ISLAND GETS <u>VERY COLD</u> AT THIS TIME OF YEAR! WE RECOMMEND WARM WOOLLY HATS COVERING YOUR EARS, AND GLOVES AND SCARVES. PLEASE TAKE CARE TO DRESS YOUR LITTLIES VERY WARMLY!!!

'What do you mean, you can't make it? What sort of talk is that?'

'I just can't make it this year.'

'I feel jolly well offended you'd even suggest such a thing!'

'Oh, Mum, please, there's no need to be!'

'Some sort of Weight Watchers *party,* did you say?'

'Not exactly. It's more of a function, I guess you'd call it.'

'Wouldn't be much of a party, would it? Everyone standing around chomping on celery sticks, looking miserable and skinny. I know where I'd rather be!'

'It's not really anything to do with Weight Watchers. It's just somebody from Weight Watchers has asked me to go to this thing.'

'And you said yes! To this *thing!* You actu-

360

ally said yes! You can't just not be here! You've always been here for the Anniversary. Every year of your entire life!'

Enigma is utterly baffled. She can't believe that Margie is being so uncharacteristically *wilful.* Laura was the naughty one. Margie was a good, pliable girl, which seemed only fair, what with all the problems that Laura caused. And now here Margie is at the age of fifty-five saying she 'can't make it' to the Anniversary and pressing her lips together as if that's all there is to say on the matter. People can't just go changing their personalities willy-nilly when they're middle-aged.

Suddenly Enigma snaps her fingers triumphantly. 'Aha! I know what this is all about. It's *The Change*!'

'Oh Lord, Mum. I'm not menopausal.'

Enigma surveys her daughter through narrowed eyes. She looks different. *Skinnier!* She leans forward and points with an accusing finger. 'Margaret Anne! You've lost weight!'

Margie sighs. 'Well, yes, Mum. I've lost two stone. I'm nearly at my goal weight. I can't believe you haven't noticed before.'

'Well, I don't look at you when I see you every day, do I? No need to get offended. I expect you do have the menopause. Your face is quite pink.'

'That's because I'm feeling frustrated. I still think we should cancel the Anniversary this year as a mark of respect to Connie.'

Enigma cries, 'Connie would *never* want the Anniversary cancelled.'

'I guess that's true.' Margie smiles slightly. Her face is thinner, notices Enigma. It makes everything about her seem more definite. 'Well, I've organised everything for the night, Mum. The staff are really very competent, you know. It will all run like clockwork. And the whole family will be there. Rose, Thomas and Debbie, Veronika, Grace and Callum, Sophie — you won't even notice I'm not there!'

Enigma decides to hold off bursting into tears. 'Of course I'll notice. Both my daughters deserting me! What will people think? My parents deserted me seventy-three years ago and now my daughters do the same thing.' It's true! Enigma is pleased to feel a genuine tickling sensation in her nose as she considers how poorly she has been treated.

'It sounds like you're starting to believe your own publicity, Mum.'

'I beg your pardon? I don't know what that means. Are you trying to sound sophisticated or something? All I know is that the Anniversary is very important to me.'

'Is it?' Margie looks at her mother curiously. 'But why?'

'What do you mean, why? It's a special family event. We have fun! And it's about my life, isn't it?'

'Oh, Mum, let's be honest. The Anniversary is about business. It's about cash flow.'

Enigma carefully pulls out her hanky from her handbag and takes a deep shuddery breath. It's time for tears.

39

I am searching for any information relating to the disappearance of ALICE AND JACK MUNRO on SCRIBBLY GUM IS- LAND on 15 July 1932. I am especially interested in meeting anyone who knew the Munros or who had parents or grand- parents who knew them. Possible mon- etary reward for QUALITY information. Please contact Veronika Gordon at veronika.gordon@hotmail.com.au

Veronika puts down her pen and blows her nose. She is at the tail end of her flu and still feels a little weak and light-headed. She ended up having to stay at Aunt Connie's house with Sophie for two days. She could barely walk! Sophie had made her chicken soup and even rubbed Vicks on her back, which Veronika found soothing, as well as . . . disturbing.

'Hello!'

Veronika looks up suspiciously. A girl with shiny black hair stands in front of her, holding a coffee mug and a plate with a large Florentine biscuit. She says, 'I know you from the gym! Boxercise for the Broken Hearted!'

It's that annoying Asian girl who always kicks with the wrong leg or punches with the wrong arm. Veronika says, 'Oh yes, I recognise you.'

'I'm so uncoordinated in that class!'

'Well, yes, you are,' says Veronika.

'I'm not sure if I'm broken-hearted any more, but the class is still fun, isn't it? Shall I join you?'

Before Veronika has a chance to say anything the girl is sitting at her table, putting her coffee and biscuit down, flicking back her hair. 'What's that you're working on?'

'It's an ad I'm putting in the paper.'

'A personal ad?' The girl dimples at her.

'Well, no. I'm trying to solve a mystery.'

'Aren't we all! Want some of my biscuit?'

'All right.'

Veronika takes a bite of the biscuit. It's delicious: sweet and crunchy. The girl raises her eyebrows at Veronika over the rim of her coffee mug. Her almond-shaped eyes are so dark they're almost black. Her fingers on the handle of her mug are long and fragile, like an artist's. She bites her nails. She's wearing a ring with a tiny green stone.

Veronika has the funniest, most exhilarating feeling that a far more interesting mystery than Alice and Jack is about to be solved.

Sophie is in her dressing gown, getting ready for her first date with Ian the Sweet Solicitor, when Grace turns up unexpectedly. The baby is in a sling against her chest, a dimpled tiny hand clutching Grace's shirt.

'Hello, Jake! Look at you!' Sophie, besotted as always, runs a finger along the curve of his creamy flushed cheek. His brown eyes rest inquisitively on Sophie and then dart away, intrigued by something over her shoulder.

'Are you going out?' asks Grace abruptly. There are purplish shadows under her eyes, which would make anyone else look haggard. They make Grace look ethereal.

'It's my first date with Aunt Connie's lawyer tonight,' says Sophie, feeling both juvenile and ancient. Here is Grace, at least five years younger than her, a mother and a wife, while Sophie is still going out on first dates.

'I'm sorry,' says Grace. 'I won't stay then. I just wanted to talk to you about something.'

'Oh, well, come in. I've got time for a quick cup of tea. I'm getting ready hours too early of course.' Why must she always *babble* in Grace's presence? 'Did your headache get better yesterday?'

Grace lifts Jake from his sling. 'Would you like to hold him? I can make the tea.'

'Oh, of course.'

So Sophie is in the middle of trying to make the baby laugh by blowing raspberries against his tummy, messing up her carefully blow-dried hair, when Grace makes her announcement.

'I'm thinking of leaving Callum.'

'Grace!' Sophie feels a thud of fear, guilt, and beneath it all a tiny, quickly suppressed twinge of excitement.

'Don't say anything to him please. Will you promise not to say anything?'

'Of course.' Wonderful. More promises to keep secrets that probably shouldn't be kept. 'But you've got to talk about this to him. He adores you, Grace.'

'No he doesn't. Not really.'

'I expect it's just both of you adjusting to the new baby. Everybody says it's such a difficult time.'

'We've been having problems for ages.'

'Oh.'

Sophie doesn't know what to say. She doesn't have the same sort of relationship with Grace as she does with her other girlfriends. With them she'd be firing questions and getting every detail. But Grace is so forbidding.

'What about the baby?' she says finally, thinking of how much Callum adores his son. He'd be devastated if Grace took Jake away.

'I don't know yet.'

'Gggggggg!' comments Jake cheerfully, trying hard to put his big toe in his mouth.

Sophie can see his whole future in an instant: being shuttled back and forth between two homes, overhearing Mum and Dad snarling at each other about child support, hating Mummy's new boyfriend (although perhaps rather liking Daddy's lovely new girlfriend?). Oh stop it, this isn't a game, this is a marriage!

'What about counselling?' she asks Grace. 'I've got two lots of friends seeing the same counsellor at the moment. Apparently he's very good and he gives you receipts that say "professional development" so you can claim it as a tax deduction. I'll get you his number. Actually, I can get you his number right now, if you want?'

Grace looks horrified by the offer. 'No,

no, I don't want to talk about it with anyone. I just thought I'd tell you. Actually, I won't stay. I'll just, well, I'll just . . . go. Have a good night.'

She lifts the baby from Sophie's arms and is gone before the kettle begins to boil.

Grace walks back up the hill, Jake's warm body swinging against her chest, her heart thudding.

Well, she sure does like your dad, Jake. She'll treat him differently now she knows I'm thinking of leaving. I've given her permission to touch his arm, to hold eye-contact. I've opened the door just a fraction, just enough to get them underway. You'll all three be very happy together. You'll have a lovely mummy and daddy. I'll give them two more weeks. I can manage two more weeks. Up until the Anniversary. I'll get the tax returns done, so Callum doesn't have to worry about it. Paperwork gives him eczema. I hope Sophie is good with paperwork. Have all the washing up-to-date. I'll leave lots of food in the freezer. Sophie only seems to make cakes — and they're not very good — but I guess Margie will help cook for them. There'll be that life-insurance pay-out, so that will be handy. It will look like an accident.

She takes a deep breath of the cold air.

Yes. She feels better than she has in weeks.

Ian the Sweet Solicitor doesn't put a first-date foot wrong. He is charming and intelligent, not sickeningly smooth but attentive and sweet. He clears his throat when they are given a table next to the kitchen's constantly swinging door and courteously but firmly asks if they can be moved. Sophie likes both the nervy clearing of the throat and the firmness.

She asks him about the scar under his eye.

'I wish I'd got it fighting a duel,' he says. 'Or at least playing some sort of rugged, masculine sport. But it's actually a chickenpox scar from when I was eleven.'

'Chickenpox!' cries Sophie. 'It's not even a nice disease!'

'Would it help if I nearly died from it?'

'Nope. It's too itchy to ever be romantic.'

He has no problem with Sophie choosing the wine. He asks questions about her life but doesn't demand to know who she votes for, or why she's still single, or whether she likes oral sex. He is interested in her work without being patronising. He doesn't show off. He is nice to their waitress. He has nice hands. He doesn't grip his knife and fork or stick his elbows out.

He drives an expensive car but doesn't

appear to be in love with it.

He is divorced, but doesn't seem bitter and weird about it.

He kisses her goodnight and it's lovely and he smells divine. His tongue doesn't slither in and out of her mouth like an eager lizard. His teeth don't smash against hers.

'I'll call,' he says, and she knows that he will.

Ian the Sweet Solicitor is an absolute catch.

As she drifts off to sleep she thinks of Callum and Grace. Their relationship probably began with a perfect first date like this. And now look.

That night she dreams she's in bed with Ian. He's lying on one elbow, smiling down at her, and Sophie is trying to hide her revulsion because he's covered in horrible chickenpox spots. 'He's just a poxy lawyer,' says Callum, sitting on the end of her bed, holding Jake. Sophie laughs and laughs.

40

Rose serenely tucks her long white hair under her hot-pink floral bathing cap while Sophie jiggles up and down on the cold hard sand, rubbing her goose-bumpy arms and saying, 'Don't you think we might be at risk of hypothermia this morning, Rose?'

'It will be lovely and bracing, darling.' Rose slowly begins to walk towards the water. Her back is milky-white with purple age spots, her spine long and knobbly. Sophie can see the memory of a young girl's beautiful athletic body in the length of her legs. Rose gets to the same mossy green rock she always chooses and dives straight in with barely a splash, emerging to do a graceful freestyle.

The woman is nearly *ninety.*

Sighing, Sophie follows. The first heart-stopping shock of the water when she dives in always makes her inwardly scream, 'NEVER AGAIN! NEVER DO THIS

AGAIN!' She comes up gasping, teeth chattering, flailing about with her nose high above the water, like a puppy. After a few minutes she calms down and remembers why she keeps doing this. The water silky against her skin, the bay gradually becoming brighter and sharper as the sun rises higher in the sky — and the fact that she will still be burning fat for an hour after this swim, so the hot chocolate and egg and bacon pastries she and Rose will have for breakfast will be like eating *nothing*!

The pastries were originally cooked by Connie. Apparently Rose's deep freeze is still stacked high with food cooked by Connie. Rose defrosts them each night, heats them up in the oven before their swim and they're still warm by the time they're ready to eat. Sophie keeps offering to take a turn at bringing the breakfast, but Rose just laughs as if she's making a joke. After their swim they wrap up in warm jumpers and beanies and sit on the sand to eat.

'How was your outing with Connie's lawyer fellow?' asks Rose.

'It was fun, actually.'

'Do you think he could be Mr Right?'

'Maybe.' She wishes she could get that stupid dream out of her mind. Whenever she thinks of Ian she imagines him covered in chickenpox spots. It's very unfair.

'Well, don't rush. You've got to hold out for the right one.'

'I can't be too fussy. I'm getting on. I'll end up an —'

Oh, God. She was about to say *old maid*. And she is talking to an *old maid*. The thought of hurting sweet, fragile Rose's feelings makes Sophie feel ill. A blistering blush shoots up her neck. The blush feels hotter and redder than usual on her cold, wet skin.

Fortunately, Rose just keeps looking at the river, steadily sipping her hot chocolate. She says, 'Connie said I was too fussy. She was always trying to match me up with someone.'

'And you didn't like any of them?' asks Sophie.

'Not really. I thought I was in love with a fairly nice chap some time in the Sixties. What year was it? I remember Connie was marching in the Vietnam protests. 1966? No, it was 1967. But I went off him after a while. To be honest, I was quite relieved. I was getting set in my ways by then. I didn't want to be cooking and cleaning for some man. He drowned a few years later. So that was lucky, eh?'

'Maybe not for him.'

Rose chuckles. 'No, not for him.'

Sophie has seen black and white photos of Rose when she was a young girl, with long hair, smooth skin and elusive eyes. Is life really so horribly arbitrary that some people just never get around to meeting the right person? Here's Sophie thinking that her life is a romantic comedy and there's no way the director will let her finish up alone because the test audiences would hate that. But in fact, it could happen. It could just accidentally, capriciously happen.

'Of course, I was such a silly, dreamy young girl,' reflects Rose. 'One day, I saw this fabric in the window of David Jones and I wanted it *so* badly. It was crêpe de Chine. A beautiful deep, rich turquoise colour. The same colour as the river on a bright sunny day. I could see the dress I would make. I needed about two and a half yards to make a dress. It was going to cost me two pounds and thirty shillings. That was an awful lot of money. We were doing it very rough. Not like now. We're very rich now. Did you know we were rich? It's lovely being rich. I recommend it. And all thanks to Connie. Anyway, the thing was, I couldn't get that fabric out of my mind. I was quite obsessed with it. I used to dream about it! I had to find a way to make two pounds thirty. And then — oh dear, darling, I'm not meant to be telling you this story until you're forty, am I? Enigma will be so cross with me. Are you forty?'

'I'm very *nearly* forty,' Sophie says hopefully.

'Oh sugar!' says Rose. 'I can't tell you any more. Enigma already thinks I'm losing my marbles.'

'Can you at least tell me if you got the fabric?' begs Sophie.

Rose smiles. 'Yes, I did. But I never made the dress.'

'And this is somehow related to Alice and Jack's disappearance?'

'Of course. It's how it all started. When we take you up to Kingfisher Lookout on your fortieth birthday, Connie will say, "We've got something to tell you about Alice and Jack. It all started with some green material that Rose just *had* to have." Green material! It was *turquoise crêpe de Chine*! Oh dear, but this is terrible. I shouldn't be telling you any of this! I don't know what's come over me lately. I've been feeling a little *wild.* As if I want to break all the rules. I wonder if I'm about to die, like Connie.'

'You're a picture of health.'

This is so tempting, thinks Sophie. The solution to the Alice and Jack mystery is right there hovering on the tip of Rose's tongue. All she needs is the gentlest nudge and Sophie could know it all. But it seems so cruel and thuggish; like capturing a butterfly. Of course, if Veronika was here she'd be tearing its wings off by now.

'Did you know that Veronika is determined to solve the mystery and write a book about it?' Sophie warns Rose. 'She's even talking about getting some forensic expert to do DNA testing on the blood stains on the kitchen floor.'

'No need for testing. It's Connie's blood. She bled all over the place that day. What a mess. Oh, *sugar*!' Rose clamps her hand over her mouth. Her eyes dance. 'I'm being so naughty today!'

Sophie puts her hands over her ears. 'I'm not listening to another word you say.'

Rose giggles. 'Thank you, darling. I appreciate it. Have some more hot chocolate.'

41

Sophie walks towards the ferry wharf to meet Rick the Gorgeous Gardener for their picnic lunch.

She feels quite pretty and appropriate and nowhere near forty. For once she has on exactly the right outfit for the occasion — a striped, subtly sailorish, flattering-to-the-waist top, with crisp white, leg-lengthening pants and flat, stylish, outdoorsy-girl shoes. Her hair is up in a bouncy, breezy ponytail. It's refreshing to go on a date without her stomach clenching, without trying not to think: *Is this it? Is this my chance? Will this change everything?* What's come over her? She doesn't care less whether Rick likes her or not. There is Ian, after all.

Someone is jogging up the hill towards her. She sees that it's Callum and now her stomach does clench with an idiotic pleased anticipation, which irritates her.

WOULD YOU STOP IT! It's just his unavailability making him seem appealing. She's acting just like a man. Callum is wearing a singlet top and baggy shorts and his face is all wrinkled with that frenzied, pained look that runners get. She waves, and when he reaches her he stops, bending forward and resting his hands on his knees.

'Good. An excuse to stop,' he puffs. 'I'm not a runner. I'm just pretending to be one.'

'You fooled me,' says Sophie.

He straightens up. 'Where are you off to? You look nice.'

'On my date with Rick.'

'The turtle-tattooed gardener?'

'That's the one.'

'Hey, Sophie?'

'Yes?'

'Has Grace said anything to you lately about . . . anything?'

Oh, nothing much! Only that you were never really right for her and she's thinking of leaving you. She hedges. 'You need to be a bit more specific. What do you mean by anything?'

His face does an awkward spasm. 'Anything about us, I guess. She's said some really strange things lately. I can't get her to talk to me. I thought maybe — well, you know, women always reveal their deepest secrets to each other. I'm not asking you to betray a confidence or anything. Although, of course, I am, aren't I?'

He tries to look flippant but only manages to look deeply unhappy. Sophie aches for him.

'I don't really know Grace that well,' says Sophie.

'No. Sorry. Of course you don't. Forget we had this conversation. It must be the unexpected rush of oxygen to the brain from exercising.'

'I'd better go.'

'Have fun. Be back by curfew, young lady.' He taps at his watch but he is too miserable to be funny. His face sags. 'OK, bye!'

She watches him go pounding off. For the first time she feels a flood of bitchy feelings towards Grace. You're beautiful. You're talented. You've got a gorgeous baby, a gorgeous husband who adores you. And you're actually considering just throwing it all away because you fight about *housework*! Well, more fool you, Grace. More fool you.

Rick the Gorgeous Gardener is wearing a white T-shirt under a blue v-necked jumper, and jeans. When Sophie goes to step into the boat from the wharf he doesn't just give her an arm. He *lifts* her by the waist and *places* her in the boat, as if this is perfectly normal behaviour. He takes her to a private beach about twenty minutes down the river, only accessible by boat. He's brought the picnic — a bottle of white wine and slab-like tomato and cheese sandwiches. The wine wouldn't have been Sophie's choice and the sandwiches are not especially nice. He's cut everything too thick and put too much pepper on the tomato. They're like sandwiches made by a schoolboy. She has to swill a lot of wine to get the sandwich down. Her head starts to feel pleasantly fuzzy.

'Very nice!' she says with relief once she's finished her last mouthful.

'Really?' He doesn't look convinced. 'A woman once told me I was such a bad cook I even ruined sandwiches.'

Sophie widens her eyes innocently. 'That's extraordinary because that was one of the tastiest cheese and tomato sandwiches I have ever eaten.'

He grins. 'Liar. I'll make you eat another one if you keep that up.'

It's very different from her date with Ian the Sweet Solicitor. Ian belonged to Sophie's Sydney world: they talked the same language; they'd been to the same films, plays, festivals and restaurants. They even discovered a mutual acquaintance. Whereas

Rick the Gorgeous Gardener 'doesn't get into town very much', doesn't even own a television and can't actually remember the last movie he saw. Ian has skied in Aspen and scuba-dived in the Maldives. Rick spent six months meditating in a Buddhist monastery in China. Ian admitted to skim-reading certain Booker prize — winning novels so he could talk about them if necessary at dinner parties. Rick only ever reads non-fiction — biographies, histories and *National Geographic.* 'I like facts,' he says, leaning back against a tree and stretching out long legs.

He makes Sophie feel frivolous and pretty and about fourteen years old. He makes her feel like suggesting they play a game of chasing and letting him catch her.

After a while there is a pause in their conversation, and for some reason neither of them break it. They just look at each other. It appears that they're having a 'staring competition' like in primary school, to see who will giggle first. Sophie's mouth twitches but she restrains herself. Rick's eyes crease slightly but his face stays immobile. They stare and stare. Now it seems to be turning into a weird sort of foreplay. Finally, to her own astonishment, she finds herself reaching over and taking the wine glass from his hand and putting it carefully on the ground, without breaking eye-contact. She puts her hand on the back of his neck. For the first time in her entire life she is *initiating the first kiss.* (Various girl-friends applaud in her head: 'About time!') Rick gets the idea and takes over pretty fast, and fortunately he doesn't kiss like a Buddhist monk. She is all melting and trembly and clawing pathetically at his clothes.

This goes on for some time until finally they pull away from each other.

'I cooked chocolate biscuits for dessert,' says Rick.

Sophie wipes her mouth and readjusts her clothing. She feels ridiculous. Was it necessary to act so eager? She's practically a *middle-aged* woman. She acted like she was gagging for it, which she was. Oh, and of course, here we go . . .

'Is that a blush?' Rick touches her cheek with his fingertips. 'Are you doing that on purpose to charm me?'

Rick the Gorgeous Gardener, just like Ian the Sweet Solicitor, is unquestionably a Catch.

42

The Trevi Fountain, ROME, at sunset

Dear Grace,
It's hot, noisy and VERY crowded here.
I've been getting terrible migraines. Two
people from our group had their wallets
stolen today. I've been keeping a good
grip on my handbag. The gelato on
Scribbly Gum is superior to any gelato
I've eaten in Italy, and as for the pizza
here — I can assure you it's nothing
special. Much too bland! We're lucky
that Australia is so clean, aren't we. The
men stare very rudely, which I find quite
disconcerting. Never thought I'd miss
Australian males. Our guide became
quite snappy today and said I needed to
'embrace the cultural differences'. Obviously he doesn't like Rome any better
than me. How is Jake? Is he teething yet?
I can't remember when they teethe. I

was thinking on the bus today about when you were a baby. One night you cried for two hours straight. I was at my wit's end. I walked over to Connie's place and handed you over to Jimmy. You stopped crying instantly. I was so furious with you. I felt like you'd done it on purpose. Silly of me.

Love,
Mum
PS. I hope you're well, Callum! Laura.

'Your mother seems to be doing a lot of reflecting while she's away,' comments Callum, putting the postcard back down on the coffee table.

'Yes. She's become bizarrely chatty.' Grace is ironing while Callum watches *Australian Idol* on television. (Grace hates *Australian Idol*. Sophie loves it and has animated discussions with Callum about who they think should win, as if it actually matters.)

'Relax,' Callum had said when he saw Grace setting up the ironing board. 'Or let me do it!' He is a terrible ironer, energetically ironing in wrinklier wrinkles and missing whole sections. Besides which, Grace doesn't want to sit down and watch television. It makes her anxious to think of sitting still. Her heart pumps and her hands tremble as if she's had too much coffee. *Move, move, move. Get this done. Get that done. Soon it will be over.*

'All these anecdotes about my childhood,' she says to Callum. 'It's infuriating.'

'Really? Why? I thought it was sort of nice.'

'She's putting on an act. Playing the Mother role.'

'That seems a bit harsh.'

'You don't know her.'

'Well, I'm hardly likely to know anything about my mother-in-law, am I, when I don't know anything about my wife.' He keeps making clumsy, nervy digs like this, trying to pretend their argument the other day had been over something trivial. Except he can't carry it off. The inflections of his voice are all wrong and his eyes are still bruised and hurt.

To distract him, she says, 'When I was ten my mother didn't say a single word to me for twenty-one days.'

Callum turns his head away from the television and speaks in his normal voice. 'You're kidding.'

'It was her special brand of discipline. She would just look right through me as if I literally wasn't there. She was very good at it. Sometimes I'd be begging her to stop it, crying, yelling at her, anything just to get her to talk to me again, and she'd just be humming this little tune to herself. I became invisible. It was quite a performance. If it was just a small offence she'd stop talking to me for a day — but if it was something really bad she might not talk to me for weeks. That was the longest. Twenty-one days. I ticked them off in my diary.'

'But that's terrible!'

'Well, she never laid a finger on me. Uncle Ron used to give Veronika and Thomas terrible beltings.'

'I'd take the beltings any day.'

Grace shrugs. As she bends over to lift another one of Callum's shirts from the ironing basket a great weight of tiredness makes her knees buckle.

Callum has turned down the sound on the television. He is far more interested in this topic of conversation than she had intended.

'What had you done when she didn't talk to you for twenty-one days?'

'I left a banana at the bottom of my school bag. It turned into black pulp and Mum was just disgusted. I can still see the expression on her face when she saw it. It was like she'd found a body.'

'A banana! Every kid does that!'

'I never did it again.'

Callum is all spluttering fascination. 'I

can't believe your mother didn't speak to you for three weeks because you left a banana in your bag. So — what — you'd come home from school and she wouldn't even say hello? What if you said sorry? If you tried to talk to her?'

'It didn't make any difference what I did. She was like the guards at Buckingham Palace. She looked right through me. Until all of a sudden one day it would be over and she'd be talking to me normally again.'

Grace flips Callum's shirt and runs the iron across the collar. She remembers how on the fifth day after the banana incident she'd forgotten her mother wasn't speaking and went running into the house and started telling her the amazing, goose-bumpy news that her painting of Aunt Connie and Aunt Rose swimming at Sultana Rocks had come first in an interschool competition. Her mother was sitting on the sofa reading a copy of *Vogue* and Grace was chatting, bubbling over with her story, when she realised Laura hadn't even lifted her head. She just flipped the page and kept right on reading her article, while Grace's words trailed humiliatingly away.

'I think that's a terrible thing to do to a child.' Callum looks at her seriously, almost pleadingly, as if he wants something of her.

What? She can't give it to him, whatever it is.

She says, 'It's hardly the worst thing that a mother can do.'

'Well, what if you'd hurt yourself?'

Grace buttons the freshly ironed shirt onto a coat-hanger. 'Actually, sometimes I thought about purposely hurting myself to get a reaction, but . . .' She really can't be bothered finishing the sentence. She really can't be bothered having this conversation. Why doesn't he just turn the television back up and stop tiring her?

'But what?'

It was when Grace was thirteen and her mother wasn't talking to her because she'd got hot-pink nail polish on the dining-room table. Grace decided to prove that Silent Time could be shattered, that it wasn't something real, that she really did exist, even during those times when her mother pretended she didn't. She bought a sesame bar. She didn't buy it at the school because all the ladies in the tuck shop knew about her nut allergy, and if she'd asked for a sesame bar they would have clutched their hearts in horror. If Grace ate a sesame bar she would DIE, a fact that kids and grown-ups alike seemed to relish. Grace's plan was to sit down at the dinner table and say,

'Mum, I'm going to eat this whole sesame bar unless you say something to me,' and then she was going to open it and slowly take a bite — *very* slowly, to give Laura time to react, to scream, 'No, Grace! *Stop!*'

The procedure during Silent Time was that her mother made enough dinner for the two of them but Grace had to serve herself. She didn't need to eat at the table during Silent Time. She could eat in her room, or in front of the television, or sitting cross-legged on the laundry floor. In fact, it didn't even make any difference whether Grace took the plate of food and upended it on the kitchen floor. She knew this because she'd tried it once and her mother didn't even flinch, which was terrifying because it must have been torture for her. But surely she wouldn't let her daughter kill herself?

Grace sat at the opposite side of the table to her mother and carefully laid the sesame bar down next to her bowl of chicken pasta and her glass of orange juice. Her mother's eyes didn't flicker. She just continued to eat her pasta, her lipsticked mouth chewing and digesting ladylike mouthfuls. 'I'm going to eat this,' said Grace, and her voice, which she had hoped would sound determined and mature, came out tentative and babyish. Laura's vague, friendly gaze just skimmed straight over her, as if she were no more interesting than a chair. Grace picked up the sesame bar. Her heart was thudding. Her mother dabbed at the corner of her mouth with her serviette. Grace tore open the packaging. Her mother reached over for the pepper grinder and put some more black pepper on her pasta. Grace held the sesame bar in front of her mouth; she nearly retched at the thought.

Her mother yawned. A genuine, slightly bored yawn.

And Grace thought, She's going to let me die right in front of her.

She took the sesame bar to the rubbish bin and then she scrubbed her hands to ensure there was no trace of sesame seed left. She took the chicken penne up to her room and climbed into bed and ate it there. Three days later her mother said, 'I think it's going to rain' when she came down to breakfast and her punishment had ended.

Now, twenty years later, as Grace irons, her grown-up mind thinks with bitter amusement, 'She won the bluff. Of course she would have stopped me.' But another less certain part of her still wonders, Would she have let me die to prove a point?

Callum still hasn't turned the television

back up. 'I can't believe you've never told me this.'

'It's not that interesting. I don't know how your parents disciplined you.'

'My father roared at me and my mother chased me around the house brandishing whatever she happened to have in her hand. They didn't ignore me for days on end.'

He is looking at her with what Grace takes to be revulsion at yet another example of her strange, cold family life, compared to his rowdy, messy, cheerful childhood.

'Can you turn it back up?' she says, but instead he stands up.

'Grace. Sweetheart.' He reaches out a tentative hand to touch her face.

'Now you're blocking the television,' says Grace, and presses the steam button so the iron hisses.

43

'Have you told your husband yet?'
   'No.'
   'I haven't told my wife either.'
   'My husband would just sneer at me.'
   'My wife would just laugh at me.'
   'Well, we'll show her.'
   'Maybe. I hope so.'
   'You're not losing your nerve, are you?'
   'Not after we've come this far.'

44

Ron is sitting in his study, desultorily working on some overdue paperwork, when he is pleased to remember that it's the first of the month, which means he can flip over the page on his Aubade Lingerie calendar. The picture for May is of a skirt flying up to reveal a G-stringed bottom, and while it's a very appealing, professional piece of photography, it will be interesting to see what June has to offer. Under no circumstances can he flick ahead. He takes pride in such small, secret acts of self-denial; they build character. He has tried to explain the importance of delaying gratification to Margie, but she only pretends to be interested while stuffing more and more food down her cakehole.

The calendar was a Christmas gift from a supplier. When Ron's daughter Veronika saw it hanging up in his study she became unexpectedly feral. They had a ferocious argument about it. She was completely irrational, of course. It never ceases to amaze him, the stunning lack of logic in women's brains. For Christ's sake, it's not like he put it up in the dining room! Besides which, this isn't something you'd see hanging up in a mechanic's workshop. It's a limited-edition collector's item. It's tasteful. It's elegant. The photos are in *black and white*!

'Oh, what would you know about art, Dad!' Veronika's lips had curled. 'This is soft porn. It's insulting to Mum! It objectifies and degrades women!'

'Don't upset your father, darling,' Margie had said. 'It doesn't worry me. It's very pretty.'

'Well, it *should* worry you!' Veronika had sounded like she was close to tears and stormed out of the room, leaving Ron to wonder out loud whether his daughter was actually stable.

(It beggars belief that this intense, contemptuous, skinny woman is the same toddler who used to be so excited when he came home from work that she spun in circles, shrieking, 'Daddy home! Daddy home!')

Sometimes Veronika makes him feel strangely inferior, strangely *lower-class,* and that's not right. Australia is a classless society. Egalitarian. He is pleased to remember the word: egalitarian. An upper-class, well-educated sort of word. He may be the son of a fitter and turner but he can use words like 'egalitarian', no problem at all.

Just because Veronika has all the benefits of the university education that Ron missed out on. A university education he damn well paid for!

To be scrupulously honest, the island paid for it.

But still.

Oh, forget it. He'll never understand her.

Ron takes down the calendar and reverently flips the page to reveal a photo of a woman with her arms raised above her head as she pulls off her sweater. Her uplifted breasts are encased in a lacy bra.

Isn't the lighting sort of . . . moody? Grainy? Doesn't that make it art? What does soft porn actually mean? Didn't Rembrandt or somebody or other paint nudes? What's the difference? Just because he's dead. And French. Was he French? The fucking French. He must look Rembrandt up on the Internet. He should do an art-history course or something.

The phone rings and he answers while still studying the woman's breasts.

'Hi, Dad.'

Ron drops the calendar on his desk as if it's hot.

'Hello, Veronika.'

'How are you? What are you doing?'

She is sounding unusually light-hearted.

'Just — paperwork, love.' He is irritated by how wrong-footed he is feeling. 'Do you want to speak to your mother?'

'Oh, OK, no time to chat I see! Well, is she there?'

'Actually, I don't think she is. She's out.'

'That's annoying. I wanted to tell her something. Something to do with the Munro Baby Mystery.'

'What is it?'

'No, no, I'll tell Mum.'

'Oh, well, the Alice and Jack business is nothing to do with me.' He tries to take a light tone but knows that he is sounding jocular and middle-aged. 'Strictly women in charge. It's a wonder they let men on the island.'

Veronika ignores this. 'Mum's always out these days,' she says. 'Where is she?'

He searches his mind and comes up blank. 'I don't know. Weight Watchers?'

'Mmmm. I don't think so. Not at this time. I'd be worried if I were you, Dad. Maybe she's having an affair now she's getting so trim, taut and terrific.'

Ron has no idea what she's talking about. Veronika says, 'I hope you've been complimenting her on how good she looks.'

Ron sighs. 'What, has she changed her hair colour or something and I didn't notice?'

'*Dad!*' Veronika explodes and sounds more like her normal self. 'Are you telling me you haven't noticed that Mum has dropped three dress sizes? You're unbelievable! Do you even look at her? All that sniping about her weight and then you don't even notice! God! You're probably too busy getting off on that pathetic pornographic calendar of yours to even look at your own wife! I wouldn't blame her if she was having an affair!'

'Is that just a pause for breath or have you finished?'

'Yes, I've finished. God! Just tell her I called when she gets home. And take a second to *look* at her! I'll see you at the Anniversary.'

'Yes, all right.'

Ron puts down the phone. He picks up the calendar and puts it back on the hook. He is used to Veronika's outbursts but this one has left him with a vague sense of disquiet.

He crosses his arms behind his head and stretches back in his chair. So Margie has been losing weight. About bloody time. She could have told him! She tells him everything else, babbles on about all sorts of irrelevant crap. Wasn't it a bit strange that she hadn't mentioned she'd lost weight? Was it some sort of trick? It is true that she has been out a lot lately. Actually, he's barely seen her over the last few weeks. She must have told him where she was going tonight but he hadn't really registered it. He knows Veronika was only joking about her mother having an affair, but thinking about it gives him a strangely familiar sort of jolt, deep in his gut. It's not necessarily an unpleasant sensation. It's a nervy, adrenaline-filled feeling like he used to get before a rugby game. He looks at June Girl's breasts and identifies the feeling exactly.

It was the summer of 1967. The Prime Minister, Harold Holt, had just vanished while surfing on a Victorian beach. His body was never found and everybody was talking conspiracy theories, but Ron couldn't have cared less about whether it was the Mafia or Martians who took off with Harold, any more than he cared what had happened to Alice and Jack Munro. He was fixated on one goal: Margie McNabb, the prettier, in his opinion, of the somewhat renowned Scribbly Gum Island sisters, daughters of the Alice and Jack baby. There were at least three other guys vying for Margie, and Ron was determined to be the last one standing. He wasn't necessarily the best looking or even the smartest of the three of them, but he knew exactly how to play it, when to come on strong with the charm, when to pull back and be a bit cool, when to be funny, when to be sensitive. He didn't consider it a done deal until the day he triumphantly slid that diamond ring on her finger. Then he knew he could relax and concentrate on other things — like work and sailing.

Margie, he remembered, used to wear a red crochet bikini, which used to send him bananas. Her breasts in that red bikini outclassed all the girls on his Aubade calendar.

It was in the Eighties that she started to really pile on the weight. It seemed to happen so fast. One day he woke up with a fat wife. Not a chubby wife. A fat wife. He didn't like it and that made him the bad guy. Apparently it's the worst thing in the world to comment on your wife's weight, even while she balloons before your fucking eyes. You can't say, 'Are you sure you need that second piece of cake?' You can't even say, 'Maybe we both should eat a bit healthier.' No, you're meant to just pretend to be equally attracted to her now she weighs as much as a small truck as when she wore a red crochet bikini. The only solution is to try and avoid looking directly at her as much as possible. That's why he hasn't noticed she's lost weight. It's not his fault.

Does he still love her? It's not something he's bothered to think about much. She aggravates him, certainly. Sometimes he can feel his nerves begin to chafe the moment she opens her mouth.

But he still thinks nothing tastes as good as Margie's cheese and mushroom omelette. He still automatically rubs the soles of her feet when she puts them on his lap while they're watching television, although maybe it's been a while since she's done that. He still remembers how he felt watching her cry her heart out at her dad's funeral. Margie was always such a Daddy's Girl, and it made him want to punch something because there was nothing he could bloody well do to fix it for her.

They haven't had sex for months, but he's never been unfaithful to her, except in his mind, and who could blame him for that?

He does give her a pretty hard time, sometimes. But she just takes it — no matter how far he goes with it — she just keeps on smiling and blinking until he wants to scream, *Are you still in there, Margie?*

The thing is, even though he knows that Veronika was only joking, if some guy, for whatever reason — maybe if he had some sort of fetish for fat women — tried to come on to Margie, then she could easily fall for some pathetic line. She's so gullible! A hopeless judge of character. The way she repeats what tradesmen tell her with such wide-eyed respect!

To his own surprise, Ron finds himself suddenly banging an agitated fist on his desk so hard that his jar of paperclips rattles.

It's past ten on a Tuesday night. Where the hell *is* she?

Rose is sitting at Enigma's kitchen table separating eggs. She does it automatically, in quick, efficient movements. One sharp crack of the egg against the side of the bowl, yolk in one half of the shell, white in the other.

Rose is working in an assembly line with Enigma and Margie, baking marble cakes for the Anniversary. They'll be sold in special 'Alice and Jack Anniversary' souvenir boxes and sold at a premium: $30 a cake. Last year they sold over a hundred on the night. Rose remembers Connie had rubbed her hands with joy after counting up the cash, as if she were still nineteen years old and destitute, not ninety years old with a share portfolio worth so much that Rose had to sit down the last time the accountant went through the figures with them. Those years of worrying about money and not having enough to eat had changed Connie forever, thought Rose. Food and money were her two obsessions until the day she died. And Jimmy, of course. And the island. She was an obsessive sort of woman, really.

'I just can't get over it,' says Enigma. 'Last night I woke up in the middle of the night thinking about it.'

Another obsessive woman! Enigma is *still* sulking over the fact that Margie will be out on the night of the Anniversary. That girl latches on to things like a pit-bull terrier.

'I'll be back by midnight, Mum,' says Margie. 'Just like Cinderella.'

'You shouldn't be going at all,' mutters Enigma.

Rose picks up another egg from the carton and observes Margie's new slimline figure. 'Margie,' she says thoughtfully. 'You're looking so pretty today. So slim!'

'Hmmph!' says Enigma, but Margie looks pink and pleased.

'Thank you, Aunt Rose. Guess what! Ron finally noticed that I'd lost weight! But he was very strange about it. He actually asked me if I was having an affair last night. He sounded a bit insecure!'

'And are you?' asks Rose with interest. Margie does seem a lot more confident these days. Someone has been putting that colour back in her cheeks!

Margie frowns down at her mixing bowl. 'Not exactly.'

Enigma throws down her sieve with a puff of flour. 'How can you "not exactly" be having an affair! I certainly hope you're not! I never got to have an affair, did I? I would have quite liked to have one at times too!'

'Oh, Mum, how can you say that? Dad was a wonderful husband.'

'He might have been a wonderful father to you, Margie, but you weren't married to him, so you have no idea if he was a wonderful husband. At times I was bored silly. But did I rush out having affairs? No! I made myself a nice sherry, bought a new Mills and Boon and put up with it.'

Margie rolls her eyes at Rose. 'Listen to Mother Theresa.'

Enigma snaps. 'I suppose that's meant to be what you lot call witty, eh? Do you see me laughing? No, you don't.'

404

The oven timer goes off and Margie puts down the beaters and goes to take out four marble cakes and put in four more.

'Aunt Connie would be pleased. We've sold out of tickets to the Anniversary even earlier than last year,' she comments. Obviously, she is not going to say anything more about the 'not exactly' affair, thinks Rose. She will have to ask her another time.

'You know,' says Rose, 'I was thinking that we should make this our last ever Anniversary celebration.'

Margie and Enigma both stop what they're doing and turn to stare at her, thunderstruck.

'It's just so much effort, isn't it,' she says. 'It's not like we need to make any more money.'

'Connie would just *die*!' says Enigma.

Rose and Margie exchange amused glances.

'Oh, I know she's already dead!' cries Enigma. 'I had noticed that, actually! I had noticed that everything is falling to pieces and everybody wants to change everything now she's dead.'

Her face is working, ready to cry.

'I'm just raising the idea,' says Rose soothingly. 'I just sometimes think we don't need to make any more money from Alice and

Jack. I just think perhaps it's time to give it a rest.'

'It's a family tradition!' cries Enigma.

'It's a family *business,*' says Rose. 'A profitable family business.'

'Well, we should keep it profitable for the children. I *knew* you were losing your marbles, Rose. We should take you to a doctor and ask him for a prescription for Alzheimer's.'

'The children don't even care about the business,' says Rose. 'Grace is busy with the baby and her Gublet books, Thomas doesn't even like coming to the island, and Veronika —'

'Veronika is writing a book about Alice and Jack!' says Enigma triumphantly. 'She's *very* interested. She wants to come and talk to me with a tape recorder. She even wanted to hypnotise me.'

'Yes, and that's going to be a problem, isn't it. What are you going to say to her?'

'Oh, I'll waffle on!'

'Yes, but we can't let poor Veronika write a book of waffle, can we. That's not fair. I think we should just tell them all the truth. Just sit them down one day and tell them all! I nearly told Sophie the other day.'

'Rose!'

'I can't help it. All of a sudden I'm just

406

tired of keeping it a secret. Let's just tell them all. I don't want them to hear it after I die.'

'Not till they're forty,' says Enigma stubbornly. 'That's the rule. *I* had to wait till I was forty, and I'm what you could call the star of the story!'

'Speaking of Veronika and her book,' says Margie. 'I forgot to tell you that she's been placing ads asking for anyone with information relating to Alice and Jack to come forward. Well, apparently she's been getting a few responses.'

'Kooks!' says Enigma. 'Veronika is a naughty girl. She shouldn't have done that. All the kooks will be coming out of the woodwork! Remember the time that psychic wrote us that weirdo letter telling us she'd dreamed that Alice's body was "somewhere mossy"? Connie laughed so much that Jimmy had to get her a glass of water.'

'Yes, well, one of the kooks says he's going to come to the Anniversary Night and give Veronika this information in person.'

Enigma chortles. 'Well, that should be good for a laugh.'

'Mmmm,' says Margie. 'Apparently he insinuated on the phone that he was related to Alice and Jack in some way and that he might therefore be entitled to some sort of "compensation" for all the money we've made from the story. Veronika says he sounded a bit creepy.'

'Well, just let him try, eh!' says Enigma.

'What if the only way to disprove this fellow is by actually telling the truth?' asks Rose.

'Oh, well, as long as he's forty,' says Margie dryly. 'That's the rule.'

'The skinnier you get, the cheekier you get,' says Enigma. 'If this chap turns up, we'll get Connie's solicitor onto him. Ian! He's a clever boy. He'll soon set him straight.'

'Ian doesn't know the truth.'

'He knows the law — and the law is on our side.'

'I don't know that the law actually *is* on our side,' says Margie doubtfully.

'Of course it is!' says Enigma comfortably.

Margie scoops cake mixture into a tin. 'I hope so, Mum.'

Rose cracks another egg and thinks of Connie at nineteen, her young, strong, determined face in the moonlight, saying, 'Neither of us is going to jail, you ninny!'

She looks down into her bowl and sees that a piece of eggshell has fallen into the yolks. 'Oh sugar.'

45

'Oh my God. Oh my God. Oh my God.'

'So I take it you found that — satisfying?'

'Satisfying! Oh my God. Oh my God. Oh my *God*!'

'Gosh.'

'I just had no idea! I'm furious with myself! All those years I wasted with big hairy apes! What a fool! Why didn't I see?'

'Well, I don't want to blow my own trumpet, but you know it's not necessarily like this with *every* woman. It might be just this particular woman.'

'Oh, I only want this particular woman.'

'Really?'

'Oh my God, really!'

46

'The gardener will be better in bed.'

'He'll have filthy fingernails.'

'Who cares about the sex? She wants to have babies! She's got to get all practical and hard-headed and pick the right father for her children.'

'I just never saw Sophie with a solicitor. I always thought she'd be with an arty type.'

'The gardener sounds a bit backward if you ask me. What about that juvenile staring competition?'

'I thought that was sexy!'

'I thought it was weird. And he made those disgusting sandwiches for her.'

'Yes, Sophie has to have a man who can cook! What are they going to eat for dinner? Novelty cakes?'

'She's got to have a man who can match her intellectually.'

'Oh, and when did Sophie become such

an intellectual giant? She watches reality TV!'

'The point is, she can't make any decisions until she sleeps with them.'

'She can't sleep with both of them!'

'She's been celibate for years. She needs to sleep with *someone*!'

'What if she gets pregnant and she doesn't know who the father is?'

'DNA testing.'

'Which one makes her laugh?'

'Which one turns her on the most?'

'Which one has the smallest head?'

'*What?*'

'That's what my grandmother always said to me, "Marry a man with a small head." She said, "You'll thank me when you're in labour." '

Sophie's high-school girlfriends rock back and forth, their faces creased like monkeys with uncontrollable, alcohol-fuelled mirth, as gale after gale of laughter sweeps the table. They're out to dinner at a Korean restaurant where you sit cross-legged on the floor around a low table. Sophie's love life is the favoured topic of conversation. There are detours: a five-year-old's sudden tantrum about going back to kindergarten after the holidays ('No, I've already done school, thank you, Mummy.'), a husband's sudden tantrum over a scheduled-for-months vasectomy ('He's scared his personality might change, like the dog's.'), a ferocious childcare centre manager, a senile mother-in-law, an outrageous parking ticket, an outrageous request for oral sex ('We'd been arguing the entire night. I seriously think his main objective was to shove something in my mouth to shut me up.'). However, no matter how hard Sophie tries to divert them they continually come back to the Sweet Solicitor/Gorgeous Gardener conundrum. Sophie is the only unmarried, childless one in this unusually fertile circle of friends, and she is therefore the sole representative of her particular lifestyle choice. (Choice? Is it a choice? They all *act* like it's her choice.) She earns the most money, she's slept with more men, travelled more and seen more movies. (Apparently you can't go to the movies any more after you have children. Sophie keeps asking what about babysitters but her friends just exchange gently patronising 'she'll learn!' looks.) Whenever she is with this particular group Sophie swings constantly back and forth between pride and shame. You're a high-powered career woman. You're a dried-up desperado who can't find a man. You've succeeded. You've failed. You're the odd one out. You're the special one.

She doesn't want to talk any more about Rick or Ian. Mention of their names makes her feel obscurely guilty.

'I got my training for doing the tours of the Alice and Jack house the other day,' she says, and is pleased when she sets off a new flurry of conversation.

'Ooh, did you learn any inside information?'

Sophie chooses her words carefully, torn between the desire to show off with some juicy gossip and island loyalty. 'Not really, although sometimes I think the old ladies know more than they're telling me.'

'My nana always insisted it was something to do with the two sisters who found the baby. She said she remembered when it happened and looking at the photos of them in the newspaper and thinking the older one had shifty-looking eyes.'

Sophie jumps to defend her fairy godmother. 'That's Aunt Connie, and she had lovely honest brown eyes. She's the one who left me the house!'

'She's also the one who wrote you the letter talking about your Mystery Man, isn't she! I'm positive she meant the gardener.'

And they're off again. They don't really need Sophie there at all. They go on and on. Sophie quietly gets the attention of the waiter and orders more wine. While she is doing this it is agreed that tossing a coin would be the most sensible idea. If it's heads, it's a win for intellect and Ian. If it's tails, it's a win for sex appeal and Rick. A gold two-dollar coin is tossed high above the table and spins down to land with a splash in somebody's goat curry.

'Which one were you hoping for before it landed?' they all yell, excited by their clever psychological ploy. 'Whoever you were hoping for is the one you LOVE.'

Sophie thinks, Gosh, mothers really are such cheap drunks. She says truthfully, 'But I wasn't hoping for either of them.'

They're cross with her. 'Come on. Of course you were. You can tell us. We're your friends! What were you thinking about?'

She was actually thinking about how that pale blue jumper that everyone said really suited her would be the perfect thing to wear when she went around to Callum and Grace's place the next night. Not that it matters what she wears, of course, but still, that blue jumper will be just right.

She says, 'I was wondering about who was going to get voted off on the next episode of Survivor.'

They all groan. 'She's not even blushing,'

says someone disappointedly.

The two-dollar coin is carefully fished out from the bottom of the goat curry. It's tails. Rick's supporters give each other high fives, a glass of wine is knocked over and the waiter arrives to ask hopefully if maybe they'd like him to bring the bill soon?

Sophie is over for dinner and Grace has let Callum light the fire for the first time since moving into her mother's place; the living room is all cosy, crackling shadows. Grace's mother only ever lit the fire when they had guests, and the next morning she would be up early, marching around with a can of hissing air-freshener held at arm's length, throwing open windows and pulling off cushion covers to be washed. But it's only a house, and Laura is so far away, on a Greek island complaining about fatty moussaka and pretending to be a different sort of mother.

(Why does no one say what they must all be thinking? Why does no one ask the question: What sort of mother decides to take a twelve-month around-the-world holiday a few weeks before her only daughter gives birth to her only grandson? And what sort of daughter has a mother like that?)

Sophie is holding Jake and sitting very

comfortably on Grace's mother's sofa, looking pretty and cheerful in a blue top. She is playing a game with the baby where she lifts him up under his armpits so his splayed legs dangle and then she buries her nose in his stomach, strands of her hair brushing against his nose. Each times she does this she makes a strange sound like: 'goobidy goobidy DOO!' Jake finds this side-splittingly funny. He convulses with anticipatory laughter as soon as she drops her head. Callum is on his knees next to them, poking away unnecessarily at the fire and laughing whenever Jake laughs.

Grace walks into the room with a heavy carafe of mulled wine and feels as though her whole body has come out in an intensely itchy rash. There is a dry clicking sound at the back of her throat. She wants to roll around on the carpet like a rabid dog. She wants to throw the carafe against the wall and see the hard glass shatter into thick fragments. She wants to scream something incoherent and stupid at them.

She says, 'Would you like to give him his bath, Sophie?'

Sophie puts the baby back in her lap and looks up at Grace in the flickering firelight. 'Oh, no, I'm not trained! I'd be frightened I'd drown him.'

Well, you'd better learn, stupid fucking bitch, with your fucking sweet dimples, or what are you going to do when I'm not around? It's like there's a mad old drunk lolling around in her head who suddenly lurches up to scream obscenities. What happens if she ever breaks free and takes control of Grace's tongue?

She smiles. 'Callum will show you what to do. He's better at bathing him than me.'

Perfect. The two of you together in a steamy bathroom with adorable splashing child away from me, away from me, away from me.

But then Callum stands up, all courteous crinkly eyed smiles, all handsome, new-age, home-improvement-show Daddy, and says, 'Why don't you two relax and have a drink while I give him his bath?'

BECAUSE I don't want to sit and make conversation with Little Miss Sweet and Clean and Cheery, can't you see that, can't you see that, I NEED, I NEED, I NEED . . .

She says, 'Sophie would probably like to see Jake have his bath,' and this time her voice has an unmistakeable, socially inappropriate hard edge that causes Callum's lips to draw together in that horrible hurt-little-boy way. Sophie stands up, pulling at the sleeves of her jumper so they cover her hands, like a teenage schoolgirl, and says, 'I'll come and hand you towels or something, Callum.'

Grace watches them go and thinks, I can't take this much longer.

Sophie sits on the edge of the bathtub holding the baby while Callum tests the bathwater with his elbow. 'So, how's it going with your two suitors?' he says. 'Anyone in the lead?'

'They're neck and neck.'

It's unsettling being in this small, brightly lit room with Callum. She can see a tiny shaving nick on his neck. He's a very large man. She feels an irresistible urge to place the flat of her hand against his chest.

'Have you got certain performance criteria? You can start undressing him, by the way.'

Sophie carefully lays the baby on his back on the change table and begins unbuttoning his suit. The fragrance of baby-bath liquid fills the room.

'Oh yes, I've got them both jumping through hoops,' she says. 'I hold up scoreboards at the end of each date.'

'I remember there was a girl in my school called Maria who kept an exercise book rating all the boys she kissed,' says Callum.

'Here — let Dad.' Jake is starting to squirm crossly as Sophie pulls ineffectually at his singlet. Callum pulls the singlet up and over Jake's head in one swift movement.

'Were you in Maria's scorebook?'

'Oh, every guy in year ten was in Maria's scorebook. We were all allowed one attempt. I thought I'd done pretty well but apparently not. I got four out of ten.'

'Oh no!'

'Yep. According to the comments, I went in too soon with the tongue. Maria specified a five-second lead-up. Also, I forgot to take my chewie out of my mouth. Apparently girls don't like that.'

Sophie guffaws. 'Oh, well, I'm sure you've improved dramatically.' She looks up at him. He is holding Jake's naked, mottled little body close to his chest. He has large hands; one hand nearly covers Jake's back. The bathroom is filled with scent and steam and the surprisingly loud sound of running water.

'Let's hope so.' Their eyes hold for just a fraction longer than is appropriate. Sophie drops her eyes and thinks, married, married, married.

Don't go there, thinks Callum, stroking his

son's soft, vulnerable head. *Don't go there, you fool!*

47

What if Connie and Rose killed Alice and Jack *together*? What if they stabbed them, their innocent young-girl faces ravaged with hatred while blood splattered, the marble cake baked and the baby slept? It's early Saturday morning, the seventy-third Anniversary of Alice and Jack's disappearance, and Sophie wakes up in Connie's bed with this thought clear and horrible in her head. Perhaps that is the family secret.

For some reason, instead of feeling happily intrigued by anything to do with the Alice and Jack mystery, today she feels not exactly frightened, but unsettled, a little nervy. For the first time she isn't thinking of it as a story to enjoy, to puzzle over, but as something that really happened to real flesh-and-blood people, younger than Sophie, who most probably didn't want to die, thank you very much.

And if Connie and Rose *did* kill them . . .

well, it wasn't very nice, was it? They'd made fools of everyone for all this time. They'd also made quite a lot of money out of their cover-up. It has been interesting to see the Alice and Jack business up close. Sophie has come to realise how cleverly they've developed the island so that everything looks charmingly comfy — never too slick. Visitors are given the carefully calibrated impression that the Alice and Jack house is a sweet family-run museum only opened as a generous favour to the public so they can share and marvel in this unusual history. Sophie herself had that impression, before she moved here. Now she knows that every possible opportunity to relieve people of their money is ever so sweetly exploited. There's nothing illegal or even especially underhand about it, of course. It's just the entrepreneurial spirit. It's good business. It's just that if it's all based on a murder, it's actually quite evil.

Sophie doesn't like the way her mind is heading. It's that same heart-sinking sensation you get a few weeks or months into a new relationship when you discover to your horror that your amazing new lover actually has a *fault*! Not just a sweet, quirky flaw but a really horrible fault, like the fact that the slow, methodical way he has of checking the bill actually indicates intense stinginess and it's not adorable at all — how could it ever have been adorable? — it's bloody ANNOY-ING. Sophie hates it when that happens.

She throws back her quilt and walks across the floorboards in her flannelette pyjamas to the window to watch the early morning shimmery haze above the river. It looks like a religious painting at this time of the morning. She doesn't want to fall out of love with the island, with her life, her new family.

But the other night, when she was out with the girls, for the first time she'd caught herself thinking wistfully about how she used to just hop in a cab and be home at her old flat in less than twenty minutes, instead of the long, rattling train trip followed by the boat trip across the water in the frosty moonlight.

Oh, but look at that view. It's worth some inconvenience.

This is the point in a relationship when you begin the process of carefully deluding yourself.

Tonight she will be selling pink fairy floss dressed up in a pink fairy dress complete with tiara and glittery wings. Apparently there are quite good margins in fairy floss.

Sophie makes tea in Connie's ceramic teapot. (Enigma saw her making tea with a teabag once and said sadly, 'Oh, darling, please don't do that', as if she'd caught a child picking their nose.)

As she waits for the kettle to boil she finds herself tentatively massaging her stomach. She's still got that feeling of apprehension she had when she first woke up. But why? Tonight will be fun. Tonight will be *great!*

Is she nervous about being the Fairy Floss Fairy? For heaven's sake, no. She'll love it.

Is she nervous because both the Sweet Solicitor and the Gorgeous Gardener have said they'll be coming tonight? Not really. She's only been on one date with each of them. She's not exactly two-timing them. Besides which, Rick will be working — apparently he does a *fire-eating* performance — and Ian is just stopping by for a while before he has to go off to some family function. So there shouldn't be time for any awkwardness. Also, in her mind she tends to sort of amalgamate Ian and Rick into the one sweet, gorgeous gardener/solicitor. She's not nervous about them. They're both *lovely.*

No, it's something to do with that picture in her head of Connie and Rose wielding knives. And it's something to do with Callum. And Grace. And how much she wanted to kiss Callum in the bathroom the other night and the expression on Grace's face when they came back into the living room, as if she knew exactly how much.

Rose is dreaming that a slimy, silver, flapping fish is trying to hug her. She wakes up with her arms wrapped around an icy-cold flaccid hot-water bottle and cries out in disgust and shoves it away from her. You horrible, vile thing!

For a few seconds she lies there trembling with disgust, and then finally she forces herself to smile. Only a dream.

She rolls over — oh, how everything *aches* first thing in the morning. Nobody knows what an effort of will it requires for Rose to just get out of bed each day. She has to give herself a pep talk. 'Come on. You can do it. One leg. Second leg. That's it!' There should be a daily award ceremony. *Congratulations on your achievement, Rose Doughty, you overcame terrible pain and got out of bed. Hooray!*

Still, there's no need to get up just yet; she's not going swimming this morning. There always comes a point in winter where one day the water just gets so laughably icy that it's time to stop until spring. Sophie had clasped her hands together in prayer and said 'Thank you, God' when Rose had told her there would be no more swimming.

It's the Anniversary, *again*. It is astounding to believe that there are seventy-three years between this day and that day. Year after year after year. She can remember it clearer than things that happened much later. What did she do in the Seventies, for example? Nothing much that Rose could recall. That whole decade seemed to have taken about a week to live through. She remembered she'd liked the fashions. Colourful. And the children had been such a pleasure. Thomas used to sit on her lap for hours, sucking his thumb. Veronika, trotting around behind her, asking question after question after question. And Grace, painting in companionable silence beside her. Sometimes Rose would reach over and take her little paint-spattered hand and kiss her knuckles. Grace was never one for cuddles.

The way Rose had felt about those three was somehow different from the exasperated affection she had for their mothers, Margie and Laura, those golden-haired Misses with their big blue eyes and sticky, greedy rosebud mouths, who were both in love with their daddy anyway. And it was different again from what she'd felt for their grandmother. Rose's love for Enigma had always been interlaced with fear: *What if we do something wrong? What if they take her away? What if they find out?* But with Thomas, Veronika and Grace it had just been unadulterated, besotted love. Sometimes she was filled with such love for them it felt almost mystical, almost sexual, almost enough to make it seem the point of . . . everything.

She reaches up one hand and pulls aside the lace curtain on her window. The sudden flood of sunshine makes her blink. The Anniversary is more often than not a beautiful day, which Rose always feels is a little fraudulent, an inaccurate representation of the actual day itself, which had been a Gothic sort of day, all grey, brooding skies, a howling icy wind whipping the gum trees back and forth, the river murky and choppy. Rose can still see Connie standing at her bedroom door, wearing red mittens and a scarf their mother had knitted, wrapped around her neck to just under her mouth. Rose could tell she had woken up with one of her earaches by the way she was holding her head tilted to one side. She was all snappy. 'This is your last chance to change your mind, Rose. After today, we can't go back. Ever.' But Rose hadn't been able to speak or move, she was trapped at the bottom of a very deep, very dark mineshaft and she didn't know how to claw her way out. She thought she was going to be there forever. She hadn't said a word. She'd had nothing to say. Connie's face had clenched with irritation and she'd said, 'Right. Well, we're doing it then.' And they'd done it.

And in the blink of an eye seventy-three years had passed.

And now, tonight, some man, some 'kook' who saw Veronika's silly advertisement will be on the island, saying that he's related to Alice and Jack Munro! It makes Rose want to laugh and it simultaneously makes her want to cry. It gives her a trembly feeling of fear and at the same time it gives her a pleasantly uplifting feeling of rage.

It really is time to get up.

The audience holds its breath in anticipation as that brave battler, Rose Doughty, overcomes horrendous pain yet again to arise from her bed.

Enigma does not dream. Veronika has told her that everybody dreams, they just don't remember it. This is nonsense. Veronika is always talking *such* nonsense. If Enigma dreamed, she'd remember it. She has an excellent memory. It's not fair that she doesn't dream. Her husband Nathaniel used to have long, complicated dreams which he always wanted to tell her about over breakfast. It was very boring pretending to listen to him. She used to sigh a lot to try and give him the hint, but he didn't take any notice, just kept droning on.

Well, here she is all alone on the Anniversary morning with nobody to bring her so much as a cup of tea in bed. She is a lonely old widow, sitting here in her bed, which is so sad, like something in a Grace Kelly movie. She sniffs experimentally.

Actually, the truth is she doesn't miss Nathaniel all that much. It's nice having all the extra space in bed and keeping the electric blanket turned up so high that she can wear her summer nightie. She'd never actually meant to marry him. There were plenty of other livelier fellows who would have suited her better than Nathaniel, with his hangdog face, always loping around behind her. Always just *there.* She'd accidentally said yes to his proposal. It was because all her friends were always going on about what a nice boy he was — so sweet, so clever — so she thought she'd look silly if she said no. It was just like when she went shopping with Connie and Rose and they told her that red polo-neck top looked so good on her, she'd be mad not to buy it. So she bought it, against her better judgement, and sure enough, did she ever wear it? Not once! It just sat there hanging in the cupboard. Nathaniel was just like that red polo-neck top. A mistake. But you couldn't keep your receipt and exchange your husband, could you? No, you were stuck with him. Well, you were back then. Today they just divorced each other at the drop of a hat. Look at Veronika. Married for all of five minutes. Enigma had given her a very expensive iron as a wedding present. Did she get it back? No siree.

She pushes back the covers and slips her feet into fluffy pink slippers, which Laura once said looked like something Barbara Cartland would wear. This should have been a compliment but Laura made it sound like an insult, which was confusing. Enigma doesn't really understand Laura a lot of the time. She supposes she is clever. Mothers aren't meant to have favourites but how can they not, when one child is so much nicer to you than the other one? Enigma has taken care not to treat Margie like her favourite daughter, but she is of course, and she should be grateful for that and she should certainly not be abandoning her mother on such an important day as the Anniversary. It's hurtful.

The house is warm and toasty as she walks to the kitchen because she kept the heating on all night. Nathaniel would have had a fit. But as she was always trying to tell him, he was married to a *celebrity*. Enigma was a celebrity, just like Barbara Cartland, and she was also quite rich, just like Barbara Cartland, so why should she have to shiver on cold winter mornings?

She's going to have a smoked-salmon omelette for breakfast, made with King Island cream, her treat to celebrate the Anniversary. Seeing as nobody else cares about her, she'll just have to look after herself. When she was a child she always got a special gift and breakfast on the Anniversary. It was like her birthday but even better because she was the Star of the Day. Rose made her a special new dress to wear, and the night before she wore rags in her hair to curl it. She looked just like a little princess and the ladies who visited the island all wanted to hug and kiss her even more than usual. 'You poor, poor darling!' they'd cry, sweeping her into scented arms. And Enigma would cry with them, thinking, 'I *am* a poor darling!' and that would make them cry even harder, thinking she was crying for her vanished mummy and daddy. This was sort of true, but not in the way they thought. Enigma's greatest fear had been that her real parents would come back to claim her and take her away from Rose and Connie and Jimmy. Every Anniversary morning she woke up terrified that this might be the day Alice and Jack would turn up, saying, 'Right. We'll have her back now, thanks very much!' And they wouldn't know her favourite foods, or how she needed to have her hair brushed as light as a feather, or her back washed upways, not crossways, or how to tuck the blanket under her neck, or anything important about her!

When Connie and Rose had told her the truth about Alice and Jack on her fortieth birthday, that had been the part that made her really very cross. All those years thinking that Alice and Jack might turn up and steal her away when there was as much chance of that happening as Santa Claus turning up on the island! It was virtually child abuse!

'But you never told us you were worried about that!' Rose had looked quite upset, as well she should have.

'Oh, for heaven's sake, Rose, we spoiled the child rotten!' Connie hadn't been at all sympathetic.

Margie dreams she is trying to kiss Rotund

Ron in a gondola in Venice, while an extraordinarily good looking Italian gondolier in a red and white striped top makes the gondola rock back and forth so much that they can't get their lips to meet. (The gondolier is doing this because he wants to kiss Margie himself!) They all three find this hilariously funny. Rotund Ron is doing his jolly fatman laugh, even though, of course, he's not a fat man any more, and Margie is giggling uncontrollably like a schoolgirl. She looks down and realises she's wearing her red crochet bikini, and this is so funny she can barely breathe. Tears of mirth stream down her face. She points out her swimming costume to the two men and they gasp and laugh with her.

'You just got a text message!'

Margie opens her eyes. 'What did you say?'

Ron leans up on one elbow and looks down at her with a suspicious, sleep-creased face. 'Your mobile phone just beeped. Someone sent you a text message. Do you want me to show you how to read it? Are you laughing? Why are you laughing?'

'I was having a funny dream.'

'Do you want me to check it for you?'

'It's OK. I know how to check my text messages.' Margie wants to get back to her dream in Venice. 'I'll check it later.'

'Well, who would be sending you a text? I didn't even know you knew how to text.'

He sounds hurt and uncertain. He thinks she's having an affair. Apparently Rotund Ron's wife is suspicious too. Both Margie and Rotund Ron agree that they quite like these wrong-footed versions of their spouses. It's a hoot! Margie compresses her lips to stop herself from giggling. She actually feels a touch tiddly, as if she's been drinking champagne. It must be nerves about tonight, or that dream, that funny dream!

'It's probably one of the kids,' she says. 'They send me text messages all the time.' This is an outright lie. The only person who sends her text messages is Rotund Ron, and this one will be something about the arrangements for tonight. It would never occur to Veronika or Thomas to text their mother. They would assume, like their father, that she wouldn't know how to read one. This is the first fully fledged, blatant lie Margie has ever told in her life, and instead of feeling guilty she feels a rush of exhilaration.

'Really?' Ron lies back down, scratching the top of his head. 'What do they text you about?'

'Oh, just whatever,' says Margie carelessly.

She gets a bit reckless. 'Sometimes Veronika sends me jokes.'

'*Veronika* sends you jokes?'

Margie's lips twitch. 'Yes. Sometimes they're quite funny too.'

There is silence while Ron digests this. Margie rolls over onto her side away from him and secretly runs her hands over her stomach under her nightie. She has 'abs' now. People know she's lost weight but nobody knows about her 'abdominals'. She flexes her legs and caresses her 'quadriceps'. Her body belongs to her again now, like it did when she was a little girl, before she developed curves and hips and that inconvenient bust. She used to wear her bra to bed every night, done up on the tightest clasp, because Laura told her that if she didn't she'd end up with breasts so big they'd be dragging on the ground. She didn't like her breasts. They were arranged by someone else to please boys like Ron Gordon and then to feed her children; they weren't anything to do with skinny, busy Margie McNabb who could turn cartwheels and climb trees with her dad.

And then, when she got fat, her body seemed to have even less to do with her; she was lost in a mountain of chicken-skin flesh. She shudders just thinking about it.

For some reason she hasn't been out yet and bought a whole new wardrobe to reveal just how much her body has changed. She prefers to keep wearing her old clothes, hanging off her and gaping around the waist. She doesn't want to share all the details of her weight loss around just yet, to hear Veronika take credit for it, to hear everyone discuss it and argue about it and make jokes about it.

The ordinary phone rings and Ron bounces upright as if to defend himself from a punch. Oooh, lovers calling from every direction, thinks Margie gleefully. 'Ron Gordon!' he growls, and Margie swallows a guffaw.

'Oh, good morning, Enigma.' Ron relaxes against the headboard. He gives an old-Ron-style smirk. 'Happy Anniversary.'

Margie hears her mother's plaintive voice spilling from the phone. 'Well, my word, Ron, you know perfectly well it's a very unhappy anniversary! Let me talk to Margie!'

Ron goes to hand over the phone but Margie silently, wickedly shakes her head.

'She's in the shower, Enigma. Can she call you back?'

'Thank you,' says Margie after he's hung up. 'She only wants to go on and on about tonight.'

'That's all right.'

It's an oddly courteous exchange. Goodness me, thinks Margie. It's all very strange in the Gordon household today. They lie next to each other in silence, as polite as strangers on a train. I've slept beside this man for over thirty years. I should be more relaxed with him than anybody else in the world, so why is it that I feel so much more like myself when I'm with Rotund Ron, who I've only known for such a short time? Relaxed enough to laugh so hard I do those embarrassing laugh-snorts. Relaxed enough to tell him whatever comes into my mind, without censoring it, without checking first if it's going to make him sneer or sigh. Like the ladybird beetles. I've never told anybody about the ladybird beetles before.

Yesterday she'd told Rotund Ron that whenever a ladybird beetle landed on her hand she liked to think it was a message from her dad, telling her he loved her, and that it was amazing how often, whenever she was feeling especially low, that sure enough an exquisite red and gold beetle would appear from nowhere, tiny wings fluttering. It hasn't even *occurred* to her to ever tell Ron this, even though he was really very fond of Dad and the two of them used to

437

have long, serious chats together about their cars and mileage or something.

'So — are you — disappointed about missing the Anniversary tonight?' asks Ron.

Lordie me! The man is actually asking how she *feels* about something.

She answers noncommittally, briskly, just like he does when asked about anything too personal. 'Not really.'

Ha! Give him a taste of his own medicine.

'Oh,' he answers. 'I thought you enjoyed the Anniversary, that's all.'

Her heart softens slightly. After a few seconds, she says, 'When I was little, every Anniversary morning I used to wake up frightened that Mum and Dad were going to disappear like Alice and Jack.'

She would lie in her bed, her heart thumping. She'd want to run and check if they were still there in their bed, but she was frozen with fear. She couldn't even move a muscle, as if that would set everything in motion. Sometimes it seemed whole lifetimes of paralysed horror passed before her dad would appear at her bedroom door in his striped blue pyjamas, his hair all sticking up, asking if she'd like a cup of tea in bed. The relief of not being abandoned was so enormous she nearly wet her pants each time.

And then, when her own children were little she became morbidly convinced *they* would vanish if she took her eyes off them for a second. She was obsessed with newspaper stories about missing children. Often she wrote letters to their mothers, telling them their child was beautiful and she was praying for them and enclosing a large cheque just in case it could help in any way. One woman in Queensland still writes back to Margie every Christmas, thirty years after her curly haired six-year-old daughter vanished while waiting for the school bus. Margie can see the faces of those missing children from the Sixties, the Seventies, the Eighties, as clearly as if they were her own children. She can remember their names, their mothers' names and what they were wearing when they disappeared. It's the unsolved ones who haunt her the most. It's better when the bodies are found. Aunt Connie always said, 'Unsolved mysteries are the best!' and Margie would want to scream at her, 'Not for the mothers, they're not!'

She has never told anybody about her 'thing' with the missing children. It's between her and their mothers.

Ron clears his throat. He sounds as awkward as a teenage boy on a first date. 'So, were you angry then — when they told you the truth about Alice and Jack?'

Yet another question about feelings! Has he been reading her copy of *Men Are from Mars, Women Are from Venus*?

'I think I already knew, without knowing I knew,' answers Margie. 'I think my subconscious had worked it out. So it wasn't a surprise, really, it was like a confirmation. I didn't feel angry so much as hurt that they felt they had to wait till I was forty to tell me.'

'Yeah. Sure. Right. I can imagine it might have been, ah . . . hurtful.'

Watching Ron try to talk about anything vaguely emotional rather than factual is like watching an uncoordinated man earnestly trying out a few moves on the dance floor. It's both touching and excruciating. There is silence. Margie takes the opportunity to quietly practise her pelvic-floor exercises. She can squeeze her pelvic floor for an impressive eight seconds now, which is not bad for a fifty-five-year-old woman with two children. An interesting thing is that these exercises often make her feel a bit sexy, or 'horny', as they say.

Ron says, 'So, this thing you've got on tonight, this Weight Watchers thing, partners aren't invited, right?'

He has already asked this three times. She

says, 'No, I'm sorry, you can't come tonight.' This new feeling of power is quite delicious. She rolls over to face him and says, hardly able to believe her wantonness, 'But we could arrange for you to come right now if you like.' He stares at her blankly. Oh dear, thinks Margie, did I get the terminology wrong? Doesn't 'come' mean orgasm? I guess I'm as bad at dirty talk as he is at 'feelings' talk! She puts a hand down his pyjama pants and takes a good, firm hold of his penis. His eyes widen in understanding. In all their years of marriage Margie has never, *ever* done such a thing without husbandly guidance. It was always Ron's role to request sex and hers to either acquiesce, or plead tiredness or 'that' time of the month. She's behaving like a real hussy this morning!

He says, rather hoarsely, 'This is unusual.'

A shadow of concern flits across his face and Margie knows he is wondering if she has developed these new habits in another man's bed, but then he obviously decides to think about it later as his eyes roll back in his head comically, like a cartoon character parodying sexual pleasure. Margie pulls her flannelette nightgown over her head, closes her eyes and imagines she is stroking the handsome gondolier's swarthy Italian penis.

And the best thing is, according to her calorie-counter book, an 'active' sexual session can burn as many as four hundred and twenty-five calories.

Grace is flossing her teeth while she stands at the end of the bed, fully dressed, watching Callum sleep. It's a strange feeling to stay awake the whole night while the rest of the world sleeps. It makes her feel tough and edgy. Sleeping seems like a dopey, passive way to spend perfectly good time. She remembers reading somewhere that the average person spends twenty-two years of their life asleep. Year after year after year. How pathetic! Callum's unshaven face is soft and facile. He's been lying there in virtually the same position for hours on end. Meanwhile, Grace has done two loads of laundry and cooked and frozen three more lasagnes. There is not another centimetre of room in the freezer. That will have to do.

The baby has slept through again. He's slept through now for three nights. Sophie won't have any trouble with him.

What will Laura think about this? Grace imagines her mother flinching with disgust. She'll be secretly embarrassed that Grace has done something so publicly emotional. (*Don't be a drama queen, Grace.*) The whole thing will seem messy to her. Grace looks at her fingertips, which are red and raw from cleaning products. Every surface in the house is shimmering and sterile in the early morning light. Of course, by the time Laura gets back Callum will have had free rein of the house for a while, so standards will have plummeted. Sorry, Mum. Did my best. I never did clean anything quite well enough for you anyway. Although I remember I once did quite a good job on the tiles in the spare bathroom. You said, 'You only missed that bit in the corner by the vanity.' How I glowed with pride! What a tender childhood memory. And what about Dad? Dentist Dad. Will he come to my funeral? Will he feel bad that he never even gave his own daughter so much as a check-up, let alone a filling? Will he send a card with a twenty-dollar note in it? *Dear Grace, So sorry to hear you killed yourself, have fun! With love from Dad.*

She grinds the floss against her gums. Her eyes are huge, dry, stinging orbs, like an alien's.

It was seventy-three years ago today that her great-grandmother Alice Munro decided to step free of her life. Veronika's theory about Aunt Connie killing the Munros is manifestly wrong. It was Alice. She knew she couldn't be a good mother to her baby so she took herself out of the picture. The only difference is that she decided to take her husband with her, whereas Grace is leaving Callum with a nice ready-made family.

Although he's sure to be upset at first. He may even grieve. She thinks of Aunt Connie's funeral. There was a moment when she happened to glance over and see Aunt Rose staring at the coffin with such naked anguish that Grace had to look away. Her pain seemed intensely private. It is unbearable to think of Callum suffering like that, to imagine the familiar features of his face distorted and ugly with grief.

But oh God, she has no choice. It will be such a relief to just stop, for good. And in the end he'll be so much happier with Sophie. It will only take a year or two. It's best for him and for Jake. No pain, no gain.

Callum's eyelids twitch as he suddenly senses her presence. 'Bloody hell!' He is instantly wide awake and sitting up, rubbing at his eyes. 'What's the matter? What are you doing there?'

'Flossing,' answers Grace.

Gublet McDublet ticked off the last thing on his LIST OF THINGS TO DO BEFORE

I GO TO THE MOON. He was feeling very happy about going to the moon. He was VERY happy. He was so happy it made him cry. Of course, he could always change his mind at the last minute. Nobody was making him go to the moon. He could change his mind right up until just before he strapped himself into the spaceship.

48

Afterwards, Sophie will always remember the Anniversary Night starting like a sedately moving merry-go-round, with smiling faces and shimmering lights and pretty music, and then gradually, imperceptibly, getting faster and faster until finally it was whirling wildly out of control, a mad, streaky blur of colour and half-glimpses of frantic mouths, which was when she decided she'd like to get off now please because she was feeling sick.

It's six p.m. and Sophie is dressed up in her Fairy Floss Fairy outfit trying to decide whether she looks gorgeous or ludicrous, when her mother rings.

'I think I might be too old for my fairy outfit,' she says, still looking at her reflection in the wardrobe mirror, and waits comfortably for Gretel's soothing cries of protest.

'Well of course you're too old for it!' cries her mother, and Sophie's eyes meet her own in the mirror with surprise. 'Why don't you take off that silly outfit and put on that stunning new green dress you got last week and come to the opera with us? Dad and I will pick you up at the station. You can stay the night. You don't want to be making that terrible long trip back late at night in the cold.'

Months before, Sophie had agreed to go to see *Cosi fan Tutte* with her parents, but it isn't one of her favourite operas and when it turned out to be on the same night as the Anniversary celebrations she'd asked her mother to see if she could give away her ticket. Apparently Pam from Pilates had been delighted to accept.

'I thought Pam from Pilates took my ticket.'

'Well, yes, she did, but I could just tell her it fell through and you wanted to come after all. We'd rather have you than *Pam*. Pam, schmam, I say!'

There is definitely something going on here.

'Well, thanks, Mum, but I don't think I can pull out now at the last minute. It would be a bit rude. Grandma Enigma is already so upset about Margie not being there.'

'Oh, well we don't want to hurt *Grandma*

Enigma's feelings. Is that what you call her now? *Grandma* Enigma! How lovely. I guess you feel like she's your grandmother now. They must be making you feel like you're part of the family. That's lovely.'

'Actually, mostly I just call her Enigma. That was a slip of the tongue really.'

'Of course, you missed out on so much, not having grandparents. So it's lovely that you think of her that way.'

'Well, I don't really think of her that way. And I never missed out on one single thing in life.'

'You did miss out on having a big family. No cousins or aunties or anything. And every Christmas you used to ask Santa Claus for a little sister or brother. I felt so mean for not giving you one. I still feel guilty about that. That's why I think it's lovely the way the Scribbly Gum family has adopted you. When we were there the other week and Margie just dropped in for a cup of tea, I thought, how lovely for Sophie! I admit I did feel a bit embarrassed when she asked you about your sore throat from the night before and I didn't even know you'd *had* one! As I said to her, I obviously would have brought some butter menthols for you if I'd known. She probably thought I was a shocking mother. I hope you haven't ever told her about how we used to smoke around you, have you? She'll get Social Services onto us! Not that she'd do that. She seems like a lovely person.'

'You've used the word "lovely" about forty times now, Mum. I think it means you don't think they're lovely at all.'

'Oh, well, listen to Freud here! You're onto me. I'm *wildly* jealous of your new family.'

'I wouldn't call them my new family, exactly.'

'Oh, I'm only teasing you, darling! I'll see you Tuesday for our manicures. You can still fit me in on Tuesday? I don't mind if you've got something on with Margie or Aunt Rose or *Grandma* Enigma or anything.'

'Of course I wouldn't miss Tuesday.'

'And I'm sure you look absolutely adorable in your dear little Fairy Floss dress.'

Sophie hangs up the phone and goes back to stare at herself in the mirror, tugging irritably at her neckline. She looks like a complete twit. Mutton dressed up as a Fairy Floss Fairy.

She needs to do something about her mother, who is obviously feeling neglected and actually sounded quite snide just then; but really, it's hardly fair of Mum — how many daughters in their thirties talk to their mothers on the phone every single day?

How many daughters join their mothers for fortnightly manicures, monthly facials and cut-and-colours every six weeks? Her mother is spoiled, that's the problem! Of course, Sophie is also spoiled. They've spoiled each other. 'You should be thankful you've only got a small family,' Claire was always telling Sophie. 'You've never had to endure emotional blackmail from your mother. Mothers specialise in it. I spend half my life feeling guilty.'

It turns out that Gretel can do emotional blackmail with the best of them. Sophie feels rather proud of her. She'll have to tell Claire that her family isn't quite so lovey-dovey after all. That fairytale façade hides conflict — issues! They're dysfunctional! Next they'll be on Jerry Springer throwing chairs at each other.

Sophie treats herself to two Turkish delight chocolates from her emergency stash next to the bed. As the familiar sweetness fills her mouth she looks at herself in the mirror and wriggles her shoulders so her glittery wings flap. She looks OK. She looks cute! The children will love it. Also, her cleavage is quite impressive. At least one of her suitors, Rick or Ian (Callum?), is sure to be weak-kneed with lust when they see her. It's true that this may indicate questionable tendencies, but still, she's been celibate for so long she'll take it any way she can get it. She lifts her pink satin skirts and hurries down the spiral staircase. She has to meet Aunt Rose to get her face painted.

Grace pushes Jake in his stroller down the main street of the island, breathing in the smells of cold air and wood-smoke, popcorn and mulled wine. Once, she and Callum were skiing in America when they walked into a bar and Grace sniffed and said, 'I just got a whiff of Anniversary Night.' After all these years of bigger and better innovations it still seems to have exactly the same fragrance it had when she and Veronika and Thomas would run wild for the night, acting like little royals and telling the other children it was *their* island and they'd better be off it by midnight or the ghosts of Alice and Jack Munro would eat them for dinner. Of course, then came their teenage years when they would just lope around looking superior and sullen and sneaking off for illicit cigarettes. One year, Veronika decided that the whole concept of the Anniversary was disgusting and disrespectful. How could they celebrate the deaths, possibly the murders, of their great-grandparents? The three of them had worn black and held a private wake for Alice and Jack on the beach at Sultana Rocks. They'd held torches under their chins and chanted incantations that Veronika had written. Aunt Connie had discovered them and laughed, which had wounded their pride, and then she had apologised, which had confused them.

It feels wrong having the Anniversary Night without Aunt Connie.

But it seems like everything is going smoothly. Margie hasn't left anything to chance. The fairy lights are on and sparkling. The island staff, who, after all, know the drill pretty well after all these years, are standing to attention behind the food-laden trestle tables which line the street. The performers are limbering up and checking their equipment. The tarot-card reader is sitting behind her table shuffling her cards. At the end of the street is a big stage and Callum's jazz band are tuning up their instruments. This is the third year they've played for the Anniversary. They were a big hit the first year, and Callum was so touchingly chuffed when Aunt Connie told him The Snazzy Jazzies was the best band they'd ever had for the Anniversary. There will be a jukebox afterwards and Callum will be giving dance lessons. He thinks rock 'n' roll, or swing, he's going to see what the crowd is like. She watches Callum's familiar body made strange by distance. He's such a good man. Kind and funny and fundamentally good all the way through. Not like Grace, who has a secret rancid core, who is capable of thinking terrible thoughts, who if somebody bumps into her in the shopping centre will sometimes horrify herself by screaming silent obscenities, DON'T FUCKING TOUCH ME! It's probably only the constraints of society that curtail her capacity for unspeakable cruelty. She should never have been allowed to be a mother. She should have been sterilised.

Early guests are starting to arrive, spilling off the extra ferries that will be running all night. Grace looks at the faces of the families walking by, flushed with excitement and probably too many clothes. They're all obediently dressed in parkas and beanies, as if they're in the Snowy Mountains, not Scribbly Gum Island.

'Excuse me?' A beaming female face swims into focus. A woman has touched her on the arm and Grace is disconcerted, as though someone on television waved at her. She feels so remote from the world, from normal people, she thought she was invisible.

'Do you know where we go for the face-painting?' asks the woman.

'Actually, I'm one of the face-painters,' answers Grace. 'We'll be setting up in about half an hour.'

'FAIRY FLOSS!' shrieks the little boy. Grace sees Sophie in her fairy outfit, surrounded by children, laughing as she swirls floaty fairy floss around a stick from her tub. Sophie is shimmery-pink and pure. She is another good person. A dear little sunflower. A sweet little sugar-cube. A sunny little honey. The perfect match for Callum.

Sophie hands an impatient child a stick of fairy floss and sees Grace walk by, pushing the baby in his stroller. She's all in black. Black jeans. Black jumper. Her hair is out, hanging straight down her back, and it looks very blonde. As she gets closer Sophie sees the impatient child's father's eyes drawn to her, flicking up and down her body. He sees that Sophie has caught him looking and says, half-apologetically, half-leering, 'That's what I call a Yummy Mummy!' Why is he talking to Sophie like she's a bloody mate in a pub? She gives her most charming smile and says, 'And that's what I call a Sleazy Daddy!' He chuckles uncertainly and drags his son away by the elbow.

'Free fairy floss?' offers Sophie brightly to

the man who appears to be next in line. He's not dressed as warmly as all the other guests. He's wearing jeans and a yellow surfy sort of T-shirt. He looks about fifty, with a paunchy stomach, stubbled jaw and an earring.

'Not exactly free, is it?' he says. 'Not when you've paid seventy-five bucks a ticket.'

Sophie notices that he is carrying some sort of elaborate vase shoved under one armpit. Has he stolen it from one of their houses?

'Well, everything is included in your ticket price,' says Sophie. 'Would you like some?'

'Can't stand the stuff. Rots your teeth.'

Aren't you the charmer, thinks Sophie, smiling beatifically.

'I'm looking for someone called Veronika Gordon,' he says. 'I've got a business appointment with her.'

Oh goodness, he's the *Kook*! Everyone has been talking about this man who responded to Veronika's ad about Alice and Jack in the paper. They'll all be delighted to see how unsavoury he looks, which will confirm their suspicions. Grandma Enigma has declared that she intends to give him a good piece of her mind. 'But what if he really does have information about Alice and Jack?' Sophie had asked. 'Well, I can assure you, he doesn't,' Enigma had said. 'He's a con-man. Ooh it makes my blood boil!'

'Veronika will be here somewhere,' says Sophie. 'But I don't know where. Are you sure I can't offer you any fairy floss?'

'If you see her, will you tell her I'm looking for her?' says the Kook. He turns and glares down at a little girl who is sighing loudly and elaborately behind him.

'Well, you're taking too long!' says the little girl, unperturbed. 'People are waiting for their fairy floss!'

'Where are your manners?' asks the Kook, suddenly looking just like a baffled grandparent, and he wanders back into the crowd, clutching his vase.

Grace is already painting her tenth child with a blue and silver face inspired by Gublet McDublet. She's painting the boys, while beside her Aunt Rose gives the girls pink and gold 'Melly the Music Box Dancer' faces.

It had been Rose's idea to give the children Gublet and Melly faces this year, in honour of Grace's books. Grace had pretended to think it was a wonderful idea. No need to mention that Gublet hadn't been himself lately.

Grace always paints the boys because it's

harder work keeping them still. She keeps a firm hand clamped on their heads and whispers that they need to sit very still or else she's liable to accidentally poke out their eyeballs. The boys like this sort of talk and give her respectful, masculine looks.

'There you go! All done!' Grace holds up a mirror in front of a grumpy six-year-old. His eyes widen as he sees his own transformed face in the mirror. 'But I want to be a scary lion!'

'Next please,' says Grace, ignoring the child's mother, who is smiling fondly under the mistaken impression that Grace finds her child as adorable as she does.

Grace can see that Aunt Rose is already drooping. She's painting much slower than usual, even with the standard 'fast-track' design. The face-painting queue is snaking all the way down the road. Dozens and dozens of squirmy, whiny, often quite remarkably snotty children. 'Why don't we ask Mummy to blow that nose?' shudders Grace as the next little boy takes the stool in front of her.

At least Grandma Enigma doesn't seem to be having any trouble minding the baby. She is sitting right next to one of the gas heaters in a comfy chair with the baby on her lap, under a sign that says *MEET THE*

MUNRO BABY — SCRIBBLY GUM'S "ENIGMA"!', graciously signing autographs and allowing people to be photographed with her. When Grace had gone over to check on them, Grandma Enigma was using Jake as a handy prop for her performances, telling people that this was her great-grandson and isn't it amazing that she was a baby just like this little darling when her parents vanished into thin air seventy-three years ago today.

'Are you OK, Aunt Rose?' says Grace, as her little boy gives a horrendously loud sniff. 'Shall I get one of the girls to bring you another cup of tea?'

'I'm fine, darling,' says Rose. 'My back hurts a bit. Next year I think we should employ other people to do the face-painting and we'll just supervise. Sophie says that's called "source out" or something like that, and it's very fashionable and fun. Are *you* OK, Grace? Happy?'

'I'm happy.'

She is happy, she realises. She has that euphoric feeling you get at the airport after you've checked in your luggage. Nothing can stop your journey. You've started sliding down the slippery dip. You're going away and leaving all your problems far, far behind. There's nothing more to do.

49

Every now and then there is a flurry of demand, but for the most part being the Fairy Floss Fairy doesn't require much effort. Sophie smiles at the people walking by, waves her wand in what she hopes is an authentically magical manner and enjoys the entertainment — the stalking stilt-walkers, the leaping-about jugglers, the garishly grinning clowns. She can see Rick the Gorgeous Gardener doing his fire-eating performance from where she stands, and it's all very primeval and arousing. He's wearing a sort of Aladdin's Cave–style vest over a bare chest and his muscly arms look impressive in the firelight as he throws back his head and lowers the flaming stick into his mouth. The watching crowd roars with approval, but Sophie wants to call out, 'Oh stop that, you'll *burn* yourself!'

It's much more relaxing to watch Callum's band. They're very good: three tall guys, one playing saxophone (who strongly reminds her of somebody but she can't be bothered working out who), one playing drums, and Callum on double bass. The music is sexy and mellow and Sophie has to keep dragging her eyes away from Callum.

It's just that it's more appealing to watch a man play an instrument than shove fire down his throat.

It's just that she has a terrible crush, which won't go away.

What would have happened if she'd just kissed him in that steamy bathroom last night? Would he have reeled back in disgust? *Excuse me, why would I want to kiss a hobbit like you with my beautiful wife in another room? Yes, but honey, sweetheart, darling, your beautiful wife is going to leave you any day now. And I sort of love you.* Oh stop it. You do NOT. You do not, you do not. Not even close. She swirls her fairy floss and feels a bit sick. Think about your potential new boyfriends, unencumbered by wives and children. She looks back to Rick the Gardener, his teeth white in the firelight. He is, truth be told, the sexiest man she has ever dated. That kiss on the picnic! It was extraordinary! And of course, kissing Ian the Solicitor in his plush, new-car-smelling Lexus, breathing in his expensive aftershave, had been very enjoyable too. Both of them are much more eligible — and, in fact, better looking — than big, messy Callum. Oh, but it's Callum she wants to kiss. She wants to kiss him very, very, *very* badly. She needs to kiss him. It's a need, not a want.

She is thirty-nine years old, wearing a fairy costume and thinking about kissing boys. She has definitely regressed. It is imperative that she has proper, grown-up sex in a bed, with a sensible-brand condom and a nice, friendly, middle-aged man, very soon. She was thinking more mature thoughts when she was twenty.

'Sophie!'

It's Veronika. Sophie feels her muscles flex involuntarily. 'Hi!'

But Veronika looks different. Her hair seems fluffier, her face softer and rounder, less manic. She's with an attractive dark-haired girl wearing a cream-coloured jumper. They're holding hands.

They're holding hands.

Holy Moly.

'Sophie! This is Audrey! Audrey, this is Sophie, who I told you about! Sophie, this is Audrey, my *girlfriend,* Audrey.' Veronika looks triumphant and expectant, her cheeks flushed.

'It's nice to meet you, Audrey,' says

461

Sophie. HOLY . . . MOLY!

'My *girlfriend,* Audrey,' repeats Veronika.

Sophie waves her wand graciously. She is her mother's daughter; she can handle an unexpected change in sexual orientation no problem at all. 'Can I offer you both some fairy floss?'

'Mmmmm, fairy floss! Yes please,' says Audrey.

'Did you hear what I said?' Veronika swings Audrey's hand. 'Audrey is my girl-friend. My *lover.*'

'I think she gets it, Veronika,' says Audrey.

'I get it, Veronika.' Sophie smiles at Audrey and hands her an extra-large stick of floss.

'It turns out that I am Gay,' announces Veronika impressively.

'Yes, you are, sweetie.' Audrey throws an arm around Veronika and vigorously pats her arm. 'Yes, you are.'

Veronika looks aggrieved. 'Well, you don't seem very surprised, Sophie. I was! Although, at the same time, I wasn't. It was like I knew it but didn't know it, if you know what I mean. I blame my repressive middle-class upbringing, obviously.'

'I'm really happy for you,' says Sophie honestly. In fact, this isn't actually all that unexpected, now she thinks about it. She wonders why she never considered the possibility before.

'I'm not just *experimenting,* if that's what you're thinking,' says Veronika. 'You're probably thinking I'm bisexual. Is that what you're thinking, that I'm bisexual?'

'Ah — no?'

'No! I'm not at all! Bisexuals are like agnostics, trying to have it both ways. My sexuality isn't in question. I have fully embraced my homosexuality.'

Sophie realises that her reaction isn't up to scratch. She understands it's annoying when people don't gasp for long enough over an unexpected event in your life. You're still shaking your head, 'I can't believe this has happened to *me*!' while they've already fully accepted it and moved on to something surprising in their own life: 'Gosh, your car was stolen, what a bummer, did I tell you the doctor thinks I might have *dislocated* my shoulder from lifting that box? I couldn't believe it!'

So she shakes her head in wonder and says, 'Well, this is quite a bombshell. I'm in shock. I'm *dumbfounded.*'

Veronika looks slightly mollified. 'Well, but, why aren't you blushing? I was sure you'd blush! I told Audrey not to be surprised and that your blush was a disorder and it didn't mean you were prejudiced against the gay community. I mean, obviously we have to deal with a lot of discrimination, just in everyday life. We're used to that. Comes with the territory.' Veronika looks noble. 'I've joined the Glass Bay Gay Rights Association, obviously.'

'Obviously,' murmurs Audrey into her fairy floss.

'Gay rights have got a long way to go. A *long* way to go. I mean — it's ridiculous! We can't even legally get married in our own country!'

'Steady on, girl.' Audrey lifts a comical eyebrow.

'Oh!' Veronika looks suddenly, endearingly embarrassed, even shy. 'Not that we're talking about marriage at this early — um — stage of our relationship. Obviously. I mean, you know, not yet.'

Why don't you get us a few glasses of that mulled wine I can smell in the air?' suggests Audrey. 'Sophie could probably do with a drink. I don't know why she has to work when you're not doing anything!'

'Because she's crazy!' says Veronika, recovering. 'I stopped helping out with the Anniversary Night years ago. I don't actually approve of celebrating murder. I'll go check out the mulled wine. Last year it was much too sweet.'

'Oh, Veronika,' says Sophie, remembering. 'The Kook is here, looking for you! The one who responded to your ad about Alice and Jack. He's walking around carrying some sort of vase, wearing a yellow T-shirt.'

Veronika doesn't look especially interested. 'I'm sure he'll find me. I might actually have to put the Munro Mystery book on hold for a while. I've got a lot of other projects I'm more interested in. I'm very busy, you know.' She walks briskly off, looking fierce and joyful. Sophie and Audrey watch her go and then look back at each other.

'I've never seen her so happy,' says Sophie. 'You must be good for her.'

Audrey tears off a piece of fairy floss and rubs it thoughtfully between her fingers into a sticky pink ball. 'You do know she was in love with you?'

'I beg your pardon?' says Sophie, and now the blush does come, engulfing her face. Because it makes perfect sense. That's why Veronika was always so possessive. If a male friend had behaved like that Sophie would have guessed it immediately and been tender and careful with him. She feels guilty and silly and somehow horribly hetero, shallow and suburban, as if she should have known and her own parochial prejudices didn't let her see it, as if she'd subconsciously encouraged and at the same time repelled Veronika's affections.

'I'm sorry, I didn't mean to embarrass you,' says Audrey. 'I could just tell the way she talked about you so much that she was a bit mixed up about you. I think she's over you now, anyway. I sure hope she is.'

'Oh, I'm sure she is!' Sophie knows her face is incandescent. She watches Audrey trying not to stare as the blush takes hold. It's a bad one. Blotches of burning colour sting her neck like an attack of hives.

'It's OK!' Audrey seems to have developed a sudden intense interest in the band's performance. 'I should never have said anything. I was just a bit jealous, I think. It's a failing of mine, and I really like Veronika. She's gorgeous. Like a porcupine. Spiky but cuddly. I just feel like, maybe this time I've finally got it right. Anyway, I can see why she likes you.'

'Thank you.' Sophie's composure returns. She saves up 'spiky but cuddly' for Callum and Grace. 'I can see why she likes you too.'

'Ha! Now you're blushing!' crows Veronika as she returns holding three large glasses of mulled wine. 'Is it a delayed reaction or what? It's OK, Audrey, you don't need to

466

pretend to look away. Sophie isn't *embarrassed* by her blushing.'

Sophie accepts the glass of wine thankfully. 'Veronika thinks of my blushing as a sort of party trick.' She takes a sip of her wine. 'Oh, this is fantastic!'

Veronika sniffs. 'Mmmm. Not bad. Too much lemon, not enough nutmeg. Anyway, come on, Audrey. I want you to meet my Grandma Enigma. Don't be surprised if she drops dead on the spot when she hears. Oh — and wait till I tell Dad! Dad will have cardiac arrest. He'll have a *stroke.*'

'You know, you don't have to tell everyone tonight.' Audrey looks panicky. 'There's no rush. You can wait for the right time.'

'No time like the present.' Veronika is already marching off, arms pumping. 'Bye, Sophie!'

'Oh God.' Audrey shrugs helplessly at Sophie and hands over her mug of wine. 'Here. Take this.' They disappear into the crowd.

It seems that Veronika won't be content with merely coming out of the closet, she's *leaping* out.

The pain in Rose's back has got so bad it feels deliberate. Malicious. It hurts her feelings. As though someone has just taken a plank of wood and violently slammed it against her lower back.

She takes a deep breath. The line of little girls waiting for their 'Melly the Music Box Dancer' faces is finally starting to dwindle. Grace has finished all the boys and is helping her out with the girls.

I'm really too old to still be doing the children's face-painting. I'm eighty-eight years old. I should be in a rocking chair with a blanket over my knees and people bringing me cups of tea. *Mum, don't you think I'm too old for this now!* Her mother had died a few weeks before Rose's fifteenth birthday, but ever since Connie died Rose has found herself missing her mother with fresh, childish grief. *My back really hurts, Mum. It's called rheumatoid arthritis. My doctor tells me to think happy thoughts. I'm afraid I thought rather a rude word. You died before you turned forty so you missed out on all the fun of getting old. Oh it's a lark, Mum.* Rose can feel the back of her mother's cool hand against her forehead. *My poor Rosie.*

She dips her paintbrush deep in pale pink and tries to smile at the little girl sitting quietly in front of her, chubby legs sticking out, hands resting obediently on her knees.

'Excuse me, excuse me!' Rose looks up from her painting to see a young fellow of

468

about Ron's age carrying some strange sort of urn and wearing a yellow short-sleeved T-shirt *without a jacket.*

Rose is appalled. 'You must be freezing! We must find another jacket for you.' The little girl looks up and solemnly informs the man, 'I'm wearing *two* pairs of socks to keep my toes extra toasty.'

'Well, I don't feel the cold,' says the man in that irritable, overly formal way of men who feel foolish talking to children. 'I've never felt the cold. Excuse me. I wanted to ask you if you know where I can find Veronika Gordon. I've been looking for her all night. People keep telling me I've just missed her. She seems to move very fast.'

'Well, you have just missed her again actually, and yes, she does move fast. Her grandfather used to call her Speedy Gonzales.' Veronika had been by with a pretty Asian girl with long, shiny dark hair. Veronika had told Rose she was feeling gay and Rose said that was lovely and she was feeling quite gay herself, even though she wasn't really because her back was hurting so much, but it was so nice to see Veronika in a good mood, instead of her normal agitated state. Then the two girls had giggled a lot about something and Veronika had given Rose a kiss on the cheek, which was also unusual for her and had made Rose feel teary.

'Look, I had an arrangement to meet this Veronika. I've got important information for her.' He pats the urn he is holding under his arm.

Rose doesn't like his tone. Suddenly she knows who he is: The Kook! 'What sort of information?' she says carefully.

'Information relating to the disappearance of Alice and Jack Munro.'

She gives him a steely look. 'I'm Rose Doughty. My sister and I found the Munro baby. I'd be very interested to hear this information. Very interested indeed.'

'I bet you would,' says the Kook. 'Because you two sure made bucket-loads of money from that little find, didn't you? Quite an operation you've got going here.' He looks around with contempt and distractedly rubs his arms, even though he supposedly doesn't feel the cold. 'You've done very well out of all this, haven't you?'

Rose can feel her heart vibrating with an old familiar terror, an ancient shame. She presses a hand to her chest. Oh for heaven's sake! This is such nonsense! She's not a teenager any more. Suddenly she is furious with Connie. It was all her idea! Her bloody idea! Rose wanted to tell everyone when Enigma was six, back in *1938*. But no, oh no, it all had to be done Connie's way. It always had to be done Connie's way, and sometimes she was *wrong!*

The Kook says, 'Anyway, it's this Veronika I've got an arrangement with, so I'll keep trying to hunt her down.' He crouches down so that he's at eye-level with Rose. He has surprisingly nice brown eyes. 'By the way, I know *exactly* what you two did.'

'We found a baby,' says Rose. She can hear herself sounding like a tremulous old woman. 'That's all we did.'

'Yeah. Good one.' The Kook bounces back up on his feet and disappears into the crowd.

'Oops-a-daisy!' cries the little girl with delight, as Rose's elbow knocks her paint palette flying, so that pink paint and silver glitter slosh all over the little girl's warmly clad legs.

Ron isn't quite sure what to do with himself. What does he normally do on Anniversary Nights when Margie is around? He can't remember. Years ago, when the kids were young, he always did the sausage sizzle. The Anniversary Nights weren't quite this glitzy back then. It seems to him that it was more fun in the Seventies. He and Laura's husband, Simon, used to cook up hundreds of sausages, stick them in bread rolls with a bit of tomato, lettuce and Margie's chutney sauce. Went down a treat. They drank a lot of beer and mucked around. Margie was always in a flap, running back and forth like a headless chook trying to keep Connie happy, while Laura just lounged around smoking cigarettes, looking sultry. Ron used to tease Margie, and Simon would say to Laura, 'Why don't you help your poor sister?' but Laura would just ignore him and tilt back her head and blow smoke rings. She didn't actually seem to *like* Simon that much; Ron remembers thinking, I'm glad Margie doesn't ignore me like that. So it was strange the way Laura reacted to Simon running off with his dental nurse. She never seemed to get over it, and every year those bitter lines of disappointment on either side of her mouth were carved deeper and deeper. Ron had missed Simon when he left and secretly felt let down by him. As if the life that was good enough for Ron wasn't good enough for Simon.

Everything was different then. With more blokes on the island it was more balanced, more normal. He misses Margie and Laura's dad too. Good old Nat, with his sweet, simple way of looking at things. And Jimmy, of course, who had a more complicated way of viewing the world and sometimes said something that really made you think. Ron is the last man standing. (Callum doesn't count — he's up there now on stage looking like a right twat plucking away at the strings of some sort of giant guitar. Ron doesn't trust men who play instruments, except for the drums.) The island hasn't exactly fallen apart without the men. As Ron walks aimlessly down the main street, watching the guests happily munching on gourmet pita-fucking-pockets or something or other, getting their tarot cards read, shelling out more money to have their photograph taken with the Munro Baby (Enigma smiling at the camera as if she's royalty) it occurs to him that this is a pretty slick event and it was his wife who organised the whole damned thing. A few weeks ago, Ron had been involved with a product launch coordinated by an 'Event Planner', a blonde in a suit who kept snapping open and shut her mobile phone, running pointy-tipped fingers through her hair and looking harried and important. That 'event' had been on a much smaller scale with a lot fewer people, but it had seemed to cause a lot more problems. Yet Margie, who certainly does not have a university degree in event planning, who did a year's worth of secretarial college when she was sixteen, had organised this whole thing, managed all the staff, organised stuff like sound equipment, without making a fuss at all. He would hear her chatting away on the phone to people, talking about their babies and their hay fever and their holidays, sounding like she wasn't doing a thing but passing the time of day, when in fact she was *running a business.*

And Ron feels a sudden painful surge of pride. That 'Event Planner' could learn a thing or two from his wife.

Ron stops to watch the fire-eating performance. It's the guy who does the gardening on the island. Bit of a blockhead. No doubt the women like him. He's well built. Probably works out every day. Ron puts a hand to his stomach. A bit flabby. He sucks it in and squares his shoulders. Maybe he needs to go to the gym himself. He thinks about the sex this morning. It was great. It was bloody great. But who *was* that woman? She sure as hell didn't act like his wife. Not even the Margie of years ago, when they were at it all the time. Ron was always the one who set the pace when it came to sex, but this morning . . . Thinking about it, Ron feels aroused and simultaneously panicked. What does it mean? What the fuck has she

474

been doing? Her body didn't feel the same either. It felt firmer, stronger. She'd lost more weight than he'd realised. She looked good. She looked bloody good.

He didn't really like it.

And tonight, when she was getting ready to go to this Weight Watchers party, she'd been excited, nervous, breathless — as if she were going on a *date*! She had her hair all pulled back to show off her new skinny cheekbones and she was wearing her diamond earrings and the perfume he'd got her duty-free on his last trip to Singapore. He'd asked again if he could go along and keep her company but she'd insisted that partners weren't invited and laughed sort of *kindly* at him, and then, as she was leaving, he thought he'd heard her phone beeping again with another text message.

If some other man had been touching his wife's body he would . . . he would . . .

'Dad! You look like you're having a panic attack!'

It's Veronika, sparky and glittery and dancing around him like a boxer.

'Veronika!' Suddenly he is feverish for information. He grabs her arm. 'Do you send text messages to your mother? Did you text her this morning?'

Veronika rolls her eyes. 'No, Dad, I guess

I didn't, seeing as I don't have a mobile phone, seeing as I don't believe in mobile phones, seeing as I know for a fact that they cause deadly brain tumours. I've read all the research. It's just like smoking and the tobacco companies. There's a massive cover-up going on. I've told you all this before. You don't listen. Anyway, Dad, I've got something to tell you. I want you to meet my friend Audrey. My girlfriend, Audrey.'

Ron drops Veronika's arm and stares at her but right through her. *Margie told him a lie.* But Margie is incapable of lying. She'd tried to organise a surprise party for him once and he'd been onto it within seconds. And on her fortieth birthday, when she'd learned the truth about Alice and Jack, she had been distraught. 'How am I going to live a lie?' she'd asked him, after she told him the true story, which she was allowed to do apparently because they'd been married for twenty years, so it was OK according to the Law of Connie, after he'd signed a confidentiality agreement, of course.

If Margie had lied it could only mean one thing. She's having an affair. His wife is having an affair at a Weight Watchers party right now. But wait a sec, there probably is no party! That's what people do when they're having affairs. They make stuff up! She's probably in a hotel! In a *Jacuzzi*! Drinking champagne with some hairy-chested dickhead, probably in *real estate*! And champagne goes straight to her head! And she'd be impressed if he told her it was Moët, when it was probably Great fucking Western! And she could be doing anything. She could be . . . she could be . . . Ron shudders with violent revulsion.

'Dad?'

Veronika swims back into view. 'I know it's a shock,' she says kindly.

She knows about the affair! She feels sorry for her humiliated father!

Ron clutches again at her arm. 'So you know everything? She's told you all about it? OK. Fine. I can deal with that. Just tell me where she is.'

Veronika's face scrunches up with irritated confusion. 'Tell you where who is?'

'Your mother, of course!'

'I don't know where Mum is, Dad. She told me she had to go to some function with her Weight Watchers friend. Oh God, this is just so *typical*. I'm trying to tell you something important. I'm trying to introduce you to my *girlfriend,* Audrey.'

The girl sticks out her hand and Ron shakes it. 'Nice to meet you, Audrey,' he says automatically. 'I'm sorry, I have to call my wife right now. There's a family crisis.'

He pulls out his mobile phone and begins to dial. 'I'm sorry,' he says again distractedly to Veronika, who has her hands on her hips, her mouth slightly open and that familiar expression of disgusted disappointment.

'Oh for Pete's *sake*!' Veronika grabs her friend's hand and drags her off into the crowd.

Margie's phone begins to ring and Ron presses his mobile to his ear with a clenched sweaty fist.

Rick has finished his fire-eating performance and has come over to see Sophie. His hair is sweatily tousled, his chest very wide. Sophie wonders if Veronika has really thought this lesbian thing through.

He says, 'You look beautiful.'

'Well, you look extremely sexy,' says Sophie. She has now had two glasses of deliciously good mulled wine and is feeling buoyant and slightly in love with everybody. 'Do you have a horrible taste in your mouth from all that fire-eating? Do you want some fairy floss?'

'No thanks. I've been wanting to talk to you. I came around yesterday but you weren't there.'

Sophie gives him a flirtatious look through her eyelashes and is conscious of her cleavage. Her heart lifts. She doesn't know why she's even been worrying about this. Rick is perfect for her. Her body knows it. Her heart knows it. Her mind knows it. He is the one. She is definitely, absolutely going to sleep with him tonight and it's going to be damned good. It will be the beginning of a whirlwind romance with sex, sex, sex, and talking till dawn and walks on the beach in chunky jumpers and frolicking in parks throwing Frisbees, and she'll be pregnant just in time for her fortieth birthday.

'I'm here now,' she smiles, and gives her wand a provocative flick. 'How can I help you? Need me to perform a spell on you?'

'It's a bit awkward. I just thought I should tell you that I've got back with my ex-girlfriend.'

OH, FOR HEAVEN'S SAKE!!!

Sophie lets her wand drop. She's going to remember that wand-flicking, eyelash-batting performance and cringe for the rest of her life.

'Oh, I see,' she says. She pauses. 'I suppose I could turn her into a frog.'

He grins ruefully. 'I should have told you when we went out that I'd only recently come out of a relationship, but I didn't want you to think I was one of those guys with all this baggage, and I really thought we were over for good. But then she sent me an email the other night and we just started being honest with each other about our feelings.'

Please excuse me while I vomit into my fairy floss.

'I'm sorry,' continues Rick. 'I had a great time with you the other day. It's just that I was with her for years and I can't turn my back on that.'

Sophie gives him a radiant smile. 'Of course you can't! I understand. Absolutely. I hope things work out for you.'

'Yeah, well, I really want to make a go of it, tie the knot, you know, all that boring stuff, settle down, be a dad. I'm ready for all that.'

He's ready to be a dad. It's hurting Sophie's face to smile. 'That's great, Rick, really. Hey, do you think you could get me another one of those mulled wines?'

Just when he thinks it's going to voicemail, she answers the phone.

'Hello?'

Except it's not Margie, it's a man's voice. It's *him.* He has a deep, salesy, I've-got-money-and-a-big-dick voice. He is definitely in real estate. He probably wears a gold bracelet and carries a man-bag. Ron feels like his head is about to explode.

Ron says, with considerable difficulty, 'Who is this?'

The bloke answers, 'This is Ron. Who's this?'

RON? '*This* is Ron!' roars Ron.

The bloke chuckles. 'Oh. Good name, mate.'

Ron speaks through grimly gritted teeth. 'Do you want to explain why you're answering my wife's phone?'

'Margie is just getting dressed. Do you want me to get her?'

Now his head does explode. 'ARE YOU FOR FUCKING REAL?'

'Oh, darling, you are *not*!' says Enigma. 'Stop being silly.'

Enigma is feeling snappy. Nobody has brought her anything to eat, except for that sandwich, which was hours ago; Margie really did go out tonight, which Enigma didn't truly believe was going to happen right until the last minute; the baby is starting to get all tetchy and squirmy — and where is his mother for heaven's sake, there has been no sign of Grace for ages; and now here is Veronika announcing, quite loudly, that she is one of those homosexuals. Enigma has no problems with those homosexuals in general. They seem like decent, kind people and they dress beautifully. She just doesn't like it when they flaunt their funny ways in public, such as that awful Mardi Gras. It's not necessary. People can do what they like in the privacy of their own homes. *However,* it is quite ridiculous to think that her granddaughter is one of them. Besides which, she thought it was only the men who were the homosexuals. Why does Veronika have to be such a tomboy?

Enigma smiles politely at the Japanese girl who seems to have given Veronika these ridiculous ideas and does her best to set her straight. 'It's just that we don't do that sort of thing in our family, dear.'

'Don't be so rude, Grandma!' cries Veronika.

'Well, we *don't,* Veronika!' Enigma is incensed. She has just made a real effort to be polite to this Japanese girl, especially when you consider that one of Enigma's loveliest boyfriends during the war was a POW in a Japanese concentration camp and came back all skinny and miserable and not at all lively any more!

The Japanese girl says, 'It's OK, Veronika.

Let's talk about this another time.' She says to Enigma, 'Is that your great-grandson you've got there?'

'Yes, this is little Jake.' Enigma immediately holds out the baby hopefully. 'Would you like a hold of him, dear? My arms are aching.'

'Oh, Grandma, Audrey isn't here to help you babysit!' says Veronika, but the girl takes Jake, which is a relief for Enigma's poor arms.

'So, you're from Japan, Audrey?' asks Enigma socially.

Veronika huffs and puffs while Audrey says, 'My parents are Malaysian actually, but I was born here.'

'Oh, well, Malaysia!' Enigma tries to think of something nice to say about Malaysia. Didn't Laura used to make quite a nice beef dish from Malaysia?

But just then a very unattractive, underdressed man comes charging out of the crowd and grabs Veronika's elbow. 'Are you Veronika Gordon? I've been looking for you all night! I've got information about the Munro Baby.'

Aha! It's the Kook! Enigma is delighted to have the opportunity to give this silly fellow a piece of her mind. 'I am the Munro Baby sitting right here in front of you,' she says firmly. 'I'm afraid you are a con-man, young man, and goodness me, you're not dressed nearly warmly enough!'

Sophie looks at her watch. They say that the time it takes to recover from a relationship is half its length, and she dated Rick the Gorgeous Gardener for approximately three hours, so by her calculations she has approximately twenty more minutes of grieving left to do. She takes another mouthful of her mulled wine. It really is the best mulled wine she has ever had in her entire life. It gives her a warm spicy glow right at the centre of her chest, which is now spreading to her knees. She tries to identify the red wine they've used. Definitely a Shiraz.

She probes tentatively at her heart. Yep, she's over him. Ahead of time! The man was entirely inappropriate. They were completely incompatible. He didn't 'especially like eating out'! He got up at six a.m. and did yoga each morning! How irritating. He was a *vegetarian*! She couldn't stand vegetarians. Clearly, he wasn't the 'young man' mentioned in Aunt Connie's letter. He was a red herring. A vegetarian red-herring. Now, where is that Ian the Sweet Solicitor? He's meant to be dropping by tonight. Sophie has always had a very clear, very definite preference for Ian. *Could it be that Aunt Connie had a premonition that Grace was going to leave Callum and she actually meant . . . ? It wasn't beyond the realms of possibility, was it? Oh, yes, Sophie, Connie was really hoping that Grace and Callum's marriage would break up just after they'd had a new baby. I'm sure she would have approved of that. Definitely. Good one. You THIRTY-NINE-YEAR-OLD LOSER.*

'Sophie! Hi!'

It's Thomas and Deborah, and baby Lily in a stroller — a stern message from the cosmos about thinking of breaking up happy families, when you could have been the mummy in this one and you let the chance go because you thought you could do so much better. The three of them are wearing matching raspberry-coloured jumpers. Lily is an adorable munchkin with creamy skin and huge chocolatey eyes. Looking at her, Sophie experiences one of those unexpectedly painful bursts of longing and regret that makes her dig her nails into the palms of her hands. *Stuffed it up, buttercup.*

'Well, hello there! Let me get you all some fairy floss,' says Sophie.

'Oh, no, Lily is much too young for fairy floss!' Deborah leaps in front of Lily's

485

stroller with arms outspread to save her child's life.

'Gosh, just in the nick of time,' says Sophie. 'I was about to ram it down her throat.'

Thomas, Deborah and Lily all stare blankly at her, and Sophie laughs merrily to try and make it sound like that was a clever witticism rather than the bitter barb of a childless ex-girlfriend.

'How are you, Sophie?' asks Thomas stiffly. 'All settled in to the house?'

'Yes, I am. I'm very happy.' She overdoes the charm trying to make up for her earlier remark. 'I'm so grateful to Aunt Connie. I'm very . . . blessed.'

Blessed? Where did she unearth such a word? She sounds like a middle-aged spinster in a cardigan and pearls. She is, of course, a middle-aged spinster in a fairy costume.

'Good!' Thomas rubs his hands together like a country minister. 'Great!'

Sophie has a sudden memory of sitting on a kitchen bench with her legs wrapped around Thomas's waist and watching his pumping buttocks reflected in the kitchen window. They had both been proud of themselves for having sex in the kitchen because it was proof of a proper movie-style passion (although they never did it again). Afterwards Thomas had made her *fantastic* scrambled eggs with Tabasco sauce and she had really thought she loved him. It is so strange that you can end up having such polite, awkward conversations with somebody with whom you once shared such intimate moments. She feels this is so interesting that it really should be commented upon, and nearly does, before realising it is perhaps not appropriate and perhaps she is a little tipsy. A drunken Fairy Floss Fairy is probably not good for Scribbly Gum Island's corporate identity.

She notices that Deborah is also holding a glass of mulled wine. 'Deborah!' she cries rapturously. 'Isn't this wine *extra-ordinarily* good?'

Deborah grudgingly smacks her lips. 'It is quite flavoursome.'

Thomas frowns. 'Not enough nutmeg. Too much lemon.'

'That's *exactly* what Veronika said!' Sophie feels suddenly very fond of them both and turns to Deborah. 'Don't you just love the way this family talks about food? They get these irritable, earnest expressions, like scientists.'

Deborah opens and shuts her mouth. She breathes in deeply through her nostrils as if she's about to sneeze. Then she says, 'I'm the sort of person who says exactly what she thinks, and I think I should say this.'

'*Deb!*' Thomas's face contorts and his arm shoots out and grabs her elbow as if to save her from falling off a cliff. Some wine spills onto Deborah's hand and she glares at him. 'Now look what you made me do!'

'We'll get you some more!' says Sophie helpfully. 'Thomas, why don't you get us both some more?'

'Because I'm starting to suspect they've overdone it on the brandy,' says Thomas.

'Rubbish!' says Deborah.

'Oh definitely not!' says Sophie.

'Oh Jesus,' says Thomas.

Deborah drains the rest of her glass, hands it to Thomas, licks her lips and says to Sophie, 'He's still in love with you. Did you know that? You're the love of his life.'

'Where are you?' asks Ron. 'Tell me where you are, right now.'

He has become icy calm. He is going to find this man and kill him with a single, efficient blow to the head.

'No need to get your knickers in a knot, Ron. We're here at the Hilton. Why, do you want to come and watch? It's no problem.'

'COME AND WATCH?'

Ron slams his expensive mobile phone to the ground and grinds it beneath his heel, much to the pleasure of a group of boys who assume he's a street performer beginning some sort of violent skit.

'Oh Deborah, I'm *not,* I know that I'm not!' says Sophie.

'She's not,' says Thomas. 'I swear to you she's not.'

Deborah wails, 'Then why did you say it? Last night? Don't pretend you don't know what I'm talking about!'

Sophie thinks, oh my goodness, he *didn't!* (Although it's hard not to feel flattered.)

Thomas looks like a man who has been kicked in the kidneys. 'This is excruciatingly embarrassing.'

'I don't care if it's embarrassing. You still love her! You said her name when we were *making love*! That's what's known as a Freudian slip, and Freudian slips mean that's what you really think deep down in your superego or something!'

'Deborah,' says Sophie earnestly, lovingly. Poor Deborah! Poor, sweet, travel-agent Deborah! 'The thing is, Thomas and I weren't at all compatible. We had a terrible sex life! Terrible!'

'Oh, God, you're both drunk,' says

Thomas.

'And you've got such a beautiful baby girl!' cries Sophie, gesturing lavishly at Lily.

'Don't you bring Lily into it!' says Deborah fiercely.

'Oh, well, I just meant —'

'I know *exactly* what you meant!'

Sophie isn't sure that she likes Deborah's tone. She was just trying to be nice. She tries to think of something devastatingly clever to say about Deborah's grasp of Freudian theories but she can't quite remember anything about Freudian theories herself, even though she got a high distinction on an essay on the subject at uni.

But then they're interrupted. 'Sophie! I've been looking everywhere for you.'

It's Ian the Sweet Solicitor, and he's perfect. He's dressed in a casual, stylish-but-not-too-stylish suede jacket and black jeans. He looks tall and funny and gently intellectual. Sophie cannot think what her problem has been. *This* is the man she will sleep with tonight. This is the man who she will have a mature relationship with over the next few months, including weekend getaways, possibly a trip to Europe, champagne brunches with friends, dinners with parents, lots of sophisticated sex in his luxury apartment, followed by one of those elegant barefoot weddings on the beach, and she'll be pregnant with her own Lily-baby just in time for her fortieth birthday.

'Have you two met Ian?' asks Sophie, all tasteful conviviality. She pats Ian's arm possessively to make it very clear in an entirely subtle way that they are an item. 'Aunt Connie's solicitor?'

'Yeah, hi, Ian! We've met! How are you?' Thomas pumps Ian's hand, looking at him meaningfully as if to say, *I've been taken hostage by these two women, save me!*

'Do you practise divorce law by any chance, Ian?' Deborah gives a tinkling laugh. 'I'm just *wondering*, that's all. No *particular* reason, except that last night my husband and I were —'

'I think it's time we found ourselves a good strong cup of coffee.' Thomas takes a firm hold of her elbow. 'Come on, Deborah.'

'Oh, well done, you remembered your wife's name! Did you have to really *concentrate?*'

But she allows herself to be led away, with Thomas pushing the stroller and Lily beaming and waving a chubby hand, 'Bye, bye! Bye, bye!' as though she's as desperate to get away as her father.

Ian watches them go and shakes his head. 'Ah, it brings back so many happy memories of married life.'

Sophie chuckles lightly in a way that indicates it will obviously be very different when they're married, and says, 'How have you been since I saw you last?'

Ian turns to her. His eyes are shining with a frightening new evangelical zeal. 'Well, actually, a lot's changed since I saw you last!'

Religion? Acupuncture? Hatha yoga? The Atkins diet? Whatever it is, she can sense the approach of a nasty sandstorm about to blast through her beach wedding.

'And it's all thanks to something you said when we went out the other night, when you were talking about seizing the day.'

Sophie stares at him. 'I have never in my life used the words "Seize the day".'

'OK, well maybe not those words, but you certainly talked about the principle of it. Anyway, it's all thanks to you, I'm giving up law and I'm moving to New Zealand to be a white-water-rafting instructor!'

Grace and Aunt Rose are packing up their face-painting equipment. They both agree that they must have surely painted the face of every child on the island and that it gets more tiring every year and next year they really should get some help. Aunt Rose is going off now to sit in the tent with Grandma Enigma and Grace is going to get them both something to eat.

Grace helps Aunt Rose to her feet and feels the delicate bird-like bones in her arm.

'Oooh, I'm an old fogy, darling, aren't I?' Rose winces and clutches at her back. 'I look in the mirror sometimes and I think, "Who *is* that old woman?" I never thought I'd be this old. Connie and I used to laugh at the thought of us as little old ladies and we'd pretend to hobble around on our walking sticks, and now look, I actually have one and it's not just for show, I need it!'

Grace just smiles. 'I'll see you at Grandma Enigma's tent. Just a cup of tea?'

'Yes, and maybe a piece of angel cake. It won't be as good as Connie's but at least they're following her recipe.'

Rose walks off through the crowd. From behind, in her long, black coat, with her hair hidden by her hat, she doesn't really look that old at all. She might need the walking stick but she hasn't lost the gliding ballerina walk that Grace remembers from her youth.

Grace pulls the note Margie left for her from her jeans pocket.

Darling, I've double-checked re the Anniversary menu and just wanted to remind you that you're fine to eat everything on the menu EXCEPT for the SATAY STICKS (well that's a pretty obvious one!!), those tiny parmesan biscuits (lethal sesame seeds!) and the SAMOSAS (walnuts, if you can believe it!). Have fun, I hope Grandma Enigma manages the baby OK while you're doing the face-painting. Don't tire yourself out! Love from your Aunt Margie xx

PS. I know this is so annoying of me but I can't help it. I just wanted to suggest that perhaps Jake could wear that little red hat I gave you — it will keep his little ears lovely and warm. I know! I'm sorry! Deborah nearly snapped my head off when I suggested Lily wear her one — so SNAP MY HEAD OFF if you like! (But I know you won't!) Can't wait to tell you all about my Weight Watchers 'party' which I've been so secretive about — it will give you all a good laugh, that's for sure.

She doesn't want Margie to blame herself, but she won't, surely she won't, and everybody will say to her, 'Oh Margie, she had the note from you right there in her pocket. It was perfectly clear! She must have been distracted and forgot. It was just a tragic accident.' But will Callum say, 'Yes, but she never forgets'? It's true that Grace never eats a piece of food cooked by anyone else without double-checking, without saying, 'I'm sorry, but could you please double-check with the chef.' Sometimes even after everybody has confirmed she's safe she will put a morsel to her nose between pinched fingers and sniff like a suspicious dog and feel a tingle of danger at the back of her throat, a vision of a quick stir with a spoon covered in quivering golden drops of deadly sesame oil, and she'll drop it back onto her plate and say, 'Mmmm, I don't trust it,' and Callum will have to be restrained from marching into the kitchen to grab the chef by the throat and demand explanations. 'My wife's life is depending on you,' he sometimes says to waitresses, so melodramatic and sweet. And he gets so mad when Grace forgets to take her EpiPen out with her, and if they're going out to dinner he makes her pull it out of her handbag and show it to him before they leave the house. But nobody will be surprised that she didn't bring it to the Anniversary Night. And Callum will be upset at first, but it will just be the shock really, and he'll know deep in his heart that he and the baby are going to be better off with Sophie.

Sophie will talk about music with him and

go dancing with him and swing her hips and jiggle her shoulders and move like a woman, not a cardboard cut-out. Sophie will make friends with that huge social circle of Callum's friends. She'll go to those loud, happy, tipsy BBQs without feeling sick flutters in her stomach, and she won't just find a chair and sit there with her arms and legs not quite right, just sitting there for the whole night, holding her drink too tightly, worrying that everybody thinks she's a cold snobby bitch and secretly thinking the steak marinade has too much salt in it. Oh no, Sophie will be flitting from circle to circle, laughing and chatting and making everybody chuckle. She'll know all their names and all their kids' names. She'll have long, chatty conversations on the phone with Callum's lovely mum, and say, 'Oh, *hi,* Doris!' She'll love Jake like a proper mother and do tuckshop duty and throw birthday parties and jump up and down on the soccer field. She'll blush and giggle and Jake will grow a foot taller than her and put his arm around her and say to his mates, 'This is my mum.' His darling little mum. And nobody will think all that much about Grace except to say, 'Oh, what a terrible tragedy.'

Jake is with Grandma Enigma right now, wearing his red woollen hat. He's warm and clean and fed and there are eleven lasagnes in the freezer and dozens of bottles of expressed milk, and all the washing is up-to-date and Sophie is just over there, the pretty pink Good Fairy waiting to step in, and Grace did the best she could but it wasn't enough, she never felt it, she never felt a thing, and it will be such a glorious relief, such a *release,* like when the pain-reliever begins its soft, fuzzy drift through your bloodstream, like cool grass on your bare feet after white-hot sand, like sleep closing down your brain after a long, exhausting day.

She looks around her and all she can see are children with Melly the Music Box Dancer and Gublet faces, her own smiling creations mocking her for thinking she could be happy, and it seems to her that the children are the only ones who can truly see her despicable core, and she can see their eyes shining at her through their painted faces and they're all saying, *Yep, do it, Grace, do it, it's time.*

'Bye everybody! So long! Au revoir!'

Gublet McDublet waved to all his friends from the window of his spaceship but nobody even lifted their head.

Melly the Music Box Dancer hadn't been to see him all night. They were all too busy playing.

Ron runs towards the wharf. He's going to take his jet-ski over, which means his clothes are going to be drenched, and if the cabbie at Glass Bay complains about him dripping river-water all over his cab he's either going to put him in a headlock and threaten to kill him or else he's going to give him all the money in his wallet and say, 'Look mate, just take me to the Hilton, my wife is there with some hairy-chested, gold-medallion-wearing guy named *Ron,* which is *my* name. I know, I can't fucking believe it either.'

He'll tell him he'll pay him double the value of any speeding tickets. Triple.

Do you want to come and watch? Was he for *real?* Had Margie got caught up in some weird trendy cult where they all practise . . . *fetishes?* Even the word 'fetish' makes him shudder. Ron does not like fetishes. He has no fetishes. He likes normal, straightforward Australian sex with a woman, and the woman should be his wife, and the woman shouldn't sleep with anyone else but him, and afterwards they should have a bit of a cuddle and fall asleep in their own bed. Simple. Bloody hell. Why did he take such simple good things in his life for granted?

As he gets to the water he sees a familiar figure in the moonlight walking towards him.

'What are *you* doing here?' he calls out in surprise, but he doesn't stop running long enough to find out.

Sophie has decided everybody on the island has had quite enough fairy floss and packed up her machine. All the children seem to be on sugar highs. Their colourful painted faces make them look like miniature demons and the older ones are running around in feral packs, making strange roaring sounds. Shouldn't they be in bed? Callum's jazz band has packed up their instruments, and loudspeakers are pounding out Latin American music. The street performers have all stopped performing. Sophie can see two clowns kissing passionately. There seem to be quite a lot of people trying out dirty dancing for the first time in their lives.

Sophie takes off her wings and puts a denim jacket over her dress. She had intended to find something to eat, but uncharacteristically she's lost her appetite. All she feels like is more mulled wine — she's drinking it like water. The more she drinks, the better it tastes. There is a gentle buzzing sound in her head.

It is so funny that both the eligible men in her life have been eliminated within half an hour of each other. Oh, it's just hilarious! The girls are going to fall about laughing. Her life should be a sitcom it's so funny. She giggles but it sounds like a hiccup. Or a sob.

The thing is, as well as being funny, it is also humiliating. Because she thought she was so great, so attractive, having two men interested in her, when she wasn't even especially interested in either of them. All of a sudden she thought she had all the time in the world. Pride comes before someone trips you flat on your face.

And now here she is, single and nearly forty. So very, very single and so very, very nearly forty. That elusive marriage and babies thing has slipped through her clumsy, grasping fingertips. She just couldn't get it right in time. There won't be a Lily baby or a Jake baby for her. She's going to be on her deathbed and thinking about her achievements as a Human Resources Director. That will be her gift to humanity. The Morale Committee will gather around gratefully. The only person who is apparently in love with her is Thomas, who is married to somebody else. And the only person she's in love with is Callum, who is also married to somebody else.

'Sophie.'

'Ha! I was just thinking about you.' Sophie looks up at Callum and feels herself pulled irresistibly to him like metal shavings to a magnet. She has to dig her heels into the ground so she doesn't suddenly superglue herself to his chest.

'Really. What were you thinking?'

'I was thinking . . .' Gosh. She has absolutely no idea how to finish the sentence. Callum doesn't seem to care. He seems bright-eyed and fidgety. 'Were you thinking you'd like to dance with me?'

'How funny! That's exactly what I was thinking!'

Callum holds out his hand and Sophie takes it. A manic happiness floods her bloodstream.

He leans towards her with wide eyes and says, 'Don't you think the mulled wine is amazing!'

'Oh,' says Sophie fervently. 'I think it's delicious.'

Rose is walking towards Enigma's tent, worrying about Grace, although she's not sure exactly why. Something about the expression on her face just then. It was so disinterested. It was wiped clean. It reminded her of someone's face from her past. Actually, she knows who it was. It reminded her of that Jenkins boy when they saw him at Dora's wedding after the war. Oh, but for heaven's sake! That's ridiculous! Grace isn't suffering from shellshock! Grace isn't about to do anything silly.

The Jenkins boy had hung himself in the family garage.

It's probably just that Rose has always been slightly worried about Grace, ever since the day Laura brought her home from the hospital and handed her over to Simon, saying, 'Here. You stop her crying. You're the one who wanted a baby so bad.'

Oh, but Grace is fine! She's got Callum, who anyone can see adores her, and the baby is thriving.

The music is too loud. Her back hurts. Someone knocks against her, 'Oh my *God*! I'm *so* sorry!' and then disappears into the crowd. There seems to be a frenetic, out-of-control feeling to this year's Anniversary. Everybody she sees is carrying a glass of mulled wine — it seems very popular, even though Rose had a taste and it definitely has too much lemon, not enough nutmeg. As she finally reaches the Baby Munro tent she can see Enigma sitting up in her chair, pointing her finger at someone, as though she's Lady Muck. (What sort of person would Enigma have been if she'd just been a plain old Beth or Agnes?) Veronika and her new friend are there too. The friend is holding Jake. It seems that everyone is talking at once to a man wearing, oh dear, a yellow T-shirt. It's the Kook. He's obviously found Veronika. As Rose gets closer she sees him hold up the strange urn and announce,

'These are the ashes of Alice Munro. My *mother*, Alice Munro.'

Veronica's mouth drops and stays dropped.

Enigma guffaws, 'Well, I don't know whose ashes they are but I can assure you they're not the ashes of Alice Munro!'

'Oh for heaven's sake!' says a familiar voice next to Rose.

Rose turns. 'What are *you* doing here?'

Ron roars across the river on his jet-ski. He's going to take her on a campervan holiday in Tasmania, he's going to finally hang up that godawful baby-in-a-flowerpot print in the sunroom, he's going to be more patient with her mother, he's going to let her watch whatever that rubbish show is she wants to watch on Sunday nights, he's going to go on picnics, he's going to put

Christmas lights on the guttering, he's going to ask her, Do you still miss your dad, because I miss him, and Do you still write to the parents of the missing children in the paper, which you thought I never knew about, and Do you still know the words to all of Buddy Holly's songs, and Do you think our children are normal . . . and, Jesus Christ, was Veronika trying to tell him she was a *lesbian* tonight?

'I thought you were in Turkey!' says Rose.

'I decided to come home early,' says Laura.

'*Laura?*' says the Kook uncertainly, lowering the urn.

'What can I get you?'

'Just one of those samosas,' says Grace. 'They look nice.'

'You're pretty good,' says Callum.

'I know I am,' says Sophie.

The music thuds inside her. They're on their own invisible island surrounded by gyrating people. They're moving like one person. He's going to kiss her very soon.

'Your mother was Alice Munro?' Veronika is ecstatic. It seems that *nothing* in her world is as fixed and boring as she thought. 'So what happened to her? Why did she leave? What happened to Jack? This is amazing! Incredible!' She looks at Audrey, who is gorgeous and calm and jiggling the baby expertly over one shoulder. 'Can you believe this, Audrey!'

Enigma says, 'He's a con-man, I tell you.'

'Oh, am I?' The Kook shakes the urn. 'How can you prove these aren't the ashes of Alice Munro?'

Laura snorts with derision. 'Oh, David, give it up!'

'Do you actually *know* this man, Laura?' says Enigma. 'I suppose you met him in some dreadful foreign country. Why are you back so early anyway? Nobody told me you were coming back early! Have you noticed that Margie isn't even here tonight? I'm here all alone dealing with problems like this!'

'I'm back early because I decided I want to spend time with my grandson.' Laura looks at Jake in Audrey's arms and pats him tentatively on the head as if he's an exotic animal. 'Is that so strange? Where is Grace? This child looks hungry. And who are you? Are you the babysitter? Don't tell me they've got a nanny? How terribly trendy of them!'

Veronika is in a frenzy. 'Audrey is my girlfriend, Auntie Laura. I became a lesbian while you were away, but I'll introduce her properly in a minute. This is important! How do we know for sure this man isn't telling the truth?'

'He's just trying to get money out of us,' says Laura disgustedly. 'I dated him for a while. I met him at Parents without Partners. I made the mistake of sharing some confidential information with him after a few too many chardonnays one night. Veronika, did you just say what I think you said?'

'Oh, Laura, that's disgraceful!' says Enigma. 'But why didn't you ever bring him home for dinner?'

'Exactly what confidential information did you share with him, Auntie Laura?' Veronika's face is pink, her hands clenched.

'You'll just have to wait till you're forty to find out,' says Enigma.

'Till I'm *forty*?'

Rose looks around helplessly for a chair. There are shooting pains up the back of her legs. She looks at the self-satisfaction on Enigma's face and the anguish on Veronika's. Oh, it's all so *silly*. It's so *tiring*. Seventy-three years of lies. Seventy-three years of thinking before you spoke. Seventy-three years of fear. Like walking along a cliff-face. How tempting to just step out into thin air.

Be quiet, Rose, orders Connie in her head.

I'm sorry, Connie. I've just had enough.

Enough is enough.

She reaches for Veronika's hand.

'We know he's not telling the truth, darling, because Alice and Jack Munro never existed. Connie and I made them up.'

'You made them up? You never found a baby? There was no baby? Or — what — why, well then, *who is Grandma Enigma?*'

Rose has a glorious sensation of freefall. 'Well, she's my daughter, darling.'

Enigma throws her hands in the air and wails, 'Oh, now look what you've gone and done!'

Callum's hand is warm on the back of her neck and he's pulling her to him, and some sober, tomorrow part of her mind is saying, Calm down, Sophie, it's only a tacky, drunken kiss, it's not a tidal wave, it's not an earthquake, it's not a *miracle,* but some other part of her mind is thinking what a beautiful and appropriate word *swoon* is and how she's swooning like a regency-romance heroine who's never been kissed in her life except that now, oh God, oh fuck, oh thank you, his tongue is in her mouth, and has every other kiss in her life been leading up to this ultimate, perfect kiss? Yes, she thinks it has.

Eating the samosa is like eating a piece of evil. Grace is committed to going ahead but she hadn't realised just how difficult it would be to go up against the habits of a lifetime. She has to physically force the hand holding the samosa up to her mouth, as though the air around her has turned into wet concrete. For a few seconds her mouth stays jammed shut while her nostrils contract in horror — nuts, nuts, we smell nuts! — but finally she manages to unclamp her lips and shovel a corner into her mouth. She is standing away from the crowds on the main street, leaning with her back against a tree. The crowd is a heaving, solid mass, faces glowing under the lights of the giant heaters. Callum and Sophie must be in there somewhere. Dancing, probably. Making life look so simple. She waits and there it is. The first warning of every allergic attack of her life. A shuddery shiver straight down her back, icy fingertips caressing her spine. She swallows convulsively and waits. There is the unbearable sandpaper scratch in her throat. It's moving faster than any other reaction she can remember. She's being strangled from the inside. Her eyes fill with water. She claws at the bark of the tree. The pain is her punishment for not loving her baby. But now it's impossible to hold on to that thought because she can't breathe. What a complete fool! What an idiotic thing to do. Every thought in her head is wiped clean except for the need to breathe. For God's sake, *she can't breathe.*

Rose is exhilarated. She wants to dance. Her backache has vanished. 'It's all over,' she says to Enigma. 'I told Connie years ago we should just tell everybody the truth. I feel so good! I feel all light and airy!'

Enigma is crying, of course, snuffling into her hanky. 'Well, I certainly don't feel light and airy! Oh! Why isn't Margie here? Laura, make Rose stop talking! Do something! It's all your dreadful friend's fault!'

The Kook has put his urn on the floor and has folded his arms aggressively across his chest. 'People are going to want to sue you. It's fraud. You women have committed fraud.'

'Well, you should know all about fraud,' says Laura. 'Because that's what you were here to commit, weren't you? You thought because you knew the truth you could get away with this pathetic stunt! Got some more gambling debts to pay off, have you?'

'Oh, dear.' Enigma is momentarily diverted from her crying. 'I don't think you should date a gambler, dear. They're awful people, gamblers.'

'For God's sake, Mum, I'm not seeing him!' says Laura. Rose notices for the first time that Laura is looking better than she has in years. She has a lovely gold tan and her forehead looks all smoothed out and she's wearing a wonderful necklace with an oval red stone.

'Laura,' she says, 'that necklace is really beautiful!'

'Don't we have a few more important things to talk about here than Auntie Laura's necklace?' asks Veronika.

And that's when somebody yells into the tent with frantic authority, 'Is there a doctor here? There's a girl having some sort of allergic reaction.'

'Grace? Is it Grace?' Enigma lifts her tear-stained face. Veronika has already sprinted from the tent, like a runner hearing a starting gun.

'What's going on?' Veronika's new friend jiggles the baby up and down in her arms. 'Who is it?'

'Where did I put my bag?' Laura kicks

violently at the ground around her. 'Somebody find my bag!' The Kook picks up a black leather bag from the ground and she snatches it from him and runs off behind Veronika, and Rose's legs shake so badly that Enigma and the Kook have to grab at her elbows to stop her from falling.

What's going on?
Some woman is having some sort of fit.
I think it's an allergic reaction.

At the moment the words penetrate Sophie's molten consciousness, Callum shoves her away from him, and it's like being wrenched awake from a beautiful dream by a shrieking alarm clock.

Grace's limbs flail in raw, uncontrollable panic. She clutches at her throat and makes guttural sounds. There is a blur of strange, frightened faces around her. And then there is a face leaning close to her and a swinging red pendant on a chain and a voice saying, 'Hold on, Grace,' and every molecule of her body is drawn to that familiar cranky voice, because of course *she* won't let her die, of course she won't.

50

The phone has been ringing at intervals for hours, it seems, but Sophie just lies in bed with her pillow held so firmly over her face that she is practically suffocating herself. She takes it away and pulls a face at the ceiling. She stretches out her mouth into an elongated oval. She scrunches her face into wrinkles and bares her teeth. She makes strange 'Yah, yah!' sounds, pretending she is insane and wishing she was. She puts the pillow back over her face.

She has a headache, of course. She knew she would have a headache, but actually it's not even that bad, just a blurry ache behind her eyes. It's a strange sort of hangover. Her mouth doesn't feel horrible. It feels quite nice and nutmeg-ish.

It would be better if she had an all-consuming run-of-the-mill hangover that would make her forget the shameful, shrivelling feeling of Callum pushing her away.

The revulsion on his face. As if he'd swallowed a fly! As if she was a desperate old tart trying to stick her tongue down his throat.

And then! It was like a nightmare. Seeing Grace's beautiful face contorting spastically, spit at the corners of her mouth, her eyes rolling into the back of her head like a frightened horse. 'Shit, I think she's actually *dying,*' somebody said in an awe-filled voice. Callum was on his hands and knees next to her, his fingers digging into the dirt, and Grace's mother took a plastic tube from her handbag with yellow and black writing, pulled off the lid, and, without pausing for even a second, took a firm hold of Grace's leg, lifted her arm high in the air and plunged it down, stabbing her, hard, murderously really, and the crowd gasped collectively but quietly, as if they were in church. Grace's body arched in the middle and then slammed against the ground, and Sophie caught sight of Veronika, also on her hands and knees, bursting into tears, and Sophie had never seen Veronika cry before, and there was Thomas shouting into a mobile phone the words 'anaphylactic shock', his face all red, and Sophie had never heard Thomas raise his voice before, and it was all so awful, so truly awful.

Twenty minutes later a police-rescue boat came roaring up the river, but by then everyone knew that it looked like the woman who had the allergic reaction was going to be fine. She was breathing normally, thanks to her quick-thinking mother, and 'Really, you'd think people with dangerous allergies would be a bit more careful about what they ate!' The Anniversary Night was suddenly over and people were trooping down towards the wharf to line up for the ferry, with sleeping, face-painted children draped over their shoulders.

Callum and Laura went off in the boat with Grace to the hospital. Veronika recovered her normal frenetic equilibrium and was going on and on about how she didn't understand how Grace would have eaten a samosa, when Mum had written her a note, and why in the world would you put walnuts in a samosa, they needed to have a good talk to the caterers, and had Sophie heard that the Alice and Jack story was a complete hoax, they never even existed. Aunt Rose had got pregnant with Grandma Enigma when she was sixteen and Connie had come up with this elaborate lie, it was such a *betrayal* really, and who was going to look after Jake tonight, she hadn't brought Audrey along to provide free babysitting, and apparently Auntie Laura had seen Dad going off somewhere on his jet-ski, fully dressed and looking quite demented, and you'd think Mum would be home from her Weight Watchers party by now, and if Auntie Laura hadn't been carrying around the EpiPen in her bag, Grace would be dead by now, no doubt about it, dead.

'Is she always like this?' Audrey had asked Sophie. 'Should I slap her across the face?'

Sophie had wondered vaguely if *she* should offer to mind Jake for the night, but it didn't seem appropriate. What if Callum came home and was horrified to find her touching his child and shoved her away again? Besides which, she was drunk, and she thought childminding was probably like driving, something you shouldn't do when you're over the limit. Luckily it soon became irrelevant because there was a family squabble over who should take Jake for the night. Aunt Rose said she'd do it, and Grandma Enigma said, 'Don't be ridiculous, you've got the Alzheimer's, you can't take care of a baby.' Thomas said he and Debbie were all set up for Lily and they would take Jake home with them, although Debbie wasn't such a good advertisement for motherhood herself, as she was sitting on the ground next to Lily's stroller with her head in her hands, shaking her head sadly over her empty glass of mulled wine, while Lily reached over from her stroller and stroked her mother's hair. Veronika said no, Jake had obviously taken a liking to Audrey, and she and Audrey would take him back to Callum and Grace's house and stay the night there, and in the end nobody had the energy to argue with her, and it *did* seem that Jake looked very comfortable with Audrey and she seemed very competent and calm. So everybody went home to bed.

Sophie had walked back to Aunt Connie's house in a daze. She'd managed to take off only one shoe before hopping into bed in her fairy dress, and obviously she'd had intentions of cleaning her teeth, because when she woke up she was still holding her toothbrush, with a carefully applied line of toothpaste. She has no memory of doing that at all.

The phone rings again. It's probably her mother, feeling guilty about last night. This time it only rings a few times before it stops abruptly, as if the caller has slammed down the phone. Sophie continues pressing the pillow down into her face and tries to think of something extremely boring and non-emotional. Tax returns. She sets herself a mental test to see if she can remember her

Tax File Number. It is a stupid test. She can't remember one digit of her Tax File Number. All she can remember is how it felt to dance with Callum, and how her lips had tingled with anticipation as he lowered his head . . . and actually her bottom lip is still tingling quite painfully now.

She takes away the pillow and gingerly puts a finger to her lips. For God's sake, that's why her lips were tingling all night — because *she was getting a cold sore.*

She hasn't had a cold sore since she was sixteen. She gets out of bed and hobbles to the bathroom, still wearing one shoe, and looks at herself in the mirror. Mirror, mirror on the wall, who is the ugliest women of them all? There is an extraordinary strawberry-shaped blotch right in the centre of her lip. She's been branded for kissing another woman's husband. Her hair is a comical bird's nest. There are half-moons of mascara under her eyes. She is a hung-over, herpes-ridden old witch. She is so ugly, it's funny.

And what's really funny is this: she does love him. It's not a silly crush. She's actually fallen in love with him. And she is never going to be with him. She doesn't even want Grace to leave him. She just wants to be living in the parallel world where he never met Grace at all and instead he met Sophie at the Pseudo Echo concert back in the Eighties and they dated and got married and had three kids and now she pretty much takes him for granted and sits on his lap like he's an old armchair and they're trying to find ways to spice up their sex life and on Saturdays they ferry their kids around to soccer and netball and on Sundays they work in the garden. She wants that life so bad.

You stuffed up big time, buttercup.

The doorbell rings. Sophie doesn't even bother to smooth down her hair. She is irretrievably unattractive. She kicks off her shoe and walks down the stairs in her crumpled-up pink fairy dress, fingering her cold sore with enjoyable disgust, muttering to herself like a mad old crone. She flings open the door.

'Good morning, darling.' It's Rose, and she's cut off all her hair. It's a white elfin cap and it makes her neck look longer and her eyes larger. She's wrapped in a stunning, richly beaded pashmina. 'You look a bit tired.'

Sophie says, 'Well, you look beautiful.'

'I've dressed up to celebrate the end of the Munro Baby Mystery.' Rose lifts a corner of the pashmina. 'This is a gift from

Laura. It's from Nepal, or somewhere like that.'

As Rose turns her head to examine the fabric, Sophie feels a shock of recognition. She says, 'I can't believe I've never noticed before how much you look like Grace.'

Rose smiles sadly. 'Well, she is my great-granddaughter, even though she doesn't know it yet. Imagine that! If she'd died last night from her allergic reaction she would never have known I was her great-grandma. I think that's terrible, I really do. I could wring Connie's neck! What have you done to your lip, Sophie?'

Sophie holds the door open and lets Rose walk in front of her. She answers, 'It's a cold sore.'

'Oh,' says Rose. 'I think you're meant to put lemon juice on it. Who told me that? I know. It was Rick. The gardener. I think he gets them sometimes.'

Sophie makes a silent gruesome face at herself in Connie's hallway mirror as she passes it.

'Have you heard how Grace is this morning?' she asks.

'Yes, apparently she's fine. Just shaken up. What a scare she gave us. We could have lost her. Thank goodness for Laura. Do you know what Thomas has done today? He's gone out and bought one of those EpiPens for each of us. So we can *all* carry one, and they cost an absolute fortune! One for you as well! But you know Tom. He's a terrible worrier. He'll be worrying over this for years after we've all forgotten it! Oh, and did I mention Ron ended up in jail last night?'

'No!'

'Yes, it's all a bit confusing. Margie had to go and get him and apparently she wasn't at a Weight Watchers party at all. Enigma wasn't making much sense because she's very cross with me and thinks I've got Alzheimer's. She won't stop crying. What a night it was! What with the Kook, and Laura coming home, and Grace, and, well, goodness me! Anyway, why don't you go and have a shower while I make us a cup of tea. Would you like me to scramble you a few eggs?'

'Oh, no, no, sit down, please!' Sophie flaps her hands ineffectually, but Rose is too much at home in Connie's kitchen. She's already taking out a glass bowl and tut-tutting as she discovers the eggs in the fridge. 'You must keep your eggs at room temperature. I thought I'd mentioned that before? Quickly, go and have your shower. You'll feel better. Then we'll put some lemon on that cold sore and you can eat your eggs while I tell you the whole story about Alice and Jack. We're going to put out something called a 'Media Release', you see, and I want everyone in the family to hear it all first before we go public.'

So, Sophie stands under the shower and lets the water spray hard on her face and thinks about how Rose meant her too when she said, 'Everyone in the family.' As she towels herself dry, the smell of scrambled eggs and coffee is drifting up the stairs and she wonders if there is something profoundly superficial about a person who can take so much pleasure in the thought of eating breakfast, even when her heart is split right in two.

51

It only takes about half an hour for the Munro Baby Mystery to be unravelled into a simple, straightforward, sad story. Sophie listens while she eats her breakfast and her cold sore throbs and sunshine floods Connie's kitchen so that Rose's eyes look especially blue and young as she talks.

Connie always started the story with my turquoise crêpe de Chine. She'd say, 'Rose went dotty over some dress fabric.' But I'm going to start a bit earlier because I'm in charge now!

It was 1932. The year Phar Lap died. You know Phar Lap? The racehorse? Sorry, darling, of course you do. Oh, you saw the movie? I don't seem to like going to the pictures any more. I can't get comfortable. Yes, I suppose I could take a cushion. Well, anyway, I mustn't digress, Veronika was nearly having a coronary this morning when

I wouldn't stick to the point. Her new friend was chuckling away. She's nice, isn't she? She seems to be a very *special* friend. Well, anyway, it was the year Phar Lap died. I can remember Dad hearing it on the wireless and stomping about, saying that Phar Lap had been poisoned by American gangsters. We didn't take much notice.

There were only two weatherboard houses on Scribbly Gum Island then. One was the house where Connie and I lived with Mum and Dad, and right on the other side of the island was our grandparents' house. You could only get there by boat then because we hadn't cleared away any of the bush.

Grandpop lived there on his own. Grandma died when I was only very little and I don't remember much about her except that she always knelt down when we visited, so she was the same height as me, and I liked that because it was like she suddenly became a child-sized grown-up. I wish I could kneel down for Lily and Jake but it hurts my knees too much. Grand-pop was Harry Doughty, who had won the island in the famous 'Ashes' bet when he was a young man. He was very proud of winning that bet. It was like his lifetime's achievement. We had to hear the story quite a lot.

Well, Connie and I adored Grandpop and

Mum, but to be quite honest we weren't that fussed on Dad. He fought in France in the war, and as Mum always said, it hadn't been a walk in the park. Poor man. He had a bad shoulder because of a shrapnel wound and problems with his right eye because of the mustard gas. He was also, how can I put this nicely, a little *soft in the head.* I guess these days they'd have him seeing psychiatrists and all that. Mum said he'd been a happy-go-lucky fellow before he went. He joined up because he thought it would be a lark and it wasn't a lark at all. He hated it. He saw his three best mates die right in front of him and he thought somebody should take the blame for that. He wouldn't stand up when they played 'God Save the Queen'. He'd ramble on and on and he didn't make much sense really. Mum said he came back different, but that was the only way we knew him, so we didn't really believe her. It was like living with a large, unpredictable dog.

Well, Connie and I had such carefree, tomboyish lives. Idyllic, really. Such freedom! Sometimes I feel sorry for the children today with their sports and their ballet and their violin lessons. Connie and I could go wherever we wanted in our row boat. Of course, we did have to go to school each day in Glass Bay, but that was all right! Connie was a star pupil. There was a lot of talk about her going off to the university. I was just average, I'm afraid. Too dreamy. After school, Connie and I would just spend hours mucking around on the island and exploring the river, fishing, swimming. We had a special shady spot down on the beach at Sultana Rocks and I'd sketch girls wearing beautiful dresses while Connie read her mystery books. We didn't go home until it was dark and we were hungry.

Actually, I think we were quite spoiled really. I didn't think until I was much older how hard our Mum must have worked and how tired she must have been. Dad couldn't get any work, you see. He was a butcher before the war but he couldn't find a job when he came back, which was just as well, Mum said, because she was sure he'd chop off his fingers, with his bad eye. He was fighting the Repatriation for years to get a pension. I can still see him at the kitchen table, angrily dictating letters to Mum because he couldn't see well enough to write. Mum had to work to support us. She had a job at a clothing factory in the city and she'd come home and Dad would be there leaning on the fence waiting to have his tea cooked for him. It never occurred to him that he could have helped around the house. Never occurred to us either. It's just the way it was. But Mum never complained. She always had such funny stories to tell us about her day. Connie and I would be in stitches. She was always losing things. She was hopeless! She would lose her train ticket and have to sweet-talk her way out of it with the guard. Well, she was so pretty, with all that curly blonde hair! That probably helped. Once she accidentally posted her pay-packet with some letters and she had to wait for hours until the postman came to empty the post-box. Oh, she was a character!

She was a wonderful cook. Better than all of us. Even Connie. And such a talented seamstress too! She made all our clothes without patterns. For Christmas each year I would draw a sketch of the dress I wanted and she'd make it for me. Well, one night in August, Mum left her only warm jacket on the train and came home chilled to the bone. Her teeth were chattering so hard it was making her giggle. She was making 'brrrr' noises with her teeth. Connie was cross with her. She said, 'You'll get sick, Mum,' and sure enough she did. There wasn't enough money for another coat for her and Mum did feel the cold. It started out as just a sniffle and then it turned into a serious chesty cough. She'd lean forward with her hands on her knees and cough and cough and cough. Well, she needed a dose of antibiotics! By the time Connie and I took her off to the hospital in Glass Bay it was already too late. She died of pneumonia a few days after. She was thirty-seven. Whenever I get a prescription from the doctor for antibiotics I look at the pack and I think, That's all Mum needed. I think, This ordinary box of pills would have saved her life. I remember Connie and me standing there at the hospital, looking at each other, not touching, not crying, just completely and utterly shocked. Our mother was too busy to die. The only time I can remember seeing her lie down was in the hospital. Is that the phone again, Sophie, love? Do you want to get it?

'It's OK.' Sophie gives a dismissive wave of her hand. 'This is more important.'

Rose smiles at her, takes a sip of tea, clears her throat and continues.

It was just one month later that Grandpop died too. I think it was the shock of losing Mum. He loved her. I think he was probably *in* love with her, actually.

Well, all of a sudden everything was different. Nothing looked familiar any more. I can remember walking out the front door and looking at the river as if I'd never seen it before. Everything was menacing and grey. My whole world looked and smelled different. There was only Connie, Dad and me on the island and it felt so empty. It needed more people to fill it up. It seemed like Mum had created enough energy and jokes and stories for ten people. It was an awful time, Sophie. We were all grieving and we didn't really know how to do it, so we just flailed hopelessly about. It was so cold too. I remember that. Connie and I couldn't get warm.

Dad went all religious in an angry sort of way. We'd always been Catholics, of course, but now Dad was reading the bible out loud every night and wanting Connie and me to kneel down and say the rosary with him. He went on and on about how Mum hadn't been to confession before she died, and Connie yelled at him, 'What would she confess? That she lost her good coat? Was that a mortal sin?' Dad slammed the bible down on Connie's knuckles and she just laughed. This horrible, bitter laugh.

We soon found out that we were in terrible financial straits. Connie had to forget about doing her Leaving Certificate and try to get a job. She walked around the city for weeks and weeks, lining up in endless queues and coming home with puffy blisters on her heels. I don't think I'd even heard the word 'mortgage' before. We didn't know we had a mortgage, or that Dad's wireless was on a time-payment plan. We didn't know it was going to take us years to pay off what we owed the grocer. We had no idea Mum was only barely keeping us afloat. She protected us from all that.

So, Connie became *obsessed* with money. All she could talk about was ways to make money. You know Banksia Island, of course? Just north of us? Well, during the Thirties, Banksia Island was a very popular picnic destination. It had quite a successful tea house. And the scones there were dreadful! So heavy and lumpy. Connie kept saying, 'If people tasted our scones they'd never go back.' But nobody had even heard of Scribbly Gum Island in those days, and why would people come to us when they could go to Banksia Island? We had to give them a reason — and of course we did, eventually, and the poor old Banksia Island Tea Rooms went out of business quick smart. Although those scones were really unforgivably bad, so we didn't feel that guilty.

Dad said Connie should stop jabbering about scones and just get tenants into Grandpop's empty house. He seemed to think it would be so easy. I can remember him shouting at Connie, 'Just go along into Glass Bay and organise for someone to let the house. We'll charge them fifteen shillings a week! That's more than fair!' He was quite oblivious to the fact there were empty houses all over Sydney because no one could afford to pay their rent. There were evictions every day. I can remember walking through the city and seeing people sitting outside their homes, surrounded by all their possessions, lamps, cushions, saucepans. But you see, Dad never left Scribbly Gum. He barely left the house. He was in his own dream world.

Well, one day Connie got sick of Dad haranguing her and told him that she'd found tenants for Grandpop's house and their names were Alice and Jack Munro. She said the Munros were good Catholic people and they were paying five shillings a week, and here was their first rent money. I remember Dad saying, 'We're not a bloody charity! They must think it's bloody Christmas!' But he seemed to accept it, and seeing as he never took the boat around to Grandpop's house he wasn't ever likely to notice that Alice and Jack were never home. Connie would chat on and on about this mythical Alice and Jack Munro. She seemed to get a kick out of conning Dad.

The rent money really came from Connie's new enterprise as a bookie. The railway workers would come down and meet her at the wharf and place their bets with her, which she'd record in a book with a red cover. It was illegal — she was breaking the law, you know! I was frightened for her but she loved it. Of course, she didn't make nearly enough money. We weren't starving, not like children in Africa. But you know, there were some days when we went to bed quite hungry. I can tell you, we never took food for granted again.

One day, a friend at school said that her sister could help me get a job at a big department store in the city working behind the cosmetics counter. So of course, I had to leave school and take it. We needed the money too badly. I hated it. I was so shy. It was agony for me to talk to those posh ladies each day. I missed my mum dreadfully.

Well, Sophie dear, you're probably wondering if I'm ever going to mention the crêpe de Chine. Do you want some more scrambled eggs? No? Yes, of course you do.

Help yourself. There's plenty.

I'd been working there for a few weeks when I happened to see a roll of fabric when I walked by the haberdashery department. It was the colour that caught my eye. I've always had an interest in colours. Certain colours make me feel like I've heard music. Mum was the same. She understood. Connie had no idea, practically colour-blind that girl! Well, this was deep turquoise, and because it was crêpe de Chine it had a rich, satiny feel to it, like a jewel. I could imagine Mum saying to me, 'Oh Rose, it's so pretty!' For some reason I became quite fixated with that fabric. I sketched the summer dress I would make with it. Just something simple with an A-line skirt and a round neckline. It seemed like if I could make that dress, I could get back my old life. I felt like it would make me closer to Mum. Well, to be honest, I don't know what I thought really. I think I just went a little mad. I *lusted* after it. I even dreamed about it, for heaven's sake. And of course, I didn't have a snowflake's chance in hell of getting it. It was expensive fabric. We didn't have enough money to eat. We certainly didn't have enough money for fabric.

Well, I may as well just come out and say this: I stole two pounds from the till.

I know. I don't look like a thief, do I? But that's what I did, and my mother would have been absolutely horrified. I didn't even think much about it. I didn't even feel guilty. I just wanted that fabric. And of course, I was caught, by the floor supervisor. I thought of him as an elderly man but he was probably forty at the most! He was a short man with a pear-shaped body and an egg-shaped head. I didn't like him at all. I secretly called him Mr Egg Head. I thought Mr Egg Head would sack me for sure, but instead he took me to the storeroom out the back and said he had a proposal for me. He said he'd be prepared to overlook what I'd done and even let me *keep the money* if I was prepared to perform some extra services for him every now and then.

Yes, darling, I can see by the look on your face that you've guessed what those services were. Well, I was such a dreamy, naïve girl. I was just so relieved that I wasn't going to lose my job or go to jail! And I could still buy my precious fabric! You know what I actually remember thinking? That Mr Egg Head had been sent by Mum to keep me out of trouble. Like he was my guardian angel. I thought I'd have to make him the occasional cup of tea.

Mr Egg Head took it very slowly. I had to

meet him in the storeroom and he'd make me close the door behind me and then it was down to business. At first it was just a kiss on the cheek and I thought, Oh, gosh, that's not so nice, I'd much rather make him a cup of tea! But then I thought, after all, I had done the wrong thing. I probably deserved it and it wasn't *that* bad. Of course, he started doing more and more and I started to feel so ashamed of myself. I truly believed I was a disgusting person. A dirty thief. And of course, one day Mr Egg Head, ah, took advantage of me, during the morning tea-break. Well, technically he raped me, but then again I never said no, of course. It didn't actually occur to me to say no. I was the bad person. I was the one being punished. I just tried very hard to think of something else.

52

Margie is bathing Ron's black eye with saline solution. He sits slumped at the kitchen table, while she stands next to him and looks dispassionately at the top of his head. That luxuriant dark hair is starting to thin so she can see his baby-white vulnerable scalp. When she first met Ron she thought he was so good-looking she was embarrassed to even meet his eyes. That was the problem. She'd thought he was too good for her and that she should be eternally grateful to him for choosing her. In fact, *he* was quite lucky to have her! When she'd shown Sophie the old photo of her in her red bikini she'd wolf-whistled and said she was like a supermodel, and then she'd said, 'No, Margie, I'm *serious,*' in that funny way of hers.

Ron winces heroically as she dabs at the cut on his eyebrow, and says, 'Do you want to go on a picnic today?'

Margie stops dabbing while a bubble of laughter inflates in her chest. 'Oh, that's OK, I don't think you're in any condition for a picnic.'

All those times he'd sneered when she tentatively suggested they take a bottle of wine down to Sultana Rocks! All those times when the children were young, when at the last minute he'd say Daddy had to stay behind and do some work in his office because Daddy made the money that paid for the nice food they were taking on the picnic, as if Mummy and Scribbly Gum Island didn't contribute a bloody cent.

'I'm OK. If you feel like a picnic?'

'I don't feel like a picnic.'

'Right. You know what I could do today?'

'What?'

'I could put that picture up for you. That one with the flowerpot.'

'Actually, Debbie saw that and she thought it might be nice for Lily's room, so I gave it to her. About a year ago.'

'Oh, did you?'

There is silence. Margie gives his forehead a last dab and says, 'Right. That should do you.' *I think it's too late, love.*

'So — ah — you had fun last night at that thing? With your friend? With . . . Ron?'

'Loved it. Can't remember the last time I

had more fun.'

'Great! It's great to have an interest!'

'Of course, it would have been nice to win first prize, not just runner-up.'

'Oh yes! Trip to Venice. Wonderful. You always wanted to go to Italy, didn't you?'

'You're thinking of Laura. She was the one who always went on about going to Europe.'

She notices he doesn't ask what they would have done if they had won first prize, which was a trip for two. Actually, she and Rotund Ron hadn't ever properly discussed it. Sometimes, their personal trainer, a blonde Amazonian called Suzie, would say, 'So what happens if you win? Are you two going to run away together to Venice?' and Ron would waggle his eyebrows suggestively and pretend to speak in an Italian accent and Margie and Suzie would make fun of him, because he sounded Indian, not Italian at all.

Last night Rotund Ron and Margie had been first runners-up in the National *'Bulges to Biceps'* Beginner Body Building Competition for Couples, sponsored by a low-fat Italian pasta sauce company. Ron had heard about the competition and suggested to Margie that instead of going to their Weight Watchers meetings they hire themselves a personal trainer and enter the competition.

'We'll probably lose the same amount of weight,' he'd said when he presented his proposal over their skim cappuccinos, 'but we'll have much more fun!' He told her that he'd picked her out of all the ladies at Weight Watchers because she looked like someone with a good sense of humour, and Margie, who had never thought of herself as having any sense of humour at all, was ridiculously flattered. To enter the competition they had to take a 'before' photo of themselves in their swimming costumes, holding up newspapers to prove just how fat they were on that particular date. Margie came out of the changing room with her robe pulled bashfully around her, ready to display the appropriate shame of a fat person, but Rotund Ron wasn't having any of that. He came strutting out like he was Mr Universe and soon had Margie quite weak with laughter and even striking Miss Universe poses herself, perhaps because she wanted to prove that she *did* have a sense of humour. It was as if she'd started to become an entirely different person, a flippant, confident, funny person — the sort of person Rotund Ron believed her to be, and damn it, maybe he was right.

Over the next eight weeks they'd met Suzie three times a week, sweating and puffing and chortling at each other. They shared their ecstasy as their bodies began to change. They tried to out-do each other when they did their sit-ups and push-ups and tricep dips and bicep curls. When it hurt too much they made very rude comments about Suzie under their breaths. They knew each other's bodies as well as their own. 'Feel that!' Ron would say, pointing at his thigh. 'Nothing but solid muscle, baby.' After each training session they'd have a protein shake in the park, sitting on a bench, red-faced, dripping with sweat and laughing, always laughing.

Margie had not had an affair with Rotund Ron. They'd never so much as kissed, but in some ways it felt like the whole experience of transforming their bodies had been more intimate, more physical, more sexy, more *spiritual* than any old affair involving middle-of-the-day sex in horrible sleazy highway motels and . . . well, whatever else those affairs involved.

On the night of the competition held at the Hilton Hotel, the 'before' photos were displayed on a giant screen behind each transformed couple flexing their spray-on-tanned biceps and triceps and quadriceps in a carefully choreographed routine. Rotund Ron and Margie had to avoid eye-contact while doing their routine — to 'Eye of the Tiger' — because otherwise they were liable to dissolve into laughter and Suzie said she was going to be furious with them if they ruined her hard work with an attack of the giggles. But on the night they'd both got caught up in the adrenaline-charged atmosphere and got all trembly and competitive before they went on stage. Afterwards they were euphoric with their achievement, even when a ferociously muscular pair of born-again Christians from Baulkham Hills won the first prize. Margie and Ron won a flat-screen TV, which they agreed to donate to a centre for kids with cancer, because Ron's best friend's son had died of cancer twenty years earlier.

It was when Rotund Ron, Suzie and Margie were all sharing a celebratory glass of champagne that Margie got the phone call from Ron and learned that he'd got into a violent argument with a taxi driver at Glass Bay who didn't want him dripping river-water all over his cab and couldn't care less that Ron was trying to get to the Hilton to drag his wife from a Jacuzzi. Unfortunately the taxi driver happened to have started an introductory course in Tae Kwan Do at the Glass Bay Evening College and after Ron threw his first clumsy punch the taxi driver executed a perfect kick to Ron's temple. The police were called, and when Ron wouldn't calm down they decided he was drunk and disorderly and threw him in the back of a paddy wagon which was jam-packed with excited, swaying young men from a drunk and disorderly bucks party. Margie, Rotund Ron and Suzie drove over to the police station to pick up Ron, and all the drunk bucks got to hear them explaining to Ron that no, they weren't having an affair; they'd been entering a body-building competition and they'd won a flat-screen TV. The glassy-eyed groom, who didn't seem to Margie to be in any state to get married the next day, became quite emotional, grabbing Ron's arm and slurring, 'She wouldn't cheat on you, mate. She loves you. She made a solemn vow to you. She's your *wife*, man! She was just doing a bit of innocent body-building and now you've got a flat-screen TV,' while the rest of the bucks competed to get Suzie's phone number by offering to arm-wrestle her.

It was all a bit embarrassing. The Glass Bay police thought it was hilarious.

She and Ron had taken the boat back over to the island in silence. Ron held an icepack to his eye, while Margie steered the boat and looked up at the stars and thought what a funny old world it was.

When they were nearly at the wharf, Ron had removed his icepack for a second and said, 'Did *you* know our daughter was a lesbian?' and Margie had grinned at him and said, 'Yes, I did. I had a lovely lunch with her and Audrey last week,' and Ron had said, 'Oh,' and pressed the icepack back to his eye.

Now Ron drums his fingers on the kitchen table and says nervously, '*We* could take a trip to Italy, if you like? You and me? A second honeymoon?'

Margie turns around from the sink and looks at him. It's as if some sort of blurry substance has been peeled from her eyes and she can see him clearly for perhaps the first time in her life — an uncertain, greying, middle-aged man with a secret terror he's not as smart or as classy as he'd like to be; a man who pretends he doesn't care what other people think when he cares desperately; a man who despises himself so much that the only way he can alleviate his feelings of inferiority is by stomping down his wife's personality with a daily stream of nasty jibes. A *little* man.

A man with a foolish wife who should simply have said, 'Don't speak to me like that.' Maybe if she had she could have saved both of them.

She sits down in front of Ron and says, 'I'm not really interested in going to Europe. What I'd really like is to drive around Australia. I've always wanted to drive across the Nullarbor.'

'We could do that. Get a four-wheel drive . . .'

'No, I mean on my own. I'd like to take a holiday on my own. For a couple of months.'

'Oh.' His face gets all pulpy with hurt. 'Oh. OK.'

'I think it might be good for us to spend some time apart, don't you? I don't mean an official separation or anything. Just a break. It seems like a good time now that we are talking about closing down the Alice and Jack business. And then we can think about what we'd like to do.'

'Oh,' he says again. 'OK. Yep. That's a good idea.'

Margie feels suddenly sick with this horrible new power.

'Well,' she says. 'I'm going to call Callum and see how Grace is.'

She stays sitting and she is about to reach over and pat his shoulder but her new, strong body doesn't move, and after a few seconds she stands up and goes to phone and leaves him sitting there studying his knuckles.

Maybe she'll call him from some outback town and say, 'Come and meet me.'

Or maybe she won't. She really has no idea.

53

Rose's story is interrupted while they move into the living room, in the hope that Rose will be more comfortable on Sophie's couch. They experiment with cushions behind her back until she says she thinks that's about as good as they can manage.

Sophie feels a sick horror over Rose's revelation. The scrambled eggs sit unsteadily in her stomach. Rose is too pure and fragile to even say the *word* 'rape'.

'That's so horrible,' Sophie awkwardly touches Rose's thin shoulder, 'what happened to you.'

'Oh darling, it's OK, it was a very long time ago,' answers Rose serenely. 'There's no need to be upset. You're just like Veronika. We only just managed to save her from breaking one of Laura's good mugs. She was *very* agitated. She couldn't understand why I didn't go straight to the police. But it's a different era now. You modern girls are a lot better informed and a lot more assertive, which is a good thing. The problem was, I truly believed *I* was the criminal.'

Rose pats Sophie's arm as if she is the one who should be comforted, and says, 'Oh sugar! I brought a photo to show you. It's in my bag still, in the kitchen.'

Sophie leaps to her feet and goes to the kitchen, conscious of how freely she can move around compared to Rose.

The photo is of Connie, Rose and their mother dressed up in hats and gloves for a day out in the city. They're walking down a street, arms caught mid-swing, and both girls are looking at their mother and laughing. 'They used to have "street photographers" in those days who would take your photo without you even knowing,' says Rose. 'Then they'd give you a card and you could go to this place on George Street and see if you'd like to buy it. Mum felt sorry for the photographer so we bought this one. It was a few weeks before she got sick.'

'You were *so* beautiful.' Sophie looks at Rose's young, laughing face. 'I bet you were like Grace and didn't even realise how beautiful you were.'

'Oh, I could be vain!' says Rose. 'Look at me with my long hair. The fashion was short bobs but I was so proud of my long blonde hair I refused to cut it!'

She caresses her mother's face with an age-spotted bent finger. 'That's the coat Mum lost in the train. It was navy. Good wool.' A tear runs down her withered cheek. 'Oh Mum, you silly thing.'

Sophie feels her own eyes sting as she looks at fourteen-year-old Rose and thinks of the terrible things that were about to happen to her. She wants to go back in time and protect her and Connie. Take them along to an ATM and withdraw as much cash as they need. Buy their mum a new coat on her credit card and take her to the doctor on her Medicare card. March into David Jones and buy a whole damned roll of turquoise crêpe de Chine. Punch Mr Egg Head in the nose and then get him charged with sexual harassment before he even has a chance to lay a single sleazy finger on Rose.

'Well,' says Rose. 'On with my story. Connie always said there's nothing worse than a person who keeps meandering from the point.'

So, it was only a few days later that Mr Egg Head got transferred to another department, and a few weeks after that I started falling asleep at the counter in the afternoon.

I was fifteen years old, Catholic and pregnant. It was quite a scandal for those days, darling. Quite a scandal. And I had an awful suspicion that my father might actually kill me. I could imagine him quite calmly picking up his bible and thumping me to death with it.

Well, Connie guessed it eventually and I told her what had happened. I remember we were sitting down at Sultana Rocks and Connie had a stick and she was making holes in the sand, and as I told the story she jabbed harder and harder until the stick broke and she threw it hard across the water. Then she gave me a hug. A very quick, hard hug. We weren't ever a very cuddly family, so it was special. It meant that *she* didn't think I was a dirty thief who deserved her punishment. Then she picked up another stick and started jabbing more holes in the sand, but this time in orderly rows, and I knew she was trying to think out a solution. I remember closing my eyes and feeling so relieved because now it was Connie's problem. I completely abdicated responsibility to her. So, I can't really complain.

The normal practice in those days for unmarried Catholic girls was that you were sent off, all very hush-hush, to a home in the country, where you had your baby and it was quickly whisked away for adoption. Well, Connie wasn't having any of that. She was determined that we would keep it. She was more interested in the baby than I was, to be honest. She was grieving for Mum too of course, and I think the baby gave her something to focus on. She was also determined to save my reputation, which seems funny these days, but she didn't want word getting around Glass Bay that I was 'used goods'. She thought I'd still meet a nice young man and settle down and get married. I remember she walked up and down the beach jabbing with her stick for ages until she finally marched back, looking very triumphant, and said, 'Alice and Jack Munro are going to have a baby.'

I said, 'Fine, Alice and Jack have a baby and then what? What happens to them?'

She said, 'They vanish! Poof! We're not even going to *try* to come up with an explanation. They're going to vanish into thin air, just like the people aboard the *Mary Celeste*. It's perfect. It's absolutely perfect.'

She had a fondness for unsolved mysteries, you see, and the *Mary Celeste* was one of her favourites. She thought this would solve everything. We could keep the baby, save my reputation, and people would hear about Scribbly Gum Island. 'Once people get a whiff of scandal they'll want to come here for a sticky-beak,' she said. 'We'll be ready and waiting with scones and tea. Light, fluffy scones! We'll put Banksia Island right out of business.'

Well, I thought she was joking, or temporarily insane, but that very day she told Dad that Alice Munro was expecting. He said, 'Well, as long as they keep paying their rent, that's all we care about.' Connie said, 'I think they're doing it tough, Dad. We'll have to keep an eye on them.' One day she said, 'I promised that if anything ever happened to the Munros that we'd look after their baby,' and Dad snapped, 'What the bloody hell did you say that for?' and Connie said, 'I was being a Good Samaritan, Dad, just like in the bible,' and that shut him up.

I didn't see how we would hide my pregnancy from Dad, but Connie said he wouldn't notice. She said he didn't look at us. I didn't see how it would be possible not to notice your daughter was nine months pregnant, but Connie was right. I just wore loose clothing and I never got very big anyway. Looking back, I think the poor man was close to being legally blind. That's why he hardly left the house.

Or maybe he did notice and he just didn't

want to know. Maybe he saw through the whole thing. Who knows?

I had to give up work, of course, when I got to three months. The ladies at the department store had beady eyes. Luckily, Connie got a job doing office cleaning and she spent the next six months turning Grandpop's house into Alice and Jack's house. She put a couple of Mum's old dresses in the cupboard. She managed to get a free crib from the Salvation Army. It was like a project for her. I think she enjoyed it. I remember the day she came up with the idea of the half-finished crossword, she was tickled pink. Well, I didn't take much notice of it all, really. I was in a funny state at that time. The experience with Mr Egg Head had quite, well, shaken me up, I suppose. I spent hours fishing and trying not to think. I honestly didn't think we'd get away with it. I thought we'd both end up in jail.

Of course, there was the problem of who would deliver the baby, when it came. We could hardly go to a hospital because what would we do about the birth certificate? Connie was thinking about confiding in a friend who was a midwife, but she really didn't trust anybody with the secret. Well, in the end we didn't have a choice. I started getting contractions three weeks early. It was one of those stormy, dramatic days. Connie took me around in the boat to Grandpop's house. The water was all choppy and I was out of my mind with fear. We got up to the house and I had Enigma on the kitchen floor in about half an hour. Connie delivered her. She cut the cord with our grandmother's old kitchen scissors. Her hands were all slippery and she was shaking so much she cut herself. So that's her blood on the kitchen floor, and probably some of mine too. I remember Connie kneeling there with tears streaming down her face, blood dripping from her hand, holding Enigma. She loved Enigma instantly. It took me much longer. Actually, to be honest, Sophie darling, I could hardly bear the sight of her for quite a few months. I was worried she had an egg-shaped head. Don't ever tell her that, will you? I still think it has a slightly eggy shape to it, at times. Connie was crying with joy, while I cried for my mother.

Well, we cleaned the baby and wrapped her up and took her home to Dad and we told him the story about going around to have a cup of tea with Alice and Jack and finding the baby. It was a test to see if he swallowed it — but he did, hook, line and sinker. At first he said we'd just have to take the baby to the hospital in Glass Bay and have it put in care, but Connie kept saying, 'We made a promise, Dad,' and then the funniest thing happened. Connie gave him the baby to hold and his face melted, went soft and smooth. He said, 'Well, as long as she doesn't wake me up at night,' and handed her back.

The next morning Connie said to me, 'This is your last chance to change your mind', as if any of it was my idea! And she went off to the police station and told them we'd found an abandoned baby. Then the newspapers sent around Jimmy to do a story, and funnily enough I think Connie and I both really started to believe in it. Alice and Jack seemed more real to me than Mr Egg Head whispering vile things in my ear. Connie was right. The very day after the story appeared a boatload of sticky-beaks turned up at the island and we were ready with a tray of freshly baked scones: tuppence and ha'penny with a cup of tea.

Connie didn't tell Jimmy the truth until after he came back from the war, and he was *furious.* The Munro Baby Mystery had been the story that started his career and he was horrified that it was a hoax. He took a long time to forgive Connie. That was when Connie came up with the idea of not telling

Enigma until she was forty. I think it threw her when she realised she'd hurt Jimmy's feelings. People don't like to feel they've been conned, do they? Especially men. Men take themselves so seriously. Connie had this idea that by the time Enigma got to the age of forty she'd be mature enough to handle it. Actually, I think Enigma was mostly worried about whether she'd stay famous.

As the years went by I started to think that maybe we could come clean about the whole thing. I wanted Enigma to know that I was her mother, but she was really more Connie's daughter than mine, especially in those first few months after she was born when I went a touch barmy. I barely touched her. Connie brought her up really. I was just like a big sister. I remember I felt hurt when Enigma asked Connie if she could call her 'Mum'. But what could I do? Connie *was* her mum. If it wasn't for her, I probably wouldn't have been able to keep her. And when Connie and Jimmy couldn't have their own children and she so badly wanted them, I could hardly say I wanted Enigma just for me.

Besides which, by then the Munro Baby Mystery had become a successful business. When Dad died in 1940 we had made more money than we'd ever dreamed of. Whenever Connie thought interest in the Munro Mystery was starting to wane, she'd come up with something new to get people talking again. After the war, she wrote all those letters from Alice to Jack and pretended to find them in the cake tin under the bed. Confidentially, Sophie, those letters were really all about Connie's feelings about her marriage to Jimmy; they were going through a bit of a bad patch. So Jimmy sat down and wrote that beautiful love letter from Jack to Alice. Connie cried when she read it. You've read it, haven't you? He could be romantic when he wanted to be, that Jimmy! Then of course, in the 1970s, when our numbers were very low, Connie read *The Female Eunuch* and decided that Alice was being 'emotionally castrated' and she sat down and wrote Alice's diary in two days and got Margie to 'discover' it under the floorboards. I remember Jimmy saying, 'Nobody is going to fall for this rubbish! How many more historical documents can be hidden in one small house?' Well, that diary caused a sensation because it implied that Alice probably bumped off Jack, and the feminists just *loved* that. After that we all agreed there couldn't really be any more discoveries.

There were so many times when I felt such a strong desire to tell everyone the truth, but Connie was like a stubborn old — is that the phone again, Sophie? No, answer it. I'm finished. That's the end of my story.

54

'Oh, you're there. I've been trying to call all morning.'

'Sorry. I slept in. I had a bit too much to drink last night.'

'Me too. The mulled wine was . . .'

'Yes. It sure was.'

'Yes.'

'Well.'

'So.'

'How is Grace?'

'She's fine, physically, but one of the doctors talked to me this morning and she seems to think that Grace has postnatal depression.'

'Oh, dear. Oh, well . . . *shit.* I should have thought of that. I had a friend who had it. I seem to have been missing the obvious lately. Oh, God, you don't think she purposely . . . ?'

'Yeah. Maybe. She says it was an accident but I don't know. She's so careful about what she eats. I should have seen it. Actually, I thought maybe she was depressed a while back, but everybody kept telling me she was fine. They kept going on about those thank you cards she made and how no depressed woman could have managed that. It wasn't as if she was crying all day. Or not in front of me, anyway. But I *did* know something was different. I should have . . . anyway, she's going to get help now. That's not why I'm calling. I wanted to say to you, about last night . . .'

'Oh no! Don't say anything! You don't need to say anything. We'll just pretend it never happened. It was just the wine. Don't even think about it! It's not important. Especially not now.'

'It is important. I wanted to say I'm so sorry for pushing you away like that and I wanted to say that . . .'

'It's OK! Please don't say anything more.'

'I don't want you to think it didn't mean anything. I don't want you thinking it was just the wine. Even though the wine — but it wasn't just the wine. Oh, fuck.'

'You don't need to say this.'

'The thing is, I really love Grace.'

'Of course you do. Please stop it.'

'I would never be unfaithful to her.'

'You don't need to say this!'

'But I just want you to know that if I'd met you before I met Grace, you know, that whole 'other lifetime' thing. This sounds like such clichéd crap but I'm serious. I just want you to know that you mean something to me, that if things had been different, then things . . . would have been different. Oh Jesus, I sound like a lunatic.'

'Please stop it.'

'OK, but do you see what I'm saying?'

'Yes, I do. Thank you.'

'OK.'

'OK.'

'I'm sorry.'

'There's nothing to be sorry for.'

'OK.'

'OK.'

'Are you laughing or crying?'

'A bit of both.'

'Oh.'

'Let's never talk about it again, all right, Callum? Not one word. Or even a meaningful look. Especially no meaningful looks. All right? You promise?'

'All right. No meaningful looks. I promise.'

'Send my love to Grace.'

'I will.'

55

Grace sits in her hospital room with her mother, looking at the lunch which has just been delivered by a sour-faced woman shoving a trolley. Callum has gone home to relieve Veronika and Audrey of Jake, and the doctors have said that he can come back and pick up Grace later this afternoon.

Grace feels shaky and surreal. Her throat is still sore, as if somebody had tried to strangle her, and her leg is aching and bruised from where her mother jammed in the EpiPen. She is not allowing her mind to form any complete thoughts about what happened last night; she's just revelling in the relief of oxygen flowing unimpeded into her lungs. In. Out. In. Out.

Laura lifts an aluminium lid from a plate and her nostrils contract with disgust. 'There is no excuse for food of this quality. It's just laziness. Look at that sandwich. Appalling. The bread is *stale.* Are you hungry?

We'll get you something when we get home. When I spoke to Veronika she mentioned the freezer was very well stocked. She counted eleven lasagnes.'

'Callum's favourite,' says Grace.

'You always said your lasagnes were better fresh.' Her mother pauses and pokes a manicured finger at the offending sandwich and says, 'Did you deliberately eat that samosa last night?'

Grace pleats the thin white hospital blanket between her fingers and breathes. In. Out. In. Out. She doesn't want to think about the failure of the Plan. She just wants to enjoy breathing.

'You're just normally so careful,' says Laura.

Grace manages to speak. 'I forgot. I was distracted.'

'Distracted,' repeats Laura. 'Distracted by what?'

Grace says, 'Do you remember that day when I nearly ate a sesame bar in front of you?'

Laura smiles, as if pleased to be reminded of a favourite joke. 'Of course I do. You were a little minx at that age.'

'I thought you were going to let me die.'

'I sure called your bluff.'

'I *seriously* thought you were going to let

561

me die.'

'Oh.' Laura rolls her eyes. 'So, what, did I psychologically damage you or something? Is that what you're saying? Because life wasn't easy for me after your father left. All very well for Margie to be the perfect mummy. She had a husband!'

'She had *Ron!*' Grace is talking in her normal voice. She feels invigorated. 'She wasn't exactly blissfully happy!'

'She wasn't a deserted wife like me.' Laura examines her nails critically and takes some hand-cream out of her handbag. 'Anyway, the fact is, I was never motherly like Margie. She played with dolls while I played with Mum's make-up. So, I'm sorry, OK? Some people just aren't motherly. I've been thinking a lot while I was travelling and I've come to realise that. I wasn't ready to be a mother. I didn't even especially *want* to be a mother, it was your father who wanted a baby! I hope that's not traumatising for you to hear, but it's the truth, and it's about time we all started telling the truth in this family. And then, when he left us for that bitch who was a size *fourteen* and couldn't cook to save her life! I never dealt with it, you see. I let it fester like an abscess. I haven't been happy for years. I've wasted my entire life mourning a *dentist,* for heaven's sake. It hit me while I was looking at the *Mona Lisa.* I had an epiphany. It was something about that knowing smirk of hers. She's thinking, Yep, all men are bastards but we women just have to knuckle down and get on with it. I decided I needed to make some fundamental changes in my life. I'm going to start by having a chemical peel because my skin is just dreadful — what?'

'You had an epiphany while looking at the *Mona Lisa* and decided to have a chemical peel?' Grace laughs and it feels like the first taste of fizzy champagne after a long period of non-drinking.

'Well, the chemical peel was just about regaining confidence in my looks. I'm going to start from the outside in. I also want to do a course. In art history, perhaps. Or ceramics. You're not the only arty one in the family, you know. You certainly didn't get your talent from your father's side of the family! And I am going to try and be a good grandmother to Jake. Not a snuggly, cuddly nana but an interested, involved, stylish sort of grandmother. You know, I'll take him to museums. That sort of thing. When he's older, of course. Not now. I won't be so much help with him now. To be honest, I find babies quite terrifying.'

Well, so do I, thinks Grace.

'Of course, you've got Margie to help you.' Laura finishes massaging the cream into her hands and offers the tube to Grace, who shakes her head. She replaces the lid and takes a deep, brave breath. 'Is there something the matter, Grace? Have you been finding it hard coping with Jake? Callum mentioned one of the doctors thought you might have postnatal depression. Look, you don't need to tell me if you don't feel comfortable talking about it. You'd better see a psychiatrist, don't you think? You can tell him. Or her. Which would you prefer? A woman would be more intelligent, obviously.'

Grace says, 'I didn't know you carried around an EpiPen. Callum said you were so calm when you used it.'

'When you were younger I used to practise giving injections to a banana. I was a nervous wreck at the thought. It's not that difficult, of course. Any fool could do it. You should have had your own in your handbag! But then, I suppose if you were trying to kill yourself, that was the point.' Laura's face crumbles slightly and Grace notices spidery wrinkles above her mother's upper lip. They make her feel protective towards her — big-sisterly.

Laura says, 'You're not going to try and do it again, are you?'

'I *forgot* the samosas had walnuts in them,' insists Grace.

'Really?' asks her mother.

'Really.'

Laura looks at her fingernails again and says, 'Grace, I wasn't going to let you kill yourself when you were thirteen. I had my hand hovering over my bread roll ready to throw it at you and knock the sesame bar from your hand. I can assure you it was never even going to get close to your mouth.'

'Oh.' Grace's voice sounds hoarse.

'I know I don't exactly qualify as mother-of-the-year material and I know I made some silly mistakes, but you're my daughter. I would have died for you, for heaven's sake.'

Grace examines her own fingernails.

'I still would. That's just, you know, the way it is.'

Grace looks up and meets her mother's eyes. Laura smiles uneasily and then brightens, peering closer at Grace's face. 'Your eyebrows look like they could do with a wax. We could get Margie to mind Jake one day and you and I could go and have facials done. Would you like that?'

'That would be nice.'

It would be awful. Grace hates facials,

they make her feel claustrophobic, but still, the principle of the idea is nice.

They lapse into silence. Grace watches her mother twiddling the red stone on her new necklace, glancing around the room with that familiar mix of tension and disdain. She imagines Laura, about the same age that Grace is now, sitting alone in the kitchen, jamming the EpiPen into a banana, two lines of fear etched between her eyes. Grace breathes in and out, in and out. Oxygen flows in through her nostrils and expands her chest. There is a vase of flowers sitting on the windowsill. The flowers are a deep grape colour, similar to the colour of Aunt Rose's new jumper. She'd like to paint them and discuss mixing the right colour with Rose. She would quite like a cup of tea. She is looking forward to having a shower and washing her hair when she gets home.

Beneath the rhythm of her breathing she can just discern a whispery thought: *Maybe it's going to be OK.*

Gublet McDublet came back from the moon to find that his mum had been off having a chemical peel and her face was all red and flaky.

'Oh, Gublet,' she said sadly. 'Why did you run away to the moon? You silly billy, didn't you know I'd miss you?'

Gublet just gave her an enigmatic *Mona Lisa* smile, because actually he hadn't known that at all.

'You seem glum today, Sophie darling,' says Rose as she's leaving, wrapping her new pashmina around her.

'I guess I've got a hangover from all that mulled wine,' says Sophie. 'And I feel especially ugly today with this horrible cold sore.'

'Oh, well, it will get better,' says Rose. 'You're a very pretty girl.'

'Hmmmph,' says Sophie disbelievingly, like a sulky teenager.

'Well, of course you are. Oh, you know, there's something I keep forgetting to tell you! I was thinking about you the other day and your search for the right man, so to speak, and you know what I suddenly remembered? I remembered that one day Connie said to me that she'd discovered the perfect man for you. The darndest thing is I can't remember who it was — although I do remember thinking that I sort of agreed with her, although I felt disloyal to Thomas.'

'Was it Rick?' Sophie touches her cold sore. 'Or Ian, perhaps?'

'I really can't remember who it was. I was just thinking about how funny it was that Connie was so *convinced* that this man was your soul mate!'

Wonderful. Fabulous. Oh, what does it matter anyway? The thought of meeting a new man at this stage, while she's still so raw over Callum, seems ridiculous and pointless.

'His name's on the tip of my tongue! It will come to me. I'll call you as soon as I think of it,' says Rose. 'Of course, you might not fancy the fellow at all!'

Rose kisses her on the cheek and Sophie breathes in her powdery scent.

'Thank you for telling me the story about Alice and Jack.'

'My pleasure, darling.'

56

It is the weekend after the Anniversary Night and Callum is taking Grace to see their house in the mountains. They haven't been up for months and he's hoping that they will be pleasantly surprised by how far it has progressed since they've seen it. Their builder has assured him that they will be thrilled, but Callum no longer likes the builder, in fact he hates him, and has secret fantasies about knocking him out with a plank of wood, sending that smug orange hard-hat flying.

Jake is in his capsule in the back seat, singing to himself. This week he has discovered his voice — a wonderful toy capable of creating a whole spectrum of interesting noises. When Jake is making his sounds he squints his eyes in deep concentration, which is exactly the same expression that Callum used to see on Grace's face when he interrupted her working on one of her

Gublet paintings. It twists his heart.

He and Grace are all tentative tiptoes around each other at the moment. They're so polite it's almost comical, but Callum can't relax because he's lost trust in his own character. He is completely appalled by himself. He thought he was superior to the sort of sleazy, shallow man who gets drunk and kisses another woman just a few months after his wife gives birth to their first child. He thought he was more *evolved* than that. And it wasn't just the mulled wine. He actually teetered on the brink of an affair. An evil, lecherous part of his mind was thinking it all out: *Where can we go? Her house? Now?* He'd wanted to sleep with Sophie. He *still* wants to sleep with Sophie. He wants to talk to Sophie, listen to CDs with Sophie, dance with Sophie, make love to Sophie, make her laugh, tease her . . . oh for Christ's sake. He is driving along with his wife beside him and his son in the back seat, having fantasies about another woman. But he doesn't want to leave Grace. Oh no. Not at all. That's not an option. All these treacherous thoughts about Sophie seem quite separate from his helpless, hopeless love for Grace. He wants to have his cake and eat it too — just like every fat, balding, middle-aged, unfaithful businessman throughout history. He is a tired cliché. A dirty joke. He has even caught himself thinking whiny, self-pitying thoughts like, But Grace doesn't *get* me the way Sophie does. *My wife doesn't understand me.*

And he doesn't understand her. He doesn't know what she's thinking any more. He doesn't know if she does have postnatal depression or not. She says she doesn't. She says the doctor who suggested that had only spoken to her for ten minutes and had no idea what she was talking about. She says she's fine. She smiles her beautiful smile and says don't worry.

He will never forget the panic he felt when she had her allergic reaction on the Anniversary Night. It was nightmarish. It was punishment for kissing Sophie. He doesn't know if Grace ate the samosa on purpose, like Laura is suggesting, because each time he goes to ask Grace, he's terrified she'll say, 'Yes, I did,' and then he'll have to say, 'Why? Why did you do that?' And what if she answers, 'Because I saw you kissing Sophie'? It gives him a stomach-lurching feeling of vertigo just thinking about it. So he says nothing at all. He acts as if it was just an accident, as if the doctor never mentioned postnatal depression, as if they're just a normal married couple, as if everything is fine, as if they still have sex, as if they still touch each other, as if a few weeks ago she didn't say, 'You don't even know me.' He talks to her each day like he's reading lines from a script. 'Good morning!' 'How did you sleep?' 'Shall I put the baby down?'

He speaks more naturally to the man at the service station where he buys his petrol each month than he does to his own wife.

He tries out one of his jovial-husband lines now. 'Do you want to stop for a coffee before we see the house?'

'No, I'm OK,' answers Grace. 'Unless you want to stop?'

'Only if you want to.'

'I'm fine.'

'Well, I'm fine too.'

Callum clenches the steering wheel and looks straight ahead at the highway peeling away before him.

57

'Oh dear. Oh damn. Where is she, I wonder? Oh. Ah. OK. Well. Here we go. HELLO! SOPHIE! IT'S ROSE! I WANTED TO TELL YOU THAT I REMEMBERED THE NAME OF THAT FELLOW CON-NIE HAD PICKED OUT FOR YOU. IT'S CALLUM'S FRIEND AND . . . oh dear, I don't think this silly machine is working, is it? HELLO? Oh sugar!'

58

Sophie wakes up early and goes to the bathroom to look at the progress of her cold sore, which looks quite pretty now, just like a smudge of pale pink lipstick. It's a pity all those horrible, humiliating feelings for Callum can't just dry up and fade away too, until there's nothing left but a nice, socially acceptable smudge of friendship.

As she's cleaning her teeth she decides to give herself her own version of electric-shock aversion therapy. Every time she thinks of Callum she will pinch herself hard above the elbow. She will train her mind like a rat in a maze. Today should be a good day to start training because she has something new to preoccupy her mind: a new life. Yesterday, at yum cha, she and her mother unexpectedly came up with a new plan for Sophie's career.

Gretel had started talking about that 'fraudulent psychic' they'd met at the

Korean baths, and 'who ever heard of a caramel aura' and 'why would *Sophie,* of all people, need a positive career-change when she was already doing so well in her career!'

That's when Sophie admitted that well, actually, she'd been coasting for the last couple of years at work and that, while she still enjoyed it, she'd really gone as far as she could go there and it wasn't really challenging her any more, and all of a sudden she was talking to her mother about how she'd always thought that when she had children — ha! — she would give up work and do something part-time, something completely different, like teaching a wine-tasting course, or perhaps using her HR skills for something different, like career counselling for teenagers or hardened (handsome, unshaven) young crims, and how she'd quite like to play violin again in a string quartet like she did when she was at uni. Her mother had said that she might have had some unrealistic ideas about just how much spare time she'd have with a baby, but seeing as Sophie owned a house outright and didn't need to worry about her mortgage payments any more, why didn't she just resign from work and take some time off and pursue some — if not all! — of these ideas.

'Why not?' cried Gretel, excitedly spilling her green tea.

'Why not?' said Sophie, thoughtfully spearing a chopstick through her steamed pork bun.

And just like that, the fraudulent psychic's prophesy came true, and today Sophie is sitting down with her notepad to consider an entirely new lifestyle and wondering why she'd never thought of it before. She thinks about how interested Callum will be and immediately pinches her arm so hard it brings tears to her eyes. She puts on her Eva Cassidy CD and thinks about what Callum said about this album — and pinches her arm again. She would have thought she might have picked things up faster than the average rat.

She is standing at the sink, pouring herself a cup of tea, when she sees a strange man standing on the balcony, with his face pressed up against the window, peering in. She jerks back in fright, spilling boiling water over her hand and dropping the mug, which shatters on the floor.

Instantly the back door swings open and a tall, lanky, pale man is suddenly filling all the space in the kitchen, saying, 'I'm so sorry for scaring you. I thought there was nobody home. I'm not an axe murderer, I'm

Callum's friend, although I suppose Callum could be friends with an axe murderer, who knows,' and while he's talking he has taken hold of Sophie's wrist and is holding her hand under the cold running water. 'Oh dear, I hope it's not too bad. I've probably scarred you for life. And was that mug your favourite?'

'I think it's going to be OK.' Sophie smiles up at him and he smiles back. He has a sad, accepting sort of smile, as if he knows life probably isn't going to work out but he's doing the best he can.

'I'm Ed,' he says. 'And you're Sophie. And I think I knew you a very long time ago. Do you remember me?'

And suddenly that mournful smile is so sweetly familiar.

'Eddie Ripple,' says Sophie, and to her own surprise she takes her wet, sore hand out from under the tap and stands on her toes so she can throw her arms around his neck.

Grace and Callum are making the bed together. He says, 'Ed is going to stop by at Sophie's place and see if she wants him to quote on painting it. He thinks he knows her.' Grace lifts the mattress and tucks in her side of the sheet. Sophie sent around a big bunch of flowers after the Anniversary Night, but Grace hasn't seen her yet and it's odd that she hasn't been around. It's also odd that Callum hasn't mentioned her before now. It seems to Grace that something must have happened between Sophie and Callum that night, and it makes her feel guilty because whatever it was, Grace made it happen. They were the unwitting puppets in Grace's plan to give away her husband to another woman and step out of her life. Then again, they're not made of *wood,* they do have their own brains, they didn't have to fall in with Grace's plans quite so willingly!

Callum says, 'Do you remember how your Aunt Connie thought Ed and Sophie would make a good match?'

'Did she?' says Grace. 'I don't remember. Oh dear. Ed Ripple. Aunt Rose always said she thought Connie's matchmaking skills left a lot to be desired.'

'I'm sure Sophie will meet somebody herself,' says Callum.

Grace looks up and meets his eyes on the other side of the bed, and he looks away and pretends to be interested in tucking in the corner of the sheet perfectly. So, she's right. Something *did* happen that night. She wonders what it was. Just a kiss? Surely they didn't sleep together? Where would they have gone? Aunt Connie's house? She imagines Callum kissing Sophie (she'd have to stand up on tippy-toes, which would be so adorable!), his hand caressing the back of her creamy white neck. When he kisses, he does this thing with his thumb on the back of your neck, a slow, delicate, circular motion, which used to drive Grace into a frenzy of weak-kneed desire when they first started going out. And Sophie, what would she be doing? Saying something funny and cute? Blushing? She probably has kissing techniques of her own. She probably does something really unusual and stylish with her tongue. Grace has no kissing techniques. She just lets Callum kiss her and enjoys herself.

Then it hits her. Callum and Sophie probably danced together. Of course they danced together; how could Callum resist dancing with a real live woman instead of a cardboard cut-out?

She becomes aware of a digging pain, as if someone is poking her in the side. It's jealousy. She wanted Sophie to marry Callum and now she's jealous at the thought of them dancing together. She lets the feeling take hold of her. It's so much better than that horrendous dull nothingness; it's a proper, human emotion. Real spiteful human blood is pumping through her veins.

She says, 'Well, would you look at this nice freshly made bed.'

Callum squishes a pillow into a pillow slip. He looks blankly at the bed and says with endearing uncertainty, 'Yeah?'

'Don't you think we should mess it up a bit?'

He drops the pillow and has her flat on the bed so fast she's laughing while he's kissing her, his hand on the back of *her* neck, his tongue in *her* mouth, and she must have been out of her mind to have thought of giving him away to another woman. 'Eddie Ripple,' says Sophie. 'I haven't seen you for thirty years. Can you believe we're old enough to say, "I haven't seen you for thirty years"? Did you ever think we'd get this old and still be us?'

She is sitting with ice wrapped up in a tea towel held against her hand while Eddie kneels with a dustpan sweeping up the broken cup. He looks up at her with exactly the same green eyes of the little boy who used to sit with her under the tuckshop stairs. The Blusher and The Twitcher. The Outcasts. The Spastics. The Retards.

He says, 'I think I thought anything that happened to me after I turned thirty would be sort of irrelevant.'

His voice is deep with the slower rhythm of a laconic Australian farmer being interviewed on TV about the drought. Sophie can feel her own voice, her own heart beat, perceptibly slowing down to match his pace. He sounds like a country boy, and of course, she remembers, that's what he'd become. His family had moved up to Queensland to live on a farm. Sophie, who only had very vague ideas about what the 'country' meant, had always imagined him going to a one-teacher school in a horse and buggy, with girls wearing bonnets, like in *Little House on the Prairie.*

'I missed you when you left,' says Sophie, remembering that all of a sudden as well. That first day at school without Eddie by her side had been like the first time she'd travelled to another country on her own. She'd felt simultaneously invisible and overly visible at the same time. She used to go to bed feeling sick about school the next day. She says, 'But guess what? Then I got popular and I didn't miss you at all.'

'How did you manage that?'

'My eleventh birthday party was a social coup. We got an in-ground swimming pool, you see, and my dad made this amazing slide into the pool. I became A-list after Dad built that slide. All the girls decided my blushing was cute and the boys pretended not to notice.'

'I don't think I missed you,' says Ed, considering, and of course that was the thing about Eddie Ripple, he was always devastatingly honest. 'Everything in Queensland was so different. We went to school barefoot. We caught yabbies in the creek at lunchtime. It just felt like I stepped into another world and you didn't even exist any more — like my old bedroom, my old street, the whole state of New South Wales had just vanished. And then, thirty years later, I'm having dinner right here in this house, with Callum's family, and they started talking on and on about this girl called Sophie who blushed, and I thought, How many blushing Sophies can there be in Sydney? And it all came back, all those conversations under the tuckshop stairs — I seem to recall discussing existential dilemmas with you, Sophie Honeywell, as well as making up bloodthirsty stories about how we'd get revenge on Bruno, and all the kids who were mean to us. Anyway, I kept remembering things while they were all talking about you, and then your ex-boyfriend, Thomas, pulled out a photo and there you were, all grown up and beautiful.'

'Thank you.' Sophie grabs hold of a blush and swiftly slays it. 'Do you still twitch, Eddie Ripple? Seeing as you've opened the door on our disorders!'

He smiles. 'Not as often, but if I'm nervous or stressed it comes back. I don't worry so much about it these days.'

Sophie says, 'How do you know Callum?'

'I met him when I moved back to Sydney. I play saxophone in his band.'

'So you were there on the Anniversary Night? Actually, I think I saw you and thought you looked familiar!'

'Yep, but I never got a chance to say hello, and then when there was all the disaster with Grace's allergic reaction I thought I'd leave it for another day. Callum told me you want to repaint this house, so I thought I'd come over and ask if you want me to quote on doing it.'

'So is that what you do, paint houses and play the saxophone?'

'I do a bit of this and a bit of that. I paint houses because I write poetry, and I've discovered the only way for me to write a poem is to paint a house. I manage a poem a room. The painting pays a lot better than the poetry. The problem is I paint slower than the average house-painter, so my clients have to be patient, but my quality is outstanding, if I do say so myself.'

'Are you a published poet?'

'Well, yeah. But it hasn't exactly flown to the top of the bestseller lists. I actually think my mother might be responsible for all of my sales. She gives them away to waitresses in coffee shops. What about you? What did you end up becoming?'

'Oh, well, I accidentally became a Human Resources Director for a company that makes lawnmowers,' says Sophie. 'Hey, did you know that our old nemesis Bruno is married with twins and working as a chartered accountant for one of the Big Six firms? I had a two-week fling with him.'

'Really? Remember Gary Lochivich?'

'I always thought he'd become a hairdresser.'

Eddie gives her a puckish grin. 'You were right,' he says. 'He did become a hairdresser and *I* had a fling with *him.*'

It seems Sophie's Fairy Godmother has made just a slight error of judgement. It doesn't matter how perfectly the glass slipper slides on to her tiny foot . . . Prince Charming isn't looking for a princess.

Enigma and Rose, Margie and Laura are having a meeting at Rose's house to decide what to do about the Alice and Jack business, now that Rose has 'gone public'. Ever since they issued their media release the phone has been ringing endlessly. Margie has organised for the Alice and Jack business to give a *very* big donation to some charity group (an overly generous one, Enigma thinks, but she is keeping her mouth shut) as a 'public apology'. Margie also has some idea about offering the Alice and Jack house as a free place to stay for families with sick children, or mothers suffering from postnatal depression, which everybody is excited about, and although it's awful to think of the house being changed after all this time, Enigma quite likes the idea of having nice, grateful people staying there. It gives her a pleasant, kind-hearted feeling.

Apparently some silly legal organisation called the Australian Consumer and Competition something or other wants to talk to them about 'misleading and deceptive conduct', which is very bad, according to Ron, and just goes to show that Rose has got them into hot water! Fortunately, Ron seems to be dealing with lawyers and talking to a lot of serious-looking chaps in dark suits, and they are working out something called a 'loophole', which sounds like a good idea. Anyway, it's nice for Ron to have something to do and to feel important, so they all act interested and encouraging when he talks about it.

Of course, nobody wants to interview Enigma any more, oh no, she's no longer the Mystery Munro Baby. She's a nobody. She'll never be on *This is your Life* now. She'll never have another *Women's Weekly* spread and nobody will ever want her autographed photo. She's just an ordinary old widow who isn't even very good at tennis. She may as well be dead.

'Is Rose talking to another journalist?' asks Laura.

'Oh, *probably,*' says Enigma. 'She's probably there right now telling the whole world that I'm illegitimate, that I'm the daughter of a rapist with a head shaped like an egg. Why does she have to say that part? What's that got to do with anything? Everybody is probably looking at me thinking *my* head is egg-shaped! There's no need to snort like that, Laura, it's very bad-mannered. Well, Laura, I blame you for this whole debacle, it is *your* awful friend's fault — he started it! I said from the beginning he was a kook, but I didn't know he was my own daughter's *beau*! People are very upset about this, you know. Very upset. Did Rose think of that before she started blabbering on? I can see you giggling, Margie. Why are you so happy these days?'

Enigma feels all itchy with irritation. Nobody is giving her any sympathy whatsoever. 'You look like the cat that swallowed the cream.'

'I think it's because she's stopped swallowing cream,' says Laura.

'Oh, ha, ha,' says Margie happily. 'You're just jealous. I'm nearly as skinny as you.'

'Well, I think actually you're in much better shape than me,' says Laura. 'You're very toned, I must say. I was admiring the back of your arms before.'

'They're called triceps,' says Margie. 'I can do tricep push-ups on my toes.'

Rose comes back into the room — another one who looks like the cat who swallowed the cream, with her sophisticated new haircut! She's *still* so pretty really, and it gives Enigma that jealous, hurt, proud feeling she'd forgotten. When she'd learned that Rose was her mother, she'd thought, I have a beautiful mother, so maybe I'm beautiful too? But nobody who knew the truth had ever commented about Enigma's resemblance to Rose. Daughters were meant to be prettier than their mothers, but Enigma knew, deep down in her heart, that she could never, ever be as lovely as Rose.

Enigma probably resembled her father. A rapist! It wasn't fair. Her blood was dirty. Enigma *hated* her father for what he'd done to Rose — a secret, powerful hatred that could make her feel quite dizzy.

Rose says, 'Sorry about that. Another journalist. Oh, Enigma, I forgot to tell you that some young girl called from Channel Nine this morning and asked if you and I would be prepared to be interviewed by Ray Martin. I said I certainly didn't want to be on TV, thanks very much, but I'd check with you.'

Enigma nearly spills her cup of tea. 'Well, Rose, of course I'd like to be on TV! It would be a good opportunity to set the record straight.' *Television!* She'd get her hair and make-up done by a professional! She'd have a tiny microphone pinned to her jacket. *Ray Martin* would look at her with those kindly interested eyes and ask her questions. All the tennis girls would video-tape it.

Rose says, 'I said I was *fairly* sure you'd be interested,' and Enigma catches her winking at Laura and Margie but she doesn't care because she's going to be on television — finally!

Sophie and Ed are in the living room talking about the colour 'duck-egg blue', which Ed thinks might be perfect to lighten the room, when Sophie says irrelevantly, 'Are you single, Ed?'

And there's the twitch. A lightning-quick spasm of all his facial features, as though an invisible hand suddenly slapped him across the face. The twitch hasn't changed at all, except that it only happens once and it's so fast that you're not quite sure if you imagined it. He says, 'I had my heart pulverised about two years ago, and I know it's hard to believe with these devastating good looks but I've been single ever since. What about you?'

She says, 'I haven't been in a relationship since I broke up with Thomas three years ago.'

'It's difficult, sometimes, being single,' says Ed reflectively, and Sophie remembers the scientific way he would examine his own feelings when the boys at school used to do horrendous imitations of his twitch. 'Most of the time I'm fine, just getting along with my life, but sometimes I just get hit by this sulky left-out feeling. Like when you played musical chairs and the music stopped and you were there feeling like a moron. You know what I mean?'

'Oh, I know,' says Sophie. 'I know.'

She watches Ed stopping to examine the framed photos that line the mantelpiece of Connie's old fireplace.

'That's my collection of godchildren,' she says. 'I've got nine of them. I'm considering telling my friends there are no new vacancies.'

Ed says, 'I've only got one, a friend's daughter called Sarah. She's a little princess. Her mum and dad and I all have to sit around having tea parties with her.'

He picks up one of the photos and says, 'I always assumed I'd be a dad. It's weird. I think I knew I was gay even before I realised what the word meant, but I also had these deeply conservative ideas about how I'd grow up and have kids and live in a house with a white picket fence.'

'I'm sure you could find a nice guy prepared to wear a flowery apron for you,' says Sophie flippantly, but then she sees the stoic expression on his face and it's identical to the one she's felt tightening her own facial muscles, when she says to women with false bravado, 'Well, my biological clock is sure getting nervous!'

She watches his profile as he picks up another photo and thinks, with a surge of anger on his behalf, Well, for heaven's sake, why shouldn't Eddie Ripple — sweet, kind, sad Eddie Ripple — be a Dad?

She thinks maybe Aunt Connie had it exactly right after all.

'Have you got to be somewhere?' asks Ed, as he turns around and finds Sophie looking at her watch.

'No,' says Sophie. 'Just checking the time.'

59

Grace is walking to the top of Kingfisher Lookout. She has the baby in a sling across her front and a backpack full of supplies, from a change of nappy to a sketchpad, just in case Gublet makes an appearance.

It's only an hour to the top of the lookout but it's been like packing for a month-long trekking expedition and Grace had begun to wonder if it was such a good idea. After all, it would be no problem finding somebody to watch Jake for a couple of hours, especially now that people are treating Grace like she's made of glass. Veronika and Audrey have even offered to take him for a whole night, so that Callum and Grace can go and stay in a hotel and have a romantic dinner together. 'I think it's crucial for your relationship,' Veronika had lectured. 'You need to see yourself as Grace and Callum again, not just in your roles as parents. You have to work to keep the romance alive, you know; it's not like in the early days when everything is just *perfect* and you can't imagine arguing with the other person, or even being annoyed by them!'

'You mean not like it is for you and Audrey,' Grace had teased, and Veronika had grinned her new sheepish grin and said, 'Well . . . yes, but anyway, love is a decision, that's what Aunt Connie told me before she died. Actually, I don't really know what her point was, do you?'

Grace hasn't done much exercise since the baby was born. It's a warm spring day and within a few minutes she can feel sweat trickling down her back. Her heart is thumping, her legs feel heavy and sluggish, the baby is a lumpen weight against her chest, while the backpack thuds uncomfortably against her shoulder blades, and she thinks miserably, 'Oh God, I should just forget it!' and then, 'Oh, no, no, stop it!' because she can feel the swirling blackness ready to suck her down and under and she's been just managing to hold it at bay for the last few days, mainly through the rediscovery of mind-numbingly good sex.

She keeps on walking and thinks about that ridiculous woman yesterday saying piously, 'Well, you know what, when I feel down, I just say to myself, Megan, *every day is a gift.*' If it hadn't been for the girl sitting to Grace's left, who'd caught her eye and pointed discreetly at her mouth, mimicking retching, Grace might have walked out of the Glass Bay Postnatal Depression Support Group at that very moment. She had only agreed to go to it to please her mother and Callum. Laura was all for getting Grace straight onto Prozac, while Callum just wanted her to see a good doctor about it. Grace was steadfast: no drugs, no doctors. No drug could make her love her baby like a proper mother. No doctor could magically cure her. Besides which, she was feeling much better — and she didn't *have* postnatal depression — she'd always been a grumpy, bitchy type of person. That was just her. The very thought of sitting in front of a doctor, with all that doctorly focus on her and her inappropriate feelings, made her feel unbearably trapped, like a pinned butterfly.

But when Callum came home with a yellow flyer pulled from the noticeboard of the Glass Bay fish and chip shop, she'd agreed to try out the support group — just once. That was the deal. At least the attention wouldn't be on her alone.

Within ten minutes she had decided she absolutely wasn't going to a second meeting, especially after pious Megan was followed by a pale wispy wraith of a woman who'd just had twins, and now had four children under the age of five, and a husband in the army who was likely to be shot at any moment in the Middle East. She talked apologetically about how some days she didn't have time to brush her teeth and she felt really down and guilty about not coping. Grace shifted uneasily in her chair, thinking, Well, of course you can't cope, you poor girl — for God's sake, who in the world could! The government should give her a full-time nanny or something. How could Grace possibly make a comment after that?

But then another woman had said, 'Well, this is going to sound really bad after what you've been going through, because I've only got one baby, who sleeps through the night, and a very supportive husband. I'm a corporate tax lawyer and I've actually always been quite vain about my time-management skills. I mean, I could achieve — but anyway, that's why I don't understand how this has happened.' She had taken a deep breath and looked around at the group with a half-fearful, half-laughing expression. 'Yesterday I sat at my kitchen table and stared at a packet of cream cheese for a whole hour.'

'Oh!' Grace leaned forward. She hadn't intended to contribute a single word, except to compliment the host before she left on her chicken vol-au-vents (actually quite stodgy, far too much cheese) but the words were just tumbling out of her mouth. 'That happened to me, but it was a carton of milk.'

'Really?' said the woman and clutched at her arm, as if Grace could save her. 'Did it really? Because I thought I was going quite loony.'

And then pious Megan interrupted with some inane piece of advice and Grace sat back and felt teary. She didn't know why it meant so much that a corporate tax lawyer had sat and stared at a packet of cream cheese for over an hour, and touched Grace's arm, but it did, and when they talked about their next meeting Grace had found herself offering to bring along mini-quiches, so she guessed she was going again.

Their 'group coordinator' had talked about the importance of fresh air and sunshine and exercise. So, seeing as Grace was ignoring all her other advice about anti-depressants, counselling and confiding in trusted family members, she had decided that the very least she could do was go for a walk.

She tightens the straps of her backpack,

takes a deep breath and forces her body to move.

60

'Do you think if we had a baby together it would blush *and* twitch?'

'That's a very strange sort of question.'

'Well, do you think it would?'

'Probably. We'd have to leave it out in the snow to die.'

'Oh. That's a bit sad.'

61

As the path up to Kingfisher Lookout starts to steepen, Grace feels her calf muscles tighten and her breathing get ragged. For God's sake, she and Veronika and Thomas used to *run* up here without stopping. Veronika always won, of course.

At least Jake isn't crying. He's looking around with interest, blinking slightly at the sunshine coming through the trees, a single droplet of saliva hanging off his bottom lip.

Grace stops with her hands on her hips to catch her breath and says out loud, 'Every day is a gift, Jake. Of course sometimes it's a really horrible gift that you don't want.'

'Ho!' agrees Jake.

Grace wonders if she could ever confide to that corporate tax lawyer that she is devoid of proper motherly feelings for Jake, but as she looks at the soft flushed curve of his cheek she is struck with a feeling of loyalty. She won't betray him. He is, after all, markedly more beautiful than the photo the corporate tax lawyer showed of her rather scrawny-looking baby. Also, Callum said he thought Jake might be musical, and Veronika's girlfriend, Audrey, who seems to know a lot about babies, said she thought he was quite advanced for his age. Grace doesn't want anyone feeling pity for Jake! People should feel jealous.

'Look,' she says to Jake. 'You're just stuck with me, OK? I know Sophie might have done a better job but I'm just going to do the best I can. I'm a better cook than her, anyway.'

Jake chuckles.

'Oh, you think that's funny, do you?'

She starts walking again. After a while her breathing gets into a rhythm and her body seems to loosen up and remember the concept of exercise. As she loops around the pathway that Uncle Jimmy and Grandpa built all those years ago, the river glitters and glares in the sunshine, so she has to stop and put her sunglasses on. The jacarandas are out and their pale frothy purple is so beautiful against the blue of the sky it hurts her chest, but perhaps that's just her lack of fitness.

She remembers coming up here to paint with Aunt Rose.

With her great-grandmother.

Would it have made everything different if she'd known that Aunt Rose and Aunt Connie were related to her? Probably not. She still would have taken their love for granted, like children do.

Veronika and Thomas have both been going on like disappointed middle-aged parents about the deceit of their family. They are disgusted that everyone has kept the truth from them for all these years. 'I was perfectly mature enough to handle it at eighteen!' said Veronika, while Thomas was baffled by his family's 'unethical actions'. But Grace quite likes the fact that you can think something is one way all your life, and it turns out you're wrong, it can be something else entirely. It makes her feel free. Nothing is rigid. Things change. You can change your mind. You can change your thinking.

Grace is just glad that Alice Munro never existed.

Finally, with her heart thudding from exertion, she reaches the top of Kingfisher Lookout and sinks down on her knees at the grassy picnic patch. At least it's a weekday and there aren't any visitors about to see her bright red face. She lays out a rug from her backpack and unhooks her sling to release poor Jake, who is sweaty from being pressed against her chest.

'Are you as thirsty as me?' she asks as she lays him on the ground. 'I've got some nice boiled water for you. Mmmm. Delicious, germ-free boiled water.'

He looks up at her and reaches out a dimpled hand to grab on tight to her hair. As she leans forward a drop of her own sweat rolls off her forehead and lands on his face. He blinks with surprise.

'Sorry,' says Grace.

'Ha,' says Jake forgivingly and grins at her.

And that's when it happens, and she can hardly believe it, because, oh my God, it *is* just like all those stupid mushy new mothers said it would be, a shot of joy straight to the heart, just like the adrenaline that saved her life — a burst of pure, mind-clearing euphoria, powerful, primal, lustful, blissful love for her son. She presses her lips to the soft springy skin of his cheek. 'Actually, I love you more than anyone,' she whispers in his ear. 'More than your daddy, even, but that's our secret.'

Jake grabs her hair tighter and gurgles contentedly, as if he never doubted it for a moment.

62

Sophie stands at the doorway of Aunt Connie's house and watches a paint-splattered Eddie Ripple loping up the footpath. He stops at the jasmine-covered archway and turns back to give her a funny, quizzical shrug. He looks very handsome and tall. Just like Prince Charming.

As he walks off there is a shriek of manic laughter from the kookaburra, sitting with his normal self-satisfied expression on the side fence. He is alone, so perhaps things aren't working out so well with his lady friend. He doesn't seem too fussed.

Sophie looks thoughtfully at her little finger. There *is* at least one very faint line there, she's sure of it.

'Well, here's how it happened. Your dad and I used to be best friends when we were little, and one day we ran into each other again because he came over to paint my house and write a poem, you know, how he does. Anyway, I didn't have a boyfriend at the time — and, umm, well, neither did your dad — but we both wanted a baby very, very much. It was exactly twenty-three minutes after one on a Saturday when I thought of the idea but it took me two weeks to get the courage up to ask him. Your dad was in the middle of dipping a paintbrush into a tin of duck-egg-blue paint (and maybe he'd just come up with a perfect line for a poem, I don't know) when I said it. At first he thought I was out of my mind. He twitched. I blushed. But then he said he'd go away and think about it, and I was pretty sure he was going to say yes.'

'So there,' she says to the kookaburra, and she goes inside to ring up Claire and invite her to come over and meet her old friend Eddie Ripple. She's pretty sure Claire will approve.

After that she's going to read a regency romance and eat a Turkish delight in the bath.

Sometimes a girl has to stop waiting around and come up with her own fairytale ending.

63

'Hi, it's me, Rick.'

'Hello, Rick. You left me with a festering cold sore.'

'I'm sorry. Can I make it up to you by taking you out on the boat again tomorrow?'

'Mmmm. What happened with your ex-girlfriend?'

'It didn't work out. She went back to her ex-boyfriend.'

'Oh, too bad.'

'So what do you say?'

64

'Hi, it's me, Ian.'

'Hello Ian. I thought you would have been throwing yourself over rapids in New Zealand by now.'

'They made me partner. It pays better than white-water rafting, and you don't get so wet and cold.'

'Well, congratulations partner-man.'

'Thanks. Hey, I've got spare theatre tickets for Friday night if you're interested?'

65

Oh my goodness.

My goodness *me.*

I think I could . . .

I think I will . . .

Cook? Sew? Have a bath?

Dance a jig?

Rose slowly, sinuously unfurls her hands above her head like a flamenco dancer. She feels gloriously pain-free. She has got back her light and free ten-year-old body. It's all thanks to Rick the Gardener.

When was it? Of course, it was the Anniversary Night — months ago now — before all the business with the Kook and Grace's allergic reaction, when Rose got chatting with Rick while he was preparing his fire-eating equipment. He'd admitted he got terrible stage-fright before he performed and that his hands shook all day thinking about it. He'd noticed Rose rubbing her back and asked if she was OK, and because he'd been so honest with her about his stage-fright, Rose told him that sometimes the pain of her rheumatoid arthritis was so bad she wanted to lie on the ground like a two-year-old and cry, and if she'd been an old dog it would have been kinder to take her out the back and shoot her. Rick said he knew just the thing to help the pain and took out a fat, neatly rolled cigarette from his jeans pocket, and Rose asked, 'Is this an illegal drug?' and Rick had answered, well, yes, sort of, but it was just marijuana and they let cancer patients smoke it, so why shouldn't she? She had put it in her jacket pocket and forgotten all about it, until tonight, when she was watching TV and saw a fire-eater being interviewed, and all of a sudden she remembered and thought, Why not? It would be better than having another chocolate biscuit.

So she sat at her kitchen table and found a match and lit it up. At first it had made her cough and splutter and burned the back of her throat, but then she had got the hang of it again. She and Connie had both smoked for years, but they gave up, at Connie's insistence, when the Surgeon-General released his findings on smoking causing lung cancer in the Seventies. 'Throw them all out right now!' Connie had said, marching over, brandishing the newspaper. Of course, Connie had been the one to get Rose smoking in the first place. Smoke, don't smoke; sun-dried tomatoes are far too fashionable for us, sun-dried tomatoes add quite a nice touch to an omelette, sun-dried tomatoes are old hat; no you can't tell your daughter that you're her mother, not until she's forty and doesn't really need a mother any more and is too old to make you a homemade Mother's Day card, no you can't be mother-of-the-bride at your daughter's wedding, no you can't stand up at Nat's funeral and tell everybody that he was the most wonderful son-in-law you could have hoped to have, no your granddaughters won't ever call you Grandma, this is business now, Rose, this is serious, this is about money.

No you can't tell the world that you're a mother and a grandmother and a great-grandmother, because where would that leave Connie? Not the family matriarch, just an elderly childless old aunt.

Rose inhales deeply and watches the smoke curling from her nostrils like a dragon's. She is ten years old and she is in big trouble from her mother, for something to do with Connie. 'Don't you know your big sister adored you from the moment you were born? She'd do anything for you! Anything!' She is twenty-five years old and she has walked in on Connie crying in her kitchen — she says it's because she's chopping onions, but nobody cries so hard from chopping onions that their eyes are all swollen, and finally Connie says that she had been a few days late, and she'd allowed herself a glimmer of hope, so stupid of her. She hadn't told anyone, not even Jimmy, and then this morning — well, she just had to bloody well accept it wasn't going to happen, didn't she, and for heaven's sake, don't just sit there, Rose, you may as well chop the carrots.

If it wasn't for Connie they would have taken Enigma away and she would never have seen her again and there would have been no Laura and Margie, no Grace and Veronika and Thomas, no Lily, no Jake. No Sophie. No children holding their faces up to be painted. No money for beautiful fabric or Christmas presents for the children or a dishwasher that left the glasses sparkling.

Rose breathes in Rick's lovely homegrown marijuana and feels a sweet melting sensation, as if she's just bitten into a chocolate truffle, as if she *is* a chocolate truffle. What will she do now? All at once she knows exactly the right thing to do. She wants to paint. Not face-painting. She wants to paint a huge canvas of big brave splashes of gorgeous colour. Grace is right! What's wrong with her? Why doesn't she try some form of art *other* than face-painting?

She floats around the kitchen and finds her paint-kit. But where will she paint? Where is her easel? She must buy herself an easel! She and her beautiful great-granddaughter Grace will paint together, and while they paint she'll tell her what she couldn't tell her before. She'll tell her to stop tying herself up in knots worrying about whether she loves Jake like a proper mother. She'll say that she didn't love Enigma like a proper mother either; she felt nothing at all, not a thing, but then one day it came — a rush of love so powerful, so raging and dangerous, it nearly swept her off her feet.

Rose sways slightly, remembering exactly how it had felt that day, how it had come from nowhere, flaring like a gas flame. She frowns and bites her lip. Of course, she won't tell Grace what happened next. It was such a long time ago and she has never regretted it, not once, but still, she wouldn't want to give Grace nightmares. Not like some of the nightmares Rose has had over the years that have left her weak and sweaty and sick in the stomach.

She looks down at the glimmering white tiles of her kitchen floor, paid for by the shadowy, mythical figures of Alice and Jack Munro, who also paid for the nice girl Kerrie to come and mop them once a fortnight. The perfect canvas!

She takes one of the cushions from the kitchen chairs and puts it down on the floor, so she can kneel on it without hurting her knees. Sensible, says Connie in her head. The paintbrush in her hand feels like it's part of her body, an extra-long alien finger.

She begins to paint, tentatively at first and then wildly. Her paintbrush moving on its own. She lies down and puts the pillow under her stomach and uses it to sort of scoot across the floor as she paints. This is fun! Funny! She imagines her daughter's face if she were to come in and see her now, lying on her kitchen floor, painting her memories. Enigma would say she had the Alzheimer's for sure.

She paints a memory of Enigma when she was a baby and learning to walk. She had such a conceited expression on her little face, as though she were the first person in the universe to crack this walking business. She tottered towards Rose's arms and Rose said, very quietly, under her breath, so Connie wouldn't hear in the next room, 'Come to Mummy. Walk to your Mummy!'

Enigma has forgiven Rose for going public about Alice and Jack. After the immense glory of her seven-minute television appearance with Ray Martin she has discovered a new career as a guest speaker. She goes around to Senior Citizens' Clubs and Rotary Clubs and Bowling Clubs and gives them the inside story on the Munro Baby Mystery. She likes to wear one of those 'hands-free' microphones so she can walk around the audience, sometimes patting her more handsome fans on the shoulder, or even the head, which they don't seem to mind. She has an appointment book and a new mobile phone, and Rose adores the expression on her face when she speaks to her 'clients' — it's exactly the same as her conceited toddler face.

She paints Laura and Margie when they were ten and twelve, showing off their diving skills to her at Sultana Rocks, screaming, 'Look at this one, Aunt Rose! We're like swans!' and then diving in with their skinny arms stretched wide.

Margie is somewhere in Central Australia at the moment. She emails Thomas photos, which he shows to Rose on his computer, photos of red rippled landscapes that stretch on forever and Margie looking relaxed and tanned and in need of a shower, standing in front of a dusty four-wheel drive. It doesn't look like she's coming home anytime soon. She made everyone promise not to cook for Ron while she's away, but of course everybody still does. It's hard not to feel sorry for him, moping around, doing projects around the house that Margie asked him to do years ago. Rose turned up the other day with a chilli beef casserole to find Thomas there, patiently cooking his father a pepper steak, while Lily crawled around his feet. Meanwhile Laura has moved back into her house on the island and is studying philosophy at the university. Laura is the least philosophical person that Rose knows, so she's a bit worried she's not going to get very good marks. Laura is also officially dating the Kook and they all have to pretend to have forgotten that the first time they met him he was trying to blackmail them with an urn full of vacuum-cleaner dust. He's a pleasant, chatty sort of fellow, but he does have a gambling problem apparently, so you have to be careful. The other day there was a discussion about the star of an old movie and Rose had said to him, 'I bet you ten dollars it was Katharine Hepburn!' and was mortified in case he should take her up on the bet and set off his problem again.

Rose sits back up on her knees and takes another deep, satisfying puff on the cigarette. She must tell her friend Marie, who also suffers from horribly painful arthritis, about this new solution. She could invite her over for a cup of tea and some marijuana.

She lies back down on the floor and paints a memory of the children when they were little. Thomas was five, Veronika and Grace were four, and they'd all got very, very dirty playing goodness knows where on the island, and Margie had put them all in a big bubble bath together and Rose helped them make beards and moustaches out of the bubble foam, and their giggles of glee bounced around the bathroom, and Rose had thought, If only we could always keep you this happy just by popping you in a bath! Then again, lately the three of them seem to be about as happy as adults can be, or at least as these particularly prickly adults can be. Veronika has moved in with her new special friend, and sometimes at family events, Rose has observed her just sitting quietly, not saying a word! Of course, it doesn't last long, but it seems as though Veronika isn't wrestling with her life like it's an out-of-control crocodile any more. Thomas will always be a worrier, but he and Debbie are worried at the moment about what sort of pavers they should choose for their new in-ground swimming pool (who would have thought there was so much to say on the subject?) and this seems to be a fairly pleasant problem to worry about, and Lily seems to be a good-natured little thing, who will keep her parents under control. Rose can tell that Thomas will always be somewhat in love with Sophie, but that's life, isn't it. Sophie seems to have a few different fellows calling on her at the moment, but more often than not she's laughing her head off with that nice tall friend of Callum's, Ed Ripple. Everybody assures Rose that no, they won't be getting married because Ed isn't interested in girls, but as far as Rose can see he's *very* interested in Sophie and he makes her happy, so who knows what's going to happen there! Grace, Callum and Jake have moved into their beautiful new home in the mountains, and Grace has finished her next Gublet book, and Rose can see that it's going to be the most beautiful one yet, and when she went over there for dinner the other night, Grace asked if she'd like to see the dedication, and Rose said, yes, of course, and it said, *'For*

Rose, my great-grandmother.' For all the world to see.

She paints Connie, tall and thin and worried, jabbing away with her stick in the sand as she came up with the idea about Alice and Jack, while Rose lay back and closed her eyes and let her take care of everything. 'One day,' Connie had said, 'we'll be sweet little old ladies and we'll forget it didn't happen the way we said it did.'

She paints her mother, before she got sick, in a beautiful silk dress, with a bell-shaped skirt and an embroidered neckline, the sort of dress she could never afford to wear, the sort of dress Rose would have bought for her from David Jones in the expensive designer part if she could have her back for one day, to show her how lovely life can be when you've got enough money.

She paints the river, green and still and mysterious and unrolling into a ribbon of lustrous turquoise crêpe de Chine. She paints the shoes she was wearing the day she went to visit Mr Egg Head to show him their baby. Connie would have had an absolute fit if she'd known her plan. Rose had told her she would take the baby for a walk around the city while she looked in the shop windows, and Connie had wanted to go to the pictures with Jimmy, so she never knew about Rose's idea to catch a train to his house in Annandale, where Mr Egg Head was at home alone while his wife was out cleaning houses. He'd been retrenched from his job at the department store and he was unshaven and unsmiling, his trouser braces dangling over his shoulders, a stained white collar. It was a bit of a shock after his dapper appearance at the store. Rose followed him into his unpleasant-smelling kitchen and he sat back down and kept shovelling spoonfuls of horrible sludgy porridge into his mouth, and Rose said, 'I just wanted you to see your daughter,' and held her up under her armpits. Rose had dressed Enigma in her very best outfit and curled up her hair around her fingertips. The baby gazed around with placid interest, while Mr Egg Head flicked her a sneering glance, snorted, and said with his mouth full, 'Bloody ugly thing, isn't she?'

Rage hit her knees so hard and so unexpectedly it was as if she'd been crash-tackled. She put Enigma back into her pram and then she turned to the messy bench-top and she didn't even look at what she was picking up with both hands until after she'd swung it against the back of his head. It made a loud 'thwack' and he tipped forward face-first into his porridge and then there was silence, except for the sharp high hum of a blowfly.

'She's a *beautiful* baby,' said Rose, to the back of his head. She'd put the bread board back down and pushed the pram out onto the street and caught the train back into the city and met Jimmy and Connie after their movie, and said she and the baby had had a lovely time walking around the city, and in all the years to come whenever people talked about the Bread Board Murder Mystery, all Rose could hear was the hum of that fly.

She very carefully paints a fractured egg dripping blood. It takes up one whole tile.

Finally, she puts down her paintbrush and gets to her feet and stands with her hands on her hips looking at her life and her family spread across the kitchen floor, before she finds the mop and washes it all away, while she steadily eats her way through an entire packet of chocolate biscuits.

The next day, when Sophie comes to visit with an invitation to her fortieth birthday party, there is a sweet smell in the air that Rose explains must be the nutmeg in her sponge cake. The floor is white and pure, and Rose looks just like a dear little old lady whose only secrets are recipes.

ABOUT THE AUTHOR

Liane Moriarty is an advertising copywriter turned author who grew up in Sydney, Australia. *The Last Anniversary* is her second novel. Her first novel, *Three Wishes,* was published in seven countries.

The employees of Thorndike Press hope you have enjoyed this Large Print book. All our Thorndike, Wheeler, and Kennebec Large Print titles are designed for easy reading, and all our books are made to last. Other Thorndike Press Large Print books are available at your library, through selected bookstores, or directly from us.

For information about titles, please call:
  (800) 223-1244

or visit our Web site at:
  http://gale.cengage.com/thorndike

To share your comments, please write:
  Publisher
  Thorndike Press
  10 Water St., Suite 310
  Waterville, ME 04901

219823191306682

CPSIA information can be obtained
at www.ICGtesting.com
Printed in the USA
FFHW010808110719
53569701-59233FF

9 781410 475299